DESERT HEARTS

THE SEDONA FILES: BOOK 2

CHRISTINE POPE

DARK VALENTINE PRESS

DESERT HEARTS

ISBN: 978-0-9883348-1-6

Copyright © 2011 by Christine Pope.

Revised version copyright © 2019

Published by Dark Valentine Press

Cover design by Lou Harper

Book formatting by Indie Author Services

CHAPTER ONE

Kara Swenson

PEACE AND QUIET. I'D ALMOST FORGOTTEN WHAT that was like. June had come and gone, and July was almost over—always a busy season here in Sedona, despite the scorching desert heat. The crowds had thinned out a little now that the monsoon storms had arrived in earnest, but the shop was still crazy-busy. I knew I should be glad, times being what they were, but every once in a while, I began to wonder just how many people out there could really be that interested in aliens and UFOs. Maybe one day I'd figure out why those people found themselves compelled to buy an alien plushie or a paperback copy of *Flying Saucers and Science* before leaving Sedona and heading home to Chicago or Omaha or Portland or wherever else they came from.

Even now, I felt as if I should be back at the shop, since Wednesday nights were usually reserved for conducting inventory or general tidying up. But Kiki had shooed me away, saying, "Even big sisters need a night off every once in a while." True, it had felt good to come home, kick off my shoes, pour myself a glass of chilled pinot grigio—already it was too hot for anything heavier—and turn on the television, but after an hour or so of that, the pleasures of a solitary evening had begun to pall.

I turned off the TV, and Gort, my wolfish German shepherd/Keeshond mix, turned an inquiring eye toward me and wagged his tail a few times. He'd already had two walks that day, but maybe what I needed right then was some fresh air, especially now that the sun had been down for a while and the air had cooled somewhat.

Only a sip or two remained of the pinot grigio, so I finished it off and set the glass down on the coffee table. "Guess what, Gort? It's your lucky day."

Gort's tail thumped against the floor again, and he scrambled to his feet and let out a low whine, dark eyes fixed on the side table where I kept his leash.

"I know, I know." I stood and retrieved the leash, then clipped it onto his collar. The drawer was also a repository for the used grocery bags Kiki and I affectionately referred to as "poopie bags," and I grabbed one of those as well and stuffed it into the pocket of my jeans. My house keys with the attached mini flashlight went into my other pocket; there weren't many streetlights out here on the edge of town.

Not that I ever worried about walking alone after dark. I'd lived here in Sedona for almost twenty years, in the house that had been my grandparents' and had come to me after my grandfather died some six years earlier. The store had been his, too. I'd gotten the whole kit and caboodle, as Kiki liked to say without a trace of resentment. True, she hadn't inherited the house or the store, but that didn't mean our grandfather hadn't taken care of her. On Kiki's twenty-first birthday, she'd gotten her share of the inheritance: a hundred thousand dollars. And, despite gloomy prognostications to the contrary from some of our circle of friends, she hadn't spent much of it yet.

Gort pulled me out the front door, tail wagging. I didn't bother to lock up—I'd only brought the keys because of the flashlight attached to the chain. Even though the sun had been down for more than an hour, the temperature hovered in the mid-eighties. I'd had always loved the way the warm nighttime breezes played with my hair and flowed gently over the bare skin of my arms.

The stars burned overhead so brightly, it seemed as if I could almost reach out and touch them. No moon yet tonight, though, and I flicked on the little flashlight and let it guide me past the end of the cul-de-sac and out onto the trail that wound around the edge of my subdivision. Snakes and scorpions didn't worry me too much, since I tended to wear jeans and hiking boots even on days like today when temperatures hit the upper nineties, but I still conscientiously ran the flashlight's beam over the path ahead of me, just in case.

Gort lifted his leg against a manzanita bush, then tugged me forward. This being Sedona, I knew all too well that there were other things—things not of this world—hiding in the darkness of the desert, but sightings were rare in this part of town. No, you had to head out toward Boynton or up Schnebly Road to see the stuff that would really make your hair curl.

Or sometimes you just had it dropped right in your store. That had happened when Persephone O'Brien showed up four months ago, asking for help. Of course, it was Kiki and the rest of the gang who got to be out in the field while I held down the fort at the store, but still, the crazy goings-on in Secret Canyon and the rescue of Paul Oliver, the famous ufologist, had proved that all the years of tracking reports of alien movements and UFO activity in the canyons surrounding Sedona weren't exactly pie in the sky. So to speak.

And now Persephone and Paul were here permanently, having decided to relocate from Los Angeles to Sedona. It was a good place for a psychic and a UFO researcher to end up, and the two were so blatantly happy that I couldn't really begrudge them their good fortune, but....

But nothing, I told myself, and tugged on Gort's leash when he seemed a little too interested in a spiky yucca plant. Being the well-behaved dog that he was, he trotted back to the center of the path without arguing.

"Good dog," I said, and he panted, the white teeth of his doggy smile flashing at me in the darkness.

Well, Gort loved me anyway. I told myself not to be silly, that self-pity didn't do anyone any good. So I was going through the mother of all dry spells in my personal life. That had happened to better women than me, and brooding over it sure wasn't going to do me any good. Besides, everything else was going great—I owned my house and the store free and clear, had a great set of friends—Michael and Persephone and Paul and Lance —

At the thought of Lance, though, my mind skidded to a stop. Yes, he was a good friend. Too bad friendship wasn't really what I wanted from him.

Gort whined then, and began to tug the leash back toward the house. I stared down at him, a little surprised. Normally, he'd try every trick in the book to extend our walks, and we'd barely been out of the house for ten minutes.

"Okay, you crazy mutt," I said, and allowed him to pull me homeward.

After all, I'd come out here for the dog. Otherwise, I would have just poured myself another glass of wine and luxuriated in the central air conditioning I'd installed a few years earlier. My grandparents had always made do with a whole-house swamp cooler, but the A/C made the place feel so much better.

As I approached the front walk to the house, a rectangle of yellow light shone down the path, illuminating the stone pavers.

What the hell?

The front door stood open, allowing anyone standing on the walkway to see straight down the hall and into my living room. No, I hadn't locked the door, but I had most definitely made sure it was firmly shut.

Just the wind, I told myself, *or maybe you thought the lock had caught, but it really didn't.*

Gort let out a warning bark, followed by a low growl deep in his throat. When I looked down, I saw the fur along the back of his neck was bristling, and his luxuriant tail—definitely inherited from his Keeshond parent—had curled itself tightly against his back.

The hair on my own neck prickled a little, but I forced myself to move forward. This was my house, dammit, and although I'd been stupid enough to go out without taking my cell phone with me, I wasn't about to stand there and shiver and shake on my own front stoop. The houses on this street had fairly big lots, but they weren't so far apart that my neighbors wouldn't hear me if I screamed.

Besides, a seventy-five-pound dog was pretty good protection.

Wrapping the fingers of my left hand around Gort's collar, I moved forward and into the entryway. Almost at once, I saw a set of dusty footprints on the gleaming Saltillo tile, and I swallowed.

It wasn't too late to turn around. I could stop, inch my way back outside, and run like hell to the Martinez's place next door.

Then I saw him. At least, I thought it was a him. From this angle, it was difficult to tell, because he lay prostrate in the middle of the living room, half of him on the Navajo rug and the other half sprawled across the tile floor.

Gort growled again, but there was the faintest hint of a whine in the sound, as if he didn't know how he was supposed to react.

Well, that makes two of us.

I moved slowly toward the stranger, barely daring to breathe. As I drew closer to him, I saw he wore some sort of tattered jumpsuit that might once have been black but was now a dingy, rusty shade of dark gray. It was torn in a dozen places and spattered with dirt and dark stains that might be dried blood. And, to put it mildly, he reeked of stale sweat.

He must have been unconscious. Otherwise, he

would have been able to hear the hammering of my heart.

Perfect. Just a few steps more to the dining room, where I'd left my cell phone lying on the table. All I'd have to do was call 911, and somebody from Sedona P.D. would come over to take the intruder away. That was the most reasonable course of action.

But something prevented me from taking those last steps. I stood there, staring down at him, and then he rolled over, gazing up at me with wide, pale eyes from within a sun-ravaged face so smudged with grime, I couldn't get a clear idea of what he actually looked like. One hand reached out feebly toward my shoe and fell short.

"Please," he whispered. "Please help me."

Lance Rinehart

He didn't know why he'd agreed to meet Michael Lightfoot and Paul Oliver so they could go out to Boynton Canyon and observe the orbs. True, Paul hadn't seen them yet —he'd been too busy giving lectures and writing his next book—but that didn't mean the scientist really needed someone to hold his hand while he went out to the canyon. Kara could have given him a map. Hell, he could've looked it up on the internet.

Besides, coming out here after everything that had gone on at Secret Canyon made no sense. Persephone had said on more than one occasion that she hadn't sensed the presence of any more of the human/alien hybrids, but that didn't mean much. She'd pulled off a pretty good trick at the underground base, destroying the hybrids with one fell swoop, but when it came to hints and hunches, she was still just as fallible as any other psychic.

At least she hadn't come along on this excursion. Lance wondered sourly how Paul was willing to give up even a few minutes of bliss with his new bride, but apparently she was accompanying Linda Santos, a member of the local Mutual UFO Network group —MUFON for short—to a seminar on UFO field data collecting. Persephone had been making noises about wanting to assist Paul with his investigations, so going to the seminar was a logical start.

Anyway, it was just the three of them out here in Boynton, sitting in the warm darkness and looking for orbs. Lance had seen them plenty of times, but even he wasn't quite able to brush them off as a commonplace.

Paul had brought along a fancy SLR. Whether or not he'd be able to capture anything with the thing was a crap shoot, given the uncertain nature of the orbs, but you never knew.

"Set off the flash," Lance told him as they settled themselves on a large, flat rock.

The other man raised an eyebrow, but he lifted the camera as instructed and pushed the button.

A bright strobe illuminated the little dell where they had paused to take their observations. Tiny points of golden light glittered in the air all around them. It looked as if someone had shaken a child's snow globe and then shone a flashlight on it. A skeptic would have remarked that the dust could have simply been suspended bits of particulate matter...except that all those gleaming specks hung still in the air, not moving, even though a warm breeze rustled through the branches of the manzanita bushes around them.

"It's beautiful," Paul said.

"You must have read about it."

"Yes...but reading's not quite the same as seeing it with your own eyes."

"True."

Michael had been watching silently, his face tilted upward to watch the sparkles until the last of them died away. "There's one," he said quietly.

It drifted in out of the darkness, a sphere a little larger than a baseball, glowing in shades of pale gold. If you looked closely, you could see variations in the colors, shadings that some people claimed looked like faces. Lance had never noticed anything like that, but then again, he'd never been one to anthropomorphize. Wasn't the presence of the orbs enough without having to give them human features?

Paul raised his camera. Lance heard a *click,* but there was no flash. He guessed that was on purpose; the ufologist knew his way around a camera pretty well. Must have adjusted the shutter speed for the darkness, knowing that the glare of the flash would fade the glow of the orb to almost nothing.

"It knows we're here," Michael said quietly.

Lance could sense it, too, a feeling of being watched. Nothing inimical, not like the cold malice that had radiated from the base in Secret Canyon, but even after all these years, he found the sensation a little unnerving.

Whether or not Paul felt the same way, Lance couldn't say. The man was a scientist, someone more centered on the left side of his brain. And although he had to be experiencing some level of awe, that didn't stop him from snapping away methodically with the camera, or pausing to pull a small notepad out of his shirt pocket so he could scribble down some notes.

The orb drifted to the top of an especially tall juniper and seemed to linger there for a moment, as if surveying them one last time. Then it blinked out of existence—no gentle fading away, no flash. It was just there one second and gone the next.

"Amazing," Paul said.

Lance shrugged. "Just wait until you see the Day of the Dead festival at Tlaquepaque."

"Orbs are old hat to you, huh?"

"Maybe." He turned away and gazed out through the darkness, but the only light in evidence was the glow from the town itself, a few miles away from where they stood. "It's exciting the first couple of times, maybe, but they don't actually *do* anything. No one's really made any contact with them. We're not even sure if they're intelligences or not, or maybe some sort of advanced observation device. But at least they give Kara and Kiki something to show off to people besides UFOs."

Paul nodded. "Reminds me of the dolphins."

Lance raised an eyebrow, and even Michael's normally placid features took on a confused cast.

"When I was a kid, my parents took me to Southern California one summer." Paul set the SLR inside its camera bag but didn't zip it closed—in case any more orbs showed up, Lance decided. "We went on a whale-watching trip, but we didn't see any whales. The tour operators made a big deal of pointing out the dolphins, though...sort of a consolation prize, I suppose. I was just saying the orbs are Kara's backup in case the UFOs are a no-show."

"Which means she's been doing a lot of orb tours lately, I guess." Lance knew there was nothing to see, but somehow he couldn't prevent himself from glancing up into the black sky, instinctively checking to see if any of those pinpoints of light had decided to move in a way contrary to the laws of physics.

A low chuckle. "It hasn't been a good summer for

UFO tours, that's for sure. Persephone's gotten an earful."

"Kara wants to blame the whole thing on Persephone," Michael added.

A little unfair, maybe, but not exactly untrue, either. After all, if it weren't for Persephone O'Brien...sorry, Persephone *Oliver*, the base up at Secret Canyon would still be humming along just fine. But with its corps of hybrid soldiers decimated and the alien-possessed humans who had been running the show deader than high-country grass, the base had gone completely quiet. None of the UFO hunters had dared to go back into Secret Canyon to see what, if anything, was happening there, but the conspicuous lack of UFO activity over the past few months seemed to indicate the aliens had taken a powder for the time being.

But because the topic of Kara Swenson was a sketchy one, for a variety of reasons, Lance settled for making a noncommittal noise. It certainly didn't help having the Olivers around as the perfect portrait of newly married bliss. Sure, give them a few more months, and they'd most likely degenerate into the petty sniping and bickering most couples of his acquaintance indulged in. In the meantime, though, the situation had only heightened the tension between him and Kara.

Most of the time, he did a pretty good job of not thinking about Kara's expectations. Over the past few years, they'd settled into a more or less friendly détente. He would allow himself to admit that he liked her and enjoyed her company, and no more. Of course, he knew he was fooling himself, and lately he'd been having traitorous thoughts about saying the hell with it and confessing that his indifference had only been an act...but he wasn't quite there.

Yet.

His tone was a little harsher than he'd intended as he said, "Kara needs to understand that there are greater things at stake here than her bank account."

Michael raised an eyebrow, and Paul suddenly found something fascinating in the sky to the northeast. At first, Lance thought he was just intentionally avoiding having to make a comment, but as Paul continued to stare upward, Lance tilted his head as well to see what had drawn his attention.

It hovered in the night sky, a flat-black triangle that blotted out the stars. Lights shimmered along one edge, then the other. With a rumble Lance felt in his bones rather than heard, it moved slowly on its axis so it faced due north, then shot upward at an angle that should have been impossible.

For a long moment, none of them said anything. Finally, Paul remarked, "Looks like they're back."

———

Kara

One agonizing sip at a time. That was all the water I could manage to get into the stranger. Each time he swallowed, he coughed, and I had to wait for the spasm to pass before I could tip the paper cup—I'd decided not to risk one of my glasses for this procedure—against his cracked lips and dribble a little more of the precious fluid into his mouth.

Somehow, I'd managed to push him up against the couch so he was basically upright. Although I knew that logically I should have picked up the phone and called 911 so an ambulance could take him to the hospital, something seemed to prevent me from doing so, had made me walk right past the cell phone on the dining room table and instead go to the kitchen to pour some bottled water into a Dixie cup.

Now I knelt next to the stranger and continued to coax the water down his throat, knowing he needed it more than anything, but also knowing that too much would only make him sick.

He shut his eyes, lashes incongruously dark and thick against the sunburned, flaking skin on his cheeks. I'd need to hit him with about a gallon of moisturizer after I was done hydrating him.

This was crazy. I'd never had any fantasies of playing Florence Nightingale or Clara Barton, so why the hell was I sitting here, patiently giving him water in dribs and drabs, when he'd broken into my home?

All right, so maybe he hadn't done much actual

"breaking," since I'd left the front door unlocked, but he'd definitely entered my home without my permission. In a way, it made sense—mine was the house at the end of the cul-de-sac, and if he'd wandered in off the desert, naturally he would have gone to the building closest to open land. Still....

"What's your name?" I asked softly.

He shook his head. Whether that meant he still couldn't speak or simply didn't want to tell me, I couldn't say for sure. Resigned, I tipped a bit more water down his throat. At least this time he didn't cough. That was a good sign. I lifted the cup to his lips again and let him drink the last of the water in the cup.

"How's your stomach?" I asked, hoping maybe he'd speak if I wasn't asking anything about his name or where he'd come from. "Do you feel nauseated?"

Another shake of the head.

The man was obviously tougher than he looked. I wondered just how long he'd been wandering around out there in the heat and the sun. Temperatures had been hovering just below the century mark for the past few days.

"Let's try some Gatorade," I said then, holding back a sigh. "Gotta replace those electrolytes."

I pushed myself up to a standing position and went to the kitchen. Although generally I thought it was pretty nasty, the sports drink did come in handy for the times I overdid it in the heat, and so I always kept some around.

After pulling another paper cup out of the dispenser and filling it halfway with Gatorade, I returned to the living room. The stranger didn't seem to have moved, although I noticed Gort had lain down next to him, as if to keep watch while I was in the kitchen. The dog whined a little as I approached, then cocked his head.

"Your guess is as good as mine, Gort," I said, and knelt down next to the man and directed my next words at him. "I hope you like raspberry."

He didn't move, so I decided to take that as a "yes." Once again, I lifted the cup to his mouth, but he surprised me by reaching up with one hand and wrapping his fingers around the fragile little Dixie cup.

"Got it," he told me. His voice was barely more than a raspy whisper, but at least he'd said something. That was a start.

"No problem," I replied, watching as he greedily drank down the Gatorade. "More?"

He nodded. "Please."

I gave him what I hoped was an encouraging smile and went back to the kitchen once again. This time, I got out a plastic cup left over from one of the MUFON meetings I'd held at the house, and filled it with the Gatorade. After that, he'd probably want something more substantial. Maybe some soup? I had a few cartons of some interesting organic stuff from my last pilgrimage to the Trader Joe's in Prescott. Sedona was wonderful, but it could be somewhat lacking in the shopping department, and I made a habit of going over to Prescott at least once a month to stock up on the things I couldn't get in town.

When I returned to the living room, I noticed at once that the stranger had pulled himself more upright so he wasn't quite as slumped against the front of the couch. Luckily, it was leather; if he left any grime on it, I should be able to wipe it off more or less easily...I hoped.

"Here you go."

He took the cup from me and drank down the Gatorade—not greedily, but in even, measured swallows, as if gauging exactly how much he needed to take in at a time for the greatest benefit. Once he was done, he handed the cup back to me. "Thank you."

Although he looked like about a hundred miles of back road—and smelled even worse—there was something about him that seemed calm and efficient, two words I generally wouldn't use to describe the desert rats one saw around town. He didn't seem to fit the type. It was more like he'd suffered some accident, some catastrophe that had left him stranded in some of the most inhospitable country in the world.

"What's your name?" I asked.

A blank, pale stare, followed by a shake of the

head. His eyes were a startling green against the sun-ravaged skin. "I don't have one."

Maybe he was a little more addled by the sun than I'd thought. "You mean you don't remember?" I'd heard of cases like that—people wandering in the heat and the sun until it cooked the memories right out of their brains. But he seemed a lot more lucid than that.

"No. I don't have a name."

It was probably best to humor him. "Okay, Kaspar," I said.

His head tilted slightly, confusion obvious in his expression.

"Kaspar Hauser," I explained. "A young man who appeared out of nowhere. He—" I broke off at the look of confusion on the stranger's face. "Never mind. We can save the history lessons for later. How about some soup?"

"Yes, please."

I essayed a half-hearted smile before heading to the pantry. Well, he might be a wacko, but at least he was a polite one. Luckily, the soup was the type you could just pour out of a carton into a bowl; a minute in the microwave, and it was ready. I used a pot holder to pull it out, dropped a spoon into it, and went back to the living room.

The stranger hadn't moved, but I noticed at once that one hand now rested on Gort's head, fingers just barely stroking the soft fur between his ears. The man had an odd, bemused expression on his face, as if he hadn't been quite sure what the dog's coat would feel like. Gort's eyes were half-closed. Clearly, whatever misgivings he'd had about the stranger had evaporated as soon as he realized the man was willing to participate in ear-scratching.

Green eyes looked at me questioningly as I approached with the soup.

"It's roasted pepper corn chowder," I offered, and held out the bowl to the man.

He took it in both hands, sniffed once, then nodded and took up the spoon. Although I guessed he must be starving, he ate neatly if quickly, with no slurping or dripping. Within a minute, he'd cleaned out the bowl pretty thoroughly.

"More?" I asked, trying not to sound resigned. Most of the time, I didn't keep my pantry all that well-stocked, since I lived alone. More often than not, I ate takeout down at the shop because I didn't have the time to do anything else. If the stranger stayed with me for any length of time, he'd end up eating me out of house and home.

Well, that was assuming a lot. My intention had only been to get him hydrated, get a little food in him, clean him up, and send him on his way.

"If it's not too much trouble."

"No trouble at all." I took the bowl from him and went to refill it, ignoring Gort's pleading doggy eyes. My fault that I'd spoiled the dog by giving him more table scraps than I should. I knew he was expecting to get the bowl to lick, but I wasn't about to do that in front of the stranger. God knows what he'd think of me.

The second bowl didn't disappear quite as quickly as the first, but the man still made short work of it nonetheless. With some food in him, he looked—well, maybe not exactly better, but the sheen of sweat had disappeared from his brow, and his eyes seemed a little more alert.

What he really needed was a hot shower and a change of clothes. I'd have to hope he could manage the former on his own, because I drew the line at sponge baths. Clean clothes—well, he was taller and slimmer than my grandfather had been, but I still had an old foot locker with some of his clothing, items I hadn't quite been ready to get rid of. Anything would be better than the foul-smelling, ragged jumpsuit the stranger had on.

"Can you stand?" I asked.

He seemed to consider, then set the bowl on the floor and pushed himself upward. Gort immediately set to on the empty soup bowl, and I somehow managed to refrain from sighing. At least the stranger didn't seem to notice, probably because he was too busy trying to keep his balance. He swayed for a second, but then seemed to regain his equilibrium.

Standing, he was even taller than I had thought. I

wasn't short, standing a little more than five-seven in my bare feet, but the top of my head barely reached his chin.

Somehow, that height seemed a little intimidating. I looked away from him, down the hallway. "How about a hot shower?"

"Yes, please," he replied. Something that might have been the beginnings of a smile touched his cracked lips. "I smell terrible."

I bit back a smile of my own. "Follow me."

Fortunately, the ranch-style house had two bathrooms, one as part of a suite in the master bedroom, and the other only a few steps down the hall, between the living room and the other two bedrooms. Since it was the bath designated for guest use, I made sure it was always stocked with clean towels. And because it had been Kiki's bathroom before she moved out, there were still a few bottles of shampoo and some soap in the caddy in the shower.

"Here you go," I told the stranger, after I reached into the room and flipped on the overhead light/fan combo. "There are towels, and shampoo and soap. I'm going to see if I can rustle up some clean clothes for you."

He watched me for a second, and nodded. "Thank you."

In reply, I only lifted my shoulders, then went down the hall toward the spare bedroom—which in actuality was more of a storage room and general dumping ground. Behind me, I heard the door to the bathroom shut, and a short time later, the water came on.

I hadn't bothered to tell him about the inadequate hot water heater, figuring he'd know it was time to wrap things up when the water began to get tepid. Still, I knew he could probably get a good fifteen to twenty minutes of decent showering in before the hot water supply began to dwindle. Plenty of time to find something for him to wear.

The foot locker was the one my grandfather had brought back from Korea, and so it had seemed fitting to use it to store the things I couldn't quite bear to give away to Goodwill: the most obnoxious of Grandpa's beloved Hawaiian shirts, some well-worn chinos, the package of underwear he'd bought only a few weeks before he died. He'd never even opened it.

Even now, the sight of those things made my throat close up a little, although it had been six years since my grandfather had passed away. Resolutely, I reached in and pulled out the least garish of the Hawaiian shirts, the pale blue one with the dark blue and red hibiscus flowers all over it, along with a pair of pants and the package of underwear. Coiled at one side of the foot locker was a belt, and I picked that up, too. Maybe the stranger could pull it to the tightest notch to keep the pants from sliding down.

I wondered then what my grandfather would think if he saw me now, calmly raiding his old clothes for some stranger who'd wandered in off the desert. Grandpa would have probably taken it in stride, actually. He'd always been the open-minded one of the family, whereas I....

Temporary insanity, I decided. *The only possible explanation.*

Back in college, my nickname had been "Careful Kara." Kara, the one who would only allow herself a single drink at frat parties, who collected keys and drove my drunk friends home. Careful Kara, who never pulled an all-nighter to finish a term paper or hooked up with guys at parties. People had teased me, even as they took advantage of my perpetual designated-driver status. I'd never bothered to explain why. Who wanted to hear about a mother who'd taken off when her children were only eleven and three, a mother who left her eldest daughter thinking she had to be responsible for her little sister and everyone else around her?

Careful Kara, who was now running a UFO shop and conducting tours to see orbs and the occasional passing spaceship. Life could definitely throw you some curve balls.

Mouth thinning a little, I piled up the clothes, then stood. The clock over the daybed ticked away. Almost ten o'clock. I kept late hours, especially if I had a UFO tour lined up, but it had been a long day. And if I was tired, I could only imagine how the stranger must feel.

No pajamas were forthcoming from the trunk, but shoved away on the top shelf of my own closet were a pair of men's sweats that had somehow gotten mixed up with my stuff when Alan and I divided our household, just before I'd come back to Sedona to take care of my grandfather. God knows why the sweat pants hadn't ended up in the charity donations, but they would do well enough for the stranger to sleep in. A T-shirt was easy; I had stacks sitting on the daybed, just waiting for me to silk-screen them and take them down to the shop.

Since the spare bedroom was a disaster, he'd either have to sleep on the couch or in Kiki's old room. The latter made more sense, although I somehow felt as if I was defiling my sister's space by letting the man sleep there. Silly, really. Kiki had moved out almost a year ago. It wasn't as if she needed that bed.

The room was more or less untouched, as I hadn't quite been able to bring myself to convert it to a second office or studio the way Kiki kept urging me to. The bright turquoise walls glared at me as I flipped on the light switch. God knows what Kiki had been thinking, going with that eye-searing combination of turquoise and lime green, but at least the space was clean and uncluttered, and the bed a queen, not the twin bed Kiki had slept on until her senior year of high school. There was no way the stranger could have ever squeezed himself into a mere twin.

I set the clothes down on the dresser but kept the sweatpants and T-shirt, along with one pair of underwear. When I emerged in the hallway, I noticed that the water had been turned off. Pausing outside in the hall, I gave a diffident tap on the door and said, "I've left some things for you on the floor out here. You can sleep in the room right across the hall. Okay?"

For a few seconds, there wasn't any response. Then I heard him say, "Okay. Thank you."

"No problem," I replied automatically, and turned away from the door.

What a lie. I had a feeling my Good Samaritan gesture was going to turn into the mother of all problems.

CHAPTER TWO

Lance

HE HADN'T GONE HOME AFTER THE MUTED goodbyes the three men exchanged, right before Paul and Michael climbed into Paul's truck and Lance got into his Jeep. They'd all been pretty quiet as they walked back to the vehicles—maybe it had been stupid to think the aliens wouldn't come back sooner or later, but he'd found himself hoping as the weeks and then months had stretched on, and there hadn't been any sign of them. There also hadn't been any chatter about a renewal of activities out in Secret Canyon, though, so maybe the aliens had decided to switch their base of operations.

Anyway, neither Michael nor Paul had seemed too interested in conversation, and Lance never liked to initiate a discussion if he didn't have to. He guessed the two of them were coming up with their own worst-case scenarios. Well, maybe not Michael Lightfoot. He'd always been pretty Zen. Most likely, right now he was sitting on the banks of Oak Creek, meditating on the situation. The man's house wasn't much, but the location was spectacular—fifteen steps would take you out the back door and right down to the water.

Paul, of course, would have gone straight home to Persephone after dropping off Michael. Lance didn't even need to use remote viewing for that; those two might as well be joined at the hip. They sure as hell didn't keep any secrets from one another, and especially not something of this magnitude.

Fine. If that worked for them, great. But he'd known exactly where he wanted to go.

Thanks to the internet and sites like Yelp and TripAdvisor, even Sedona's few remaining neighborhood bars could be overrun with tourists. But Lance liked the Sundowner because it was cheap and because Rose, the bartender, seemed to instinctively know when to simply hand him a cold bottle of MGD and leave him alone.

This was definitely one of those nights. He took the beer from her and laid a fiver on the bar, then grabbed a stool and surveyed the crowd. For a Wednesday night, the place was pretty full. It was the usual mix of locals and those tourists—mostly kids in their twenties—who were brave enough to get off 89A's main drag and go prospecting. There were a few exceptions, though....

The woman looked like she was probably in her mid-thirties, tanned and with hair a little too blonde to be natural. Great body, though, and in that clingy tank dress, she obviously didn't mind showing it off. He noted the diamond studs in her ears, the gold bracelet draped over the Omega watch on her left wrist. No wedding ring. Either she was doing well for herself on her own, or she'd gotten the worst of some poor bastard in a divorce. Either way, he didn't really care. It wasn't as if he planned to settle down with her.

She apparently noticed him looking and flashed him a smile. Great teeth, too.

He didn't exactly smile, but gave a little nod. That was about all the effort he was willing to put forth. If she came over and engaged, great. It had been a while, and after seeing the huge ship hovering over the desert, he was thinking it might be a good thing if he could distract himself, if only for an hour or two.

It seemed to be enough. She moved toward him, and he caught a drift of perfume. Something familiar. Chanel, maybe.

"Hey," she said.

"Hey," he returned. "Don't think I've seen you in here before."

"No, it's my first time in Sedona."

Her voice was higher-pitched than he liked, with a little bit of a nasal quality he instinctively associated with Southern California. The Valley, to be precise. Well, he really hadn't planned to have a long, drawn-out conversation with her.

"Liking it so far?" he asked.

"Oh, yeah. The red rocks are so gorgeous!" It almost sounded as if she said "gah-jous," and he tried not to wince.

"Here alone?"

"In the bar or in Sedona?"

Maybe that was her version of trying to be cute. He took a drink of MGD and replied, "Both."

"Alone here at the bar, but I'm visiting Sedona with my friend Lindsay. But she was pooped after going on one of those massive Pink Jeep tours today, so I came out alone tonight. I wanted to get a taste of the nightlife before we bailed."

"You're not here for long?" This could be great. If she was leaving tomorrow, then he really wouldn't have to worry about there being any strings to this encounter.

"No, unfortunately. We're sort of making the rounds. Tomorrow we're going to a spa in Scottsdale, and then after that it's back to Newport Beach. We've got a wedding to go to."

He would have preferred she not said the "W" word, but he just replied, "Oh."

"So...." she said.

"So?"

"You a native?"

"You make it sound like I should be wearing a loincloth or something."

"Oh, you!" she exclaimed, and gave him what she most likely thought was a girlish slap on his arm. It stung a little bit more than she'd probably intended; it looked like Ms. Newport Beach had already had a few. "You know. You live in Sedona?"

"For the past ten years. My condo's just up the road."

There was no mistaking the gleam in her eyes. "Is it?"

"Yes. It's not all that much, but it works for me. And I have much better booze there."

"I'm dying for a martini. This Corona is okay, but...."

Lance allowed himself a smile. "Gin or vodka?"

Kara

I awoke to the sound of the television drifting down the hall toward my bedroom. For a second or two, I had the muddled thought that Kiki must have come over and plunked herself in front of the TV, as if trying to relive the Saturday mornings of her childhood and adolescence. However, these were more or less adult-sounding voices I heard now, not the kids' fare Kiki used to watch.

Then it came back to me. The stranger. He must be up already. Odd—you'd think with the shape he'd been in, he would have slept for at least twelve hours or more. I sat up in bed and realized that my madness of the night before seemed even crazier in the clear light of day. Well, it couldn't be helped now. Besides, if he'd intended to rob the place...or worse...he would have done the deed and taken off already. I doubted anyone intent on committing a crime would have paused to watch the Saturday morning newscast before looting the house.

Normally, I would have just crawled out of bed as-is, in my tank top and underwear, but I thought that probably wasn't a very good idea, given the circumstances. Instead, I pulled a pair of cropped yoga pants out of the bottom drawer of my dresser and put them on, then stopped in the bathroom to run the brush through my hair a few times. Probably lip gloss would be a bit too much, but I did give my lips a quick flick of some Burt's Bees balm before I headed out to the living room.

The stranger was sitting on the rug in front of the couch, much as he had the evening before. This morning, however, his eyes seemed bright enough, and I had to keep my mouth from dropping open in shock at how much he'd recovered in just a single night. I'd expected his skin to still be bright red and flaking from the repeated sunburns he'd obviously suffered, but now all I could see were a few reddish patches high on his cheekbones. Otherwise, his skin looked as bronzed and healthy as that of someone who'd paid a lot of money for tanning sessions, followed by heavy-duty moisturizing treatments.

Despite the baggy T-shirt and high-water pants he wore—he had several inches on my grandfather— he looked good. Okay, scratch that. He looked amazing. Last night, I would never have been able to guess he was even semi-attractive, let alone someone Kiki might refer to as "smokin' hot." Judging by his skin tone and the high cheekbones, I guessed he might have some Native American a generation or two back, something that was pretty common around these parts. Maybe he really was a local.

I noticed that Gort again lay by the stranger's side, getting his head scratched. Strange, as the dog really wasn't a big fan of strangers, especially male strangers. Since Gort was a rescue dog, I had always assumed he must have been mistreated by a man at some point in the past. In fact, I usually exiled Gort to the backyard whenever I had male guests, since I could never be sure how he would react to them. But there he was, sitting next to the stranger with his eyes half-closed, obviously in the doggy equivalent of nirvana.

"Feeling better?" I asked, forcing myself to concentrate on the matter at hand.

The stranger nodded. I noticed that he had a Dixie cup of water on the table in front of him—carefully set down on one of my sandstone coasters. "Much. Did the television wake you?"

"No. It was about time for me to get up." A quick glance at the clock on the wall above the TV told me it wasn't quite seven-thirty. The shop didn't open until ten.

Oh, great, the shop. What the hell was I supposed to do about that? I couldn't even call in Kiki for backup, since she was heading out to L.A. in a few hours. I hadn't been that thrilled about the Los Angeles trip from the start, but now I was even less happy. What was I supposed to do with the stranger? Drag him along to the store?

That didn't seem like much of an option, but neither did just leaving him here.

He said, "You're troubled."

Oh, God, please not another psychic. Right then, I felt as if I'd met my monthly quota of weirdness. I shook my head. "No, it's just—well, I have to go in to work in a few hours, and I'm not sure what I should do with you."

His gaze didn't flicker. "I can leave. You've done enough already."

Any protests that he wasn't well enough to do so would sound silly, considering he looked like he'd just spent a weekend getting expensive spa treatments instead of wandering around in the desert.

Then again, just because he seemed okay didn't mean he necessarily was. I cleared my throat. "I don't know if that's a good idea. You probably still need to get hydrated, and it's supposed to be a hundred degrees today." He still looked uncertain, and I added, "Besides, where would you go? Do you know anyone in town?"

"I know you."

From anyone else, I would have said such a remark was disingenuous at best, but I could tell he spoke what he thought was the simple truth. That must have been some knock on the head he'd gotten, even though there was no longer any evidence of the injury. It couldn't be simply sun exposure that had cooked the memories right out of his brain.

"Yes, you do," I replied, in tones that sounded a little too hearty even to me. "Anyway, if you don't mind hanging out here while I'm at work, then that's cool. I can come home at lunch and check on you."

"All right." His gaze shifted from me to the two talking heads on the television set. "I was hoping they might have some actual information to impart, but it doesn't sound that way."

"Well, that's what you get for watching the local news. Except it's not even that local—all the stations are based down in Phoenix, and they pretty much ignore what's going on in this part of the state unless it's something pretty spectacular." And what had he been looking for, anyway? I'd hadn't heard of any bus accidents or plane crashes in the area within the past few weeks, and surely he couldn't have been wandering around for much longer than that. It was a mystery, all right.

An even bigger conundrum was what I was supposed to feed him. I'd never been much of a breakfast person, but he looked like the sort of guy who could routinely eat large helpings of protein each morning. Well, he'd have to make do with the multigrain waffles I had in the freezer.

"You like waffles?" I asked.

He looked puzzled, then gave a half-hearted nod. "I—I don't remember."

"Well, let's find out."

It felt odd to be at the shop, knowing my house was occupied by a stranger who at the moment could be cheerfully clearing the place of everything valuable it contained. Somehow, I didn't think that was the case, though. He'd offered to clean up the breakfast dishes so I could get ready, and when I left, he was watching a broadcast of the BBC news on cable, a slight frown pulling at his dark brows. Nothing about him seemed to give the impression of someone who was just biding his time until he could call his friends to back a van up to the garage so he could take everything that wasn't nailed down.

In the end, it was Gort's behavior that decided things. To anyone else, that might have sounded stupid, but I implicitly trusted the dog's instincts—one time I'd brought home a date who turned out to be a little too grabby, and Gort became positively wolfish in my defense, scaring the guy into a hasty retreat and even taking me a little aback. I hadn't thought my pet had it in him, since he usually was one of the sweetest-tempered dogs I'd ever met. So if Gort thought having the stranger around was okay, then it must be all right.

At least tonight I didn't have any UFO tours scheduled. Word had gotten out that UFO watching in Sedona wasn't what it used to be, and although I missed the business, today especially I was glad that I could go home when the shop closed at six. Thank God that in Sedona, everyone except the restaurants and bars rolled up the sidewalks at around five or six.

I'd just started restacking the T-shirts—a group of boisterous teenagers had played havoc with the neat piles, and then wandered out, with one of them buying a stupid two-dollar magnet after all that—when the bells on the front door jingled. Hands still full with T-shirts, I turned to give my customary greeting of "Welcome to the UFO Depot"—only to see it was Persephone Oliver who'd just entered.

"I thought you'd be on the road by now," I said.

Persephone pushed her sunglasses up on top of her head and lifted a Walgreens bag by way of explanation. "Just getting some last-minute supplies. Apparently Paul's allergies have no problem with the juniper around here, but the combination of ragweed and L.A. smog is just deadly." She paused and gave me a searching glance. "Everything okay?"

"Why shouldn't it be?" Even though I'd realized a while back that Persephone was not a mind reader *per se*, it was still tough to figure out exactly what my friend could sense and what she couldn't. For all I knew, Persephone could simply sniff out the fact that I had a strange man with no known origins currently camped out in Kiki's old room.

"I don't know. Just...something." Another hesitation, and Persephone frowned. "I mean, I know you're not exactly thrilled about Kiki going along on this trip—"

"Not really," I said, figuring I might as well be honest. "That is, I'm glad you and Paul are sort of running interference, but I don't really like Kiki's sudden fascination with Jeff Makowski."

That was putting it mildly. I knew I had no right to butt into my sister's personal life, and of course I'd known that Kiki's relationship with her former boyfriend, Adam, had never been one for the ages. Kiki was only twenty-two, and Adam, though nice enough, had never seemed to have that certain something I knew my sister deserved. However, that didn't mean I wanted Kiki to start showing an interest in Jeff, the hacker who'd assisted our group in defeating the alien forces out in Secret Canyon. Even though I had to admit that he did have a certain brilliance, I also thought he was surly, insensitive, and rude, and in fact demonstrated the paranoia I associated with the worst of the tinfoil hat–wearers from the lower dregs of the conspiracy forums.

But when Persephone told all of us that she and Paul were going to L.A. in August for her friend Ginger's wedding, Kiki had piped up and asked if she could tag along, that she and Jeff had been corresponding online and talking through Skype, but there were certain things he wanted to show her that could only be done in person. From anyone else, I would have thought such a suggestion was the lowest form of come-on, but although Jeff was many things, a lech he was not. Probably Kiki had more sordid things on her mind than he did.

Even so, I'd tried to dissuade my sister from going, telling her that August, although not as busy as July, could still be pretty hectic, and that she would be needed at the store. To those remarks, Kiki had only shrugged and pointed out that I could call in Michael for relief if strictly necessary. After all, Kiki was trying to grow her computer consulting business in Sedona, and having a few of Jeff's tricks under her sleeve could only help.

Any further protests would have made me sound as if I didn't want my sister's business to succeed, so I'd shut up then. It was true that Michael had helped out on occasion when Kiki had other plans or I was sick and things were busy.

Lord knows I'd never ask Lance to come in and play shopkeeper, that was for sure.

I must have frowned, because Persephone said, "I know you're not happy about it, but we'll keep an eye on her as best we can. At least Bettina Croft got us adjoining rooms at the Marmont, so there's a limit to how much running around Kiki can do."

"I suppose."

Persephone's expression softened. Despite Sedona's fierce sun, she was still as pale as the day she'd walked into the store, looking for help rescuing Paul. "Kiki will be okay. She may not be on the path you wanted her to walk, but she'll be fine."

"Is that a prediction?" I asked, trying to keep my tone light.

"I'd say it's more from my years as a family counselor than any psychic vision, but yes." A shadow seemed to cross over her face then, and she shook her head. "Actually, it's you I'm more worried about."

"Me?" I forced a laugh and prayed she couldn't actually see into my mind. I really didn't feel like going into explanations about the stranger inhabiting my house, mostly because I couldn't explain what I'd done even to myself. "What's to worry about?" I went on. "I'm Careful Kara, the one who always sits back and minds the store."

Persephone didn't seem convinced, either by my

words or the self-deprecating tone in which they were delivered. "I don't know. I'm not getting any clear signals, but...." She lifted her shoulders, which were as pale as her face. Even so, there was something about Persephone's looks that turned heads whenever she walked in a room. She was exotic, with her curly dark hair and hazel-green eyes, making me wish I wasn't quite so all-American girl-next-door in appearance. "There's something...like that sensation you get during a thunderstorm when lightning's about to strike. Like a smell of ozone. And besides, didn't Lance tell you?"

"Didn't Lance tell me what?" Despite my best efforts, I could hear a hint of acid seep into my tone. Lance had always been quicksilver, but lately he'd seemed even worse, dropping out of contact for days at a time. Maybe he thought with the aliens gone, our little group of UFO-busters didn't need to keep in touch all that often.

Persephone's gaze shifted upward, as if piercing the shabby acoustic tile of the shop's ceiling to watch the skies above. "They're back."

"*What?*" I exclaimed, glad no one else was in the store to overhear the shock in my tone.

"That was about my reaction," she said. "Paul and Michael and Lance went out last night to see the orbs. I guess they saw a little bit more than they'd bargained for."

I finally recalled the T-shirts I was holding and

set them down more or less in place before I hurried over to my laptop and lifted the lid. Fingers poised over the keyboard, I asked, "Where exactly was it? What type? Was there any contact, or—"

Since she knew the drill, she delivered the facts in a crisp, succinct way. "They were out in Boynton. Triangular. No contact." She shrugged again and waited for me to finish typing before adding, "It shot off to the north and disappeared. Paul says he doesn't know if it spotted them or not, but they weren't doing anything to hide themselves, so who knows."

Persephone's tone was deliberately casual, but I could tell she was trying to hide her own worry. Here we'd thought we'd successfully vanquished the aliens. Obviously, it wasn't going to be as easy as that. I supposed I should have known; after all, even aided by Persephone's unexpected talent for wiping out hybrids and alien-infected humans alike, we UFO hunters were still just a small group of very fallible human beings. Of course, the aliens would return at some point to try to pick up where they'd left off. I supposed I'd just been hoping that it wouldn't be quite so soon.

"Guess I'll have to stay on my toes, then," I replied lightly.

"I'm sure you'll be safe here in town...." But even as she spoke, Persephone looked less than convinced.

I wasn't convinced, either. Voice tight, I asked,

"What about my tours? I don't have anything tonight, but I'm booked both Friday and Saturday."

"Then make sure you take either Michael or Lance with you. Preferably both."

Persephone was serious, I could tell Michael, sure, but I could just imagine Lance's reaction if I tried to get him to babysit one of my tours on a Friday or Saturday. He never talked about his personal life, but Sedona was a small town. Word got around. Kiki once derisively referred to Lance as a "man-whore," and although I wasn't quite ready to admit that about him, I also knew he didn't spend much time at home on weekend evenings.

But maybe the situation wasn't quite as bad as I feared. "The aliens could just be, I don't know, reconnoitering."

"I suppose so. But they could also be regrouping." Persephone pulled her sunglasses off her head and dangled them by one of the arms. "The timing on this couldn't be worse, but I know Ginger would have my head if I begged off matron-of-honor duties just because Paul saw some lights in the sky. But we'll back late Monday night."

"I'll be fine," I said. I was glad for Persephone's concern, but really, I'd been doing this sort of stuff for years now. I knew how to take care of myself.

All the same, I knew I'd be calling Michael for backup just as soon as Persephone left. No sense in taking any unnecessary risks.

We made our goodbyes and then Persephone left, squinting a little as she stepped out into the sunlight, glaring even at barely ten-thirty in the morning.

I drummed my fingers on the countertop, then sighed and began to reach for the phone. I'd barely wrapped her fingers around the receiver before the door opened and Kiki came sailing in. Probably not a coincidence—Kiki had already promised me that she'd drop the UFO Night Tours van off at the shop before she left town, and so she and Persephone had no doubt arranged to meet here. Why Persephone hadn't stuck around, I couldn't say. Well, actually, I could. Persephone most likely wanted to make herself scarce in case we exchanged any choice words on the subject of Jeff Makowski before Kiki left.

But I had already been down that road with Kiki, and I didn't see any point in going back over it now.

"Here are the keys," Kiki said, setting them down on the counter. "And I filled up the van on the way over."

It was Kiki's way of offering an olive branch, and so I smiled. "Thanks. You guys heading out now?"

"Yep. We're going to swing by and collect Paul and then get on the road. We should make it into L.A. around five, five-thirty."

And probably at the height of rush hour, but that was Persephone's problem. Or maybe Paul's, depending on who was doing the driving. At least it wouldn't be Kiki.

Thank heaven for small favors. Kiki behind the wheel in L.A. traffic was not something I really wanted to contemplate.

"Well, have a good trip," I said.

To my surprise, Kiki maneuvered around the counter so she could give me a quick, fierce hug. "Persephone told me about the sighting last night," she said. "You going to be okay?"

"Of course," I said automatically. Why was my throat so damn tight? Kiki was going away for five days, not forever. "I've got Michael and Lance, and the whole MUFON crew if I need them. I'll be fine."

A short honk sounded from the parking lot, and Kiki said, "That's Seph. She went to get gas while I stopped in here, but the lines weren't too long this morning. Gotta go! 'Bye!" And she heaved the embroidered linen backpack she used for a purse over one shoulder and dashed out.

Well, that was that. I wouldn't let myself sigh—that seemed a little melodramatic—but this was the first time since I'd moved back to Sedona that my sister and I had been separated for more than a few days. Kiki had moved out of our grandfather's house almost a year ago, true, although we spent so much time together between the shop and the tours and the MUFON meetings that it hardly seemed as if she had her own place.

I glanced up at the clock. Not quite a quarter 'til. I usually took my lunch around one, and with Kiki gone, that meant seeing if Michael could spell me at the shop for that hour or so. Half the time, I just ordered in and didn't stir until it was time to hang the "Closed" sign on the door, but I had to go home today. I'd told the stranger I'd be home for lunch, and so I would.

If he was even there. Sure, Gort seemed to like him, but that didn't mean I wouldn't get home and find the place cleaned out, right down to the big sixty-inch TV I'd splurged on a few months earlier.

This time I did allow myself a sigh, right before I picked up the phone and finally made that call to Michael Lightfoot.

CHAPTER THREE

THE FIRST THING THAT GREETED ME WHEN I opened the door that led from the garage to the house was the scent of the all-natural lemon verbena cleaner I used to mop the floors and spray down the countertops. Wrinkling my nose in confusion, I looked around and noticed that everything in the kitchen was sparkling clean. The chrome faucet practically glittered in the fluorescent light from overhead.

"What the...?"

Gort came bounding up to me, mouth open in a doggy smile as he headed toward the bag of sandwiches I held.

"No chance in hell, Gort," I chided him. "It's kibble time, and you know it." After setting the bag on the unnaturally gleaming counter, I went to the top shelf in the pantry where I kept his big bag of dog food. It was the only place I knew it would be safe. I took it down, still looking around in confusion. Now, I was a more or less neat person, mostly because I hated clutter. However, my schedule was hectic enough that my cleaning routine mainly consisted of wiping things down and hoping for the best. It had definitely been a while since the house looked as if a professional had gone over it.

The stranger appeared around the corner between the kitchen and the dining room, a roll of paper towels in one hand and the spray bottle of verbena cleaner in the other. "Hello."

I startled and dropped a few stray pieces of dog food, which Gort happily pounced on. "Um...hi." Pointing with my free hand at the model-home perfection of the kitchen, I asked, "Did you do this?"

"I hope it's not a problem," he said, looking a bit sheepish. "I felt as if I should be doing something besides sitting and watching the television."

A problem? No, having a stranger who looked like an underwear model doing maid duty while I was at work was definitely *not* a problem. "That's— that's great. Really. I just haven't had much of a chance to clean lately...."

The slight frown that had creased his dark brows erased itself. "Good. I got the idea from a commercial on your television."

It figured. Daytime television tended to be dominated by advertising geared toward stay-at-home moms—cleaning products, educational toys, the odd ad for a vocational college for those who might decide that getting out of the house sounded like a really good idea after the umpteenth diaper change that day. I found myself staring at the swell of his biceps below the baggy Hawaiian shirt and forced my gaze upward. Not that that really helped, either; those eyes were the most amazing green I'd ever seen.

"I brought some sandwiches," I said hastily, recalling the bag on the counter. "Hope you like chicken pesto."

"I—I don't remember."

"You'll be fine." If his appetite this morning as he put away all the remaining multigrain waffles had been any indication, he'd most likely devour pretty much anything I put in front of him. Not that I'd met anyone yet who turned up their nose at the Wildflower Bread Company's sandwiches... well, unless they ate a gluten-free diet. And since the stranger had happily devoured those waffles earlier in the day, I figured the sandwiches must be safe.

I took the bag over to the small café-style table next to the window, then went back to retrieve a couple of glasses and the pitcher of sun tea from the refrigerator. He seemed to understand what I had planned, and so he took one of the seats and waited for me to sit down as well. After I pulled one of the sandwiches out of the bag and handed it to him, he said,

"Grayson."

"Excuse me?" I paused with one hand still inside the paper bag.

"You can call me Grayson."

A little thrill went through me. Maybe he was finally starting to remember something. "That's your name?"

He shook his head. "No. I saw someone named that on one of the shows on your digital recorder, and I thought it sounded like a good name."

Good thing I didn't have anything more incriminating than old episodes of *Drop Dead Diva* on my DVR, episodes I refused to erase even though the show had been canceled years earlier. Then again, the name wasn't a bad choice. After all, the fictional Grayson was also tall, dark-haired, and gorgeous. "So...Grayson...you still don't remember anything?"

Another head shake. I noticed he was careful to finish chewing before he replied, "Nothing. Just darkness. Everything was black...and then I saw the lights of your house, and I followed them."

Pouring iced tea for both of us gave me time to think. "So, nothing at all...no explosion, or bright light, or anything like that?"

"No." He frowned as he reached for his glass of tea. "That is...I'm not sure." The frown deepened. Up close like this, I could see a few more traces of the damage he'd incurred in the desert, the smallest patch of flaking skin on his forehead, a slight redness in his eyes. Still, he had shown remarkable powers of healing. If those powers continued at this rate, by the following day, there shouldn't be any trace left of his time in the desert.

I remembered that I had a sandwich to eat and took a few bites of my own food. "You're not sure? So maybe there's...something?"

"I—I don't know." He set down the glass of tea and stared across the table at me, eyes like chips of green glass against the browned skin. "There was...a light? I don't know if that's the right word. Something that burst over me...everyone around me...and then darkness. I don't remember anything after that."

It could have been a crash of some sort. True, I hadn't heard anything about an accident like that, but that didn't mean much. Just because the aliens had been scared off didn't mean the government wasn't still testing all kinds of crap in the deserts of Arizona and New Mexico. Grayson could have been part of some sort of failed test flight or something. But I'd never heard of government agents leaving one of their own behind, especially if the person in question was a highly trained pilot.

"It's okay," I said in soothing tones. The look of distress in his eyes was real, and I suddenly wished I hadn't tried probing into his origins quite so soon. Yes, at some point I'd have to do my best to track down who he was and where he came from, but for God's sake, the guy had just collapsed in my living room the night before.

"I don't know," he replied, and that green gaze seemed to shift from me to some indeterminate point down the hallway, beyond the front door. "I don't know if it is."

Lance

He hadn't really intended to go into the UFO Depot today, but after last night's sighting, he figured he owed it to Kara to at least give her the straight scoop in person. Paul, of course, had already told Persephone, and Lance guessed she'd passed the information on to Kara. If he didn't go in and tell her what he'd seen with his own eyes, he knew she'd be more than a little put out. Michael she'd let off the hook because this was the high season for him as well—he was off this afternoon conducting one of his "spirit walk" tours of the vortexes. Even shamans had to pay the rent.

The roughly paved lot outside the store only had a handful of vehicles parked in it, one of them Kara and Kiki's garishly painted "UFO Night Tours" van. It made good advertising, but Lance knew Kara hated it and only used the van when actually ferrying tourists out to one of her tours. Kiki, on the other hand, loved driving it all over town. Subtle, Kiki was not.

A pair of tourists chattering away in Japanese pushed past him as he entered the store. They clutched multiple shopping bags against themselves as they went, so it seemed at least Kara had made a decent sale. Good. Maybe that would put her in a better mood.

As he entered the store, a blast of cold air greeted him. With the monsoon rains had come their accompanying mugginess, and he was glad Kara had decided to put comfort ahead of her electric bill. This type of conversation could be tricky enough without dripping with sweat into the bargain.

"Hey, Kara," he said, knowing it was probably better to launch a preemptive strike rather than let her get the first word in. "I suppose you heard about last night."

"Persephone might have mentioned something," she replied. Her expression didn't seem particularly irritated, but he knew her well enough to recognize that certain lift of her chin, the one that meant she was more than a little annoyed.

"Well, I figured the grapevine would get to you first, so I could take my time. Not as if anything was likely to change between now and then." Which was more or less true. The aliens in general were active at night, using the darkness to conceal their doings.

"I suppose." She made a show of tucking a credit card receipt under the money tray and then closing the cash register. "Seph thought I should ask you to come along tomorrow night, but Michael already said he would."

Hell. It would make more sense for both him and Michael to be there, since there was no telling what the aliens might be up to. Kara was smart and tough —and could both drive and shoot pretty well—but those skills might not be enough when push came to shove. When going up against extraterrestrials, you stood a better chance if you had something a little extra yourself to bring to the table.

But dragging a bunch of rubes out to Boynton or up Schnebly Road on a Friday evening wasn't exactly what he had planned for the weekend. Then again, after going four rounds with Ms. Newport Beach the night before, he thought he might be okay for a while.

He said, surprising even himself, "I'll come, too."

Kara's blue eyes widened before she recovered herself and gave a quick lift of the shoulders. "I don't need a babysitter, Lance."

"It's not babysitting. More like...running interference."

She raised an eyebrow. He had the stray thought that she was looking particularly good this morning, despite her obvious annoyance. If he didn't know better, he'd have said she'd gotten laid. Kara wasn't the type for casual flings, though, and he hadn't heard that she was seeing somebody. Still, she seemed somehow changed, as if something—or someone—had happened along to give her life some spice.

He wasn't sure how he felt about that Actually, he knew exactly how he felt about that particular possibility, but he didn't want to deal with it at the moment. Brushing away the unexpected stir of jealousy, he added, "You weren't out there at Secret Canyon—"

"You're right. I wasn't. I never get to be, do I?"

"Trust me, you wouldn't have wanted to be there."

"But I'm never given the choice."

She didn't even sound petulant, like a child begging for something she didn't understand. Her tone was calm enough. Maybe it was because she knew she was right. They never did give her the choice. She didn't have his or Michael's...skills...and Kiki was always jumping in feet first and worrying about the consequences later. Kara had to be the sensible one, the person who kept everything going. It couldn't be easy for her, always standing back, but also knowing she was the public face of their group, knowing that the computer at the shop and the desktop she kept at home were probed routinely by agencies so secret, they didn't have names. She kept enough on those computers to make sure the snoops had something to look at, but all the important stuff lived in the MacBook Air she carried with her everywhere in her oversized purse.

"Sorry, Kara," he said, and he found he genuinely was. It was times like these when he wished he could kick his scruples aside and take her in his arms and hold her the way he'd dreamed of a thousand times. But he wouldn't do that to her. He *couldn't* do that to her. "I'd feel better if I came along."

"Suit yourself," she said with a shrug. "Just no cracks that the tourists can overhear, okay?"

"Is it all right if I think them real loudly?"

Her only response was a roll of the eyes, but he thought he caught a glimpse of a smile ghosting its way around her full lips. Which meant it was okay.

So why did he feel as if things were decidedly *not* okay?

Kara

After I hung the "Closed" sign on the door at exactly six o'clock, I took a detour down to the outlet stores in Oak Creek to pick up a few odds and ends for Grayson. I had no idea how long he was going to be around, but I did know that he deserved better than high-water pants and the loudest Hawaiian shirts this side of Arnold Schwarzenegger. It seemed reasonable to pick up a few pairs of jeans, a jacket, some flip-flops. T-shirts weren't a problem; I had stacks of those back at the house. I'd have to take him somewhere in town to get some real shoes, but that could wait. Right then, I wasn't sure how I was even going to handle parading around town with the guy. Practically everyone knew me...and way more about my personal life than I would like...and someone was bound to ask questions.

I also stopped at Whole Foods to get some organic food to heat up for dinner—veggie quiche, their amazing spinach turnovers—before finally pointing my Prius toward home. By then, it was almost seven, and I hoped Grayson wasn't too worried that something might have happened to me. Besides, I knew Gort would be jonesing for a walk.

All seemed quiet enough as I pulled into the garage and parked on the left side. The right side of the garage was sacred to my grandfather's beloved Indian motorcycle, which hadn't run in more than fifteen years but which I steadfastly refused to sell. I grabbed the bags of clothes and food and headed on inside, wondering what sight was going to greet me this time.

The kitchen was still spotless, of course, but otherwise I didn't see any real evidence of Grayson's presence. More notably, Gort hadn't come running to see me, which was even stranger. Normally, the dog would be waiting at the garage door, tail wagging in anticipation of his evening walk, which he loved even more than a full bowl of kibble.

I put the takeout from Whole Foods in the refrigerator and left the bags of clothes sitting on the counter—it wasn't as if the jeans were going to spoil. It was as I turned away from the kitchen and toward the sliding glass door which opened onto the patio that I realized where Grayson had gone.

During most of my childhood, the backyard had been planted with grass that my grandfather stubbornly refused to plow under, even though the hardiest of Bermuda tended to wilt under Sedona's scorching summer sun. After I inherited the house, I had the whole thing rototilled and planted with drought-resistant trees and shrubs, with tasteful groupings of native rock, and a few years ago, Michael had come over and spent several weekends constructing a medicine wheel in the far corner of the lot. While I did my best to maintain the yard, during the summer, I had a tendency to let things go, and weeds had sprouted here and there. Not anymore. A healthy pile of bindweed and other unsightly scrub was stacked off to one side, and the spots where some of the rocks in the medicine wheel had shifted out of place were now correctly filled in.

I didn't have to look far to locate the architect of all this orderliness—Grayson stood off to one side, Hawaiian shirt knotted around his waist. His torso and arms were paler than his face and neck, but he was still pretty stare-able despite that, stomach flat and rock-hard, biceps knotted with muscle.

He seemed to notice me then, and quickly untied the shirt and pulled it back on. The slanting shadows in the backyard made the light chancy, but I could have sworn he blushed. For the first time, I noticed Gort sitting at attention a few feet away from Grayson.

"Housekeeper *and* gardener?" I asked, trying to force back some of the heat that had risen in the pit of my stomach at the sight of him half-naked. "Pretty soon, I'll have to start paying you a salary."

"Room and board is enough for now," he said, coming toward me. His posture seemed a little more relaxed now; maybe he was glad I hadn't done or said anything to give undue attention to his previously half-clad state. "Sorry about the pile of weeds—I didn't know where I should put them."

"It's all right," I replied. "There's a bin around the side of the house I use for composting. But you can leave them for now. Hungry?"

"Yes."

"Then come inside."

I went back in, both Gort and Grayson trailing behind. The dog pushed past both of us and went to his bowl, which he nudged with a metallic clank when he realized it was still empty.

"Getting to that, Gort," I told him, and poured

out his cup of kibble. He immediately set to, and I turned to the oven and got it preheating. "I'll have to walk him after he's done eating," I said to Grayson, who had been watching from the other side of the counter. "But I'll start things heating up before that so we don't have to wait too much longer for dinner."

"Do you want me to go with you?"

"'Go'?" I repeated, and then realized he was asking if I wanted him to tag along on the dog walk. As much as I would have liked that, I knew it would be opening a real can of worms if I went sauntering down the street with Grayson in tow. Sooner or later, people would find out I was shacked up with a man who had wandered in out of nowhere, but I preferred to put off that day for a while longer if possible. "Oh, no, that's okay—I thought you'd probably want to relax after working out in that hot sun all day. Maybe take a quick shower?"

"Are you saying I smell?"

His mouth quirked a bit as he asked the question, so I guessed he was teasing me. "Not as much as you did when you showed up here last night!"

I thought he'd smile for real at that comment, but instead his expression sobered abruptly. "I hope not." He ran a hand through his hair, as if trying to gauge its level of greasiness, and shrugged. "I understand. You don't want to have to explain me."

Once again, I wondered if I'd stumbled on yet another psychic. Or maybe I just wasn't used to a guy so capable of picking up on subtext. "Maybe not tonight. It's been a long day." Those green eyes suddenly seemed a little too probing, and I looked away from him. Recalling the bag on the counter, I picked it up and handed it over. "Thought you might like some clothes that actually fit."

He took the bag from me almost without thinking, but then he actually looked inside. Something in his face seemed to brighten, as if that one simple act had helped to reassure him that I didn't mean to kick him out any time soon. "Well, I definitely need to take a shower now. Don't want to put clean new clothes on top of this sweat."

"Good idea," I said, relieved that he wasn't going to discuss the dog walk any further.

He flashed a grin at me and headed down the hall toward the bathroom, carrying the clothing with him. Gort let out a little questioning whine, and I smiled, too. "Yes, you silly mutt. Let's go."

After that, the evening passed normally enough—or at least as normally as it could, considering that I still knew nothing about Grayson or where he'd come from. Aside from a complete lack of knowledge as to his past or his identity, he seemed sharp enough. Nothing in any of his reactions or his conversation seemed to indicate that he'd suffered any sort of long-term cognitive loss due to his ordeal in the desert. Judging from a few comments he made, I gathered he didn't know too much about current events or popular culture, either, unless that was just another manifestation of whatever trauma had caused him to lose his memory.

I really would have liked some wine with dinner, but alcohol was probably not a good idea for Grayson, and it didn't seem very fair to drink in front of him. So we both had iced tea, and I shooed him out to the living room when he offered to do the dishes. Enough was enough. Maybe he was bending over backward to show how useful he was so I wouldn't kick him out, but I didn't feel comfortable taking advantage of the poor guy.

Even now, though, as I told him good night and watched him close his bedroom door, I couldn't keep my mind from ticking away at the problem. Maybe it was long overdue, but I thought I should at least make a call to the Sedona P.D., see if anyone had been reported missing. I wasn't too worried about tripping any alarms; I knew the chief detective, Lieutenant Gonzales, well enough. He was a straight-up guy. Had to be, since he'd married my college roommate, Jennifer Morales.

So I went to my office and shut the door, then picked up the phone. Of course, the Sedona P.D. was a pretty small outfit, all things considered, and I had no way of knowing whether Joe was on duty that night or not. If he wasn't, no big deal. I'd try again and call him in the morning.

However, when I dialed the number, it was his voice I heard on the other end of the line.

"Gonzales."

"Hey, Joe, it's Kara." Silly of me to feel such a sense of relief in knowing he was there. Then again, he'd helped me out more than once in the past—minor stuff, like a break-in at the store that turned out to be the work of some bored high school kids, another time when someone managed to walk out of the UFO Depot with a couple hundred dollars' worth of merchandise without my noticing.

"Hey, Kara. What's up?"

"Are you busy? Because I can call back—"

He let out a not very professional-sounding snort. "Busy? My hottest case is the theft of some-one's riding mower up in Shadow Rock. I think I can spare a minute or two."

I probably should have expected that. Sedona wasn't exactly a hotbed of criminal activity. Most of what went on was petty theft, residential burglary, minor drug possession. "Thanks, Joe. Actually, I was calling to see if anyone had filed a missing-persons report lately."

"Why? You find somebody?"

"More like he found me, but yeah."

A note of warning entered Joe's voice. "Kara..."

"Come on, it's me. The guy is harmless. He

weeded my backyard for me this afternoon without my asking. What do you say to that?"

"I think you should ask him to marry you."

"Very funny. Anyway, have you heard anything?"

Joe let out a little chuckle. "Description?"

"Early thirties, I think. Six foot three, one-eighty, maybe one-ninety. Dark hair. Green eyes."

"Sounds like you ordered him from Tinder or something."

I wish.... Trying to sound businesslike, I said, "So have you got anyone on file like that?"

"Let me check."

I heard a clicking noise on the other end of the receiver that I guessed was Joe looking up the information in a database. Were there really that many missing persons in a town as small as Sedona?

A minute later, Joe was back on the line. "Here in Sedona, I got nothing, unless you count Mrs. Haskell calling me for the umpteenth time to complain about her husband disappearing to go fishing on the Verde River. Guess that's not the sort of thing you meant...and anyway, Philip Haskell is anything but a thirty-something stud with dark hair and green eyes."

"I never said he was a stud."

"You didn't have to. I heard it in your voice."

I bit back a sigh and began to regret making the call in the first place. There were other people I could have asked. Then again, Lance was one of the people I looked to when I needed someone to dig into law enforcement data, and right then, Lance was about the last person I wanted to know anything about Grayson.

"Anyway, over in Cottonwood, I've got a man who got in a fight with his girlfriend and took off. Haven't heard from him since, but I don't think he's your guy, either, because the party in question is Hispanic and five foot eight. No one up in Flagstaff, and nothing down in Camp Verde or all the way over to Prescott. I can check Phoenix if you like."

"No, that's all right," I said absently, my brain turning over the information Joe had just given me. Somehow, I knew in my gut that Grayson hadn't wandered here all the way from Phoenix. "I thought I'd check with you just to be sure."

"Are you sure everything's okay, Kara?"

"Of course it is," I said, an automatic response. "You know how careful I am."

"True. You have a good night."

"You, too, Joe. And tell Jen I said hi."

I hung up and stepped away from the desk, arms crossed as I considered what to do next. The call to Joe had been a long shot. At least I knew he would let it alone, wouldn't try to press me for more information. After all, wasn't I Careful Kara? I couldn't possibly be involved in anything as crazy as letting a stranger with amnesia crash at my house.

Right.

Even though the missing-person angle was a dead end, there had to be something, some scrap of evidence that would help to explain the mystery of Grayson's origins. But he'd wandered out of the desert with nothing on him, no I.D., no car keys, not a single piece of jewelry, not even a watch. All he'd had was the clothes on his back.

The clothes on his back....

Struck by a sudden thought, I strode out of my office and into the garage. I'd discarded Grayson's wreck of a jumpsuit out there in a messy pile by the washer and dryer, not knowing what else to do with it. Even now, I didn't relish the thought of picking up the dirty, malodorous garment, but there didn't seem to be anything else for it. Using only my fingertips, I lifted the jumpsuit from the ground and spread it across the top of the washer, looking for anything out of the ordinary, anything that might provide a clue.

The stink of it rose from the rusty, grayish-black fabric, and I did my best to breathe through my mouth so I wouldn't have to smell any more than was absolutely necessary. Nose wrinkling, I turned the garment over, but it just looked like a worn-out jumpsuit. It was stained everywhere, holes worn through the knees and the elbows, and with a jagged tear at the bottom of the left leg where it must have gotten caught on some rocks or been ripped by a juniper branch or something similar. Grayson obviously had gone through hell, whatever had happened to him.

As I flipped the jumpsuit back over again, a flash of white at the back of the neck caught my eye. That piece of white was the garment's tag. Simple enough —it had a stylized American flag and the words "Patriot Uniform Company" woven into the fabric, with the legend "proudly made in the USA" written out below that in smaller type. On the back, it said, "100% cotton, machine wash," but below that was a tiny number, so small that I had to lift the jumpsuit closer to the bare lightbulb on the wall above the washing machine so I could read it: "23112056." It must be a serial number of some sort.

"Gotcha," I said aloud. Of course, it was too late to be calling this Patriot Uniform Company, whoever and whatever they were. But I'd look them up online and get the information together so I could call from the shop in the morning. If they were meticulous enough to be weaving a serial number into their jumpsuits' tags, then there was a good chance they'd have some information stored on who they'd sold the garments to.

The jumpsuit suddenly seemed too precious to be left lying on the garage floor, so I folded it up the best I could and tucked it into a spare garbage bag before turning off the light and heading back inside. I paused in the hallway outside the room where Grayson lay sleeping, but I heard nothing. Good. I wasn't sure if I wanted him to know about my latest Nancy Drew trick or not. He obviously seemed troubled by the subject of his past, but whether that was because of his inability to remember anything, or whether he actually had begun to catch glimpses of something unpleasant, I didn't know.

The phone rang as I was halfway down the hall to my office, and I hurried to pick it up, hoping I'd caught it before it woke Grayson. I glanced at my watch. Five minutes after ten. Usually, I didn't get calls at that hour unless there was an emergency. My heart rate sped up a little as I grabbed the receiver and said, "Hello?"

"Hey, Kara, I know it's kind of late, but we've been so busy running around that I didn't really get a chance to call—"

"It's okay, Kiki." I willed my heartbeat to normalize, then said, "So you got into town okay?"

"Oh, yeah, but the traffic was a *nightmare*. We didn't even get to the hotel until almost eight. And then Ginger wanted to take us all out—she is so cool, totally bought drinks for the whole table. And we've got the coolest rooms at this Chateau Marmont place—"

"Well, that's good," I cut in, knowing if I didn't do so, I'd probably be subjected to a long description of everything else "cool" in Kiki's immediate vicinity. "So, what's on the agenda for tomorrow?"

"Seph has to do some wedding stuff with Ginger,

and Paul is meeting with some members of the local MUFON group. Jeff said he'd pick me up here in the morning and take me back to his place, since he doesn't live far."

Jeff. I was still less than thrilled about the whole thing, but Kiki was an adult. Let her make her own mistakes. I couldn't figure out what the hell my sister saw in that scruffy, antisocial computer hacker. He might be halfway decent-looking if he was cleaned up, but a good haircut and a shave probably wouldn't do much to improve his attitude. And there were plenty of presentable young men in Sedona who would be more than happy to date Kiki, now that she and Adam had broken up, but she was having none of them. Oh, well.

"Going to do a little hacking 101?"

Kiki sighed. "Oh, please, Kara, we're way past 101. But yeah, he has some stuff he really wants to show me."

I hope it's just code he wants to show you, I thought. However, I only said, "Well, it's good you'll have something to keep you occupied while Seph and Paul are busy. Doing the same on Saturday, then?"

"Probably. Ginger invited me to the wedding, but I don't really know her, and I'd feel weird going without a date. And Jeff said he absolutely wouldn't go any place where he was expected to wear a tie, so...."

"I didn't think they wore ties in L.A.," I said absently.

"Well, at *weddings*."

"I guess that makes sense."

There was a short pause. Then Kiki asked, "Is everything okay? You sound a little weird."

My response was automatic. "I'm fine. It's been busy, so I'm tired. I was just about to get ready for bed when you called, since I've got a long day tomorrow."

Another hesitation. "Maybe you should cancel the tours this weekend. I mean, with *them* showing up again and all—"

"I am not canceling. It's two full tours. That's too much money to throw away." *I'm not going to let those aliens chase me out of my own backyard.* "Besides, both Michael and Lance are coming, so short of heading out there with a bunch of Army Rangers, I think I'm doing about the best I can."

"Lance is coming? Really?"

"Really."

"Well, I guess if Michael is there as a chaperone, you two kids should be safe enough."

"Very funny." I wouldn't let myself think about how much that casual joke stung, about how much I would have liked to drive out somewhere under the stars and have Lance hold me as the warm night wind swirled around us. I cleared my throat. "Okay, Keeks, I've really got to get to bed. Call me at the shop tomorrow if you have a chance, but otherwise, I'll try you."

"I'll call you when I can. Jeff has a cellular jammer at his house, so calls can't get in."

Of course he does. "Well, all right, but if I don't hear from you, I'm going to have no choice but to call Persephone to check up on you."

"I'll call, I'll call!" Kiki exclaimed in mock-horror. "Even if I have to go out on the street corner to do it. One big sister breathing down my neck is enough."

"I'm not so sure about that," I replied. "But okay. I'll talk to you later."

"'Bye."

I heard the line go dead and replaced the handset in the receiver. It was silly to be worrying about Kiki—she had Seph and Paul with her, and they'd make sure she was fine. No doubt they'd be worrying about me if they knew I had a strange man sleeping in Kiki's old bed.

Well, I hadn't been lying about one thing. It really had been a very long day. I'd worry about tomorrow, tomorrow.

Or maybe I wouldn't. It seemed as if I already had plenty of people worrying for me....

CHAPTER FOUR

Mornings were generally quiet at the store. Oh, sure, you had the diehards who were eager to hit the shopping trail as soon as they were done with breakfast, but most of the time, the real crowds didn't show up until well after lunch, and often liked to linger until I shooed them out at closing time. I sympathized with their frustration over most of the stores closing by six—there wasn't much to do in Sedona except shop, hike, or go out to eat—but that didn't mean I wanted to be stuck at the store at all hours just because someone was used to shopping until nine back home. When in Rome....

At any rate, after the early birds had come and gone, I figured it was safe enough to try making a call to the Patriot Uniform Company. I'd already looked up their contact information on my laptop—no point in letting the snoops know what I was up to—so it was just a matter of timing.

No one had pulled into the parking lot. I figured I'd have at least a couple of minutes free. Better to do it now.

I picked up my cell phone and dialed the number, reading it off the site I'd cached on my MacBook Air.

A vaguely hostile female voice said, "Patriot Uniform Company."

Since I had dealt with a lot worse over the years than snotty-sounding operators, I replied calmly, "Hi, I was wondering if you could provide me with some information on one of your products?"

"Would you like to talk to someone in our sales department?"

"Sure." That sounded reasonable enough. After all, it was the salespeople who would probably know more about which items were sold to whom. I waited as the operator patched the call through.

An infinitely friendlier male voice came over the line. "Hi, this is Ben Parsons. Can I help you?"

"Hi, Ben," I said. "My name is Karen Sherman, and I'm with an outfit in Boulder, Colorado." I knew better than to give the guy any real information, no matter how friendly he might sound. And my phone had all its caller ID information blocked, so anyone on the other end of the line wouldn't be able to figure out where I was calling from...unless the Patriot

Uniform Company had far more sophisticated equipment than I thought.

"Sure, Karen. How can I help you?"

"We're looking to purchase approximately one hundred jumpsuits. I was thinking black, with utility pockets on the legs. A friend recommended your company, and said he thought the ones numbered '23111056' might be a good fit."

"Let me check on that—we produce a large number of items, and I don't have all the SKUs memorized."

"No problem." I shifted the cell phone from one hand to the other and looked over at the door when I noticed movement outside, then relaxed. Just someone using my parking lot as a throughway to the ATV rental place next door. At another time, I might have mentally cursed the person in question for using my lot as an auxiliary road, but right then, I wasn't going to worry about it.

"Ms. Sherman?" Suddenly, Ben Parsons didn't sound quite so friendly.

"Um, yes?"

"I don't know where your friend got his information, but we've never manufactured a jumpsuit with that particular SKU."

"Really?"

"I'm afraid so. Maybe he got the name of our company mixed up with someone else."

"Oh, wow, I'm so sorry," I said. "I'll have to

double-check with my friend...he could have written down the wrong SKU or something. I apologize for wasting your time."

"It's no problem. You have a nice day." And he hung up abruptly, as if he didn't want to run the risk of me asking any more questions.

What the...? I didn't pretend to be psychic, but I thought I was a pretty good judge of people, and though I didn't know this Ben Parsons from Adam, I had the distinct impression he was lying. Why, I couldn't begin to guess.

Unless Grayson really was involved in some sort of secret government test or project. I suppose if that's what's going on, then this Mr. Ben Parsons would have plenty of reasons why he wouldn't want to say who those jumpsuits had been sold to...or even admit that his company manufactures them at all.

Of course, that took me right back to the beginning. I'd already suspected Grayson might have been involved in some sort of covert operation, but if that was the case, I couldn't understand why he'd been left to wander around in the desert. Lance had already filled me in on just how sophisticated the government's scanning and surveillance equipment was; if some secret operation had lost a man out in the wastes between Sedona and the New Mexico border, you could be damn sure they'd be able to find him. Hell, according to Lance, they'd probably be able to pin a scorpion down to a single square yard, let alone a grown man.

Lance. I wished I could discuss Grayson with him, but that wasn't going to happen—I could only imagine the lecture he'd give me for taking in a stranger and not reporting it to anyone. Not to mention the weird baggage between us, the baggage neither one of us wanted to acknowledge. After all, we were just friends.

Right.

At least I was able to admit to myself that I was attracted to Lance, wanted something more from him than friendship. He'd always maintained a neutral stance with me, but every once in a while, I'd catch an odd look in his eyes, something that told me maybe he wasn't quite as disinterested as he wanted me to believe.

Or maybe I was just flattering myself.

One time, after Lance had just left the UFO Depot, Kiki remarked in overly dramatic tones, "I'm a rebel, Dottie...a loner." I'd stared at her blankly for a moment until I realized my little sister was quoting a line from a PeeWee Herman movie where PeeWee was trying to give the brush-off to a female friend who was just a little too interested in him. Trust Kiki to pull up some obscure bit of '80s pop culture and apply it to Lance.

In a weird way, it did fit, though. Lance had done a pretty good job of cultivating his "lone wolf" persona. I knew he'd been in Special Forces before he was recruited for the Army's remote viewing project, but other than that, Lance hadn't revealed squat about his past. Maybe he was hiding some deep, dark secret, something he believed would keep us apart...or maybe he only maintained that pose because it made a good excuse for holding me at arm's length.

Contrast that with Grayson, who seemed almost too giving, too open. Not that he had much to be open about, because at the moment, his past was apparently a deep, dark hole, but at least I could tell he wasn't hiding anything from me on purpose. And now that the jumpsuit was apparently a dead end, I didn't have a clue as to where I should look next.

Well, that wasn't precisely true. Even though Persephone was out of town, I knew I didn't need a psychic to delve into Grayson's past. Among my acquaintance were several hypnotherapists who'd probably be willing to lend a hand. It wouldn't exactly be a past-life regression, since all I really wanted to know was who Grayson was and where he'd come from, but maybe a hypnosis session would help to get past that barrier, shine a little light into the dark that shrouded his origins.

First, though, I had to get through the UFO tour tonight. I'd already explained to Grayson that I had to go out that evening, although he'd only raised an eyebrow when I tried to describe a UFO night tour to him. He was too polite to say anything, but I got the distinct impression he was thinking, *Wow, people actually pay for that?*

At least by that point, I knew I could leave him at the house with no negative repercussions, but something still felt wrong about it. Maybe it was only that I hadn't left him there alone at night before this, or maybe I was beginning to pick up some of what Persephone referred to as her "spider sense." Either way, it didn't really matter. I wouldn't cancel the tour, not when almost a grand was riding on it.

"Everything is going to be fine," I said aloud to the empty store, although at the moment I couldn't say whether I was trying to reassure the universe...or just myself.

Lance

He leaned against the side of his Jeep and tried not to scowl as he surveyed the group Kara had assembled for the night's UFO-watching tour. Ten in all, which was probably why she had refused to cancel the trip. That was a serious chunk of change. Even now she stood in front of the motley assortment of tourists, holding the military-spec night-vision goggles she used for the tours and explaining how they worked.

One group of four appeared to be college-age

kids, all of whom were trying to look serious but who couldn't help but trade typical twenty-something side-eyes at each other as Kara described the various types of UFOs that had been spotted over Sedona and how to track them. Lance wondered what the hell they were doing on a UFO tour if they didn't believe in the phenomenon to begin with. Maybe a dare. Or maybe they were already bored with Sedona's limited nightlife and were looking for something unusual to do.

In addition to the kids, there were two married couples, one probably in their early thirties, the other somewhere in their mid-fifties. They all seemed pretty serious, listening intently as Kara gave her spiel. The last two were both women who looked to be in their late forties, with the sort of wide-eyed but also piercing gaze that Lance recognized all too well from countless MUFON meetings and UFO symposiums. These were true believers, come here to either reinforce some previous close encounters, or desperately trying to prove to themselves that what they believed wasn't just smoke and fairy tales.

It's a lot of things, but fairy tales it ain't. Some days, he wished it really was all crap. Maybe then he could have some peace. But the aliens seemed to have returned from their sabbatical, and he had to stay on guard.

His gaze moved to Michael Lightfoot, who was a watchful shadow near the rear end of the UFO

Night Tours van. Lance had driven Michael here, and they'd take Lance's Jeep out to the site. Kara would drive the van. Luckily, this group seemed okay with being driven to the site; sometimes people stubbornly insisted on taking their own vehicles, even if they weren't suited for the terrain. The Night Tours van might look shabby on the outside—he still recalled Persephone's crack about it being their "Scooby van"—but it had a beefed-up suspension and run-flat tires. Not true four-wheel drive, unlike his Jeep, but it could handle the ground at the sites Kara used, unlike some tourist's rented Chevy Malibu.

"Everybody got it?" Kara asked, and the group responded with a variety of head nods and "uh-huh"s. They all piled into the van as she headed to the driver's-side door.

He approached her and said, "Boynton, right?"

"Yep," she replied. "I figured if the UFOs don't want to come out and play, we have a better chance of seeing the orbs in that area than up on Schnebly."

Her tone was casual, but something in her expression made him pause and give her a sharp look. It wasn't worry—he would have understood that—but instead something close to preoccupation, as if her thoughts were someplace else. And that bothered him, because tonight she needed to be sharp. Chances were, nothing would happen, but if it did....

He asked, "You okay?"

"I'm fine." She shrugged, her hair slipping over her shoulders as she did so. Even in the uncertain light of the one street lamp in front of the shop, those long strands gleamed gold.

He'd always wondered what that hair would look like spread out on a pillow next to him.

Well, you're not going to find out any time soon. "All right. We're right behind you."

A nod, and she turned away from him to climb into the driver's seat of the van before slamming the door with a resounding thud. He didn't know if the slam had been intentional or not. He got the distinct impression she wasn't all that happy to have him and Michael along as babysitters. When it came down to it, Lance had a thing or ten he would rather have been doing tonight, too, but Kara's safety overrode everything else. Frankly, he didn't really give two shits about the tourists, although he supposed it would be bad for business and tourism in general if one of these trips went sideways and word got out.

He went back to the Jeep and slid behind the wheel. Michael was already waiting in the passenger seat.

"Hope you packed a flask, my friend," Lance remarked, to which Michael only gave him a level stare and a small head shake.

Sometimes Lightfoot had absolutely no sense of humor.

Kara

I bounced the van along Boynton Pass Road, fingers gripped around the steering wheel. Luckily, the tourists were busy talking amongst themselves and didn't seem to notice my preoccupation. That is, the group of four college students were being almost too boisterous, chattering and laughing. Maybe they were feeling uneasy and were overcompensating. Didn't really matter. Their commotion made it easy for me to avoid engaging any of the other passengers in conversation.

The road was paved, but it had been years since it had gotten anything more than a casual patch job, and it was giving the shocks a run for their money. I didn't mind too much. It gave the impression that we really were going way off the beaten path, far from the restaurants and shops that lined 89A, the town's main drag.

Out here was pure inky darkness. In a few hours, a quarter moon would rise, but in the meantime, there wasn't anything to interfere with the view. I remembered the first time Grandpa brought Kiki and me out here to see the stars. Of course, Kiki had run around, looking at everything but the sky, but I'd been transfixed by the expanse of the Milky Way that revealed itself in the indigo-blue skies above the desert town. I'd never realized that many stars filled the heavens. I'd fallen in love.

It took me a few years more to realize not everything that glittered in the night sky was that beautiful.

I pulled off to the side of the road, at a spot where a trailhead dead-ended. We'd hike out into the juniper and mesquite from here. Not too many snakes in this area, thank God, not that they'd be much of a problem even on a warm night like this. Our group actually ran more risk of startling some javelinas and having to scurry out of the way of the odd-looking boar-like creatures. They did tend to be pretty territorial.

"Okay, we're here," I called over my shoulder, and the chatter dropped in volume somewhat but didn't stop altogether. Fine. With any luck, the twenty-somethings would scare off any wild animals within a quarter-mile radius.

We all climbed out of the van and stood waiting in the gravelly sand at the road's border. A few seconds later, Lance's Jeep pulled in and parked a few yards away. The two men got out, Michael towering over Lance by half a head, although Lance was certainly not short. They paused a short distance away from the group, obviously waiting for me to give the rest of my little speech.

"I know you're all eager to get out there, so I'll make this quick," I said, using the brisk, no-nonsense tones I found worked best for these tours. "We all need to stick together. No wandering off—it can get disorienting out here, especially if you're not used to the wilderness. And there's no moon yet to help guide you, so that goes double tonight.

"The binoculars I handed out back at the shop will do most of the work for you. It helps if you stay as still as possible as you're watching the skies. And please, no playing jokes with camera flashes. You can temporarily blind someone."

The twenty-somethings murmured amongst themselves, as if possibly plotting something, but I shot them a quelling look and they subsided.

"Remember," I went on, "you'll be able to tell the UFOs from other objects such as satellites or planes by their movements. UFOs are known to exhibit non-ballistic movement, which means they can stop suddenly, shoot off at odd angles, disappear altogether. Believe me, you'll know when you see one."

Again some *sotto voce* chattering, this time from everyone in the group except the two women I'd already pegged as serious UFO believers. They gripped their binoculars and looked around them as if they expected a couple of Greys to emerge from one of the manzanita bushes.

"Michael?" I called out, and he nodded.

"Follow me," he said.

They fell into line behind him, not questioning him taking the lead even though I was the tour operator. Funny how everyone expected the Native American to be the trailblazer. I knew my way around here pretty well, but if I had Michael along, I sure as hell was going to put him in the lead. He could probably be dropped into one of these canyons blindfolded and still find his way out without breaking a sweat.

Lance took up the rear, one hand resting casually at his hip. I hoped to God he wasn't carrying. Probably not—most likely, such a stance was second nature to him, even if he was unarmed. Still, it unnerved me a little. Or maybe it was just having him directly behind me, watching as I negotiated my way over the rough ground. At least I wasn't wearing shorts. One particularly hot night, I tried that and came away with manzanita scratches all over my bare legs. Ever since, I'd worn jeans and hiking boots when conducting these tours, no matter how warm it might be.

The spot I usually chose for UFO watching out in Boynton was only about ten minutes off the road, so it wasn't too long before Michael stopped on the little rise that was our destination. The other UFO tour operators knew this was my stake and didn't intrude; there was certainly plenty of open ground around Sedona to choose from. True, not all of it was prime UFO-watching territory, but there weren't so many of us that we had to worry about tripping over each other. Besides, I'd heard that Craig's group was going up to Schnebly tonight, which was part of the reason I'd come out here.

"Okay, everyone," I said. "Eyes to the skies. If you see something, call it out so the others can have a chance to look in that quadrant. It's usually better if you decide in advance which part of the sky you're going to watch so there isn't too much overlap."

A hurried convo among the participants followed these instructions, and then almost as one they strapped on the binoculars and swiveled their heads upward to view the heavens. I heard a few gasps and *oohs* and *ahs*. So many visitors to Sedona came from big cities, and they'd never before seen the glory of a desert sky at night.

Even after so many years, I wasn't completely jaded, but I didn't need the binoculars to see the constellations, and in fact preferred to keep them off. It was easier to go to a particular client if necessary when I wasn't encumbered with the night-vision lenses. I stood off to one side and watched as they pointed upward and chattered and compared notes.

Something moved lazily overhead, a bright star I could see even with my naked eyes. I watched it for a few seconds, then realized Lance had come to stand next to me.

"Space station?" he asked.

"Think so. The time would be about right." I kept my tone casual and tried not to think about how close he stood to me. His proximity probably had far more to do with not wanting to be overheard than because he was trying to create some sort of intimate moment. I knew better than that.

"A couple more weeks, and it'll be time for the Perseids," he remarked.

"Yeah, I know. I hate that."

He arched an eyebrow.

"Oh, come on, Lance, you know what a pain those things are. Everyone thinks they're seeing crashing UFOs. I should just close up shop that week and go to Vegas or something."

"Didn't know you gambled."

"I don't. I'm all about the buffets."

He actually halfway grinned at that remark, white teeth flashing in the darkness. It was nice to see him without his ubiquitous mirrored sunglasses, the ones that made him look like a cop even when wearing jeans and a T-shirt. Then again, that was probably the whole reason he wore them in the first place.

Michael came up on the other side of us. "Nice group tonight."

"Yes," I responded, glad of his presence. It was somehow a lot easier to stay focused when Michael was around. "I was sort of shocked that I actually got a full booking. Things have been kind of sparse the past few weeks. Apparently, word's gotten out that UFO watching this summer is not it's all cracked up to be."

"Hmm." His gaze was fixed eastward, where a few flickers of lightning showed above the ridge that marked the edge of the Mogollon Plateau. A short time later, thunder rumbled toward us, and I heard one of the college-age girls gasp out loud.

"It's miles off," I called out to the grcup. "No worries. We might see some rain before dawn, though."

That was how it worked out there. The storms came rumbling in from the Gulf of Mexico, hot and laden with moisture. When the rain finally cid come, it was cool and refreshing, if short-lived. A lot of people disliked the monsoon flow, and the latter part of the summer tended to be the slowest because of visitors trying to avoid it, but I had always enjoyed the turbulent weather. Something in the storm clouds and the sudden, jagged flashes of lightning called out to me. Then again, I loved Sedona in all its seasons, whether the red rocks were crowned with thunderheads in August or tipped with snow in January.

"Hey!" one of the boys called out. Travis, I thought his name was, though I couldn't remember for sure. "What's that?"

Nine other heads swiveled upward to where he was pointing. I followed his gesture as well, although I didn't really expect to see anything besides a low-flying plane. You got those out here, even at night; Sedona's airport closed at dusk, but Prescott and

Flagstaff weren't that far off, and they had much longer hours of operation at their airports.

But the object skimming the ridge line to the west didn't look like an airplane, or a helicopter. I'd seen that shape before, just once—only then the enormous triangular craft had shot almost directly upward at a speed no human-built craft could manage. This one, though, kept dropping lower, heading straight toward us like an old-style fighter plane coming in for a strafing run. A beam of white light shot out from underneath, illuminating a narrow band of scrub brush to almost daytime brightness.

"Take off your binoculars!" Lance shouted, bolting past me toward the group of sky-watchers, who didn't have even enough time to become frightened, judging by their general air of confusion. "Down! Everybody down!"

I had never heard that note of command in his voice before, but even the boisterous college students recognized it for what it was and dropped to the dirt. The ship moved closer, and now I could feel the hair on my arms and along the back of my neck prickling, smell the tang of electricity in the air.

...that sensation you get during a thunderstorm when lightning's about to strike. Like a smell of ozone....

Persephone's words rang in my mind, and I wondered if that was what the psychic had meant.

Lance's voice cracked like a whip. "Kara!"

I knew I should be moving, should be scuttling in the dirt along with the rest of the group, all of whom had taken shelter beside a nearby clump of manzanita. Something seemed to hold me in place, though, kept my boots rooted to the ground as if the sandy soil had become magnetized. My reply got stuck in my throat, like those times when I'd awakened with night terrors, trying to scream but finding no air to fuel my cries.

The beam of light moved closer. I knew it would be on me next, burning me with its white heat.

Must move....

But still my muscles wouldn't obey my brain's commands. The sand sent up little wisps of steam into the night air as the light traced its way to me. Was I the aliens' target, or only collateral damage of some kind of probe?

Something hard hit me, forcing me to the ground, pushing me out of the path of the light beam. It was only after a dazed second that I realized it was Lance who had landed on me, who was sheltering me with his body. Past his shoulder, I saw something dark standing between me and Lance and the aliens' beam, a tall shape that raised its arms as if warding off the probe.

Michael. It sounded as if he was chanting something, but between the earth-shaking hum emanating from the ship and the shrieks from the tour group, I couldn't tell hear what he was saying. I wanted to scream at him to run, to move out of the way of the beam, but still my voice felt strangled in my throat... or maybe Lance had knocked the wind out of me when he pushed me out of harm's way.

For a few seconds, the ship didn't move. It hovered a hundred feet off the ground, beam stationary, as Michael stared up at it, arms still outstretched, the low monotone of his chant a counterpoint to the throbbing drone of the enormous vessel's engines. Then the beam disappeared and the ship shot almost directly upward, disappearing into the night sky.

For a long while, no one moved. Finally, I felt Lance shift off me and climb to his feet. He brushed at the dusty knees of his jeans and shot an incongruous smile at the group of terrified tourists.

"Well, kids, looks like you just had your first close encounter."

CHAPTER FIVE

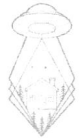

Kara

Lance insisted on driving me home Just as well, because my hands still shook so much, I didn't know if I could have even inserted the key in the ignition, let alone maneuvered the van back onto the road and down to town. He'd given his own keys to Michael so he could drive the Jeep. The tourists, shaken and quiet, had piled into the back of the van with such alacrity that I almost smiled, despite everything that had happened. Obviously, they were more than ready to get the hell out of Boynton Canyon.

At least no one even mentioned a refund. I'd had the thought in the back of my mind—in the part of my brain that didn't feel like scrambled eggs, that is—that one of them might ask for their money back, since the tour had barely lasted ten minutes. However, everyone seemed to be sufficiently freaked out that they only hurried to their cars once the van pulled into the UFO Depot's parking lot. Probably most of them were headed out to get a good stiff drink.

God knows I needed one.

I wished I could have asked Michael exactly what the hell he had done to drive off the UFO, but that would have to wait for later. At the moment, my biggest problem was making sure Lance dropped me off quickly and didn't try to loiter around the house, making sure I was all right. I had the feeling I'd completely melt down if I had to attempt explaining Grayson to Lance right now.

He was grimly quiet as he piloted the van down 89A and headed into the quiet residential neighborhood north of the highway where my house was located. We pulled into the driveway, and he shut off the headlights before killing the engine and pulling the key from the ignition.

"Thanks, Lance," I said. I'd managed to sound almost normal, though I wasn't quite sure how. "You can take the van. If you drop it off at the shop tomorrow morning, I'll drive you home—"

"What the hell are you talking about? You think I'm just going to drop you here after what happened?"

"Well, yeah. Everything's okay now, so—"

"Everything is not okay. You think they won't come back? You think I didn't see how they were headed straight for you?"

"That was probably just a coincidence," I said, although my voice shook a little and I knew I wouldn't have sounded convincing to anyone, let alone Lance.

"Coincidence? Nothing with these bastards is a coincidence, and you know that!"

I knotted my hands in my lap and forced myself not to raise my voice as I replied, "Okay, fine, but you know as well as I do that you can't stop them if they really want to come after you."

"Michael did," Lance said, his tone flat.

"Yes, all right. But I sure don't know what trick he used, and I'm guessing you don't, either. So I really don't see the point in you staying here and being my babysitter."

"Let's go." Lance opened the door and got out, so I had no choice but to do the same and then wait as he locked the door and came around the back of the van to meet me. "I'm not going to argue with you, Kara."

"What, are you going to pick me up and throw me over your shoulder so you can carry me into the house or something?"

"If I have to."

And he had the balls to do precisely that, if I continued to cross him. Scowling, I stalked past him and up the front walk, mentally rehearsing a litany of plausible lies about Grayson. *He's my cousin from San Francisco...he's my college roommate's brother... he's a member of the Phoenix MUFON group and needed crash space....*

Anything except, *Oh, he's this stranger who almost dropped dead in my living room after wandering around in the desert for God knows how long. And by the way, his memory is shot, but I have a sneaking suspicion he's connected somehow to a secret government test program.*

"The light in your garage is on."

Startled, I looked past Lance to see a thin outline of yellow light marking the edges of the garage door. It had to be Grayson, but I didn't want to admit that to Lance. No sign of Gort, either, which meant the dog was out in the garage as well. Thank God I usually put Gort outside when I had male company, so Lance probably wasn't in the habit of looking for the dog. "I must've left the light on when I was out there doing laundry."

He apparently found the explanation plausible, because he shrugged and followed me up the walk to the front door. I turned the key in the lock, praying that Grayson wouldn't be sprawled out on the living room couch, watching some embarrassing chick flick on the DVR, or wandering around in his underwear.

Silence greeted us, and I sucked in a little breath as I went inside, Lance a pace or two behind. The lights were on, and the air conditioning hummed away in the background, but other than that, there were no obvious signs of anyone being anywhere around. So Grayson must be out in the garage. I could only hope whatever was occupying him would keep him out there until I could get rid of Lance.

"See?" I said, after I dropped my purse on the dining room table. "All's quiet. Just go home and get some rest."

He ignored me and went into the kitchen. Thank God Grayson was such a neatnik. I'd left takeout for him to heat up for dinner in my absence, but the counters were spotless, the dishes hidden inside the dishwasher.

"I've got some leftover Indian food in the fridge if you're hungry," I suggested.

"I'm not hungry." In the fluorescent light, his eyes looked almost like molten silver, and far too sharp. "You always leave the air on like this when you go out?"

"I was in a hurry. Normally, I turn up the thermostat before I leave. What, are you the conservation police now?"

"No. Something doesn't feel right."

"Of course it doesn't feel right," I snapped. "We almost got strafed by a UFO tonight. So if you want to go look under my bed for little gray men, feel free, but I doubt they're hiding in the fridge."

For a minute, he didn't say anything, but only surveyed the kitchen with that gray laser-beam stare. "Kara, what aren't you telling me?"

Over the years, I'd wondered exactly how psychic Lance really was. He always denied it. However, I didn't see how someone could be in the army's remote-viewing project and not have at least some latent abilities. I had to hope to hell he wasn't reading my mind now, but instead interpreting some wordless tell that had betrayed me without my knowing it.

"I'm not *not* telling you anything, Lance. Well, okay, besides the fact that I'm tired and want a long soak in the bathtub. I'll just have to hope the aliens don't want to jump in and play with my rubber duck."

His gaze flickered at the mention of the bath, although he didn't say anything at first. Finally, he stalked out of the kitchen and through the living room, then down the hall. I found myself holding my breath as he peered into Kiki's old room. All it would take was one sock left in the middle of the floor, one abandoned flip-flop, and I'd find myself having to invent explanations I really didn't want to make.

But here again there was no visible sign of Grayson's presence, and after doing a quick survey of the office, the bathroom, and my room, Lance seemed almost satisfied.

"Not going to look under the bed?" I inquired after he'd completed his sweep and headed back into the living room.

"It looks clear."

"It *is* clear."

Still, he stood there, looking oddly irresolute for Lance. I tried not to recall how it had felt to have the weight of his body against mine, the heat of his breath on my neck as he shielded me from the aliens. It was the closest physically we'd ever been. He'd only done it to protect me, though. Maybe in the movies such contact would lead to other things, but I knew better than to hope for such an outcome here.

Hoping to mollify him, I said, "If I notice anything strange, I'll call. I promise."

"I might not get here fast enough."

I asked, "Isn't that a risk I've taken ever since I got mixed up with you guys?"

It was only the simple truth, but before that moment, I'd never had the guts to say such a thing out loud. For the first year I'd run the shop, I'd thought of it as a harmless enough endeavor, the legacy of a beloved grandfather who had a fascination with UFOs. I hadn't believed in any of it until Michael Lightfoot approached me one night, spoke to me gravely about the the real situation in the depths of Secret Canyon...took me to see the orbs, and then the mysterious lights in the sky. From then on, I'd been a believer, had used the shop as the nexus of the underground UFO activity that swirled around Sedona and through the greater desert Southwest.

Lance's mouth tightened. "Maybe it is. But it sure seems a hell of a lot worse now."

"Then we're all facing it. And unless you're suggesting that we all bunk down together someplace, present a united front, I'm guessing the best thing to do is just keep calm and carry on."

A hesitation, and then he replied, "Keep calm, fine. But no more UFO tours until we get this figured out. It's too dangerous."

I couldn't even argue with that. Only an idiot would go back out there after what had happened earlier that night. Yes, it would hit me in the wallet, but better broke than dead...or worse. "No tours. I'll contact my clients for tomorrow's tour and let them know there's a family emergency or something. That satisfy you?"

"What would satisfy me is to know those bastards are gone for good, but yeah, it's a start."

His expression hadn't changed all that much as he spoke, but I thought I detected a hint of relief in his voice. "Then can we call it a night? I'm bushwhacked and just want to get cleaned up, okay?"

"Okay. I don't like it, but...okay. But you call Michael or me the second you smell something that doesn't seem right."

"Absolutely." Funny how I never thought I'd be so glad to be getting rid of Lance. Most of the time, I'd daydreamed about what it would be like to be alone with him, just the two of us in my house, but now all I could think about was whether he was finally about to give up on the hovering and head out.

He fished the key to the van out of his pocket. "Michael's going to meet me at the shop with the Jeep. I'll leave the van in its usual space, and then I'll drop him off at home. But one call, and I'm right back here."

"Got it," I said. For some reason, I didn't think that call would be necessary. Wishful thinking, maybe, but whatever the aliens had been after, I didn't think they'd found it. That white light could have burned me to a crisp on the spot...or laid all my thoughts bare. I'd heard of both sorts of things happening, although a lot of the UFO enthusiasts didn't want to hear the darker stories, didn't want to admit it wasn't all peaceful exploration and happy hand-holding "Kumbaya" scenes like the end of *Close Encounters*.

They knew who I was. They knew where to find me. If they were going to come, there wasn't a whole hell of a lot I could do to stop them.

In the meantime, I was going to live my life.

Another one of those hesitations. Lance was being awfully irresolute for him. I had the wild thought that maybe he was going to try to kiss me. He stood just a little too close, was focused just a little too intently on my face.

That thought didn't last long, though.

"Okay, I'm heading out," he said. "Make sure you turn on the alarm."

"Will do."

And then, finally, thankfully, he was gone. I turned the deadbolt, but I didn't engage the alarm. Not yet.

First I was going to find out exactly what Grayson was up to in the garage.

Lance

He drove away into the darkness, cursing the aliens, cursing himself, even cursing Kara for being so damn stubborn. Maybe that was what he'd been hoping for —that she would be all nervous and afraid, and would beg him to stay. Maybe that would have finally given him the *cojones* to do what he probably should have done months or even years ago.

Instead, she acted as if she couldn't wait to see the back end of him. Not very flattering, and somewhat mystifying. You'd think she'd want someone around after an experience like that. Hell, he had to admit he was a little glad he wasn't going right back to his empty condo, but rather dropping Michael off at his place before heading home. And after an experience like that, there was a very good chance that Michael might invite him for a little of the surprisingly world-class tequila he kept around the place.

The Jeep was already waiting in the lot at the UFO Depot when Lance pulled in and parked the van in its regular spot on the north side of the building. Michael stood next to the driver's-side door and extended one hand with the key as Lance approached.

"That didn't take very long."

"No," Lance replied curtly as he took the key and got behind the wheel. He waited while Michael crossed to the passenger side and got in. They pulled out onto 89A and headed south. For a few minutes, neither one of them said anything. Finally, Lance asked, "So how did you do it?"

"Do what?"

"Push back a two-thousand-ton alien spaceship with your bare hands?"

Michael stared out the window. "I'd rather answer that over a shot of Alquimia."

"Done."

Sedona designated itself as a "dark sky city," which meant it was careful about the lighting on its streets. On the twisty little side road that led down to Michael's property, the lighting was nonexistent. Lance flipped on his high beams and navigated the Jeep the rest of the way to the house, pulling up in front of the garage next to an ancient El Camino. Michael swore it still ran, but Lance had never seen the man actually drive it.

Michael's transportation issues weren't his concern right now, though. Lance watched Michael open the front door—which he never seemed to lock —and wend his way toward the kitchen.

Even though Lance had been here scores of times, he still found the place slightly unnerving. His own condo was as spartan and military as one might have expected, given his background—furniture chosen for utility rather than style, walls bare of paintings or any adornment, plain vertical blinds on the sliding glass doors. And Kara's was warm and comfortable, maybe a little too typically Southwest for his taste, but welcoming and attractive all the same. Whereas Michael's shabby little two-bedroom house looked like a row of Sedona's kitschiest tourist traps had exploded inside the place.

Every inch of the floor was covered in Navajo rugs. The walls were painted a dark adobe color and covered with tin road signs, metal sculptures, woven dream catchers, and shelves crowded with statuettes, old copper kitchen implements, and potted plants. The furniture was a similar hodgepodge, from the table of carved juniper to the old barstools lined up against one wall.

Lance had asked Michael about the place once, since its hectic melange seemed completely opposed to Michael's outwardly calm and serene demeanor. He'd just shrugged and said, "People like to give me things," and left it at that.

Maybe some of those things included the row of tequila bottles in the liquor cabinet. Funny thing was, Michael really didn't drink that much. He'd nurse one shot in the same amount of time that Lance could put back three or four. And the levels in the tequila bottles didn't seem to change all that much between Lance's visits.

Some of the precious fluid already gleamed pale gold in the two shot glasses sitting on the pink tile counter, more kitsch from the early '60s when the house had been built. Lance reached for one of the glasses, but Michael put out a hand.

"Outside. It's better."

Mystified, Lance could only shrug and follow the other man through the kitchen door and onto the patio, which, in direct contrast to the rest of the house, was completely bare, except for a wrought-iron bistro set and a couple of potted cactus. Oak Creek rustled and chattered to itself only a few yards away; the house might be kind of a dump, but the location was incredible.

After they'd sat down and shared their first ceremonial swallow of tequila, Lance asked, "You going to reveal the mysteries of the universe now?"

Michael smiled, head tilted upward to the sky. The moon had begun to rise at last, a thick crescent just appearing above Wilson Mountain. "We're not the only ones who don't want the aliens here. She doesn't, either."

"'She'?" Lance repeated, mystified.

"The earth. The mother goddess. I asked to borrow some of her strength, and she lent it to me."

"Simple as that."

"The simple things are often the strongest."

Great, so now Michael was going to lapse into some of his shaman mumbo-jumbo. Lance was tempted to make a comment about leaving that sort of thing for the tourists, but he remained silent. He didn't pretend to understand what Michael had done, and apparently Michael had no explanation that wasn't couched in mystical terms. All the same, the alien ship had gone, which, at the end of the day, was the most important thing.

"Think you'll be able to do it again?"

"I won't know until the time comes."

It must be nice to be that placid, that unconcerned. Lance had never been able to achieve such a Zen-like state, even though his training in the remote viewing program had allowed him to detach his emotions when necessary. But he couldn't maintain that state indefinitely, whereas it seemed to be an integral part of Michael's being.

Lance took another sip of his tequila, let the mellow, smoky heat of it work its way down his throat. If he drank enough of it, he might be able to achieve nirvana. On the other hand, he wouldn't be able to drive home.

"Kara was acting strange," he remarked.

"She had a shock."

"I don't think that was it." Lance mentally replayed his conversation with Kara, noting the strain in her voice, the way her gaze kept flickering down the hallway toward the bedrooms. He could flatter himself and try to think she'd been looking for a more physical form of comforting, but he knew that wasn't it. She'd been on edge, nervous. True, she'd almost gotten flattened by a UFO. Somehow, he didn't think that was the cause of her agitation, though. Something else...something he couldn't quite put his finger on. And that bothered him. He thought he knew her pretty well. She was a stand-up girl, not one to dodge the truth. So what could be so important that she'd risk lying to him?

"Everything will be revealed in its own time."

"Thanks, Confucius. Do I get a fortune cookie with that?"

Michael's smile flashed white in the darkness. "No fortune cookies around here. We're on the edge of something. I can feel it, but it's not here yet. So drink up. Worry about tomorrow, tomorrow."

Sound advice. Lance drained the rest of his tequila and considered going back inside for a refill. He'd still be okay to drive after two shots. Something stopped him, though, something that told him he needed to be relatively clear-headed. Michael had said to worry about tomorrow when it came, but that wasn't good enough. Sometimes storms arrived earlier than when they were forecast.

"I think I'm going to head out," he said, and got up from the little wrought-iron chair.

Michael's eyes were a darker gleam in the black night. "Be careful."

"I always am."

And Lance set the shot glass down on the table and left.

Kara

I waited until I was sure Lance had backed the van out of the driveway and headed out toward the highway. Then I turned the knob and went into the garage.

It was stiflingly hot, even with the two fans I kept out here for laundry days going at full blast. The fluorescent shop lights overhead illuminated the space above the workbench, showing Grayson hunched over my grandfather's Indian, a clutter of sockets and wrenches and other tools scattered around him. A few paces off, lying on a carpet remnant, was Gort. He thumped his tail at the sight of me but didn't get up.

"What are you doing, Grayson?" I asked. I wouldn't let myself get upset that he was monkeying around with Grandpa's bike—after all, the thing hadn't run for years, so it wasn't as if he could do much to screw it up any more than it already was.

He looked up. A smudge of grease traced its way across one cheek, and sweat gleamed on his forehead. Somehow, that made him look even more distractingly attractive rather than disheveled. In answer, he reached over and turned the key in the ignition, then touched the throttle.

The Indian roared to life, the sound of its engine shockingly loud in the enclosed space. I took a step backward despite myself, then shook my head and moved back toward Grayson. "How the hell did you do that?"

He lifted his shoulders before reaching down and shutting off the bike once more. "It wasn't that complicated. Two of the lifters had gotten knocked out of place, and after I fixed that, it was just a matter of adjusting the carburetion."

Never mind that I didn't even know what a lifter was, let alone why having one knocked out of place was a bad thing. But maybe this unexpected display of mechanical prowess had provided a clue to his past. "So...does this mean you're a motorcycle mechanic?"

An expression of confusion passed over Grayson's regular features, and he slowly shook his head. "I don't think so. That is, I don't remember anything about motorcycles specifically. More that I could just tell where it had gone wrong somehow, and the best thing to do to repair it. It needed to be fixed."

Well, I couldn't really argue with that, had felt guilty about letting the bike go for so long. Not that I could have ridden it even if it was up and running. But I knew that Grandpa, wherever he was, would be glad the Indian had finally been brought back to life. He'd loved the damn thing, had held on to it long after his riding days were over.

How exactly Grayson had been able to hone in on what was wrong and correct it, I couldn't begin to guess. Maybe he was some kind of mechanical savant. That didn't seem any more implausible than any other explanation I could cook up.

"Well, maybe you can try a test drive tomorrow when it gets light," I said, my tone deliberately casual. I wouldn't let herself get worked up over this. After all, it was possible that he'd been some kind of mechanic or bike builder and simply couldn't remember. "It's stifling out here, though.

Since the Indian is back from the dead, how about you come inside and have some water or something?"

Grayson put up a hand to his sweaty brow, as if realizing for the first time how hot it actually was in the garage. "That's probably a good idea."

But before he would follow me inside, he carefully picked up all the tools and put them back in their various cases and boxes, then slid the containers back onto the shelves under the workbench where they usually resided. I began to offer to help but realized I didn't even know which bits went in which cubbyholes—most of that stuff had been untouched since my grandfather's death.

Until now.

Gort let out a little grunting bark of relief at coming back inside in the air conditioning and went immediately for his water bowl. Strange how he'd stayed out there by Grayson's side, despite how hot it was. Gort was a loyal dog, but he loved his comforts. It was always a struggle to get him to go outside in the summer during the daylight hours; coaxing him out of the house usually involved some sort of doggy treat bribery.

Grayson ran a hand through his shaggy hair as he entered the kitchen, obviously trying to get some of the air flow on his overheated brow. "I guess it was pretty hot out there." He frowned then, seeming to take in my appearance more closely in the brighter light of the kitchen. "What happened? Are you all right?"

For the first time, I looked down at myself, saw the smudges of dirt on the knees of my jeans and up one side of the tank top I wore. My elbows smarted, and I realized I must have skinned them when I took that header into the dirt. "Oh, it's nothing—I took a spill. Wasn't paying attention to where I was walking."

"It looks a little worse than nothing. I didn't know UFO tours could be dangerous."

You don't know the half of it. I gave a shrug that I hoped looked realistic and replied, "I guess they can be if you're a klutz like I am."

The crease between his brows only seemed to deepen, as if he somehow knew I wasn't telling him the whole truth but couldn't figure out how to challenge me on the subject. "But it went well?"

"The tour group definitely got an eyeful." That wasn't even a lie, but I still couldn't quite meet his gaze. To cover up my discomfort, I went to the cupboard and pulled out a couple of glasses. "Water?"

"Sure."

I busied myself with pouring some cold water from the pitcher in the fridge and then adding a few ice cubes to each glass. Grayson took his from me without comment, but those green eyes were too speculative. He obviously could see that something was wrong. I had no idea what to tell him, and he seemed reluctant to ask too many questions. Just as well; I had no idea what I would even say.

After an uncomfortable silence that lasted about ten seconds too long, I said, "Well, I'm beat. It's a long day when I have to do a tour. Feel free to stay up and watch some TV or something if you like—I know I'll sleep right through it."

"That's all right—I could do with some sleep, too." He drained the rest of the water in his glass. "Mind if I get more?"

"No, go ahead."

Even sweaty and mussed as he was, I had to admit he was awfully easy on the eyes. It was a pleasure to watch him cross the kitchen and pour himself some more water.

And not ten minutes ago you were standing in the same spot and wondering whether Lance was going to kiss you. You really need to get a grip, Kara.

Well, it wasn't a crime to feel attracted to two men at the same time, especially when the odds of anything happening with either one of them seemed pretty damn slim. Sooner or later, I'd have to do something about the Grayson situation, but after all, he'd only been here two days. I wasn't about to shove him out on the street, especially since his memory showed no signs of returning.

And making any kind of a decision when I was exhausted and wrung-out and more stressed than I wanted to admit was definitely not a good idea. I didn't know if the world would look all that much better when I woke up the next morning, but at least I'd be a bit more rested.

So I allowed myself to utter the only words I trusted myself to say.

"Good night, Grayson."

CHAPTER SIX

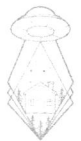

I blinked at the line of bright sunlight peeking past one edge of the blackout curtains in my bedroom and thought, *I need a day off.*

Oh, sure, I'd already planned to cancel the tour tonight. I'd start making calls and sending texts as soon as the hour was a little more decent. But this was something different. I wanted nothing to do with the store, knew if I forced myself to go in, I'd end up walking right back out an hour later.

Once or twice in the past, I'd gotten like this, but I'd had Kiki to fall back on, or Michael if Kiki was busy. With Kiki in L.A., it would have to be Michael...only I knew I wouldn't even bother to call him. It was Saturday, and Saturdays were generally his busiest days. Usually the busiest day at the shop, too, but really, if I was going to manufacture a family emergency to beg off from doing tonight's tour, then why not go whole hog and shut down the store for the rest of the weekend?

The thought alarmed me at the same time it thrilled me. I honestly couldn't remember the last time I hadn't worked through a weekend; that was just part of being a shop owner in a tourist town. My normal days off were Mondays and Tuesdays, although half the time, I ended up working Mondays, too, especially if Monday fell on a holiday when a lot of other people would be off work. It was nuts to shut down on a weekend, on the days when I got the vast majority of my sales. But....

Not too long ago, Kiki accused me of having a scarcity mentality. At the time, I'd brushed off the remark, putting it down to something my sister had probably heard one of her psychic clients say. After all, Kiki was only three when our mother disappeared, leaving me to finally call our grandparents in a panic after Kiki and I had been alone for four days. Kiki probably didn't remember much about moving from one crappy one-bedroom apartment in Phoenix to another, or having to live off Top Ramen and mac and cheese from a box because our mother was too busy spending what little money she had on cigarettes and booze.

No, if God was merciful, Kiki had forgotten most of that, but I was eleven when we came to live with our grandparents, and so I recalled far more than I ever wanted to. The memories of those days lurked somewhere far back in my mind, and so even though I knew intellectually that I was doing just fine—the house and store were paid for, and I had about fifty grand in the bank—for some reason, I kept pushing myself, worrying that one day the bottom would fall out of everything and I'd be back to the bad old days of Top Ramen. Stupid, I knew. I could close the shop for a whole month and not feel it too badly...except for whatever customers I might piss off by being shut down for that amount of time.

Okay, that seemed to settle it. The world would not end if the UFO Depot closed its doors for one weekend. The tourists would just wander a few shops down and find something else to spend their money on, and if they were here in town for a longer stay, they might try back in the middle of the week if they really couldn't live without an "I had a close encounter in Sedona, Arizona" T-shirt.

I hadn't even realized what a weight had been sitting on my shoulders until after I made my decision. It would feel so, *so* good to play hooky.

But now that I had a day off, what was I going to do with it?

Lance

He swung by the shop to check on Kara before he

went to get his ritual morning cup of espresso at the Secret Garden Café. To his surprise, he saw a sign in the window of the UFO Depot that read "Closed for the weekend due to family emergency. We apologize for the inconvenience." It had been printed on Kara's laser printer in big block letters that could be read clearly from the parking lot. Trust Kara to be conscientious even about blowing off her customers.

Well, he couldn't blame her. Maybe it would be better if she laid low for a few days. After what happened last night, it was probably a good idea for her to keep a low profile...at least until Paul and Persephone got back in town and they could all discuss their next course of action.

Lance's mouth thinned slightly at that thought. He really didn't like the idea of waiting for anybody —after all, the group had gotten along just fine before the Olivers took up residence in Sedona—but he'd seen what Persephone had done to all those hybrids and alien-infected humans. It would be stupid to do much of anything without her around.

A quick glance at his watch told him it was just past nine-thirty. A little early for a social call, but it couldn't hurt to swing by and make sure Kara was okay. Even though she was taking the day off, he knew she had to be up and around because of the sign on the shop's door. And if part of him was just curious to see what exactly she had planned for a Saturday where she wasn't at the store, well, fine.

Better that she be a little annoyed with him for being nosy rather than have something actually be wrong. She could have been coerced into making that sign. You never knew.

Thus determined on his course of action, he headed back to the Jeep. He'd just put his hand on the door handle when he heard a half-familiar female voice say, "Lance? It *is* Lance, isn't it?"

No choice but to turn toward the woman. When he saw who it was, he had to force himself to keep from gritting his teeth. "Hi...." Oh, shit, he'd completely forgotten her name.

"Taylor. Taylor Bradford."

Great. She sounded like a law firm or something. "Taylor, of course. Sorry, I was thinking about something else."

"I know, isn't it a bummer?"

"What?"

She pointed toward the door with a perfectly manicured hot pink fingernail. "I *so* wanted to check out this store before we headed down to Phoenix."

"I thought you were supposed to go to Phoenix on Thursday...or Scottsdale, I mean."

A wide flash of toothpaste-commercial teeth. Maybe she was pleased he'd remembered that much about her itinerary. In the harsh light of day, she didn't look quite as good as she had in the bar—skin too taut from an overdose of Botox, tendons standing out in her neck. He had to revise her age upward a few years, closer to his own. But damn, her body was amazing.

"Well, we were *supposed* to, but then Lindsay had to go have the worst allergy attack, and she's spent the past two days up at some holistic center in the canyon getting hot rocks on her back and herbal inhalers and I don't even *know* what else to try to fix her sinuses. But our flight leaves for L.A. at two, so I thought I'd come by this place to see if it was open. I wanted to get one of those alien T-shirts...it would've been so *cute* for the gym."

He wondered if she would find the aliens quite so cute if they were swooping straight down at her. Probably not. In his mind, he saw Kara again, pale hair blowing in the unnatural wind kicked up by the alien ship, her clean profile outlined by its harsh, glaring lights. She'd looked like a Valkyrie...well, right up until the second he'd tackled her.

"That's too bad," he said, trying to sound somewhat sympathetic and not sure he'd succeeded. "Stuff happens, I guess."

"I guess," Taylor replied, and sent him a significant look.

Shit. He was in no mood to go for round two with her, not with the alien threat hanging over all their heads, not with the memory of Kara's body beneath his just a little too vivid. But he also knew it would be a supremely assholish thing for him to just blow her off. Looked like he'd have to postpone that visit to Kara's house.

"Have you eaten yet? Because I know this great place down 89A...."

She nodded enthusiastically and climbed into the Jeep with him. He tried not to sigh as he pointed the 4x4 down the highway to the Coffee Pot restaurant. They were famous for their breakfasts, and a local hangout, so that should satisfy her. He was damned if he was going to take her to the Secret Garden, his special sanctuary. A man had his limits, after all.

Kara

I used my time on the treadmill to send off all the necessary texts and make phone calls to those who didn't text, letting them know the tour had been cancelled and that I'd be refunding their money just as soon as possible. Thank God I could log directly into my merchant account to do that and wouldn't have to call the bank. Everyone sounded disappointed, and a few tried to ask questions, but I dodged those inquiries and stuck to the party line about there being a family emergency.

By the time I was done, I heard Grayson emerge from the shower in the other bathroom, so I judged it safe enough to get cleaned up. The house's water heater couldn't handle two showers at once, as I'd learned to my dismay not long after moving in with my grandparents. I really should see about replacing that crappy old thing at some point.

"I'm going to shower," I called down the hall. "Are you okay with cereal? That's all I've got left in the house."

His voice drifted back to me. "Sure. I'll eat and then go check on the motorcycle."

It all sounded so normal, so prosaic. Hard to believe that three days ago, I hadn't even known him. Then again, I really couldn't say I knew him now. No past, no memories, a name borrowed from a TV show. I really was nuts.

I shook my head and went into the bathroom.

The day was bright and sunny, but once again, thunderheads loomed to the south and east. Hard to say if they'd make it all the way over here, but I stood in the driveway and squinted at the sky anyway, trying to figure out what the weather was going to do. Or maybe I was just attempting to avoid the curious gaze of my next-door neighbor, Felicia Martinez, who was making something of a show of watering her rosebushes but who was probably just gawking at Grayson.

Not that he wasn't eminently gawk-able. He sat astride the Indian in the middle of the driveway, my grandfather's old motorcycle helmet dangling from his left hand as he adjusted the mirrors with his right. The muscles in his arms did interesting things under the close-fitting gray T-shirt, and I had to force myself not to stare.

"Be careful," I said. "You don't have a license."

"It would have been a lot easier if I did, wouldn't it?" he asked, all seriousness. Then he planted a pair of Ray-Bans on his nose—the sunglasses were another relic of my grandfather's—and pulled on the helmet before fastening the strap under his chin. "Anyway, I'm only going down the street and back. It'll be fine."

"Okay."

I watched as he twisted the throttle and brought the Indian to roaring life once again. For a second or two, I'd thought that maybe it wouldn't start, that maybe last night had been a fluke, but no, the bike sounded healthy and ready to rumble. Grayson flashed me a grin and rolled out of the driveway, balancing expertly even at that low speed. Then he was off down the street, obeying the residential thirty-mile-per-hour speed limit, although the motorcycle sounded almost petulant at being reined in like that.

"Who's your friend?" asked Felicia, obviously unable to contain her curiosity any longer. Water was beginning to overflow the garden bed, but she didn't seem to notice.

"Grayson?" I responded, in what I hoped was a convincingly casual way. "He's a...friend of a friend. Actually, a friend of one of my roommates from college. When I mentioned I really wanted to get the bike up and running, she suggested him. He's a genius at that sort of thing."

"I'll bet." Felicia's gaze was tracking down the street, where Grayson had already disappeared around a corner.

"He's just fixing the bike."

"Of course he is."

I had to repress the urge to stalk back inside. Instead, I made a show of turning toward the end of the cul-de-sac and looking for Grayson to reappear. It didn't take long; within the minute, he was back in sight, slowing down as he took the turn with casual grace. A few seconds later, he was back in the driveway.

"Runs great," he said. "A little rough on the idle, though. She really needs a long, hard ride."

At that statement, Felicia Gomez made an ostentatious throat-clearing noise and Grayson looked over at her, clearly mystified.

"Let's get the bike back in the garage," I said, sounding a little strangled myself.

Luckily, Grayson didn't argue, but only got off the bike and rolled it inside. I hurried past him and hit the button for the garage door opener so Felicia couldn't eavesdrop on any more of our conversation.

"What was that about?" he asked.

"Nothing. Anyway, I'm sure you're jonesing for a road trip, but I'm not sure that's such a great idea."

"Why not?"

"Well, there's your total lack of a license, for one thing," I said. "If we get pulled over—"

"Why would we get pulled over? You saw I can handle the bike just fine. It's been sitting so long, it really needs a good run to blow the carbon out of the engine."

I didn't have an immediate answer to that. All through the years, I'd dutifully paid the registration on the motorcycle, even in its defunct state, because I never knew when I might get it up and running. It was easier to do that than register it as non-operable and then have to re-register it later. So as long as Grayson obeyed the speed limit and didn't do anything fancy, we'd probably be safe.

Yeah, right. A hundred things could go very wrong.

On the other hand, a thousand things could go right. And, as Kiki liked to remark from time to time, *Sometimes you just gotta say, "What the fuck."*

"Okay," I said. "I think I know just the place...."

———

Lance

He wasn't able to get rid of Taylor until almost eleven, and even then it required repeated texts from her travel mate Lindsay before Taylor finally climbed into her rented Camry and headed off to collect her baggage and head for Phoenix. It would take a miracle for her to make a two o'clock flight. Thank God she really did have a wedding to go to that night, or she probably would have invented yet another excuse to remain in Sedona.

Save me from clingy women. He shook his head and was just about to back out of the parking space and head up toward Kara's when one of Sedona P.D.'s two unmarked police cars rolled up next to his Jeep and Joe Gonzales got out.

"Morning, officer," Lance said.

"Lance," Gonzales said, his tone guarded.

The two of them had never been buddies, mostly because Gonzales, with his cop instincts, seemed to know there was a lot more in Lance's past than he cared to let on. Also, Gonzales knew Kara from way back and tended to be a little protective of her—his wife had been roommates with her in college or something. Anyway, he'd never warmed up to Lance, which usually wasn't that big a deal but made their interactions, when they occurred, less than congenial.

The detective looked over at the sign on the UFO Depot's door. "Closed? On a Saturday?"

Lance shrugged. "Family emergency."

"I didn't know Kara had any family anymore except Kiki."

Well, that was the simple truth. But although Kara hadn't heard from her deadbeat mother in years, as far as he knew, the woman was still alive and kicking, more or less. He manufactured a lie and said, "I think her mother surfaced down in Tempe or something. I don't have all the details."

"Oh," was all Gonzales said, but that one word held a weight of meaning. He also knew a thing or two about Kara's family history. "Well, hell, sorry to hear that. I just thought I'd check in on her. She called me the other day, sounded sort of strange, and I wanted to make sure everything was all right."

"'Strange'?" Lance repeated. Alarm bells started to go off in his head.

"Yeah, she was asking about a missing person. You know anything about that?"

"Can't say as I do. Did you get a description?"

"Wasn't much. Early thirties, dark hair."

"I haven't seen anyone like that around. Maybe she was asking for a friend or something."

"Maybe. Kara does have quite the network, that's for sure." Gonzales squinted up at the sky and adjusted his sunglasses. "Looks like we'll have rain by nightfall. Well, if you see Kara, let her know I was following up for her, okay?"

"Sure, no problem."

Gonzales got back in his Chevy and headed north into the heart of the touristy section of town. Lance watched him go, then climbed into his Jeep, mouth grim. Missing person? What the hell?

His brain picked apart Gonzales's words as he drove to Kara's house. Now he was sure she was hiding something. And he aimed to find out exactly what it was.

When he pulled into her driveway and got out of the Jeep, however, he was stopped partway to the front door by a woman's voice.

"She's not home."

Lance turned around and saw a Hispanic woman in her late fifties regarding him with an amused look. In one hand, she held a pair of clippers, and on the ground in front of her was a basket into which she'd apparently been dead-heading her roses. She was stocky and no-nonsense in her striped T-shirt and khaki crop pants, but something about the tip-tilted dark eyes told him she'd probably been a pretty hot tamale back in the day.

"What?" he replied.

The woman gestured with her clippers. "She took off about a half an hour ago, on the back of Jim's old Indian. Has some friend staying with her who she says fixed up the bike."

"Friend?"

"Well, that's what she *said*," the woman remarked with a knowing grin. "A man who looks like that, I'm guessing is a little more than a friend."

"So what does he look like?"

"Dark hair, green eyes. Body like—" She broke off and rolled her eyes. "Well, I wouldn't kick him out of bed for eating crackers. Just don't tell Mr. Martinez that."

"Is he in his early thirties?" Lance rasped, ignoring the comment about the crackers.

"Mmm...yeah, could be. Somewhere around there. *Muy caliente!*"

"Thanks...Mrs. Martinez."

Since he'd already heard far more than he wanted to, Lance stalked back to the Jeep and got in, then backed out of the driveway a little more quickly than he should have. God damn it. So this was what Kara was hiding—the fact that she had some guy shacked up with her? Was this eighth grade? Why the hell should he care who she was seeing?

Good question.

Gritting his teeth, he maneuvered the 4x4 through the clotty traffic on 89A. His thoughts roiled. What he really wanted was a drink, but it was way too early in the day for that. Besides, he knew better than to crawl into a bottle when things got rough.

He'd had his chance with Kara. And he'd blown

it. She'd been giving him signals for years, and he'd ignored them. What had he expected, that she should live like a nun until he finally pulled his head out of his ass?

Based on his actions so far, that was exactly what he'd expected. And look where it had gotten him.

The thought surfaced, *I was only trying to keep her safe*, and he couldn't quite ignore it. Yes, he'd been an asshole, but there'd been a reason for it...a reason he'd never wanted to discuss with her, or anyone, for that matter. Digging up the past usually made things worse, not better.

But maybe if he had...maybe if he'd trusted in the universe the way Michael had always admonished him to....

Maybe then she wouldn't be out riding around somewhere on a motorcycle with her arms around Mr. *Muy Caliente*'s waist.

That was a mental image he did not need. Well, it was way too early to start drinking, but he'd go do the next best thing. Thank God he always kept a packed gym bag stowed in the back of the Jeep.

If he was lucky, he could wash away thoughts of Kara in another man's arms by sweating them out instead of drowning them.

Kara

The road up into Jerome twisted and turned, but Grayson maneuvered the bike with casual confidence around every switchback, every loop. Now a tourist town and burgeoning artists' colony, the onetime mining mecca clung to the side of the mountain with gravity-defying tenacity. Well, mostly gravity-defying. Some of the buildings were still sliding despite preservationists' best efforts, and every once in a while, a structure had to be torn down in the name of public safety.

I didn't know exactly why I'd thought of Jerome as a getaway. Once, a long time ago, I'd come up here with Alan. He hadn't cared for it, found it claustrophobic and vertigo-inducing at the same time. Or possibly he just didn't like the way the place got crowded with bikers on the weekends. They were mostly well-behaved, but they did give the place a sort of rough-and-ready atmosphere.

Riding behind Grayson, I understood for the first time the appeal of a motorcycle—at least for all those women I'd seen over the years riding pillion behind their significant others. It was strangely intimate, the sensation of being pressed up against his back, of feeling the hard muscles of his stomach under my arms, of having to move with him as he shifted his weight to accommodate the ever-changing rise and fall of the highway. All the same, I was almost relieved when we finally pulled into town and began hunting for a place to park. Being so close to Grayson had made me start to think about being with him in even more physical ways, and I wasn't sure I really wanted to go there yet.

Since it was a Saturday toward the tail end of summer, the place was packed. However, because we'd ridden in on a motorcycle instead of a car, we found a spot at the long end of a row of Harleys in front of the Spirit Room, a popular hangout. Even though it was barely noon, the sound of live blues-tinged rock pounded out of the place.

The crowds milling around looked more than a little rough, and I began to question the wisdom of coming up here. Still, there didn't seem to be much I could do except climb off the bike, since Grayson had already throttled it down and begun to unfasten his helmet.

An enormous individual in a black leather vest and faded jeans paused on the curb, looking down at the motorcycle. He probably could have put me, Grayson, and the Indian through a wall without breaking a sweat. I swallowed.

Then the guy gave us an approving nod and said, "'46 Chief, right?"

"Right," I managed.

"Good job." And he gave us a thumbs-up before disappearing back inside the bar.

"What was that?" Grayson asked as he looped his helmet's straps around the handlebars and reached back to take my helmet from me.

"I think we just got the stamp of approval. Which means I guess it's okay to park here."

"Why wouldn't it be? It's a public place, isn't it?"

"Yeah, well, there's public and then there's public. But I guess this old bike has a certain cachet. Just go with it."

A look of confusion passed over his face, but he only nodded and fastened my helmet around the other handlebar. Normally, I would have worried about leaving the helmets there like that where anyone could take them, but I guessed that probably wasn't going to be an issue here.

We headed off down the sidewalk. I didn't really have a destination in mind, although I figured we'd grab some lunch fairly soon. In the meantime, though, Grayson didn't appear to have any problem with wandering in and out of stores, looking at mineral specimens and antiques and all sorts of Arizona- and mining-themed tchotchkes. I'd never had the luxury of doing so with Alan, because any kind of shopping that didn't involve buying food or electronics bored him silly. Grayson, on the other hand, appeared to be fascinated by everything, whether it was a hunk of glittering amethyst crystals or an old copper coffee pot. We spent an inordinate amount of time in a shop that specialized in kaleido-scopes, examining everything from small plastic models obviously intended for kids all the way up to an enormous brass-bound specimen that used real pieces of crystal and other minerals to create the kaleidoscopic effect.

"You should have gotten it," Grayson protested after we finally emerged from the store. "It was beautiful."

"It was also three thousand dollars. A bit above my pay grade. Besides, it would have been too big to bring back on the motorcycle."

"You should have beautiful things."

I didn't quite know how to respond to that. He looked so earnest with the sunlight glinting in his jade-colored eyes as he gazed down at me. Obviously, the constraints of living within a budget were not something he recalled very clearly.

Keeping my tone light, I replied, "Right now, what really sounds beautiful to me is some lunch. You hungry?"

"I could eat."

That was an understatement. I'd never seen him not ready to pack away a serious amount of calories. I had no idea where he put it, either. Maybe in his shoe. "Okay, well, that place a few doors down looks good. Let's see what we can rustle up."

"Sure."

It turned out the restaurant had marvelous food. We started with stuffed portobello mushrooms and moved on from there to sandwiches—a burger for him, a chicken salad sandwich for me. Feeling a little daring, I ordered a glass of pinot grigio for myself and asked Grayson if he'd like something to go with his burger.

"Maybe a glass of zinfandel?" I suggested.

"I don't know what that is, but sure." He smiled across the table at me.

Something in that smile made me feel just a little melty. It wasn't the heat of the day outside; the restaurant had great air conditioning. And it was probably reckless to order wine, what with the impure thoughts I'd had about him on the drive up here, but at the moment I really didn't care.

"Zinfandel, check," the waitress said, with a smile that seemed more than a little knowing.

If Grayson noticed anything, he didn't give any indication. He picked up his water and took a few healthy swallows. It had been a hot and dusty ride up into Jerome. Then he looked around the restaurant with an air of lively curiosity, as if the odd assortment of tourists and bikers was one of the most fascinating things he'd ever seen.

"So, this is what people do?" he asked.

"I don't follow."

"Go out to public places and eat. Look at things."

That must have been a hell of a knock on the head he'd gotten. How he had retained enough knowledge to resurrect the Indian from the grave and yet still seemed puzzled by some pretty basic human behavior was beyond me.

"Among other things, yes," I replied. The waitress appeared with our wine, and I took my glass of pinot grigio gratefully before allowing myself a good swallow. "I mean, do you *really* not remember doing anything like this?"

Grayson reached out and picked up his own glass of wine. "No. I don't remember...anything."

"But there must be *something*," I protested. "You fixed the bike. You rode it up here like someone who's done that a thousand times before. I don't understand how you can have retained those sorts of skills and yet can't recall anything of who you are or where you came from."

An eloquent lift of his shoulders was his only reply. Then he took a cautious sip of zinfandel, as if wanting to distract himself from the conundrum of his existence. An expression of something close to joy spread over his features and lit up his green eyes, and he followed the sip with a much healthier swallow.

"Easy there, big boy," I cautioned him. "We still have to get down the mountain."

"It's supposed to have some sort of effect?"

"Um...yeah. Okay, maybe not after just a couple of sips, but still...." I drank some pinot grigio and nodded. It wasn't enough to even start getting me tipsy, but I could still sense something of its effects. "You really don't feel anything at all?"

He drank again, two more big swallows, then shook his head.

Nice party trick. "Well, I'd still be careful. Sometimes it sneaks up on you." *On the other hand*, I thought, *I might have found the world's best-looking designated driver.* "Anyway," I continued, not about to let him permanently change the subject, "I really do think we should get you in to see someone. I have a friend, Janelle Russo, who's a licensed hypnotherapist. Does past-life regressions, that sort of thing. Not that we need to send you back to a past life—we just want to find out what happened to the one you were living up until three days ago."

Another shrug. "If it's important to you."

"Isn't it important to you?" I asked. Part of me just couldn't understand why he wouldn't want to find out about his past. Having everything be such a total blank would have driven me crazy.

"I'm not sure." He drained the rest of his zinfandel and started looking around for the waitress. "Maybe there's a good reason why I can't remember anything."

Those words sent a little shiver through me. Maybe he was right and we should just let well enough alone. But I knew it wouldn't do him any good to keep blundering on without knowing who he was and where he had come from. Even unwelcome knowledge was better than ignorance.

I'd have to keep telling myself that.

CHAPTER SEVEN

EVEN THOUGH TEMPERATURES HAD PUSHED INTO the mid-nineties, Jerome was rocking and rolling that afternoon. The crowds spilled out of the Spirit Room and flowed into the side street that ran along the bar's western side, turning the narrow lane into an impromptu block party. Local law enforcement didn't seem too worried, but just let the people go where they wanted.

The pounding bass line got into my blood, and I grasped Grayson by the hand and pulled him toward the music. Already, people were dancing in the street, keeping themselves hydrated by passing around bottles of water and sometimes dumping the water right on their heads or down their necks. Looking bemused but game, he followed along after me as I pushed my way into the throng.

"Don't suppose you remember dancing, either," I

said, raising my voice so he could hear me over the music.

"No."

"It's easy."

My daring probably had its origins in that second glass of pinot grigio I'd drunk, but I wasn't going to worry about it right then. The music settled down into a slower piece, and I put my hands on Grayson's shoulders and drew him to me. He gave a quick glance around, as if to observe what other people were doing, and then wrapped his arms around my waist, bringing me even closer.

This close, he was far more intoxicating than the wine. I could sense the heat of his body through the T-shirt—which was getting damper by the second in the brutal July sunshine—feel his muscles moving under my fingers as he swayed with me to the music. When was the last time I'd danced with somebody like this? Years, definitely.

Scratch that. I'd never danced like this, out in the sun and the wind, energy seeming to swirl and shimmer in the very air. And I'd certainly never been with anyone like Grayson. Truth be told, I didn't think there *could* be anyone else like Grayson.

He seemed to feel it, too, his smile flashing white as he gazed down into my face, watching me closely. God knows what I must have looked like, with sweat plastering my hair to my brow and lips bare of gloss, since I'd forgotten to put some back on after lunch...

but he didn't seem to mind too much. If anything, he moved closer, our bodies now locked from shoulder to hip. Once upon a time, I might have cared about such a public display of sensuality, but everyone around us was doing pretty much the same thing.

The force of the desire that passed over me was so strong, I would have staggered if he hadn't been holding me so tightly. It reminded me of the one and only time my mother had taken me to California and brought me to the beach. No real altruism there —Marybeth Swenson had been pursuing some man or the other at the time—but still, I had gotten to stand in the water, feel it rushing around my legs and feet. And then I'd gone out a little farther and almost been knocked down when a wave came out of seemingly nowhere and engulfed me up to my waist.

The sensation was similar now, of being surrounded by a force I couldn't control or even resist. And that wasn't like me. Not Careful Kara, who always looked before she leaped.

Grayson's hands slipped from my waist, and I realized the song had ended. I put my hand up to my forehead and felt how overheated I'd really become.

"I think we'd better go inside for a cool drink."

He smiled at me.

"Not *that* kind of a cool drink. Just some ice water."

"All right." His tone was casual, and if he'd had

the same kind of physical response to me that I'd had to him, he sure wasn't showing it.

We went in the bar and overpaid for a couple of glasses of ice water, but I didn't really care. It was only fair to give the place some custom, considering we'd been dancing to the lounge's musical offerings for free. And after we'd cooled down sufficiently, we headed back out to the street. Not to dance; I thought I'd skirted the edge of danger there, and since Grayson hadn't shown any particular interest in going another round, better to head on to something a little less...fraught. A storefront just down the hill from the Spirit Room seemed to catch his eye, and he paused.

"Wine tasting?" he asked, staring at a sandwich board propped up on the sidewalk. "Isn't that what we did at lunch?"

"Not really," I said. "We ordered wine with lunch. When you do a wine tasting, you generally get a sampling of the different wines from one particular winery. We've got quite a few around here, believe it or not. A lot of them are down in Page Springs, but there are wineries all over the Verde Valley."

"Let's try some. I want to see what a wine tasting is like."

"I'm not sure I'm cooled down enough for that—"

"You like wine, don't you?"

Since I knew he wouldn't believe me if I

answered in the negative, I only lifted my shoulders. "Sure I do. But we can only buy one bottle if we find something we like. I couldn't fit anything more than that in my bag." I'd transferred everything to my one purse that was backpack-style so I could wear it over my shoulders while we rode, but since it wasn't a true backpack, it had a limited carrying capacity.

"No problem."

He held the door open for me as I went in, and I had to smile inwardly at his contradictions. He didn't seem to notice or care that I was dropping a good chunk of change during this little outing of theirs, and yet he always made sure to open doors or do the sorts of things my grandmother used to refer to as "gentlemanly." Oh, well, I could afford to splurge every once in a while...although if he suggested dinner at L'Auberge or Rene's once we were back in Sedona, I'd have to put my foot down. Enough was enough.

Any irritation I might have felt evaporated once I crossed into the wine-tasting shop. The space was light and airy, with high-beamed ceilings, but what immediately drew the eye was the amazing full-wall window on the southeast side of the building. It looked out over the Verde Valley, offering an incredible vista of desert canyons and golden-brown hills. The day was clear enough that you could see all the way to the San Francisco Peaks in Flagstaff, although a mass of bruise-colored clouds had begun to build up above the Mogollon Plateau, bringing with it the threat of the monsoon storms. I'd have to keep an eye on that—riding back in the rain didn't sound too appealing.

We crossed to the bar and made our selections, a mix of whites and reds. I liked both, and obviously, Grayson didn't recall enough of his previous existence to have a preference one way or the other. For all I knew, he'd been a beer-drinking guy back in the day.

He didn't show much evidence of that as he sampled the offerings with me, though. All of them seemed to meet his approval.

"Just one, remember?" I said.

A flash of those green eyes as he grinned. "All right, if I have to choose, I like the red blend. The one with the moo—"

"Mouvedre," I supplied.

"That one."

The shop's proprietor—I got the feeling he was the owner, too—packaged up the wine for us. If he was a little disappointed that we were walking away with only one bottle, he didn't show it.

"You two have a nice rest of your afternoon," he said.

We thanked him and headed out. I was surprised to see that the sun had already begun to dip behind the mountain. Sunset was still a few hours off, but I hadn't thought we'd spent so much time in Jerome. I glanced down at my watch and saw it was pushing on toward six o'clock.

"That was a great view," Grayson commented. "Any place else we could find something like that?"

"Almost anything in town, probably, but I think I remember there being a lookout spot a few levels up. Ready for a climb?"

Another one of those quick, flashing grins. "Are you?"

"It'll give me a chance to work off lunch. Come on—I think we need to take those stairs over there."

The narrow little concrete staircase did in fact lead up to the next terrace, but the overlook in that spot was still crowded with tourists, so we gamely pressed on to the next one, which was deserted. It figured. People in general were only willing to go so far to get a great view.

Up here the wind was stronger, pulling at my loose hair. It whipped around my face, and I had to reach up to push it back. Good thing my sunglasses did a decent job of protecting my eyes from the wayward strands.

Grayson gazed to the east toward the Mogollon Rim, which was now barely visible beyond a dark mass of thunderheads. "Is that a storm?"

"Looks like it. With any luck, it'll keep blowing west. It won't be fun to drive through a downpour, but it's sort of a hazard in these parts at this time of year."

He nodded, fine profile outlined against the mottled sky. Even here in Jerome were faint traces of high cirrus clouds, the outriders of the storm front. I squinted eastward, gauging the strength of the wind and the size of the mass of clouds building some forty miles away.

"It's not looking too good," I said. "Maybe we should head back now, try to—"

I'd been about to say, *try to outrun it,* but I didn't get the chance, because Grayson had turned to me with one swift movement and pulled me against him, then buried my mouth under his.

A brief second of shock, and then I let myself fall into the kiss, tasted him as he kissed me with an urgency and a thoroughness I really hadn't expected. Not with the way he had walked so casually away from the dance, as if our bodies hadn't been pressed up against one another for all the world to see. His hands moved through my hair, fingers strong as they moved down my neck, brushed against my collarbone.

The air was thinner up here in Jerome. That had to be the explanation for my sudden lightheadedness, for my difficulty in drawing enough breath into my lungs. I clung to him, feeling the strength of his body, the coiled power in those muscles.

Gently, very gently, he released his hold on me, letting me drift away just enough so he could look down into my face. I could only stare back up at him, at the green eyes with their heavy fringe of dark lashes, the high cheekbones with the smooth brown skin pulled tightly over them, the trace of dark stubble along his jaw.

Anything I might have said would have been woefully inadequate. So I settled for, "Wow."

"You didn't mind?"

A shaky laugh bubbled its way up my throat. "Mind? No. That is…no, I didn't mind at all."

"I've wanted to do that all day." He shook his head. "No, actually, I've been wanting to do that ever since I first saw you."

"Even though you were almost dropping dead from dehydration and exposure?"

"Even then. When I saw you bending over me, I thought you must be an angel. No one else could be that beautiful."

From anyone else, I would have thought that was the mother of all lines, but as I watched him, saw the earnest expression on his face, I realized he spoke simply, from the heart. Something inside me seemed to turn over, and my breath caught. Could it be that finally, when I least expected it, something pure and lovely had come into my life?

I wouldn't call it love. It was too soon for that. But it was…something.

The moment was too intense. I wasn't ready for this. Better to take refuge in brittle, ironic words. "I think even Nurse Ratched would have looked beautiful to you right then if she'd been carrying a glass of water."

"Who's Nurse Ratched? And you are beautiful, you know. Then, and now."

Heat flooded my cheeks, and I stared out into the wind, hoping the rising breeze might help to cool my blush. As I watched, I saw the clouds racing, dropping lower, the blurred darkness beneath them a sure sign of a desert downpour.

"Okay, if you say so. But I really think we need to get going. It's starting to look pretty grim out there."

He followed my gaze, appeared to take in the looming clouds to the east. "I think you're right. It's probably the kind of evening where you want to stay in."

Since I was already a little flushed, I couldn't do much more than nod without looking straight at him and then head down the narrow, treacherous staircase. No one else seemed to be in much of a hurry, but maybe they'd come from points west and north, or maybe they were willing to stay and see if they could ride it out.

After all, desert storms, while spectacular, were usually short-lived.

Lance

He picked up the Ruger, aimed it at the can on the rock some thirty yards away, and pressed the trigger.

Blam!

The can flew up into the air and fell with a metallic *clank* among its brethren, which now numbered an even two dozen. With no sense of satisfaction, Lance re-sighted, fixed his aim on the next can in the lineup, and squeezed the trigger again.

Again, the can shot skyward and then dropped to the earth. He paused for a second to wipe away the sweat from his brow, replaced the clip, and went on to the next one. *Blam!* And so on.

Usually, a few hours spent in target practice helped to settle his mind. Today, even though his aim was as unerring as always, he couldn't quite achieve the Zen-like state he'd hoped for. His thoughts swirled in his head, bringing with them unwanted images of Kara in some stranger's arms. It didn't seem to matter whether he was shooting the Ruger or the rifle or his beloved Glock—he couldn't force his mind to more useful subjects.

At least he was alone out here. The gym had been hectic and noisy, typical for a Saturday, and he'd packed it in after only forty-five minutes. A cold shower hadn't helped, either, so he'd loaded up the Jeep and headed out to one of his favorite spots above Oak Creek, along one of the trails that led up into U.S. Forest Service lands. You could shoot safely there, and most of the time, the place was pretty deserted. It was cooler, too, up above the heat in Sedona proper. The sky was starting to look ugly, though. He guessed he had maybe half an hour at most before he'd have to stow everything in the Jeep so it wouldn't get soaked.

It was stupid for him to be this upset. For all he knew, that Mrs. Martinez had just been yanking his chain. And even if she wasn't, he didn't have a claim on Kara. She could do whatever the hell she wanted.

Nice try. But it wasn't working.

He remembered the first time he'd really noticed her. Oh, sure, she'd been in and around Jim Swenson's shop during her college years, which was right after the time Lance had relocated to Sedona. He'd liked Jim but of course hadn't paid any attention to Kara. Lance was many things, but a cradle robber wasn't one of them. Besides, trailing after Jim's college-age granddaughter would have been a little bit too much like pissing in the guy's pool. Then she'd gone up to NAU for her last two years of undergraduate work, and appeared ready to stay on for several more years so she could get her master's. But when Jim had his stroke, she came right back to Sedona, leaving a bad breakup with her fiancé and a half-finished post-graduate degree behind her.

After Jim died, she took over the shop, got involved with Sedona's UFO community. And it was when she came to one of the local MUFON meetings for the first time that Lance realized sometime in the intervening years she'd gone from a girl to a woman...and a beautiful one at that. It wasn't just her looks, though—it was the way she'd carried on and made a life for herself, picked up her grandfather's work even though it had been his passion, not hers. Took over raising her little sister after both her grandparents were gone. Lance respected that.

It had been hard to appear uninterested, to be just another piece of the UFO network here in Sedona, when what he'd wanted more than anything was to get close to her, to be there for her so she wouldn't have to keep going it alone. But he knew all too well the consequences of getting too close. He was on too many radar screens. So far, he'd skated along, tried to appear as harmless as possible. Just a washed-up relic of a now-defunct program the Army didn't even want to claim, one that was something of a laughingstock.

It had been real, though. It had all been real. Too real. He'd thought he could have it both ways, and she'd paid the price.

Natalie.

Try as hard as he could to remember the good things about being with her, what had been burned into his brain cells for all time was that last image he had of her lying sprawled out on the kitchen floor in the house they'd just rented together. Blood trailed away from the back of her head, and those dark eyes he'd loved so much stared sightlessly at the ceiling.

And a small piece of white paper with block letters printed on it, placed carefully on her chest.

LEAVE IT ALONE.

He'd tried hunting them down, had a good idea who was behind the hit. But the problem with dirty government agents was that they could hide behind a huge, faceless bureaucracy. They were quicksilver. So he'd gone along, hating in his heart, hoping one day he could get his revenge.

In the meantime, he had to play it safe. No attachments. Present the appearance of a washed-up operative who'd thrown his lot in with the tinfoil hat–wearers. And in the meantime, disseminate as much information as he could, by means of data so heavily encrypted he knew no one could hack it. Sometimes it helped to have savants like Jeff Makowski on your side.

And if the current casualty appeared to be his heart, well, he could live with that. Better to have the pain and know that Kara was safe.

He could handle a lot, as long as he knew she wouldn't get hurt.

Kara

The storm hit us just as we passed the turn-off for

Page Springs. It pounded down, soaking right through my T-shirt, turning the road into a slick nightmare. Thank God Grayson seemed to have no trouble with the sudden change in conditions; he throttled back slightly, but the tires held as we continued down 89A, the rain a drumbeat on my helmet.

I clung to him, eyes slitted behind my sunglasses. Hopefully, he could see better than I was able to, because right then the whole world looked like one big blurry mess.

He turned off 89A onto Soldier Pass Road. Funny how I didn't even have to remind him of the route. Somehow, he just knew. Another turn, and we were in the neighborhood of modest but well-maintained homes that had been my world for almost the past two decades.

As we turned the corner onto my street, I let go of Grayson with one arm so I could reach in my bag and fish out the remote control to the garage. Sheltering the device from the rain as best I could, I hit the button and sighed a little in relief as the door opened. The motorcycle slowed to a stop in the empty spot to the right of my Prius.

I stowed the remote back in my purse and reached up with chilled wet fingers to undo the strap of my helmet. Underneath, my head was more or less dry, although the ends of my long hair, unprotected by the helmet, dripped with rain. The rest of me was a sodden mess. Blue jeans did not improve with soaking.

Gingerly, I climbed off the bike and watched as Grayson removed his own helmet and stood up as well. Like me, he was pretty much soaked from the neck down, but he didn't seem fazed by that. He flashed me a grin and said, "Some ride, huh?"

"It was something," I agreed. I got the house keys out of my purse and went to unlock the door that led from the garage to the house. The alarm immediately went off, but I typed in the code without thinking.

Gort came rushing toward us, panting and doing the little half-jumps that indicated he wanted a walk.

"Not yet, kiddo," I said, pointing toward the window. "It's pouring rain. Give it a half hour or so."

The dog let out a resigned whine and padded out of the kitchen to the living room, where he could take up his favorite spot on the Navajo rug and wait out the storm.

"It's always something—" I began, but I didn't get much farther than that, since Grayson had come up behind me and turned me around so he could kiss me once again.

That was all well and good, but now that I was out of the wind, my jeans and T-shirt had begun to stick to me, soggy and cold and more than a little uncomfortable. I came up for air and said, "Grayson, I have got to get out of these clothes—"

"Good idea."

And he grasped the bottom of his sodden T-shirt and pulled it over his head, revealing a stomach so hard and flat, I had a feeling I could have bounced a quarter off it. He dropped the shirt on the floor and reached toward me, taking hold of my own tee so I had no choice but to raise my arms so he could pull it off as well.

"I have a hamper for that stuff, you know," I said in mock-prim tones, but inwardly, I could already feel the heat rising in me, the need.

"Show me, then."

With a laugh, I dashed away from him, running back toward my bedroom. He followed close behind and caught up with me a few paces away from the bed, his fingers feverishly working on the button of my jeans. Since everything was soaked through and clinging together, my underwear came down along with my pants, but somehow I didn't mind. All I could think of was getting rid of Grayson's jeans as well, removing the last obstacles to this, the inevitable end to our day.

His pants dropped on top of mine, and then we were on the bed together, his hands moving over my body, finding the clasp to my bra so he could remove my final piece of clothing. And oh, God, the feeling of his breath hot against my chilled skin, the delicate sensation of his lips moving down from my neck to my exposed breast, his mouth warm on my nipple, sucking....

I let out a cry and moved myself closer against him. His arousal was as hard as his muscles against my hip, and I reached down so I could take him in my fingers, move my hand up and down, listen to him moan, the sound muffled somewhat by my breast. One of his hands traced its way down past my hip bone, down across my thigh, and then in between my legs, stroking me, using the wetness of my own arousal to intensify my pleasure.

This was crazy. Some part of me knew that, but my body had taken over, was clamoring for the release it had been denied for so long. I let myself relax into his touch, pressed against him, surrendered to the heat and the delicate yet insistent pressure of his fingers. And when the climax came, I had to bite back a sob, and instead kissed his arm, his chest, anything to keep myself from completely falling apart.

He shifted so he could kiss me on the mouth, his tongue insistent, strong as the rest of him. I could tell he wanted to push into me, but I wasn't that far gone. Not yet.

"Wait," I whispered and he paused, looking at me with curious eyes.

It had been a while, and I had to hope that condoms didn't have a shelf life or something. But the little foil containers were still there in my night-stand drawer. I pulled one out and ripped it open.

"What's that?" he asked.

I didn't bother with the conundrum of him knowing how to repair a motorcycle but not recognizing a condom when he saw it. "For protection—against pregnancy, against disease. You know."

"No, I don't. How could I have a disease? I've never been with anyone else."

"That you remember."

His frown told me he didn't quite know how to reply to that remark. Luckily, his confusion seemed to be entirely mental—his erection hadn't flagged at all. So I bent over him and rolled on the condom. He didn't seem fazed by the procedure, and even let out a little sigh of his own as my fingers brushed against him.

"It's okay now?" he asked.

"Very okay."

And then he was on top of me, face close to mine, as he pressed inside me and I rocked my hips to take him in. Oh, yes, this was what I'd wanted, had hoped for since he'd held me in his arms on the street in Jerome only a few hours earlier. Or maybe it had been even before that, if I wanted to admit the truth to myself.

No time left for any self-examination, any doubt. It was only his body and mine, joined in a consummation that seemed ever so right, sweat and rain mingling as our disparate selves became one. He cried out as he came, a guttural, shocked sound, as if he hadn't known what was about to happen. Maybe that was yet another thing he had forgotten. My own climax came almost immediately afterward, a wash of red heat throughout my entire body, better than I had ever remembered.

Better than it had any right to be.

We both lay there for some time afterward, too spent to move. Finally, I kissed him on the cheek and murmured, "I need to go clean up."

He shifted off me then and lay sprawled on the bed as I got to my feet and went into the bathroom. My legs shook a little as I staggered to the sink and splashed some cold water on my face. Even the shock of the water wasn't enough to quite dispel the after-glow, however. I looked at myself in the mirror then, at the fair hair plastered to my forehead and cheeks, at the inky stain of mascara below my eyes. The Kara I saw in the mirror didn't appear all that different, although I did look, as my grandfather used to say, as if I'd been rode hard and put away wet.

Well, both of those statements were equally true.

But as I stared at myself, some of the glow began to ebb away. Oh, it had been great sex, marvelous— better than I'd ever had with Alan, if I wanted to be perfectly honest. So what was the problem? I should be ecstatic. After all, Grayson was pretty much my perfect man: fun, honest, sweet...and amazingly good-looking.

Why, then, did I feel so guilty?

CHAPTER EIGHT

AFTER PULLING ON A TANK TOP, FRESH underwear, and some yoga pants, I went back over to the bed and smiled at Grayson, who had pulled up the sheet to cover himself but who otherwise didn't seem to have moved much.

"Did I wear you out?" I teased.

He appeared to consider my question seriously. "No, I don't think so. But I think I might be hungry."

"Well, we can fix that. But I really need to walk Gort. It sounds as if the rain is letting up."

"Do you want me to come with you?"

For a second or two, I considered it. Gort seemed to love Grayson, and I'd always wanted to share that intimacy with someone someday—to bond over the dog, to make it seem as if we were a family. But with Felicia Martinez doing her Gladys Kravitz impersonation next door, it would probably be better if I went on my own.

"It's okay," I said. "We're just going to do a quickie around the block. But when I get back, we can order pizza, if that sounds good to you."

"Sounds great."

It sounded great to me, too. The afternoon in Jerome had been wonderful—magical, almost—but now I was home, I only wanted to cocoon and have someone bring the food to me.

"Back in a few," I promised.

Gort was already waiting for me in the kitchen, his luxuriant tail beating on the Saltillo tile floor.

"Okay, Gort," I told him, "but if the skies open up again, we're running for home. So poop early and poop often, all right?"

A doggy smile, and he was on his feet, standing at attention as I got out his harness and fastened it around him. I detoured briefly to grab my cell phone out of my purse—I'd been completely distracted up in Jerome and hadn't looked at it once, so I thought I'd better check to see if I'd gotten any messages. Then we were off.

The air always smelled wonderful after one of those rain showers, redolent of pungent juniper and sun-warmed rock. I breathed in deeply as Gort bounded ahead, pulling at the leash just enough that I had to quicken my pace to keep up with him. It was only when he stopped to sniff a promising patch of gravel in a neighbor's front yard that I had time to pull the cell phone out of my pocket and take a look at it.

Three messages. Not too bad, all things considered. Briefly, I wondered if one of those messages might be from Lance, and then decided I really shouldn't be going there right now. Not after what had just happened between Grayson and me.

However, when I looked at the "recents" screen on my iPhone, none of the numbers were Lance's. One was an 800 number, which meant it was probably some kind of junk call; one had a Sedona prefix, though I didn't recognize the number itself; and the third was from Kiki. She'd called a little after five-thirty, probably right around the time Grayson and I were getting pelted with rain on 89A.

After wedging the phone between my shoulder and my ear so I could pick up Gort's business with the plastic bag I'd brought along, I listened to Kiki's message.

"Hey, Kara," Kiki's voice bubbled in my ear, "Jeff's showing me all kinds of really great stuff. Seph and Paul just headed off to the wedding, so I'm not planning on hearing much from them for the rest of the night. Anyway, I just wanted to let you know that I've decided to stay here in L.A. for a few more days after they head home. Jeff already said he'd drive me back to Sedona—probably on Thursday or Friday."

I permitted myself an eye roll as I followed Gort around the corner. He'd somehow gotten the vibe from me that I wanted to stay in the housing tract instead of heading out onto the wilderness paths as we often did, but that didn't mean he wasn't going to try to maximize his walk. A quick glance upward told me the rain seemed to be holding off for the moment. Still, I could smell it on the air. This storm wasn't done with us yet.

"Anyway, I wanted you to know what's going on. I'll let Seph and Paul know tomorrow—I have a feeling they're going to be back late tonight. Hope everything's going well over there, and I'll try you again sometime in the morning. Hugs!"

The message ended, and I reeled Gort back in a bit. I'd just felt the first few raindrops hit my bare arms, so the time for leisurely sniffing was over. He gave a little shake but obediently moved in closer to me and pointed his nose toward home.

What was I supposed to think about Kiki extending her stay in Los Angeles? Not much, frankly, but in one way, I was almost relieved. I hadn't really looked forward to Kiki intruding on my idyll with Grayson, to be perfectly honest. Maybe there was a way to explain the situation so it didn't sound completely insane, but I hadn't thought of it yet.

As for this possibly developing relationship with

Jeff Makowski...well, I was less than thrilled about that, too. I didn't care how brilliant he was. He didn't seem like the right person for my sister. On top of that, Jeff Makowski was definitely not the sort of person you wanted pissed off at you. One bad breakup, and you could find yourself with a heinous credit report and a rash of unpaid parking tickets...or worse.

On the other hand, I mused, brightening slightly as Gort and I headed up the walk toward the front door, if Jeff Makowski screwed around with Kiki, Lance would probably break the computer hacker over his knee and bury him in some forgotten canyon somewhere. Lance could be a prickly sort—Persephone had more than once compared him to a cactus —but he was someone you could trust to have your back.

Not that it would come to that. One of these days, maybe I'd learn to stop borrowing trouble. Most likely what would happen was that Jeff would suffer some sort of unrequited angsty lust for Kiki, an attraction she wouldn't reciprocate, and then he'd go off to brood over the latest conspiracy theory on his favorite website. Kiki was awfully good at getting guys to fall for her, but so far I had yet to see any deep involvement on her side. Sure, she cared for her boyfriends, but she never exhibited any of the signs of being crazy nuts in love. Maybe that was a good thing.

At least you couldn't get your heart broken that way.

Grayson was dressed by the time I got back. Gort went bounding over to him, tail wagging, and Grayson bent down to give the dog a good scratching behind the ears.

"He feels a little wet."

"Yeah—it's trying to rain again. Good thing we decided to order in. So, what do you like on your pizza? Please don't say anchovies."

He got that puzzled look again on his face, the one that seemed to indicate he realized he was supposed to know the answer to a question but didn't. "What's an anchovy?"

"A horribly salty little fish thingy people put on pizza."

"Why would they do that?"

"Good question." I wandered into the kitchen and picked up the phone; I'd kept my grandfather's land line more out of nostalgia than anything else. But conveniently, the phone had Moon Dog Pizza on speed dial, so I pressed #3 and waited. In the meantime, I put my hand over the mouthpiece and said, "I'll get us some pepperoni. It's hard to go wrong with that—and it's pretty obvious you aren't a vegetarian."

A grin was Grayson's only reply.

I placed the order and hung up, then asked, "Want to pop open that bottle of wine?"

"Sure."

My bag was sitting on the kitchen table. I extricated the wine and dug through the utensil drawer, trying to locate a corkscrew, scolding myself for the umpteenth time about not putting the corkscrew in a separate drawer so it would be easier to find. At last, I dug it out and brandished it with an air of triumph.

"Do you want me to do that?" Grayson asked, having watched the previous procedure with an air of bemusement.

"Do you know how?"

After appearing to think it over for a few seconds, he replied, "I'm not sure."

"Well, I'd rather have you experiment on something a little less special, if that's okay."

Even as I said the words, I realized maybe they sounded a little harsh. Maybe I should have just let him try. I didn't want to offend him or make him think I didn't have confidence in him. But he hadn't sounded certain, unlike his conviction that he could ride a motorcycle just fine.

But he didn't appear to have taken offense. "You're probably right. I'd hate to break off a cork in there or something."

I smiled. "Okay." *Wow, he really* is *that nice....*

Soon afterward, the cork had been safely

removed, and we relocated to the living room with the bottle and a couple of glasses in tow. I wasn't sure what the proprietor of the wine tasting room would think about the two of us drinking his proprietary blend accompanied by pepperoni pizza rather than something a little more exalted, but then again, Moon Dog's pizza wasn't exactly supermarket frozen-case stuff, either.

We settled down on the couch with the wine. Outside, the rain began to beat down heavily once again. With it the temperature dropped, enough so the air conditioning clicked itself off. Too bad it hadn't truly cooled down enough so I could start a fire in the hearth, but weather that accommodating wouldn't be along for a few more months.

Still, it was cozy enough in here, with just the one lamp on its lowest setting and Gort curled up a few feet away on the rug. While we were still in the kitchen, it had seemed easier to keep Grayson at arm's length, to act casual, as if nothing of any real import had happened between us, but now that he sat next to me on the couch, so close I thought I could smell the scent of shampoo in his damp hair and feel the heat coming off his body, it was a lot harder to act cool and collected.

"So," I said, after allowing myself a bracing swallow of wine, "anything 'click' while we were out riding around?"

"'Click'?" he repeated.

"You know...look familiar. Maybe on the road out toward Cottonwood?"

He appeared to mull over my question, tanned fingers wrapped around the stem of his wine glass. Then came a reluctant shake of the head. "No. Not really."

Well, I should have known it wouldn't be that easy. "Then I think you should see my friend Janelle. She's done some amazing stuff with helping people retrieve lost memories. It's not all past-life regressions and telling people they were Napoleon or Cleopatra or something."

By that point, I was used to the expression of confusion that would flit across Grayson's features any time I brought up something he didn't understand, but it still unnerved me a little. Could he really not remember famous historical figures like Cleopatra and Napoleon? How he could have lost such fundamental knowledge, yet still be able to maneuver a bike up a curvy canyon road as if he did so every day?

It was a puzzle I couldn't begin to unravel. Maybe Janelle would have better luck.

"You can call her, if you want," Grayson said. "I guess I keep hoping that my memories will start to come back on their own, but maybe that's the wrong way to go about it. It's been several days, and still nothing."

I nodded. Janelle didn't work on Saturday

evenings, of course, but from time to time, she'd see a client on a Sunday if it was a special case. If we were lucky, she might even be able to work with Grayson the next day.

"Just a quick call," I promised. "Let me get my wallet in case the guy with the pizza shows up while I'm on the phone." If I'd been thinking, I would have brought it in with me already. At least it only took a short minute to retrieve the wallet from my purse and then, after thinking about it for a second, pull out a twenty and a five and leave them on the coffee table. "That's enough to pay for the pizza and the tip."

"Got it."

That handled, I went back into the kitchen so I could make the call. Of course, Janelle wasn't on speed dial, but the phone table drawer contained stacks of business cards, and the hypnotherapist's was in there somewhere. After sorting through the cards for a minute, I located the one I was looking for and dialed the number. On a Saturday night, I expected to get Janelle's voicemail, but the phone picked up on the second ring.

"Janelle Russo."

"Oh—hey, Janelle, it's Kara." Since there wasn't any way to put it without sounding like an imposition, I just plowed ahead. "I know it's the weekend and everything, but I was wondering if there was any chance you could see a friend of mine tomorrow."

"A friend?" Janelle paused. There were indistinct sounds of people talking all around her, so I guessed she must be someplace public—maybe a restaurant. It was almost seven on a Saturday night, after all. "My day's pretty open, actually. We'd been thinking about going hiking, but with the weather so unsettled, we called it off. So sure. What's the session for? Past-life?"

"Actually, no. I've got someone who's experienced complete amnesia—he can't remember his name or anything about his past. I was hoping you might be able to help."

Janelle's tone sharpened slightly. "Was it caused by some sort of trauma? Because if that's the case, he really should be seeking medical attention."

"There might have been trauma, but he doesn't remember it. He looks fine now. " *Really fine*, I added mentally, recalling just how amazing his body looked once there weren't any clothes to conceal those muscles or that flat stomach.

"You're sure."

"As sure as I can be. Really, he's got no bumps or bruises, nothing to show what—if anything—caused the memory loss."

"Well, I'll admit the case sounds a little intriguing. At least it'll be a break from having people find out they were sixteenth-century Flemish peasants instead of Alexander the Great."

I had to chuckle at that remark. "I hear you. So what time would be good for you?"

"How about eleven?"

"Great. We'll be there."

We exchanged a few more bits of chitchat before we said our goodbyes and hung up. One thing resolved, anyway. Or maybe not. Who knew what can of worms we were going to open up when Janelle put Grayson under?

The smell of pepperoni pizza greeted me as I returned to the living room. Gort had moved a few feet closer to the coffee table and was shifting his gaze from the unopened pizza box to Grayson and back again. The dog knew he wasn't supposed to have pizza, but he probably was trying to figure out whether Grayson would be a softer touch than his mistress.

"Thanks for waiting," I said, plopping myself back down on the sofa and reaching for the pizza. Good thing the delivery guy had left some paper plates along with the food, because I'd completely forgotten to get any plates while I was in the kitchen.

Grayson didn't do the same, however. He remained where he was, looking at the pizza with an odd expression on his face. For a few seconds, he didn't say anything. Then, finally, "I'm taking advantage of you."

"What?" I replied. Actually, it came out more as "wha," since my mouth was full. I swallowed, grabbed my glass of wine, and washed the taste of pepperoni from my mouth. "What are you talking about?"

He gestured toward the pizza. "This food. This whole day, really. You gave me a place to stay, tried to help me, and now you're spending all this money—"

So it had been bothering him. I set down my half-eaten slice of pizza and turned toward him, stared up into those eyes, which in the dimmer light of the living room looked like cloudy jade. "It's okay, Grayson. It's not as if I can't afford it. Besides, you fixed Grandpa's Indian. I'd say you've more than earned your keep, if that's what you're worried about."

"But—"

"But nothing. You don't need to stress about it. If it bothers you so much, I'll make you wash the dishes."

"These dishes are made of paper."

I grinned. "Okay, you got me. Guess I'll have to take it out in trade." And I leaned forward and kissed him, kissed him thoroughly enough that for a while, neither one of us thought about much of anything else.

Luckily, the pizza wasn't *quite* cold by the time we got back to it.

Lance

He returned to his condo, not because he considered it any sort of particular refuge, but mostly because he couldn't think of where else to go. Barhopping didn't sound remotely appealing. What else was he supposed to do? Go to a movie by himself? Drop in on the wine and cheese mixer the local MUFON group was having down at Barbara's house in the Village of Oak Creek?

Not bloody likely.

Instead, he found his thoughts drawn north and west, to the facility out in Secret Canyon that once had housed alien/human hybrid soldiers, alien-infected humans, and the men and women who were either too corrupt, too stupid, or too scared to do anything except what their alien overlords told them to do. Persephone had said she hadn't picked up any vibes from the place since she'd blasted the whole kit and caboodle of them out of existence. Maybe so, but that UFO the other night hadn't exactly acted as if it was out on some sort of pleasure cruise.

He didn't like to talk about his time with Project Aurora, partly because describing his experiences there was like trying to describe the color blue to someone who'd been blind since birth, and partly because he just wanted to put that period of his life behind him. Most people—when they thought about it at all—didn't believe such a thing as remote viewing was even possible, and thought the Army had been funneling money into a bogus program that was yet another spectacular waste of taxpayer dollars.

But it had been real. And he'd been good at it.

Too good, some people had thought. Well, maybe so. Because he'd seen things he wasn't supposed to...and the base at Secret Canyon was one of them.

For all he knew, it could have been what brought him here to Sedona in the first place. Remote viewing wasn't like looking at Google maps or something; just because he could visualize a place didn't mean he knew exactly where it was located. But after he'd left the service, and after Natalie was dead, he'd drifted this way and that, moving westward, until one day he drove up Interstate 17, took the turn-off for Sedona, and saw the red rocks for the first time...and realized he'd come home.

The condo was a bank foreclosure, and he'd gotten a good deal on it. Money wasn't a problem, as long as he didn't get too extravagant. Maybe the Army looked on his generous pension as a leash, a way of keeping him quiet. Keep your mouth shut, keep collecting the checks.

Joke was on them. The NSA might have some damn good analysts and programmers, but Jeff Makowski could run rings around them in his sleep. So far, no one had yet figured out that some of the leaks of information the government would have preferred never saw the light of day had come straight from Lance, encrypted ten ways from Sunday, thanks to Jeff's code-writing skills.

Now, though, Lance thought it might be time to bend his own thoughts toward Secret Canyon, to see if he could discover anything there. It would have been better to have Persephone here—the woman could be annoying sometimes, with her smart-aleck attitude, but she hadn't steered them wrong the last time. Her instincts were good. *Clairsentient rather than clairvoyant*, was how she liked to put it. Meaning she knew things without knowing how she knew them, but she couldn't necessarily always see them the way Lance did.

He'd always worked best seated in a chair, so he pulled out one of the hard-backed little jobs from his dinette set and placed it in the dead center of the living room carpet. Right then, he was just trying a little fact-finding; he wouldn't bother with the notepad and pencil. Time for that later...if he had any success on this go-round.

Eyes shut, he placed his hands palm down on his knees and waited. Sometimes, it took a while to come to him, especially if he hadn't attempted a viewing for weeks or even months. But he couldn't be impatient. He couldn't be anything except an empty vessel, waiting for the visions to come.

That wasn't exactly the right way to think of the

process, but it was close enough. Maybe it was more like slowly scanning across radio bands and waiting for one to come in clearly amidst all the static. The one thing he needed was to be completely blank, to shut out everything around him.

Including the unwelcome vision of Kara on the back of her grandfather's Indian Chief, arms wrapped around some muscle-bound character in a tight-fitting black T-shirt. The guy was wearing a helmet, so Lance couldn't see his face. Not that it mattered. Mrs. Martinez had already stated that the guy was *muy caliente*.

No. He couldn't do anything about any of that. It was not his problem. Time to focus on something else.

The darkness and stillness in his mind were always the precursors to the viewings. He had to get to that headspace before anything else could happen. Somehow, he managed to get there, to let go of everything in and around him so he could do what needed to be done.

Outside, it was full dark, but levels below the ground, the base blazed with light. This was an easier viewing than many because he'd already been there; his mind filled in the details of that which was known and concentrated instead on what had changed.

You'd never know the place had been dead and quiet only a few weeks earlier. Now the corridors were filled with people, many of them the blank-faced hybrids Persephone thought she'd destroyed all those months ago.

Incongruously, a mangled version of the old slogan from a potato chip commercial surfaced in his mind. *Kill all you want...we'll just make more!*

He gave the slightest of head shakes. Focus...he needed to focus, because even that stray thought had caused the scene in his mind to waver, like a television picture broken up with static.

It wasn't just the hybrids, though. He also saw people who looked human but whose movements and expressions told him they'd been taken over by aliens. So maybe the grand plan to enslave a good chunk of the world's population had failed, but obviously the aliens were still acquiring puppets as the need took them.

And then he saw...others. Aliens in their true forms, with no need to hide or dissemble, which meant that no actual humans existed at the base. And that meant....

Nothing good. Previously, there had been some sort of agreement between the aliens and certain corrupt members of the government, but if the base was all aliens, all the time, then most likely even the compromised humans were being kept in the dark.

What were the aliens plotting? He had no idea, could tell nothing from the shapes, both human and inhuman, walking to and fro within the base's corridors. They moved quickly, as if intent on some purpose, but what that purpose was, he didn't know.

Don't get frustrated. Just observe.

Easy to say. Not so easy to do. He had to let the images come to him, couldn't force them or try to make them go someplace else. It would have been better to see inside one of the labs, or even the motor pool. Any place but these interminable hallways.

But as he drew in a deep breath and tried to regain his ragged focus, it dissolved before his eyes. All he could see was the black behind his eyelids, and he knew he'd lost the vision.

"Well, shit," he said aloud to the empty room, and opened his eyes.

He glanced down at his watch. Nine o'clock. So he'd been out of it for almost an hour and a half. His stomach grumbled, telling him it had been way too long since lunch.

Lance ignored the rumblings and headed instead to the cabinet in the kitchen where he kept his liquor. A shot of Jack went into a glass, and he took it quickly, gulping it down without really tasting it. Some booze was meant for savoring, but not ol' J.D. That was for when you needed to get your head together real quick.

For a second, he contemplated calling Paul but realized that was a stupid idea. The Olivers were at a wedding in California; most likely, Paul had his phone shut off in order to avoid any uncomfortable interruptions. Besides, they were going to be back the day after tomorrow. The aliens looked busy, but Lance hadn't gotten the impression that they were ramping up for a final push. There was probably plenty of time to plan a counter-strike before the shit really hit the fan.

Probably.

CHAPTER NINE

Kara

JANELLE RUSSO'S OFFICE WAS LOCATED AT THE west end of town, on the second floor of an office building done in adobe-colored stucco to coordinate with Sedona's ubiquitous Southwest vibe. Even the McDonald's a few blocks down the street had a set of teal-colored arches rather than the regulation gold.

I'd driven, although Grayson had offered. The motorcycle was one thing, but I would rather he stayed out from behind the wheel of my Prius, just in case. Besides, as I'd pointed out to him, I already knew where we were going.

So he'd shrugged and finished clearing away the rest of the breakfast dishes. Apparently, he'd been serious about pitching in around the house as a way of paying off his perceived "debt" to me.

Well, if he didn't want to feel like a kept man, I couldn't really blame him. Never mind that we'd already fallen into the sort of easy routine I recalled from my time with Alan...although with Alan, there had always seemed to be bickering over whose turn it was to do the dishes or take out the trash.

I had to remind myself that Grayson had only been with me for four days. Somehow, it seemed as if he'd been a part of my life for much longer than that. But he hadn't, of course. And we were here to try to find out just where he'd been before those four days began.

We pulled into a space directly in front of the staircase that led up to the second-floor offices. Janelle's Honda sat a few spots away, but otherwise, the parking lot was empty; after all, it was a Sunday, and no one else had any real reason to be at the complex.

Grayson followed me up the stairs. We hadn't said much on the drive over. Most likely, he was worrying about the session and what it might reveal. And some people were just hinky about being hypnotized. I'd always rather enjoyed it, since I really did come out of a hypnotic trance feeling refreshed and relaxed. Then again, I'd only had sessions with somebody properly licensed, not some entertainer trying to make people squawk like chickens or hop around on one foot for five minutes.

Janelle opened the door just as we approached. "Come on in," she said. "I was keeping this locked since I'm the only one here."

"No problem," I replied, moving past Janelle. Grayson also entered, looking around with some interest.

The office was small but well-furnished, with a reclining leather chair in a deep smoke color rather than the typical black. Two more office chairs were covered in the same gray leather, and the walls were painted a soft, soothing shade somewhere between gray and blue. Graceful palms sat in two of the corners.

"Hi, Grayson," Janelle said, putting out her hand. "I'm Janelle Russo."

He took her hand somewhat uncertainly and shook it.

She pointed at the recliner. "You can go ahead and take a seat in that chair."

A wary glance in my direction. "Kara can stay, right?"

"Normally, I prefer to see my clients alone, but if it makes you feel more comfortable, that's fine." Janelle flashed a quick smile at him, but her dark eyes seemed to be intent on me, as if she was attempting to figure out exactly what the relationship between the two of us might be. "Kara, you can sit over there."

The second of the two office chairs was located about three feet away from the recliner and the chair where Janelle would conduct the session. I went over to the office chair and sat down, then gave Grayson what I hoped was an encouraging smile. "It'll be fine."

His expression was dubious, but he took his seat in the recliner and folded his hands in his lap. "What do I have to do?"

"Nothing difficult," Janelle said in soothing tones. Even though I knew the hypnotherapist had been here in Sedona for more than ten years, she still had a touch of East Coast sharpness to her accent. "I want you to close your eyes and breathe in and out, slowly and deeply." She paused to make sure Grayson was doing as she requested, then continued. "Okay, I'm going to count backward from ten. When I get to one, you'll be relaxed and open, ready to receive your memories. Ten, nine...."

And she went through the countdown, as Grayson's dark lashes fluttered against his cheeks and his breathing grew slower and deeper. Even though I had seen this many times, it was still fascinating to me, that a person could so easily be guided into a trance state.

"All right, Grayson," Janelle said, "we're going to take you back to Wednesday night. Can you tell me where you are?"

A pause, and then he said, his words slow and his tone oddly flat, "The desert."

Well, that really narrowed it down. I refrained from letting out a sigh, reminding myself that I needed to be invisible while this was going on. Besides, Janelle had only begun. She was merely setting the stage right now.

"Can you tell me about this desert?"

"Dark. Hot. I see lights."

"Lights from where?"

"Houses." He hesitated, then said, "I know I'm not supposed to go there, but if I don't, I'll die."

Janelle's brow furrowed a little, and she pushed her glasses up with one finger so they settled more firmly on the bridge of her nose. "Why are you afraid you're going to die?"

His hands, which had been resting limply against his jean-clad thighs, clenched. "Haven't eaten. Haven't drunk. Too much sun."

That seemed to jibe with my speculation about his condition when he first showed up on my doorstep. I held my breath as Janelle asked, "How long have you been in the desert?"

No answer. Only his sun-browned fingers digging into the flesh of his thighs.

"It's fine," Janelle soothed him. "You don't have to tell me that right now. Can you go past the desert, back to where you were before you were out in the heat and the sun?"

A frown. His jaw muscles tensed. "Number D-7957."

"Excuse me?"

"Number D-7957."

"Is that an apartment or house number?"

No response. This time, I could actually see the muscles in his throat and jaw tense as he seemed to wage some kind of internal war. Finally he said, "No."

"No, it's not an address?"

"No."

Janelle frowned, just the smallest bit, then sat up a little straighter. "Okay, Grayson—"

Voice emphatic, "That's not my name."

Without missing a beat, Janelle asked, "Can you tell me your name?"

"No."

"You don't remember it?"

"No name."

Again, a frown creased the olive skin between Janelle's eyebrows as she sat back in her chair and appeared to contemplate Grayson for a moment. "Are you afraid to tell me your name?"

"I can't."

"All right, let's leave that for now." The hypnotherapist's voice was still soothing, still unruf-fled, although I guessed she must be feeling frus-trated. God knows I was frustrated enough for the two of them. "Can you tell me about where you came from? Were there other people there?"

"Yes."

"Many people?"

"Yes."

"Was it a city?"

"No."

"A smaller town, then. Like Sedona?"

"No."

His voice still sounded flat, expressionless, so unlike himself. Or maybe this was the real Grayson, and the man I thought I'd come to know over the past few days was someone else entirely, a construct built on our interactions and nothing more.

No, I refused to believe that was true. It was something about the hypnosis, something in the way he was reacting to it that made him sound like an entirely different person...and not one I wanted to know.

"Can you describe this place?"

"No. It's not allowed."

"Can you explain that? Did someone tell you not to speak about where you came from?"

"No one is supposed to talk about it. I shouldn't be talking to you now." Finally, some emotion seeped into his voice; he sounded tense, almost nervous.

Janelle obviously picked up on it, too, because she said, her tone even more gentle than before,

"You're safe here, Grayson. If you don't want to speak of it, you don't have to."

"No. It's not safe."

"Can you tell me why you would say that?"

His hands were knotting and unknotting themselves against his thighs, and I could see a sheen of sweat on his brow, even though the office was air conditioned and more than comfortable. "Because they're looking. They're looking, and they'll find me. I know they will. They won't stop. They never stop!"

He almost shouted these last words. I sat up a little straighter and shot a worried look at Janelle. Grayson seemed so agitated, surely the therapist would pull him out of the trance now.

We seemed to be in accord, because Janelle gave a grim shake of her head and said, "All right, Grayson, I want you to take in a deep breath. Breathe in, then out."

Although his hands were still clenched, his respiration did seem to slow. He shut his eyes and breathed as he'd been instructed.

"Very good, Grayson. Now I'm going to count backward from ten. As I count, you're going to come slowly up to consciousness. You'll awake refreshed, and you won't remember anything that took place here, unless you want to. All right? Ten... nine...eight...."

I looked on as Grayson's breathing grew more shallow. As Janelle said "two," his eyelids fluttered, and then he opened his eyes and stared up at the ceiling in an unfocused way, as if he couldn't quite recollect where he was.

"Doing okay?" Janelle asked. "Some water?"

He shook his head. "No, I'm all right." A tentative smile, the warmth in his expression so different from the flat intonation he'd used while under hypnosis. "So, did I say anything important?"

Janelle and I exchanged a glance, but luckily, Janelle spoke up first. "We weren't able to find out much about who you are or where you came from, unfortunately. But this was only a light trance... maybe if I put you under a little deeper...."

"I don't think that's a good idea," I said, surprising myself. After all, this had been my suggestion. Now, though, I was thinking we probably should have left well enough alone. "Unless you really want to, Grayson," I added.

For a few seconds, he didn't say anything. Then he replied, "No, I think you're right. If we didn't find out anything, maybe there's a reason." He got up from the chair and extended a hand to Janelle. "Thanks for taking the time to see us."

"I'm sorry I couldn't be of more help." Now she was the one sounding neutral, although in her case it was probably because she wasn't quite sure what to make of the little she had heard.

"It's all right," he said.

I stood up, too. "We've interrupted your day

enough, Janelle. Thanks again for letting us come over."

"It's no problem. I was taking advantage of the peace and quiet to do some paperwork anyway." Her eyes met mine for a second, as if to say, *We'll talk later.*

That's going to be an interesting conversation, I thought, but I only smiled. "Still, it was an imposition, and I'll make it up to you."

"If you insist—maybe you can take me out on one of your UFO tours."

"Sure." *If I ever have another one, that is....* That was crazy, though. Of course I'd host more tours, once the group had determined it was safe to do so. When exactly that would be, though, I didn't have a clue.

Grayson and I left then, hurrying down the stairs through the heat so we could get to the car as quickly as possible. He waited until we were inside and back out on the street before asking, "So what *did* happen in there?"

"You really don't remember anything?"

"No. It's just...black."

Like everything before you came here. He'd revealed so little, and the tiny pieces of information he'd let drop had been far from reassuring. So "they" were looking for him. Who exactly were "they"? He hadn't said anything, but if my theory was true and he really was some sort of lost test pilot or something, then of course whatever branch of the military he was with would be doing everything it could to track him down. If that were the case, then calling Joe Gonzales and asking after any missing persons fitting Grayson's general description probably hadn't been such a brilliant idea. That kind of inquiry could have sent up all sorts of red flags. Then again, if that were true, wouldn't they have already found him?

I had no idea. Right then, I didn't know much of anything, except that, despite everything, I was very glad he had come into my life.

Almost of its own volition, my hand moved from where it rested on the gearshift—a habit I found hard to break even though the Prius was an automatic—and lay down on top of Grayson's. He gave me a startled look and then smiled.

"We're okay?"

"Oh, yes," I said, "we're okay."

———

Lance

He watched as Michael carefully poured sun tea out of the incongruous glass container with strawberries on it that he used to make the concoction and into a pair of tall glasses filled with ice. As much as Lance would have liked the drink to be something a little stronger than iced tea, he figured three o'clock on a

Sunday afternoon was a little early to start bending the elbow.

Although normally, he would have called Kara and discussed what he'd seen with her, he'd held off, waited instead for Michael to be available. Somehow knowing that Kara was running around with Mr. *Muy Caliente* had put a damper on Lance's desire to share confidences with her. He'd tried calling Paul, since the wedding was over and done with and Persephone and Paul should have been more or less available, but he'd only gotten voicemail. The information he wanted to divulge wasn't the sort he felt comfortable leaving on a cell phone's voicemail system, so he hung up. The Olivers would be back in Sedona Monday evening. Things could wait until then.

So he'd come over to Michael's once the shaman had finished his medicine wheel talk or whatever the hell he had going on today. Lance couldn't really keep track, and it didn't matter much one way or another.

They made their way outside. The sky was heavy with clouds again, shifting light and shadow. No rain yet, though, so they sat out in the yard and listened to the creek burble a few yards away. At least the cloud cover brought the temperature down enough that it was fairly comfortable to sit outdoors, and the cottonwood and sycamore trees that ringed the patio helped by providing shade.

"Have you spoken with Kara?" Michael asked.

"No."

He shot a curious dark look at him. "Why not?"

"Didn't feel like it."

Silence for a moment, as Michael regarded him carefully before taking a large swallow of tea. "Usually you would share these things with her."

"Yeah, well, she's not sharing a lot with the rest of us right now."

A lifted eyebrow. "How so?"

"Guess she's met someone." Lance shrugged, and then hoped it didn't look too calculatedly casual. "At least, that's what I heard."

"Ah," said Michael, which could have meant anything at all. He drank some more iced tea and then gazed upward, apparently contemplating the shifting clouds as they turned the sky alternating dark and bright, dappling the ground with unexpected patches of sun and shadow. "It bothers you."

"This isn't junior high. I couldn't care less what she does with her private life...unless it compromises our work."

Another one of those heavy pauses. Michael had always been good at that, at using silence as a tool more eloquent than any words. If he thought you were holding something back, he'd just wait. And wait. And wait.

Well, two could play that game. Lance drank his own tea and stared off toward the creek, which he could hear but couldn't quite see, except for the occasional shimmer through the branches of the trees that stood between Michael's property and the water.

A smile then, but one that seemed almost inwardly directed, as if Michael was smiling at himself for having his own strategies thrown back in his face. "So you say. But you should talk to her."

"I will." *Eventually.* "I figured since Paul and Persephone are going to be back tomorrow anyway, it could wait. Like I told you, I didn't get a sense that anything requiring immediate action was going on."

"And what 'action' do you think we should take?"

Good question. "I guess that's for all of us to figure out. Persephone was pretty effective the last go-'round, but I have no idea whether that trick is going to work again or not. I suppose that's up to her."

"She'll do what she has to, just as we all will."

That remark sounded vaguely ominous. "You know something I don't?"

Michael looked unconcerned as he drained the last of his iced tea. "No. But I know her. And you."

That makes one of us. Lance didn't like feeling so unsettled, so uncertain. He'd thought he knew where things stood, how to handle Kara. But she'd upset part of the equation, and in doing so had forced him to re-examine pieces of his life he'd taken for granted. Damn it, things were complicated enough already. Now he was going to have to factor in a possible addition to Kara's world, and he found he didn't care for it much.

I don't know who the hell you are, mystery man, Lance thought, *but you're already causing way too much trouble.*

———

Grayson went out, saying he wanted to go for a ride, clear his head. I hadn't much liked the idea, but I also couldn't think of a way to articulate my concern that didn't sound like some over-protective mother hen. Yes, Grayson shouldn't be riding without a license, but we'd gone all the way to Jerome and back without incident. The only difference this time was that I wouldn't be riding along.

So instead I'd settled for writing my cell number down on a scrap of paper and slipping it into the pocket of his jacket. "If anything happens—if you get pulled over for some reason—you call me. I know the local cops. I can probably get it to go away. But don't admit to not having a license, whatever you do. Okay?"

"Okay," he replied, and for the first time since leaving Janelle's office, he looked amused, as if my fretting was something that didn't merit much concern. Then he added, "You shouldn't worry so much," before disappearing into the garage.

A minute later, I heard the Indian start up with a

low rumble that seemed to shake the house. I couldn't hear the garage door opening over the sound of the motorcycle, but since I'd left the spare remote on the work table, I assumed he must have found it and taken it with him.

It felt weird to be all alone in the house. Okay, mostly alone; Gort looked up at me and gave a faint whine, as if he could tell something was troubling me but couldn't quite figure out what it was.

"I'm okay, Gort," I said, and bent down to ruffle the dog's ears. How could I explain to Gort why it seemed so strange to be by myself when I'd spent most of the past year living that way? Four days spent with Grayson didn't seem to be enough to balance out five years of not having a man in my life.

Or maybe I just didn't want to admit how much he'd come to mean to me in such a short amount of time. The sex had been great, obviously, but I thought it was more than that.

Unless it was simply because I *needed* it to be more than that.

I wished I could stop trying to analyze everything. But, as Kiki had pointed out on more than one occasion, I had never been all that good about living in the moment. How could I, when I'd spent so much of my life having to look out for other people?

There was also that nagging sense of guilt trailing after me, shading everything I did with Grayson, as if I was betraying Lance by being intimate with someone else. Even more stupid, since I was pretty sure Lance didn't give a rat's ass who I was sleeping with. For all I knew, he'd be relieved to find out about Grayson. If I was hooked up with someone else, then I wouldn't be mooning after Lance, and he wouldn't have to worry about any more awkward pauses or uncomfortable glances.

That old song, "Torn Between Two Lovers," had always annoyed the hell out of me. Certainly, I'd never expected to be in that position.

You're not in that position, I told myself as I went into the kitchen to pour myself a glass of water. *'Cause Lance sure as hell isn't a lover. He's a—I don't know what. The guy you've wasted too much mental energy on already. Don't screw up this thing with Grayson just because some part of your brain won't give up on Lance.*

That all sounded very sensible. And all right, maybe it was crazy to be falling for someone I'd only met days ago, and even crazier to be risking my heart when I knew absolutely nothing about him. Forget the lost test pilot idea—he could have a wife and three kids down in Phoenix or Tucson.

Somehow, I didn't think so, though. I did not get that vibe off him at all. And, as tanned as his hands were, you'd think there'd be at least a faint line where a wedding ring used to be.

My cell phone rang, and despite myself, my

heart started thudding. *Don't let that be Grayson, pulled over somewhere....*

It was not. I recognized the number immediately as Kiki's, and picked up. "Hey, Keeks, I—"

"Oh, my God!"

I had to hold the phone away from my ear before replying, "Um...Kiki?"

"It's all over the place! Why didn't you *tell* me what happened? It's already gone viral!"

"What's gone viral?"

"The video of your UFO tour! I can't *believe* you guys got buzzed by a UFO and you didn't tell me!"

Oh, hell. Still keeping the phone a safe distance from my ear, I replied, "I figured I'd tell you about it when you got back. Waiting wasn't going to change what happened, was it? Anyway, where the heck did the video come from?"

"Well...I guess not." A pause, and then Kiki continued. "And the video was uploaded to YouTube about an hour ago. Jeff has all these alerts set, so of course when one of them went off, we stopped the routine we were running and checked it out. It's not great quality—off someone's cell phone, obviously, but *still*."

Privately, I was a little impressed that one of my tour group had maintained enough presence of mind to keep the cell phone camera going during a close encounter, but I wasn't about to tell Kiki that. "Do you know who uploaded it?"

"Well, the YouTube username was sundevil588, so we guessed it was someone from ASU. Jeff looked into it. Turns out the guy's name is Travis Dooley. He's a junior at the college."

Travis. I remembered him. Smart-ass. It figured he'd be the one holding his iPhone high even while getting strafed by a UFO. I wondered why he'd waited so long to upload the video. Fear? He didn't seem the type to get frightened by much, but maybe he'd just needed a while to work up the nerve to do it. Even a non-believer might worry a little bit about the kind of shitstorm such footage would stir up.

"It's amazing!" Kiki exclaimed. "The way you just stood there, staring up at it? Even Jeff was impressed. I mean, I *think* he was."

"It's not like I planned it that way. I just... couldn't move."

"You mean they had you pinned in place by their ray or something?"

"Or something. I don't know exactly what happened. But if Lance hadn't pushed me out of the way—"

"Yeah, that was amazing, too! The way he just tackled you! Guess you two had your own close encounter, didn't you?"

I couldn't even laugh. The memory was still too raw. And I wasn't about to admit to my sister how I'd continued to feel the weight of Lance on top of me long after we'd both gotten to our feet.

"If you say so."

Whatever Kiki's faults, no one could accuse her of being unperceptive. She must have caught the edge to my voice, because she said quickly, "I'm just glad you guys are all okay."

"Yes, we're fine. I'm not doing any more tours, though, until we can all get together and discuss the situation. You're sure you don't want to come back with Paul and Persephone tomorrow?"

A pause, during which I heard something muffled that might have been a comment from Jeff in the background. Kiki said, "Well, maybe we'll come back on Wednesday instead of Thursday. But I can come back sooner if you really need me."

Meaning she really didn't want to hurry back to Sedona, for whatever reason, but would do so out of duty if necessary. I didn't quite sigh, but I found myself letting out a breath before replying, "No, I'm fine. It's been really quiet around here since then, actually, so there's no point in cutting your trip short."

"If you're sure—"

"I'm sure."

"Okay, well, I've got to go, but you should really check out the video. It's epic!"

I bet it is. "I'll take a look. You take care of yourself, Kiki."

"Looks like you're the one who should be taking care of yourself!"

I managed a laugh, then said my goodbyes and ended the call.

At first, I had no real intention of looking at the video—why would I want to relive such a terrifying event?—but curiosity got the better of me. If nothing else, it would be interesting to see how many views the video had gotten.

I got out my laptop and surfed over to YouTube, then saved time by looking up sundevil538's channel. The Sedona video was right at the top, but I wasn't sure I believed the number I saw on the page. How could it have gotten almost half a million page views when it had only been up for a couple of hours?

Kiki was right—the video shook and wobbled, and the angle showed that it had been shot from someone down on the ground, holding their phone upward. The light from the UFO was so brilliant that it overtaxed the camera's white filters, and therefore the image was that much more degraded. But even so, you could see the glare outlining my body as I stared up at the huge alien ship, my hair blowing back in the wind it created. From this angle, it did look as if I was trying to face down the thing single-handed, even though I knew that was definitely not what had happened. I watched, waiting for the moment when Lance tackled me and Michael stepped forward as the little group's true defender.

That moment never came, though. The image

jiggled a little, and then the YouTube viewer went blank and was replaced by the message, "This video has been removed by user."

What the hell? Maybe Travis Dooley had decided the video was a little too hot.

No, that was too easy. *Somebody* had decided that video needed to be pulled...but I had a feeling that someone wasn't Travis Dooley.

Either way, it was probably for the best. God knows I had enough crap to deal with already.

The doorbell rang, and I automatically shut my MacBook Air and then, almost without thinking, slid it into the drawer that held placemats and other assorted linens. I didn't get many visitors, but maybe it was Michael dropping by to check on me, or maybe Felicia Martinez had invented an excuse to come over so she could get another peek at Grayson. She was going to be disappointed when she found out he'd gone off on an extended ride.

I pushed my hair back over my shoulders and went to answer the door, somewhat relieved that I'd put on a nice top to go with my jeans and had taken a little care with my makeup this morning, since Grayson and I were going to see Janelle Russo. Not that either Michael or Felicia really cared what I looked like, but I didn't want to be viewed as a slob.

What greeted me when I opened the door, however, was neither Michael nor Felicia. Instead, two unsmiling men in black suits stared down at me.

"Kara Swenson?" the taller of the two asked.

Throat tight, I could only nod mutely. I knew it was pointless to deny my identity. They knew who I was.

He didn't exactly smile, but he seemed somehow pleased.

"We'd like to ask you a few questions...."

CHAPTER TEN

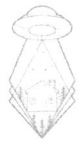

Men in black! I thought. I've got a couple of real live MIBs in my house!

I didn't know whether I should be completely freaked out...or possibly more than a little excited. Sort of like UFOs, men in black were the kind of thing whose existence you doubted until you saw them in the flesh.

They certainly looked solid enough as they stood on the Navajo rug in my living room and regarded me with a notable lack of expression. Some people claimed the MIBs weren't human at all, but some sort of extraterrestrial clean-up squad. These two looked like ordinary men, though.

Scratch that. They didn't look like ordinary men. They looked like ordinary government agents.

They could have been anywhere between thirty-five and forty-five, both Caucasian, one slightly darker-haired than the other. Their suits were identical, as were their dark ties and polished wingtips. I supposed they could have been alien-possessed humans, although I didn't get that feeling from them. Then again, how would I know? Unlike Persephone, I wasn't psychic.

The taller one asked, "You are Kara Swenson, owner of the UFO Depot?"

I thought I'd already verified that I was Kara Swenson, but what the hell. "Yes."

"And where were you the night of Thursday, August tenth?"

Come on, boys, is that the best you've got? "Here in Sedona."

Two sets of eyes, one brown, one blue, narrowed.

"I was leading a UFO tour in Boynton Canyon."

"And how often do you lead these...tours?" asked the shorter of the two men.

I couldn't help noticing that they hadn't given me their names. Sure, they'd flashed a couple of badges at me, but the cases that held those badges were opened and shut so fast, I didn't have time to read the names on their I.D.s. "Depends. Sometimes just once a week. During the busy season, as many as three or four."

"And do you believe in UFOs, Ms. Swenson?"

"Is that a trick question?"

Identical stony expressions were the only response.

"I believe there's *something* out there, yes. Exactly what, I can't say. I wouldn't make a very good UFO tour guide if I didn't believe in what I was selling, now, would I?"

The two men exchanged a brief glance. "Is it your assertion that you encountered a UFO on the night of August tenth?"

"I encountered something," I said warily.

"Could you elaborate on that?"

"I don't know."

"You don't know."

I could tell they were less than thrilled with my responses, but I wasn't an idiot. Confessing that yes, I'd seen a UFO would be all the excuse they needed to make sure I disappeared somewhere. I wouldn't be the first...and I wouldn't be the last. But if I muddied the waters enough, I just might be able to get out of this interview relatively unscathed.

"No, I don't know," I said. "There was a bright light in the sky, and a lot of wind, but so what? It could've been a helicopter. We've got tons of helicopters around Sedona. All the sightseeing, you know."

"That a fact."

"Yes."

"So why would someone be buzzing your tour group with a helicopter?"

"How would I know?" I crossed my arms and hoped I wore a convincing combination of exasperation and confusion on my face. "I'm not the only UFO tour operator in Sedona, after all. It's entirely possible that one of the other tour owners got a friend with a helicopter to come in and mess up my tour."

"Why would they do that?"

No one could be that obtuse. I refrained from snapping, *It's the economy, stupid,* and instead replied, "We're all competing for the same slice of the pie, you know? So maybe someone wanted to scare me off."

The agents exchanged a glance. The taller one said, "You'd swear an affidavit to that effect?"

"No."

Two sets of eyebrows lifted.

"I'm not going to swear to anything when I don't have all the facts," I told them. "I don't know exactly what happened. It could have been little green men...or it could have been someone taking the opportunity to try to put me out of business. But which one do you two gentlemen think is more likely?"

"You tell us."

I stared at both of them, certain that I couldn't make a single misstep or I'd be in a world of hurt. On the other hand, I was acutely aware of time passing. Grayson could be back at any moment—and I just couldn't risk the two agents still being here when he arrived.

"Look, I run a business devoted to UFOs. You

know that. But I think we also know it's far more plausible that a competitor was trying to give me a scare. In fact, I'd love it if you could find out who it was. There has to be a law against that sort of thing, doesn't there?"

For the first time, they looked a little uncomfortable. The taller agent said, "I'm afraid commerce isn't our department, ma'am. But I'd say it was unscrupulous even if it wasn't illegal."

He didn't exactly smile, but something in his face seemed to soften the slightest bit, and that was when I knew they were both as human as I was, even if they were doing their best to toe the company line. It didn't mean I was going to invite them over for dinner, but I also knew they were most likely just doing their best to plug a leak that had their superiors scrambling for plausible deniability. My crazy little story about a competitor buzz-bombing the tour group was probably a welcome lifeline they could hold on to and take back with them.

I wished I could feel more relieved that at least they weren't alien-infected humans or hybrids, but the knowledge didn't change the fact that I still wanted them out of my house before Grayson came back. Somehow, I managed a smile and replied, "Sounds like we're on the same page here, then. I wish I could help you out more, but...."

"It's no problem—" the taller agent began, but his compatriot broke in, saying,

"Then you won't mind if we take a quick look around?"

"Not at all," I said at once, uttering a silent prayer that I'd had the presence of mind to stow my laptop under the placemats in the linen drawer. Technically, I could have demanded to see a warrant. That would have been a bad move, though—better to let them have their look-see and get out, rather than raise their suspicions once again by mentioning a warrant.

They nodded and went their separate ways, the tall agent going down the hall toward the bedrooms and my office, the shorter one looking around the dining room and then the kitchen. I held my breath, wondering if he was going to start pawing through the drawers, but it seemed he was content with just a cursory glance before heading out to the garage. Thank God Grayson was as neat about the work-space out there as he was with his bedroom; neither agent would find any real evidence of his presence in the house, unless they dug through the trash and found the bristles from his morning bout with Grandpa's old electric razor.

Or the used condoms in my own bathroom trash can.

Heat rose in my cheeks, but I somehow managed to look on with mild interest as they continued their inspection. After about ten minutes, they reconvened in the living room, each giving the other the smallest of head shakes.

These aren't the droids you're looking for, I thought, and bit back a chuckle. "Everything okay?"

The tall agent gave the slightest of nods, but the shorter one asked, "You live here alone?"

"Yes."

"Lot of space for one person."

"I inherited it from my grandfather. My sister lived here with me until about a year ago." *Which I'm sure you knew already....*

He gave me a hard look out of those dark eyes, a look that seemed to say he thought I was up to something but couldn't find enough evidence to press the issue. Then I saw just the slightest lift of the shoulders under the black suit, as if conceding me the point in this match.

"I think we're done here, Ms. Swenson," he said. "Sorry to take up your time. However, I'd advise you to stay local, just in case we need to ask you any more questions."

"I'm not planning on going anywhere. I've got a business to run."

"So you're going to reopen tomorrow?"

Damn. I'd forgotten about the sign on the door about the shop being closed for a family emergency. Smoothly, I said, "That was the plan. After Thursday, I needed to take a few days off, but I'd be stupid to miss out on the last few weeks of summer, you know?"

"Very good." Another searching glance. "Then we know where to find you."

And he nodded at the taller agent, who seemed almost embarrassed by his partner's brusque behavior but knew better than to say anything. They went out and shut the door behind them without a goodbye.

Not that I cared. The important thing was that they were gone.

The relief that coursed over me was so intense, I actually felt my hands begin to shake. I pulled out one of the chairs to the dinette set in the breakfast nook and sat down, staring out the window at the carefully arranged rocks and desert plants in my backyard without really seeing them.

God, what next?

———

Lance

When his cell phone started vibrating in his pocket, he had half a mind to ignore it. He'd come up to Airport Mesa after leaving Michael's house, hoping maybe the wind and the sky could clear the cobwebs in his head. True, the place was overrun with tourists, but he knew a couple of hard-to-get-to spots that only the most intrepid scenery-seeker would attempt. Actually, he was halfway surprised he even got cell phone service out here.

But he knew ignoring the call wasn't really an option. Not that many people had his number, and almost any of them would have a damn good reason to be calling him.

He pulled out the phone and looked at the display. Kara.

Hers was about the last number he expected to see. Without thinking, he pressed "Accept" and held the phone up to his ear. "Kara?"

"Oh, hey, Lance."

She sounded shaken, and icy fingers of worry started to trail down the back of his neck, despite the lingering heat of the day. "What's the matter?"

A brittle little laugh that didn't fool him for a second. "Guess who just paid me a visit?"

"Who?"

"A couple of MIBs."

"*What?*"

"That's right. Oh, they were very polite, but... they wanted to know about Thursday night. Don't suppose you saw the YouTube video."

If he didn't know better, he would have thought she was getting some perverse pleasure out of piling on the shocks. "What video?"

"I guess one of my clients got around to uploading the footage off his phone earlier today.

According to Kiki, it went viral. It's down now—says 'Video removed by user,' but I'm guessing it wasn't Travis who took it down."

No, probably not. Lance stared out westward, roughly in the direction of the base in Secret Canyon, then said, "What did you tell them?"

"Not much. I hinted that I thought it was a rival tour owner out to scare off my customers by getting a friend with a helicopter to buzz me."

"Nice." Trust Kara to be able to think on her feet. He wouldn't say that nothing fazed her, but she'd been hit with enough disasters in her life that she didn't rattle too easily. "Do you think they bought it?"

"I think so. It's times like this I really wish I were psychic like Persephone. But I do think they were... like us. Regular people. Not...*them*."

Interesting tidbit. Sounded like the right hand didn't know what the left hand was doing. Or, maybe more accurately, the right hand was going about its business while the feet were carrying the whole damn thing someplace that ol' right hand really didn't want to be.

"Are you okay?" he asked abruptly. He wanted her to say she wasn't. He wanted her to say that she'd been shaken up by the whole experience and that she needed him to come over.

She hesitated. "Sure. They weren't that scary, actually. One of them was almost nice."

His tone flat, he repeated, "'Nice.'"

"Okay, not *nice* nice, but...anyway, I'm fine. Of course they gave me the standard line about not leaving town. Stupid. I mean, where would I even go? I've had a few days to get my head together, and I need to get back to work tomorrow."

He and Kara didn't have the sort of relationship where he could feel comfortable asking about what she'd done with those few days. Besides, thanks to the intelligence he'd gotten from Felicia Martinez, it was pretty clear what Kara had been doing with at least part of that time. He really didn't want to think about that, though.

She added, in an overly cheerful tone of voice that was probably intended to reassure him but in fact did just the opposite, "Well, we'll certainly have a lot to tell Paul and Persephone when they get back in town. Hard to believe it's only been four days!"

"You could put it that way."

A pause. "Everything okay, Lance?"

"Everything's great," he rasped. He wasn't about to tell her what was really bothering him. "I just don't know if it's such a great idea for you to be there by yourself."

"I'm not by myself—I've got Gort to protect me."

"Yeah, well, unless he can shoot laser beams out his eyes like the original Gort, I'm not sure how much good he'd be in an actual crisis."

She actually laughed at that gloomy remark, and

her laughter this time sounded genuine, with nothing of the forced cheeriness he'd heard from her just a minute ago. "That would be something. But no, you're right. I love Gort, but he's just a big pussycat. Good thing he looks fierce enough that most people don't try to find out whether his bite is worse than his bark."

Lance considered offering to stop by and then decided against it. Hovering wasn't his style, and if he pressed the issue much more, Kara might begin to realize that his solicitude stemmed from something more than just friendly concern. "Well, then, thanks for the update. I'll let Michael know what's going on, and once Paul and Persephone are back, we'll try to set up a time we can all get together and discuss our next steps."

Once again, she hesitated, just for a fraction of a second, but enough so he noticed. "Yeah, sure, that sounds good. Let me know."

"Will do. 'Bye."

He ended the call and shoved the phone back in his pocket, then stared once more out toward the western horizon, where the sun was finally beginning to touch the edge of the Black Hills. The wind had started to pick up as sunset approached, and he lifted his face into it. Right then, it was taking just about every ounce of determination he had not to go back to the Jeep, drive down the hill, and head over to Kara's house. If the shit really was about to hit the fan, he wanted to be with her, watching out for her. He sure as hell didn't want her relying on Mr. *Muy Caliente*, whoever he might be.

But in that direction, as they say, lay madness. He took a breath, then another, and forced himself to stay where he was.

Kara

Grayson came back almost an hour after the agents had left. After I'd ended my conversation with Lance, I roamed the house, unable to do much of anything constructive, although I did some general tidying-up as a way of expending my nervous energy. I'd opened my laptop, but when I saw sixty-seven unread messages in my inbox, I decided to put that off for another day. Probably most of the emails were from people who'd seen the video and now wanted their own extra-special close encounters.

Sometime the next day, I'd have to update the store's website to say there weren't going to be any more tours in the immediate future, but I knew I couldn't deal with that right now. Kiki had designed and built the website and put the whole thing in WordPress so it would be easy to update...theoretically. More than once, I had managed to blow up the whole thing, though, so I thought it better to avoid logging in until I felt a little more settled.

I'd just shoved the laptop back into its bag when I heard the automatic garage door open, followed by the deep rumble of the Indian. At once, Gort got up and assumed his waiting position on the rag rug just inside the door to the garage.

"Yeah, well, I'm not sure Grayson is going to want to go on a walk right away," I warned him. Still, I thought I knew how the dog felt. All that time, I couldn't stop myself from worrying about him, about the fact that he was out riding around alone in a town he didn't know, on a motorcycle that didn't belong to him, all the while with no driver's license. I probably should have tried harder to keep him from going, but he was a grown man. There was only so much I could have done.

But when he entered the kitchen, he looked considerably more cheerful than when he had left. His hair was mussed from the helmet, and he grinned at me as he bent down to scratch Gort behind the ears.

"Beautiful country around here, isn't it?"

I nodded. Not much argument with that. "Did any of it look familiar?"

"Not really. Not except for the part I saw yesterday, that is."

I should have expected as much. Could I really fault him for getting out and trying to see things on his own, without someone else's input to possibly skew how he was looking at the area around town?

Some part of me had wanted to be angry with him for being foolhardy, but as he looked at me with that melting smile, I knew I couldn't hold on to that anger. There was something so open and joyous about him, so lacking any subtext, that I just couldn't be upset with him for very long. He was so different from any of the other men I had known.

So different from Lance.

With an inner grimace, I pushed that thought aside. Maybe the brooding hero was a standard romance-novel archetype, but he was also sort of a pain in the ass to deal with on a daily basis. Grayson was so much easier to get along with.

I smiled back at him and stood, going to him so I could give him a hearty kiss. He immediately pulled me more tightly against him so I could feel the heat of his body, the strength of those arms as they folded around me. From somewhere, I heard Gort give a discontented little whine, as if he knew all too well where this was heading.

Sure enough, Grayson scooped me up in his arms and carried me down the hallway to the bedroom. I couldn't protest, not without sounding like a fool, because I knew I wanted him just as badly as he wanted me. At least I was pretty sure the MIBs had taken themselves off for the time being; I'd gone out front to pick up the neglected newspaper from my driveway as a pretext to do a brief scan of the neighborhood, and I hadn't seen any cars I didn't recognize. No, they'd probably dismissed me as harmless...for the time being.

So it was perfectly safe to let Grayson lay me down on the bed, to reach out and pull off his slightly sweaty T-shirt, to say the hell with the foreplay and wrap my legs around him and draw him into me, our bodies joining in a rush of heat and need. In that moment, I let myself forget about everything in the world.

Except him.

The next day, I dragged myself into the store, even though I would have happily continued my hiatus for a few more days. However, I couldn't justify that, even to myself. And though Monday was usually one of my days off, I didn't have Kiki to spell me, so I would be stuck there the whole day.

Grayson didn't seem too put off by my declaration that I had to get back to work, but instead commented that he thought the Indian was running a little rough, and so he planned to re-jet the carbs. I had no idea what that meant exactly, so I nodded and said that sounded like a great idea.

The deluge of emails I'd received after the video

surfaced—albeit briefly—translated into an unaccustomed rush at the store when I opened the doors at ten. After explaining to approximately the twentieth person that I wasn't going to be hosting any tours in the near future, I pulled out a Sharpie and composed a sign that read "All UFO tours suspended until further notice" and taped it to the front door. I still had to explain myself to the more stalwart diehards, but the looky-loo types read the sign and departed for greener pastures without ever coming inside. It was something, at least.

Even so, the day seemed interminable, and because Kiki was out of town and Michael unavailable, I couldn't even take a break to go home for lunch. I'd prepped Grayson for this eventuality by pointing out some of the frozen dinners in the freezer and giving him a quick primer on how the microwave worked, but it still seemed wrong that I would be kept away all day.

The day improved slightly when I got a text from Persephone saying they were on their way home and should be getting into town around seven that evening. I forwarded the text to both Lance and Michael and suggested a meeting for Tuesday night, but Michael already had a workshop scheduled for that evening, so we made tentative plans for Wednesday instead.

In an impulse, I sent a follow-up text to Persephone. *If you two aren't too tired, could you come over for dinner on Tuesday around seven? There's someone I'd really like you to meet.*

The reply came back almost immediately. *Sounds great. Do you need us to bring anything?*

Just yourselves...and a bottle of wine, if you'd like.

Will do! See you then.

Maybe I was being a little impulsive, inviting the Olivers over so soon, but I secretly hoped Persephone's powers would prevail where hypnotherapy had not. Sooner or later, we'd have to get through the impenetrable wall that seemed to have enclosed Grayson's past. Best that it should come from Persephone, who would be sympathetic no matter what happened.

Funny how someone I'd only known for a few months had become my best friend. My circle was large, but I counted most of those people as acquaintances and not close friends. Kiki and I had always been very close, of course, though that wasn't quite the same as having a friend of your same age and experience, more or less. Until Paul Oliver came along, Persephone's love life hadn't been all that great, either. She knew what it was like to be a single woman in her early thirties with the sort of job that tended to scare off any halfway decent prospects.

Anyway, I had to hope that Seph would like Grayson and want to help. I really didn't see how anyone could *not* like Grayson, but maybe Persephone would think I was rushing things. Maybe so. I didn't want to admit it to myself, but I knew the current state of affairs couldn't continue indefinitely.

———

On Tuesday, I put together my famous Greek stew in the crockpot so I wouldn't be rushing around at the last minute, trying to get everything ready in the scant hour between the time the shop closed and when the Olivers were due for dinner. I tried to impress on Grayson the need to be ready for company at a little after six, and he nodded, but I wasn't sure how much had sunk in. He'd been preoccupied with the motorcycle, whose carburetor was proving to be a little more temperamental than he had planned.

So I wasn't all that surprised when I got home around six-thirty and found him still out in the garage, grease smudges on his chin and cheekbone, and his hands not fit for company in their current state.

"You have got to take a shower," I said, wrinkling my nose. "My friends are going to be here in half an hour."

"That's plenty of time," he replied, fiddling with some unidentifiable slender brass part.

"Um, no, not really. Come on, Grayson—you've been messing with that thing all day."

"All right." An expression of irritation passed

over his features, but almost at once, he relaxed and shook his head, as if annoyed with himself. "Sorry, Kara. I'll go make myself pretty."

"You're pretty right now," I said, and gave him a swift kiss while avoiding the grease smudge on his chin.

He got up then and went inside the house, thankfully in the direction of the master bath. For the last few days, we'd given up any pretense of him having separate accommodations in Kiki's old room.

Somewhat relieved, I went back to the kitchen to crumble the feta cheese and get the kalamata olives ready to be added to the stew. Since it was a one-dish meal, about all that was left was to prep the salad and heat up the loaf of bread I'd bought at Wildflower on my way home from the shop.

I didn't know whether Persephone had been an on-time sort of person prior to hooking up with Paul Oliver, but the couple could always be counted on to be punctual. So I wasn't surprised when the doorbell rang at one minute past seven. Grayson, of course, was nowhere in sight. I'd have to make excuses for him and hope he wouldn't take too much longer.

Persephone enveloped me in a hug as soon as I opened the door. "We've been so out of touch—but Lance told us about the UFO and the MIBs—"

"Yesterday's news," I said, with what I hoped was an airy wave of the hand. "Come on in."

Persephone and Paul followed me into the kitchen, where Paul sniffed the air appreciatively.

"That smells amazing."

"It's Greek stew."

He threw a look of mock-dismay at his wife. "So you're half Greek, Persephone, but it's the Swedish gal who ends up making me Greek stew?"

Her hazel eyes danced. "If you thought you married me for my cooking, we're both in a world of hurt."

"No, it was all your other sterling qualities, fortunately."

They exchanged fond glances, and I felt something inside me twist a little. This was what I wanted with Grayson—this feeling of being so easy, so relaxed. But was that possible when so much of him was still hidden from me?

"My apologies for Grayson," I said then. "He got a little caught up in working on the bike, and I had to pry him away from a carburetor. He should be out of the shower in a few minutes."

"No problem," Paul said. "My stomach can hang on for a little while longer." He glanced out the sliding glass doors, where the red rocks above the backyard were beginning to turn even redder with the coming of sunset. "You mind if I take a look at your yard? I still haven't had a chance to really check out the medicine wheel Michael made for you."

"Absolutely."

"But only if you open the wine first," Persephone put in. She handed Paul the bottle of cabernet she was carrying.

"Opener?" he asked, looking resigned.

Suppressing a smile, I went to the odds and ends drawer and pulled out a corkscrew, then handed it to him. He struggled a little with the foil but eventually got the cork out. "Glasses?"

I produced those as well, and he poured a decent measure into each wine glass before snagging one for himself and letting himself out into the yard.

"Poor dear," Persephone remarked. "I'm probably better at that than he is, but I like to make him feel useful."

"Yeah, right. I'm guessing he's more than a little useful."

She cocked her head slightly and twisted a dark curl around one finger. "Oh, okay. He's definitely useful. And decorative. But enough about my husband. Tell me about this mystery man. We're gone five days and you've already found someone?"

"More like 'finally found someone,' but yes. It seems kind of crazy, but—"

"These days, I don't worry about crazy so much. It's easier that way. How did you meet him?"

"Well, that's kind of complicated." Even now, I wasn't sure exactly how to explain what had happened, although I knew the truth would have to come out at some point. I drank some wine, hoping that might make the confession a little easier. "He just sort of...stumbled over my doorstep, in a manner of speaking."

"Ah." If Persephone the psychic had picked up more from my statement than its face value, she didn't seem to show it.

But then I thought I heard movement down the hallway, and I looked past Persephone to see Grayson cutting through the living room on his way to the kitchen. His hair was still a little damp, but otherwise he looked more than presentable, in clean jeans and the one button-up shirt I'd bought him, with the sleeves rolled back slightly because of the warmth of the day. "Here he is. Grayson, this is my friend Persephone. Persephone, this is Gray—"

The word broke off abruptly, because I watched as Persephone shifted her position to greet Grayson... only to see her turn dead white. She was always pale, but right then she looked as if she was going to faint. The wine glass slipped from her fingers and fell with a crash to the floor.

"Oh, my God," she whispered.

Grayson looked at Persephone in confusion, then over at me.

I asked, past the constriction of worry in my throat, "Seph, what's the matter?"

Persephone shook her head. "It's not possible. He's...he's one of *them*!"

Somehow, I managed to ask the question, even

though my own hands had begun to shake. When a psychic had a reaction like that, it was not a good thing. "One of who?"

It was Paul who answered. Apparently, he had headed back toward the house as soon as he'd seen Grayson appear. The astrophysicist shut the sliding door behind him and said, "One of the alien/human hybrids."

CHAPTER ELEVEN

I SHOOK MY HEAD, WANTING TO DISBELIEVE, knowing the only way I could handle this was to deny what Persephone and Paul had just told me. "That's not possible," I said, my tone flat.

"We were there," Paul stated, looking grim. He glanced over at Grayson, who had watched our exchange with an expression of complete bewilderment on his face. "We saw them. We know what they look like."

"Oh, come on," I protested. "He's as human as you and I are."

"No, he's not." Persephone continued to stare at Grayson, glassy-eyed, rather like a small desert rodent mesmerized by a snake. "He may look like it, but he's really not."

For the first time Grayson spoke. "What are you

saying? That I'm...what? Some sort of science experiment?"

"You could put it that way," Paul replied. He, too, was watching Grayson with extreme care, but more the way a cop might regard someone with whom he'd had questionable dealings in the past. "So, you don't remember anything?"

"No." Those brilliant green eyes were harder than I'd ever seen them, glittering with repressed emotion. Was it anger? Confusion? Could he even feel those things?

Had he ever felt anything for me at all?

"I think I'm going to be sick," I whispered, and I turned from them and ran, ran down the hallway to the guest bathroom, where I dropped to my knees and vomited up the wine I'd just drunk and the little that remained of my meager lunch. I clung to the bowl and gasped, thinking of his hands on me, of him *inside* me, when all the time he'd been some alien *thing*, some construct—

I retched again, over and over, until it felt as if I was puking up my very guts, as if I was trying to expel the alien taint from within my body. Then I realized my frame was racked not just with sickness, but sobs, as I wept over the loss of what I'd thought I had with him, of what I'd thought Grayson had meant to me.

Someone's hand then, gently stroking my hair. Persephone's voice. "I'm so, so sorry, Kara."

Doubled over with wretchedness, I could only continue to cling to the toilet, the cold porcelain under my fingers somehow holding me down, the only thing connecting me with reality. I choked, "I—I didn't know."

"Of course you didn't." From somewhere, Persephone brought out a damp washcloth and began to wipe the heat and the sick from my cheeks. "I'm sorry I broke it to you like that. But when I saw him— it just came over me in a wave, and...it just sort of spilled out."

"It's all right." Somehow, I found the strength to loosen my grip on the toilet bowl, to force my shaky legs into a standing position. "It's better that I know."

"Paul's with him now. He seems a little...shell-shocked."

As well he might, I supposed. If hearing the truth had been terrible for me, what must it have been like for Grayson? To find out that you weren't *you*, not a real man, but something built by aliens for their own inscrutable purposes?

The nausea had passed, and now I only felt spent, as if I'd just spent a day running uphill in the heat. I got one of the little paper cups cut of its dispenser and rinsed out my mouth, not once, not twice, but three times, and then pulled out another cup and drank down enough water so I wasn't feeling quite so dehydrated. Now my body had been more or less taken care of.

I wished I could say the same thing for my spirit.

"What am I supposed to do now?" I whispered. "How can I go back and face...him? Is he a he? Or is he an it?"

Persephone gave me a look that seemed to say, *You'd know that better than I would....* But she only replied, still in the gentle, soothing voice usually reserved for her clients, "He's a he. Of course he is. And it's obvious he's not under their control...at least it doesn't feel that way. Something very strange is going on."

"Well, that's Sedona for you," I remarked.

A twitch of Persephone's finely arched brows, as if she knew all too well the hurt I was doing my best to hide under a glass-sharp edge of brittle humor. "Do you want to wait here? We'll figure something out if you don't want to see him...."

I shook my head. What good would hiding in a bathroom do? I had to face him, face what he was. A convulsive spasm of my hand, and the little paper cup was crushed flat. I threw it into the trash. "I'm all right."

Persephone didn't look all that convinced, but she didn't say anything, only nodded and let me exit the bathroom and head back into the kitchen. Grayson was sitting at the little table in the nook, head down, hands buried in his thick hair as if he was trying to feel his way through it to the secrets buried within his skull.

Seeing him like that, I felt a stab of pity go through me, unexpected as a knife thrust. It was fine for me to run to the bathroom and moan the loss of what might have been, but at least I was still myself. I hadn't lost my identity, only to discover the truth in all its horror.

Paul looked over at us. The set of his mouth was grimmer than I'd ever seen it. "You okay?"

I nodded but didn't quite trust myself to speak.

"You get anything?" Persephone asked.

A shake of the head. "He still claims not to remember anything."

At that remark, Grayson finally glanced up. His green eyes glinted as he said, "I *don't* remember anything. I don't know what you people are talking about!"

"I know you don't," Persephone said, and her voice still sounded curiously gentle. She added, her gaze fixed on Paul, "He really doesn't. I don't know what's going on, and I doubt we'll figure it out tonight, but I'm not getting anything bad off him."

"Except that he looks like about a hundred other men back at Secret Canyon who tried to kill us."

Improbably, a dimple flickered into existence next to her mouth for about a second before it disappeared again. "Well, yes, besides that."

The timer on the oven went off, and I started. Oh, right. The damn bread.

I hurried across the kitchen, glad to have something to do, glad I could busy myself with locating some pot holders to pull the bread on its cookie sheet from out of the oven. The watching eyes of the trio at the table in the nook felt heavy on the back of my neck, and after I set the cookie sheet down on the counter, I turned around and snapped, "Well, what was I supposed to do? Let it burn?"

"Of course not," Persephone said, voice still calm, soothing. "In fact, I think we should all just sit down and have something to eat and try to figure this out."

"You *what*?" Paul demanded, in tones that suggested he thought she'd completely taken leave of her senses.

"Yes," she said serenely. "Kara, do you need help with anything?"

Not sure of exactly the best way to respond, I pointed at the refrigerator. "Um...salad?"

"Got it."

And Persephone sailed over the fridge, got out the bag of romaine lettuce and the package of tomatoes and a bottle of Caesar dressing, and set to, since the salad bowl and tongs were already sitting out on the countertop. Grayson and Paul looked at each other in bemusement, as if they didn't quite know what to do with themselves.

"Paul, darling," she said, "can you get the wine glasses? And Grayson, the bottle of cab? Although I think we'll probably end up needing more than just the one...."

"I've got plenty in the wine rack in the dining room," I said faintly. I didn't quite know what I should do, but I thought—after I'd forced myself to eat something—getting mercifully drunk might be a very good idea.

"Great." Persephone sprinkled some Parmesan cheese on top of the dressing, added the succulent little grape tomatoes, and then finished off the salad with a handful of croutons.

The two men silently gathered up the wine and the glasses and headed out to the dining room. Persephone picked up the salad and followed them. Feeling as if I'd just been dropped into some bizarre alternate reality where it was considered perfectly normal to sit down to dinner with an alien, I took up a pair of pot holders and lifted the ceramic crock out of its metal housing and carried it over to the dining room. I'd already set down a trivet to protect the table from the crock, so I put the container of stew there, then murmured that I'd be back in a bit with the bread and butter.

They were all hovering around the table, as if unsure as to where they should sit. *No surprise*, I thought. Neither Paul nor Persephone probably wanted me sitting next to Grayson, but if we were seated across from one another, things could be even more awkward. I was pretty sure I couldn't manage to make it all through dinner while staring into those green eyes and trying to decide if I still saw anything human in them.

But we also couldn't all stand there like a bunch of overgrown partygoers in the world's most awkward game of musical chairs. I cleared my throat and said, "Grayson, how about you sit at the head of the table, and Paul on your right, and Persephone on your left...."

They all hastened to take the places I'd indicated, and I sat down in the chair at the foot of the table. Yes, I'd still be across from Grayson, but since the table was a rectangle, there was a lot more space dividing us than there would have been if we'd taken the seats Paul and Persephone now occupied.

For a minute, none of us said anything. There was the food to occupy us, the ritual passing of the salad bowl, the breaking of the bread, the pouring of more wine. I forced myself to put a bite of salad in my mouth, then another. To my surprise, I found it tasted good. The sweetness of the tomatoes and the crisp flavor of the greens seemed to erase the last of the sick taste from my mouth. There was water in addition to the cabernet Paul and Persephone had brought, and I drank some of that, too, made sure I had taken at least three healthy swallows before I allowed myself to drink any of the wine.

But even so, there came the inevitable time when the salads were done and the empty bowls pushed aside. Ladling out the stew and passing around the bread took up a few more minutes, and at last Persephone said, "Since I know none of you know what to say, I'll start."

Paul lifted an eyebrow, and Grayson looked a little alarmed.

"Don't worry—I don't bite." Her gaze slid to Paul for a second, and she added, with the faintest hint of a smile, "Well, unless you ask. Anyway, Kara's probably mentioned that I'm a psychic."

Grayson's expression was still wary, as if he wasn't quite sure that she wasn't about to jump up from her chair and lay hands on him or something. "I had that general impression."

"I hope you're going to hold off on the mind probes until after dessert," Paul remarked. He seemed to have relaxed slightly as he watched his wife. Since she appeared to have gotten over her initial alarm, he probably had decided to take a step back and see where things went.

I wished I could be that calm, that composed. My hand still shook slightly as I lifted my wine glass and drank. But if Persephone could somehow manage to face Grayson and address him as if he were any other dinner guest, I supposed I should try to do the same thing.

"You know I don't work that way." She turned back toward Grayson and gestured with her half-full wine glass. "I mostly work off vibes. And I'm not getting any negative ones from you, so...." She shrugged. "But I am seeing something."

"You are?" Grayson and I demanded, pretty much simultaneously. Then we exchanged an embarrassed glance before I forced myself to look away from that green stare, to focus on the food on my plate.

"I am." Persephone's hazel-green eyes seemed to go blurry, as if she was looking at something very far away. "I see the base at Secret Canyon...the empty hallways, the bodies of the aliens and the hybrids. And then...." Her words trailed off, and her mouth tightened.

"And then...." Paul prompted, after an awkward few seconds had passed. He'd been there, seen the aftermath of Persephone's psychic blast or whatever it was, and probably didn't want her to dwell on it.

"And then I see one of them stumble to his feet, stagger down the hallway. He's heading to the exit off Level Three, where the motor pool used to be. And then he's out, moving into the darkness and away into the desert. After that, he disappears."

I didn't want to believe it, but I'd seen too much evidence of Persephone's powers already and knew she wouldn't be making any of this up. "So...you're trying to say he's been out in the desert for the last *five months*? How could anyone possibly survive out there that long?"

An expression of troubled pity passed over

Persephone's features. "But he did survive it, somehow. All those months, hiding by day, hunting by night..."

"...finding water when I could, sheltering in caves, hungry...always hungry." Grayson's voice was faint, almost as if he was reliving those days of agony all over again. Maybe he was. "I *remember*."

Unexpectedly, Persephone said, "I'm sorry."

The expression of anguish on Grayson's face was so naked, I wanted to look away from it. I'd seen his unclothed body, had been as intimate with him as another person could be, and yet I suddenly felt as if I was observing something I shouldn't.

"I don't want to remember." His fingers tightened around the fork he held. "What did you do to me?"

"Nothing. All I did was see, and when I told you what I saw, the words unlocked what had been hidden in your mind all this time."

Easy for her to say. I could tell Grayson didn't want to believe it. Honestly, I didn't want to believe it myself. But Persephone's visions, or feelings, or whatever you wanted to call them, were rarely wrong. Sometimes they didn't come when she wanted them to, but once that peculiarly tuned muscle in her mind's eye locked on them, they tended to be something you could take to the bank.

He set down the fork on his plate with a clatter, then stood. "I need some air." And he went to the sliding glass door, opened it, and slipped out into the dark.

I began to half-rise in my own chair, but Persephone's words stopped me. "Don't. He needs to be alone for a while."

It somehow didn't feel right to allow him to wander around in the darkness by himself, but I did as Persephone had instructed and resumed my seat. "Is he going to be all right?"

"I don't know."

"What, your second sight suddenly desert you?"

Paul began, "Now, that's not fair—" but Persephone only shook her head slightly.

"It's all right, Paul." She shifted in her seat so she faced me. "You know I can't see everything. I'm not sure I even want to. But he needs to come to terms with this on his own." Her tone softened a little, and she added, "And what about you? Are you okay?"

"That's a hell of a question." I finished off the last half-inch in my glass and wished the bottle of cabernet was in arm's reach so I could pour myself some more. "I'm...I don't know what I am. I'll live, if that's what you're asking. It's just—I thought—I thought Grayson and I—" I shook my head, feeling like a complete idiot. How could I confess to Persephone and Paul that I'd thought Grayson might finally be the one, when I'd only known him for a few days? Maybe if I was alone with Persephone, I'd have the guts for that, but not with Paul watching me, too, even though his expression seemed sympathetic enough. Anyway, I'd already proven myself to have completely failed in judgment when it came to Grayson. No point in making the situation even worse than it already was. "Anyway, it doesn't matter what I thought. What matters is what we do next."

"And what *are* we supposed to do next?" Paul asked. His words had been directed toward both of us, but I noticed that he was looking at Persephone as he spoke.

"I guess that depends on Kara." Persephone pushed her plate away slightly so she could rest her hands on the tabletop. "What do you want to do?"

I wanted to say I didn't know, let it all fall on them, let them take care of it. Suddenly, I was so very, very tired. The events of the past week seemed to be catching up with me all at once. But I managed to reply, "I'm not sure. But I do know we need to keep him safe."

Paul's gaze sharpened. "Are you saying he's in some sort of danger?"

"I don't know. Maybe." The words spilling out, I described our visit to the hypnotherapist, Grayson's non-answers, that final outburst: *They're looking, and they'll find me. I know they will. They won't stop. They never stop!*

After this revelation, Persephone and Paul both sat there, silent, appearing to absorb the unwelcome information. Finally, Persephone expelled a heavy breath and said, "Well, I suppose that's not really unexpected. I mean, if nothing else, they're going to want to find him to figure out why one of them survived when the rest were all...destroyed."

I had the feeling that Persephone had almost said "killed," substituting the other word at the last minute. Although she had done what she thought was necessary, it couldn't be easy having all those deaths on your soul...even the deaths of hybrids and alien-infected humans. And maybe it was worse now that she'd found out not all hybrids were exactly created equal.

"I think we should have him stay with us for a while," Paul said. "If nothing else, it's probably safer that way—you have to be gone at the store for large parts of the day, Kara, but I'm home all the time. And Michael and Lance can take turns in providing any necessary defenses."

It sounded logical, but I found myself unwilling to agree. So I was supposed to just kick Grayson out like that? *Sorry, hon, it's been great, but this whole alien thing has kind of put the kibosh on any romantic entanglements, you know?*

Well, what else could I do? I certainly didn't want to abandon Grayson to the mercies of his former masters. On the other hand, I knew we couldn't go on as we had been. Even now, the thought of him touching me made me...well, not sick, not the way I'd been less than an hour ago, but I couldn't help shivering a little. He wasn't who I'd thought he was...*what* I thought he was.

And I really didn't want to think about what Lance would say when he found out what I'd been up to...and with whom. My cheeks flushed, but thankfully, I'd dimmed the light over the dining room table as I'd set out the tableware, thinking it made for a more intimate setting. That was a laugh.

"So that's that," came Grayson's voice from the sliding glass door.

I started, and Persephone looked a little troubled. But Paul only gazed at the half-alien man steadily and nodded. "I'm not proposing anything permanent. But from a security standpoint, it makes more sense, and I don't think any of us can fault Kara for needing a little space."

A little space. That sounded good right now. A chance to breathe, to think. And Kiki would be home the day after tomorrow. God only knew what she'd make of the whole situation, but if nothing else, it would be a comfort for me to have my sister back in town. Kiki wouldn't condemn. She, who knew more than anyone else how much I had given up over the years, might just begin to understand.

"Just for a few days," I began, but Grayson lifted a hand.

"I get it. Let me go pack my things. I assume you won't mind if I take the clothing you bought me?"

"Of course not," I faltered, hearing in his voice

an echo of the cold, flat intonation he'd used while under hypnosis at Janelle Russo's office. Had my suspicions then been true? Was this the real Grayson, or was he just trying to mask his own hurt and confusion under a veil of indifference?

Impossible to know for sure, and of course I couldn't say anything else of a personal nature, not in front of Paul and Persephone. Maybe later Grayson and I could find some quiet time to talk, but at the moment, I thought maybe it would be best if he simply went away. I couldn't seem to think clearly with those green eyes, now hard and cool as polished jade, staring at me.

The briefest of nods, and he moved past the table and down the hallway. For a few seconds, no one said anything. Then, finally, Persephone let out a little sigh. "Come on, Kara. I'll help you get this cleaned up."

Lance

So Mr. *Muy Caliente* had turned out to be a hybrid. Lance halfway wanted to laugh, but he guessed neither Paul nor Persephone saw anything too amusing in the situation. And it wasn't, really. He knew he couldn't begin to explain to them how he'd been wracked with jealousy over someone who wasn't even human. Or maybe he could, but he really didn't want to.

"And you just left Kara alone, after all that?" he demanded, after watching the so-called "Grayson" disappear down the corridor in the direction of the Olivers' guest bedroom.

"She said she wanted to be by herself." Persephone pushed a wayward dark curl off her forehead. In the uncertain light of the one torchiere lamp that illuminated the living room, she looked very tired. "I offered to stay with her, but she said no, that I'd just gotten back from out of town and that she didn't need to be babysat."

"That sounds like our Kara. Always has to be tough, even when it's the worst thing for her."

Both the Olivers looked at Lance in some surprise, as if they really hadn't been expecting such an insight from him, nor the almost compassionate tone in which it had been spoken. He lifted his shoulders, annoyed with himself for revealing even that much. He must be slipping.

Good. He suddenly realized he *wanted* to be slipping. God, he was sick of the lies he'd told all of them...told himself.

Persephone sat quiet and still on the love seat, Paul just a few inches away from her. Their fingers were intertwined, resting along the crack between the two seat cushions, a casual intimacy that said far more about their relationship than a more showy display might have. Her eyes, watching Lance, were gentle and a little sad. He'd often wondered how much she really saw of what went on his head, although she'd never said or done anything to indicate that she knew anything more than any other acquaintance would. Still, feeling her gaze on him now, he guessed she knew everything.

Well, in that case....

He stood. "I'm going to go check on her."

Paul said, "I'm not sure that's such a good idea, Lance. She was pretty adamant about wanting to be left alone."

"Yeah, well, after everything she's been through, she might not be thinking very clearly. Besides, she's already had one visit from a couple of MIBs. I don't think any of us want them making a return trip while she's in her current mental state, do we?"

As he'd expected, the Olivers exchanged a worried glance. Persephone looked back over at Lance, and something in her expression told him she knew exactly why he wanted to go to Kara now...and why she wouldn't say anything to stop him.

"We'll keep an eye on Grayson," she told him, and he nodded.

Paul had a mystified expression on his face, but he somehow seemed to sense that now was not the time for any more protests. "Michael said he'd stop by after his talk was done."

"Good." And that seemed to be as good a sign-off

as any. Lance nodded at the couple, then let himself out, his pace quickening as he crossed the neat stamped-concrete driveway and got into his Jeep.

He had no idea what he would say to Kara when he arrived at her house. He had to trust he'd figure it out in time.

CHAPTER TWELVE

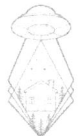

Kara

After everyone had left, I wandered back into the living room and sat down on the couch, my hands hanging limply over my knees. I found myself wishing Persephone had left me with a pile of dirty dishes, but my friend, trying to help, had made sure the kitchen was spotless before she and Paul led Grayson out of the house and into Persephone's Volvo. So now here I was, in an empty house with nothing to do.

Gort nudged me with his nose, and I reached down to ruffle him behind the ears. He whined a little, as if sensing my disquiet. "It's all right," I said. "My heart's already been broken once. I know it can heal. But the process may require many pints of Ben & Jerry's."

The dog cocked his head to one side. He was a fiend for ice cream, since I let him lick the bowl of anything that didn't have chocolate in it.

I had a feeling this might require more than a bowl of Cherry Garcia, though. This was...I didn't even know how to articulate the feeling inside me. Hurt, yes, of course. But beneath that, something else. Betrayal? Maybe. Stupid, really. It wasn't as if Grayson had purposely set out to deceive me.

Or had he?

No. I refused to believe that. Whatever else happened, however things ended up between us, I knew he'd truly not known who...or what...he was. Besides, Persephone had flat-out stated that she didn't feel anything bad coming from him. And she would know. She'd tried once or twice to describe to me how it had felt to touch the consciousness of the aliens and the hybrids, and even that bit had been enough to tell me I was glad not to have that sort of perception, not if it meant being exposed to that kind of evil.

Grayson wasn't evil. I'd know it.

Wouldn't I?

The doorbell rang and I started, even as Gort gave a short, sharp bark and dashed toward the entry. His tail was wagging, though, which indicated he knew who was waiting on the other side of the door. Persephone, coming back to babysit despite my protests to the contrary?

I let out a breath and stood, automatically pushing my hair back off my shoulders. This was an argument I really didn't feel like rehashing, but if Persephone needed to be told for the fifth time....

I opened the door. On the other side waited Lance, for once without his mirrored sunglasses.

"Oh," I said lamely. Lance was about the last person I really wanted to see right then, for a variety of reasons. "Aren't you supposed to be standing watch over the alien captive or something?"

The keen gray eyes didn't blink. "I wanted to talk to you. Can I come in?"

Since I couldn't refuse without sounding completely rude, I lifted my shoulders and stepped aside. Gort looked up at the intruder with wary eyes, but because he recognized Lance's smell, he moved out of the way and went back into the living room to occupy his favorite spot on the rug, the one that in the winter was touched by the heat of the fireplace.

Following his lead, I took my own place on the couch, pushing myself back into one corner as I stared up at Lance, arms crossed. "I hope you're not here to read me the riot act. I know I screwed up, okay?"

His brows drew together. "That's why you think I came over here?"

"It's not?"

"No." With a restlessness quite unlike him, he paced over to one side of the coffee table, hands jammed in the pockets of his cargo pants. "How could you have known?"

What he said was true enough, but I couldn't quite figure out what to make of his words. Lance wasn't exactly known for his gentle, forgiving nature. And seeing him here like this, after everything that had happened—well, I hoped I would be able to hold it together long enough for him to speak his piece and be done with it. I had a hard enough time concealing my feelings from him on a normal day; right now, with all my nerve endings flayed and raw, the thought of looking at him as if he didn't mean anything more to me than anyone else of my acquaintance made me feel almost physically ill.

Or maybe the sickness gripping my belly was just echoes of my reaction to Grayson's true identity.

"Okay," I said, uncrossing my arms and cupping my palms over my jeans-clad knees, "so why *are* you here? It's been kind of a rough night, and I'm wiped."

"I didn't like the thought of you being here alone."

That comment made me lift my head and look up at him sharply. The expression on his face was so unexpected that at first I didn't even recognize it. Worry, yes, but something else. It couldn't be need. Not from Lance. All the day's shocks must really be getting to me.

"I'm fine," I said, those two words of denial that

had gotten me through so many things—my mother's abandonment, Alan's betrayal, my grandparents' deaths. By that point, the phrase hardly meant anything anymore.

"No, you're not."

I didn't like how he stood there, looming over me. Without replying, I rose and moved past him to pause a few feet away from the mantel. Absently, I thought I had the air conditioning turned up too high. That must be what was making me feel suddenly chilled.

"Okay, and what if I'm not fine?" I asked, wrapping my arms around myself, feeling the goosebumps on my bare flesh. "How is admitting it going to make any difference?"

"I don't know if it will. But denial sure doesn't help."

The retort shot out of my mouth before I even realized what I was saying. "Oh, you'd know all about that, wouldn't you?"

He didn't blink, even though something in the taut lines of his mouth told me I'd scored a point with that one. Not that I'd really been intending to. I didn't want to hurt Lance. I just really didn't want him there right then, not when I felt so close to losing it.

Plowing forward, since I didn't know what else to do, I said, "Look, I know I was an idiot—"

"You're not the idiot around here." He hesitated, but that piercing ice-gray gaze never left my face. "I am."

That confession came from so out of nowhere that for a few seconds, I could only stare up at him. Finally, I said, "I don't follow."

One sun-browned hand reached up to push its way through his close-cropped fair hair. "If I'd had the balls to say something to you before this, then this whole Grayson thing would never have happened."

He couldn't possibly be saying what I thought he was saying.

Or...*could* he?

Now, after everything, he'd come over here to announce his feelings for me? Never mind that for years I'd hoped for such a declaration. But how could I possibly accept it now? He couldn't think that I'd just forget what had passed between Grayson and me, that I'd put those feelings aside as if they'd never been.

Or maybe he could. Men's thought processes never seemed to work the same way as mine.

I gave a shaky laugh. "Wow, Lance, your timing is really spectacular."

He didn't appear to take any offense. He just stood there, back as straight as if he were in a military review. "Would you rather I didn't say anything, that we just keep lying to one another?"

"I don't know, Lance—it's worked out pretty well so far!"

His mouth twisted then, and before I could really understand what was happening, he reached out for me and pulled me against him, held me close. No attempt to kiss me—just his arms around me, his heart thudding beneath my cheek. He felt very different from Grayson, leaner, more wiry, but just as strong in his own way. And the warmth of his body seemed to surround me, to finally take some of the chill from my flesh, as if he was lending that strength to me when my own had begun to fail.

Maybe I should have tried to push him away. My thoughts didn't seem able to stay in one place—they skipped this way and that, first telling me that this was nuts, that I couldn't go running to Lance just because things with Grayson had fallen apart, then whispering insidiously that this felt too good, and hadn't I wanted this all along, settling for Grayson because I had thought there was no hope of ever being with Lance?

I didn't know anymore. The one thing I did know was that I didn't want to leave the circle of Lance's arms. I'd dreamed of this for years. Was I really going to push him away now?

Somehow, I did. I moved back a step, then another. "Is it just jealousy?"

He blinked, but, surprisingly, he didn't bother to dodge the question. "At first."

"'At first'?" I repeated. I didn't bother to hide the skepticism in my tone.

"Well, I think that's what made me finally wake up. I kept thinking everything could go on the way it was because there wasn't anyone else in your life. But when I found out about Grayson—" A shrug, followed by a narrowing of his eyes. "I found I really didn't like the idea of you tooling around on the back of a motorcycle with some random guy...and I liked even less the thought of you shacked up with him."

"How the hell did you find out about that?" I demanded, although I thought I could guess.

"Your neighbor is the chatty type."

Thanks, Felicia. But at the moment, I was too tired to feel anything except mild annoyance at Mrs. Martinez's loose lips. At least she'd done her blabbing to Lance and not someone much more dangerous, like the two government agents who'd stopped by earlier that afternoon.

Or worse, whoever or whatever the aliens had out looking for their one lost soldier....

Still, I couldn't think about that now. I didn't really know what I should be thinking about, because the tumult of the past few days seemed to hit me all at once...the UFO...the MIBs...Grayson...now Lance...and I couldn't seem to focus on any of it.

Lance was staring at me intently. When he spoke, his voice was far gentler than I'd ever heard it, lacking its usual irony. "You've had a hell of a time, haven't you?"

"You could say that," I managed.

"And I haven't made it any easier. I get it. But you don't have to go through all this alone."

Meaning what, exactly? That he wanted to be with me now? Surely I should be happy about that, but somehow, all I could feel was an enormous leaden weight of weariness.

"Thank you for that, Lance. But right now, I think I just need to go to bed. I just...I just can't process this right now."

He didn't move, but only stood there, staring down into my face. If he reached out to hold me again, I wouldn't stop him...mostly because I didn't have the energy at the moment.

"I don't think I should leave you alone."

"So, what, you're expecting to stay the night?" I asked caustically. "That's asking a bit much, don't you think?"

The ironic glint returned to his eyes. "I don't know...that couch looks pretty comfortable."

Oh, right. Of course he wouldn't be stupid enough to ask to crawl into bed with me. Not now, anyway. If I'd been functioning a bit better, I probably should have been able to figure that out on my own.

"You don't need to sleep on the couch, Lance.

I'm fine. The bug-eyed monsters aren't coming to get me."

"Maybe not...but I'd still feel better if I did."

Something about his stance, about the set of his jaw, told me he was willing to stand there and argue the point until I capitulated. And since I felt about ready to fall over from exhaustion, it wasn't worth the effort.

"Okay," I replied. "It's your back. Hope you've got a chiropractor on speed dial. Let me get you some blankets at least."

He seemed to relax slightly. "Okay."

And I made myself go to the linen closet, retrieve a lightweight cotton blanket and a spare sheet, then return to the living room and hand off the bundle to Lance. "Here you go. You know where the bathroom and the kitchen are, so—make yourself at home."

He took the blanket and sheet from me and set them down on the couch. For a second or two, he watched me carefully, as if trying to gauge exactly what might be going through my head. "You sleep well."

So much for worrying about whether he was going to try to kiss me. I didn't know what I would have done if he'd made the attempt, but it looked as if I wouldn't have to deal with that particular scenario. At least, not tonight.

"Goodnight, Lance," I said.

That shuttered expression was back on his face. "Goodnight, Kara."

And that seemed to be it. I left him standing there in front of the couch, and went to my own empty bed.

Lance

Kara might have been able to sleep, but he knew it was still a long ways off for him—if it ever came it all. If so, this certainly wouldn't be his first sleepless night.

He untied the desert boots he wore and lined them up at one end of the couch. Gort, still lying Sphinx-like on the rug, watched him with a mixture of curiosity and wariness, as if not sure what to make of this intruder who'd taken up residence in the living room.

I'm not sure what to make of it, either, Lance thought, and lay down on the couch. Even if he wouldn't be able to sleep for a long while—if at all—he figured he might as well make himself comfortable.

Should he have kissed her? Maybe that would have been smarter, to just push ahead after he'd held her in his arms. But she'd looked so tired, shadows under the deep gentian blue of her eyes, that he hadn't the heart to force the issue. She'd had enough shocks already. He hadn't mistaken her regard for him—no, that had been clear enough in her face. There'd been confusion, too, and guilt, as if she inwardly berated herself for caring for him and Grayson at the same time.

Grayson. Lance wondered then how the half-alien man fared, tucked away into the Olivers' spare bedroom. Probably not too great; that bed had to be a lot colder than the one he'd been sleeping in up until today.

That might not have been the best thing to think about. Lance really didn't want to imagine Kara tangled up in the hybrid's muscular arms, and he certainly shouldn't be thinking about her now, sleeping just a few yards away down the corridor. He wouldn't go to her, of course not, but his loins tightened a little at the thought of her lying in her bed, golden hair spread over her pillow.

Go ahead, drive yourself crazy, he mocked himself, and the wave of heat subsided somewhat. He wanted her, yes, but he could give her all the time she needed. He'd made her wait long enough.

He didn't want to think about how much time any of them had left.

Kara

I awoke with a start, eyes straining at the darkness in my room. One hand reached out to touch the space where Grayson should have lain. Then I paused, fingers tangling in the cold sheet. Of course, he wasn't there. He was clear on the other side of town, in the Olivers' guest room.

A noise then, just the slightest whisper of movement, coming from somewhere down the corridor. I reached under my bed for the Louisville Slugger I kept there—another relic of my grandfather's—and eased myself from underneath the covers, the bat clutched grimly in my right hand.

Blinking the cobwebs of nightmares away, I crept down the corridor, padding along in my bare feet. I didn't know how someone could have gotten in without tripping the alarm, but—

Lance's voice came to me in the dark. "Forgotten about me already?"

Of course. My sleep had been so disordered, my waking so sudden, that I'd actually forgotten that Lance had insisted on staying over. The bat dropped down to hang limply at my side. "Maybe." I squinted into the dining room, realized he was sitting at the table and staring out into the backyard.

"Hmm."

I advanced a few paces, then stopped. In hot weather, I slept in my underwear and a tank top, which was fine if I was alone. Not so great for parading around in front of the man with whom you had a good deal of unresolved sexual tension. On the other hand, to turn now and flee back to my bedroom would only show him exactly how uncomfortable I was. So I moved on into the dining room, silently grateful that at least Lance hadn't turned on any of the lights.

"Couldn't sleep?" I asked.

"No." His gaze flicked toward me, lingered for a second, then moved back to the sliding glass door.

Great. Apparently, the darkness wasn't quite as concealing as I'd hoped it would be. Movement out of the corner of my eye made me startle for a second, until I realized it was only Gort, padding from the living room to a few paces from where I stood. He whined.

"No three a.m. treats," I said.

He whined again, then lay down on the rug, resignation clear enough even in the gloom.

I returned my attention to Lance. "Did you see something?"

"No. That is, I thought I heard something, but nothing's out there."

Sitting down seemed safer than standing up so he could see everything. At least that way, he wouldn't be staring at my striped bikini underwear. I pulled out the chair nearest me and settled into it, my eyes becoming more and more accustomed to the lack of light. The solar lamps in the backyard made little pools of blue-white light, but there wasn't much for them to illuminate.

"Probably a cat," I offered. "Felicia Martinez lets hers roam all over the neighborhood, even though everyone tells her the coyotes are going to get them eventually."

"Maybe."

He didn't look as if he'd attempted to sleep, since he was still fully dressed, although his shirt was untucked. Something pale moved near the floor, and I realized it must be his bare feet. So at least he'd allowed himself to relax that much.

"You don't really think they're watching my house, do you?" I asked. "I mean, if they knew Grayson was here, you'd think they would have already tried to retrieve him."

At my question, Lance shifted in his chair so he could meet my gaze. "You're probably right. But it doesn't have to be the aliens, come in search of their prodigal son. Could be the MIBs. Just because you got rid of them temporarily doesn't mean they're gone for good."

"Well, that's a cheery thought." I watched him carefully, but his eyes seemed to be more or less intent on my face, and not the amount of cleavage exposed by the skimpy tank top I wore.

His shoulders lifted. "Or I could just be jumpy. But I keep wondering...why? What's so important here that the aliens have come back, even when we wiped out their forces, basically compelled them to go back to square one?"

I could have made a snide answer about the aliens wanting to get a spa treatment or a psychic reading, but something in his voice stopped me. He actually sounded tired and a little worried, which was not the Lance I knew. While I appreciated him showing something more of himself to me, part of me wished for the snarky, confident man who never seemed to get rattled, no matter what the world might throw at him.

"I wish I knew," I said when the silence between us grew too unsettling. "I suppose Paul and Persephone will try to get more information out of Grayson...." I trailed off, realizing I should be there for that interview, and not sure whether I was really up for it.

"True, but he may not know that much, even if his memory has returned." Lance sounded a little more brisk now, as if glad he could talk about Grayson on a more abstract level, as part of the alien puzzle to be solved and not the man who'd made himself a part of my life. "After all, even though it's clear something strange has happened to him, he was only a soldier. Soldiers do what they're told. They don't have to have the big picture to get the job done."

"Are you speaking from experience?"

"Yes," he said shortly, then turned to look back out the window. "The brass always thinks the grunts are too dumb to master the intricacies. Besides, we can't divulge information we don't know, can we?"

I supposed that was true enough, but I still didn't like the sound of it all that much. Maybe I was too much of an individualist to appreciate the nuances of military service.

"Grayson," Lance repeated, and gave a short, humorless laugh. "Did you name him that?"

"No. He heard it on TV and told me he liked the way it sounded." I wasn't about to tell Lance that Grayson had picked it up from a frivolous rom-com show I'd had languishing on my DVR.

"Ironic."

"How do you mean?"

Once again, Lance turned to look at me. "Grayson. Gray's son. Considering he's an alien/human hybrid, I'd say the name is pretty apt. Maybe his subconscious was trying to tell him something."

Now that he'd pointed it out, I wanted to smack myself for not making the connection before. "Wow —that is kind of crazy."

"You could say that." He showed no signs of resuming his inspection of the backyard, but remained swiveled in his seat, eyes fixed on me.

I didn't know what he expected me to say. Was he thinking now was the time when I'd reveal why exactly I'd allowed Grayson into my house and my bed, would explain what the hell I'd been thinking? Well, if that was what Lance wanted, he'd be waiting a long time to get it. I didn't even know if I could explain it to myself, let alone a not entirely unbiased audience like Lance.

"So what do we do next?" I asked, hoping the question would shift his thoughts away from my relationship with Grayson and on to bigger concerns.

"We'll meet up tomorrow. Paul sent me a text a while ago saying he wanted everyone over at his house tomorrow around eleven. You should have gotten one, too."

Probably I had, but my phone was buried in my purse, and of course with everything going on, I hadn't bothered to dig it out and look at it. "Council of war?"

Lance nodded, his mouth very grim. "I'd like to say I hope not, but considering our past history with these adversaries, I'm guessing that's exactly what it's going to be."

Great. Well, I'd always bemoaned my role in this group, thinking I was going to be continually shuffled off to the sidelines, always kept out of the important goings-on. Now I was stuck right in the middle of things, and it wasn't quite as exciting and thrill-packed as I'd thought it would be.

"Kiki and Jeff are going to be showing up sometime tomorrow," I pointed out. "Wouldn't it be better if we waited until they were back in town?"

"I've already briefed Jeff on the important elements," Lance replied.

Irritation flared in me. "Oh, you have? Did you ever stop to think that maybe I'd like to reveal certain things about my private life to my sister in person?"

Lance looked singularly unperturbed. "I said I told Jeff...and what I told him was in confidence. All Kiki knows is that there's a situation going down here, and that they're to be in Sedona ASAP. They're actually leaving before first light tomorrow, to beat the traffic. They may make it here by noon if all goes well. They're not going to miss that much—I told Jeff to drive straight to the Olivers' place."

Despite the seriousness of the situation, I couldn't help feeling a little amused at the thought of Jeff having to rouse Kiki at o'dark thirty to get on the road. My sister had never been an early morning person. "Okay, then...guess you've got it all worked out."

"Not really."

I lifted an eyebrow. "You could have fooled me."

Lance didn't reply, but only gazed at me steadily. It didn't take a rocket scientist to figure out what he was thinking. He wasn't thinking about Jeff or the Olivers or the "council of war" anymore. He was thinking about the situation between the two of us.

Damn. And we'd been getting on so well there

for a while, discussing things as if nothing had happened, as if he hadn't held me in his arms just a few short hours ago. How long had it been, actually? From where I was sitting, I could squint and just make out the digital clock on the microwave in the kitchen. Two forty-four. Somehow, it felt much later than that.

"Maybe we should just worry about that later," I said.

"How much later?"

The question sent a small spark of fury along my veins. What a thing to be asking, considering everything that was going on. I had no idea how I even felt about Grayson, and there were aliens outside town plotting God knows what, and the man I'd been hopelessly in love with for years had finally gotten the balls to admit that he cared for me as well, and what the hell was I supposed to do with that particular piece of information?

I was so wrapped up in my thoughts, I didn't even realize at first that Lance had gotten out of his chair and now stood next to me.

"Kara."

A look upward, and those keen eyes caught me and seemed to hold me, seemed to prevent me from moving or speaking. He reached down and took my hands, drew me upward. Then his mouth on mine, his hands in my hair, his body crushed against me. I could feel so much more of him now that I wore only the tank top, feel his taut muscles against my breasts, the strength of his fingers and the warmth of his flesh. There was my own heat as well, working its way from the pit of my stomach down between my legs, the need, the ache, the desire for something I'd dreamed of for so many years.. .

Somehow, I managed to back away, to put a few inches of distance between us. Lance did nothing to stop me, as if he knew I needed to claim that space for myself.

Oh, I was in trouble. Big trouble. Even though I'd wanted this for so long, some part of me had hoped that when Lance kissed me, I wouldn't react all that much, and I could dismiss the infatuation as simply that, and no more. But....

Kissing Grayson had been amazing. No doubt about that. God only knew how a human/alien hybrid with no experience of women could manage to be even half that talented, but wherever he'd learned his technique, it was damn good.

Kissing Lance, though....

Kissing Lance was like coming home. It felt right, more right than anything ever had. He was too old for me, scarred and ironic and distant, and yet I knew now that what I'd felt for him all these years had been my soul crying out for its mate, for the person who understood me and knew everything about me and still loved me anyway.

I stood there for a long moment, staring up at

him. Still, he didn't move, but only watched me with those steel-gray eyes of his, eyes that had seen far too much and yet lingered on me with a sort of wondering joy, as if he couldn't quite believe that we had finally come to this moment.

Somehow, I found my voice. "Is this crazy?"

One corner of his mouth lifted. "Probably."

"Well, as long as we're in agreement on that." My body ached with need for him, but, as right as things felt with Lance, I knew I couldn't take the next step, not until I had time to let Grayson know how things stood between us. And Lance would just have to understand. Stumbling over the words, I went on, "I want to, Lance. But not yet. Not before—I should talk to him, let him know—"

"It's all right."

Startled, I stared up at him. The lighting made it difficult to read his expression clearly, but he just looked resigned and possibly a little amused.

"I've waited this long to say anything, Kara. Do you think a night or two is really going to make that much of a difference?"

I wanted to smile back at him. Instead, I planted my hands on my hips and tilted my chin. "How do you know it's going to be only 'a night or two'?"

"Wild guess."

And then we were kissing again, bodies locked in an intimacy that might have been a tease but which I knew was really a promise. It would have been so easy to take him by the hand, lead him down the hall to my bedroom. Time enough for that later, though. I knew I could never forgive myself if I didn't set things straight with Grayson first.

Whether he'd be open to hearing my explanations was an entirely different matter....

CHAPTER THIRTEEN

LANCE LEFT SOMETIME EARLY THAT MORNING. When, I wasn't exactly sure, but his Jeep was gone when I staggered out of bed at around seven-thirty, feeling seriously hung over even though all I'd had to drink the night before was approximately a glass and a half of wine. Well, sometimes hangovers could be mental rather than physical.

I tried to put away the feel of his lips, the warmth of his flesh, as I took a shower and prepped myself for the meeting at Persephone and Paul's house. The timing meant I'd be hanging another sign on the door at the UFO Depot, but I wasn't about to skip out on something so important just because the store was open. Luckily, Thursdays tended to be slow as well—not quite as quiet as Wednesdays, true, but it wasn't as if I was shutting the place down on another weekend day.

So I printed out yet another "Closed for family business" sign on my laser printer and laid it on the front seat of my Prius before heading out. I found myself glad to be leaving the house—even with Gort there, the place still felt empty with both Grayson and Lance gone. But as intense as that exchange with Lance had been the night before, I wasn't quite sure where we were headed. Into bed, I had no doubt, but after that? Could Lance give up his freewheeling bachelor status to settle down with me?

I found I didn't want to think about that right then, not with the memory of his kiss still tingling on my lips. Neither did I want to think about the upcoming interview with Grayson. How on earth could I make him understand that I had responded to Lance because I'd been in love with him for years, and not because I was rejecting who Grayson was and where he had come from?

Could I have come to overlook that part of Grayson's background if Lance hadn't been part of the equation? I wanted to say I could, but I had no way of knowing for sure. Sure, he was sweet and fun and considerate...and half-alien. And not even the good kind of alien, like Persephone's spirit guide Otto, who had turned out not to be a spirit at all, but some sort of highly evolved humanoid being. No, the aliens currently re-infesting the base in Secret Canyon were much more the abduction/medical experiments/mind-fuck kind of aliens.

Whatever their reason for creating human/alien hybrids, it definitely wasn't for the betterment of mankind.

Mouth grim, I pulled into the parking lot of the UFO Depot at five 'til ten—the store's usual opening time—and strode up to the door. I'd just ripped a piece of tape off the roll I'd tossed in my purse when a half-familiar voice said,

"Been having a lot of family emergencies lately, haven't you?"

I turned and forced a noncommittal expression on my face as I saw one of the MIBs from the other day—the tall, friendly one, fortunately—standing a few feet off. Behind him was parked a black Ford that practically screamed "unmarked law enforcement vehicle."

"If you knew my mother, you wouldn't be surprised," I remarked as I began taping the sign to the front door of the shop.

"I know *of* her," he said. "So no, I'm not that surprised. What does surprise me is that her last known location was Taos, New Mexico. You planning a road trip, Ms. Swenson?"

Taos? I thought in some disbelief. The last time I'd talked to my mother, she'd been back in Phoenix. No big surprise, though. Marybeth Swenson always did have itchy feet...especially if a man was involved. And, to be fair, we hadn't been in contact for years.

I shrugged and said, "Oh, right. I'm not supposed

to leave town. Well, unless I'm under arrest, I'm going."

"Why do you think I'd want to arrest you?"

He seemed genuinely interested in how I would answer that question. Despite the bright morning sunlight, he wasn't wearing his sunglasses, and his eyes—a clear gray-blue—looked guileless enough. Actually, I realized right then that he was very good-looking, and just as quickly put that particular thought aside. I already had plenty of men on my plate, thank you very much.

"Where's your partner?" I asked.

An incongruous grin. "He had an attack of some chile relleno that didn't agree with him."

"Oh. Too bad."

The grin broadened a little, as if he knew all too well that I wasn't a bit sad about his partner's current condition. "You didn't answer my question."

"Well, I don't know," I said, since it seemed obvious he didn't want to let it go. "I guess usually if you don't want someone to skip town, you have a pretty good reason for it. And if you want someone to stay put, then generally you types can come up with a reason to arrest them. Or are the movies and TV shows getting it all wrong?"

"I'd say they're exaggerating."

"So I'm free to go?"

"Since it's up to me...." He made a show of shrugging, then reached in his pocket and pulled out a card and handed it to me.

I took it, since I didn't know what else to do. "*Martin Jones, Special Agent, FBI,*" I read. That was all, except for a phone number with a Phoenix area code.

"You find you need any help, Ms. Swenson, you give me a call."

When pigs fly, I thought, and then chided myself. He seemed friendly enough. Maybe I was flattering myself by even entertaining for a second or two the notion that his interest in me might not be entirely professional. Briskly, I added, "You think I'm going to need help in the near future?"

Another shrug. "You never know." He fished his sunglasses out of his jacket pocket and planted them on his nose. "Time to go see if Agent DeSalvo has pulled his head out of a toilet yet. You have a good day, Ms. Swenson."

"You, too."

And I watched in bemusement as he got into his unmarked car and drove off, heading west on 89A, which meant the two agents were probably staying in one of the cheaper motels out toward the edge of town. At least he hadn't hung around to watch which direction I would go when I left the parking lot. Paul and Persephone's house was on the southern border of Sedona proper, down toward the Village of Oak Creek, and the opposite direction from the one I would have had to take if I really was heading up to I-40 so I could go rescue my mother in Taos.

Well, I couldn't hang around here all day and wonder what exactly the MIBs were up to, if anything beyond some pretty basic surveillance. Although the "council of war" was scheduled for eleven, I had already checked with Persephone to see if it was okay for me to come over a little early. Not that I was all that eager to have a confrontation with Grayson, but I figured it would be better if I spoke to him first, before everyone got there.

The Olivers' house was in a newer subdivision, halfway up a hill off Chapel Road. I had wondered how they'd managed to swing the purchase of the house, considering the neighborhood where it was located and its relative size, but Persephone had just laughed when the question came up and said, "Paul and I both had some money saved up. Besides, our mortgage here is less than what I was paying for a two-bedroom apartment in West Hollywood. Rents in L.A. are insane."

Maybe that was true. I'd never had the slightest desire to find out how much it cost to live in Los Angeles—I was a northern Arizona girl and always would be.

I pulled into the driveway and got out. Once again, clouds were beginning to move up from the southeast, bringing with them fluttering shade and shadow. The day still promised to be mind-achingly hot, though; even at this hour, I could hear the faint whir of an air conditioning unit off somewhere along the side of the house.

Maybe it was Persephone being psychic—or maybe she heard my footsteps along the stamped-concrete walkway that led to the front door. Whatever the case, the door opened before I even had a chance to knock. Persephone stepped out of the way with a smile. One would never know to look at her that she'd had a half-alien houseguest the night before.

She led me into the living room, where Paul and Grayson were waiting, both looking distinctly uncomfortable. Unfortunate, since it was the sort of room that invited you to be comfortable. The style of the furnishings and flooring was more Tuscan villa than desert Southwest, but everywhere were warm tones, plumply upholstered furniture, and mismatched antiques that still coordinated beautifully.

You couldn't say the same for the two men sitting on the couch and in one of the armchairs. Paul shot a grateful look in my direction, obviously only too glad to have me take over babysitting duties. And Grayson...well, Grayson looked as if he hadn't slept all night, which might just be the simple truth. His green eyes were bloodshot and shadowed, and he stared up at me with a sort of desperate hope.

I swallowed. Grayson was obviously expecting

some sort of lifeline, and I'd come bearing an anchor instead.

"Hi, Grayson," I said, relieved that at least I sounded mostly normal. "I thought maybe we could talk before everyone gets here."

He only nodded, eyes still fixed on me as if trying to read his fate in my face.

"We can go into the family room—" Persephone began, but I shook my head.

"I thought Grayson and I could talk out in the yard. You don't mind, do you?"

"Of course not," Persephone replied. Paul just looked grateful that whatever we were going to hash out, at least it wouldn't be in the house where he'd have to pretend not to overhear.

The yard was as lovely as the house. It had been pretty much laid out and landscaped when the Olivers bought the place, although they'd added a water feature to the area next to the house where a pergola covered in grapevines provided some much-needed shade. A redwood bench, aged silver by the elements, waited there, and that was where I led Grayson, who still hadn't spoken.

I sat down, and after a second or two, he took a seat next to me, body tense, jaw set. Whatever he'd seen in my expression, apparently he could tell it didn't bode well for our future.

"Grayson, I—" I began, and he shook his head.

"Just tell me the truth. I may not be a man, but I deserve that much."

Had he spent all night harrowing himself with that thought, that he wasn't human, but something devised by the aliens for some unknown purpose? More gently than I had intended, I reached out and took his hand. It felt very real and very human, from the warmth of his flesh to the calluses on his fingertips. There was even still a spot of grease under one of his fingernails, left over from working on the Indian.

Throat a little tight, I said, "You're Grayson. That's all that matters. I'll admit that last night I was shocked by what Persephone said, and maybe I didn't handle things as well as I should have. I'm sorry for that. But I wanted to tell you that what's happening with me doesn't have anything to do with who you are or where you came from."

"'What's happening'?" he repeated, looking confused.

Oh, this was awful. It wasn't fair that he was watching me with that half-worried, half-hopeful expression, like a puppy unsure whether it was going to get a treat or smacked with a rolled-up newspaper. How on earth could I explain to him what had happened between Lance and me...not when I wasn't sure if I could even explain it to myself?

I let go of his fingers and rubbed my damp palms over the knees of my jeans. Damn, it was hot out here, even in the shade. The jeans suddenly felt as if they weighed a hundred pounds.

"I just want you to know that we're going to watch out for you, keep you safe, no matter what happens. We won't let them get you."

One eyebrow went up, as if he guessed there was some subtext to my words beyond the offer of protection. "Well...thanks, I guess. Don't be offended when I say I'm not sure what you can really do to defend me from *them* if they get wind of where I am."

He had a point there. I wasn't sure, either, but since Persephone, Lance, and Michael had somehow come out victorious in the last go-'round, there had to be some hope that they'd prevail again. "That's more Persephone's deal, I guess...and Lance's, and Michael's."

Another guarded look, as if Grayson had heard some alteration in my tone when I said Lance's name. "Ms. Oliver mentioned them. They're part of your UFO group?"

"I guess that's as good a way of describing it as any. Look, Grayson, I've always been the one to wait it out on the sidelines. I'm not a psychic or a shaman or a soldier. So I don't know what they have planned. But I suppose we'll discuss that when everybody gets here."

"Probably the smartest thing you could do is just hand me over, you know. *They* might take it as a gesture of good faith."

I stared at him, not sure whether I should be more horrified by the suggestion itself or by the way in which Grayson had said it—voice flat, detached, as if he was discussing someone else entirely. "We would never do that."

"No?"

"No." Restless, I got to my feet and stared off past the cottonwoods that ringed the yard. The red-hued top of Courthouse Butte was just faintly visible through the lacy green foliage. Absently, I thought that view had probably added at least another twenty or thirty grand to the price of the house. "For one thing, even if we were that cold-hearted—which we're not—we know it's pointless to try negotiating with them. They don't see us as much more than insects, right? So how could we trust them to ever keep their word about anything?"

An unwilling smile touched his mouth. "You know more about it than you let on."

"I listen to what people have to say."

He nodded but didn't speak at first, instead gazing past me into the garden with its carefully groomed gravel walks and the assortment of drought-tolerant plants and grasses that grew in the spaces between the walkways. At length, he said, tone too casual, "This Lance person. Your voice changes when you mention him. Is there something you're not telling me?"

There's a whole lot of something I'm not telling

you.... Somehow, I forced myself to nod. "I've known him for almost six years."

"You were...involved?"

"No."

Grayson's expression brightened a little, and I spoke quickly, not wanting to feed him any false hope. "That is, we weren't. I—wanted to. But—"

"But?"

"But I didn't think there would ever be anything between us. So I tried really hard not to think about him that way."

"And I was...what? The consolation prize?"

I wondered how he, a hybrid grown by aliens in a lab, could even know what a consolation prize was. Then again, how had he known how to repair the Indian, or to kiss me, or....

That line of thought was dangerous. I pushed it away. "No, of course not. I was attracted to you. We had a wonderful time together. I thought things could be really good between us. But...." And I let the words trail off, because I didn't know how to say it without it sounding dreadful, without intimating that yes, he was my second choice, since the wish of my heart had been denied me.

"But you loved him first." To my surprise, there was no condemnation in those words. Grayson had spoken them slowly, thoughtfully, as if turning over the concept in his mind, trying to familiarize himself with it.

No point in trying to deny it. "Yes. I've loved him for a very long time. I just didn't think he felt the same way."

"So what changed?"

"He stopped trying to run away from it, I guess," I said. "I don't know why. We haven't had much of a chance to discuss the situation. But I wanted you to know that what's changed between you and me isn't because of what—of *who*—you are. It's because of what's between Lance and me."

Silence again, as Grayson appeared to absorb this statement. Then he said, "Thank you, Kara."

Startled, I stared down at him. "For what?"

"For being honest. For treating me like a person."

"You are a person," I said softly. "You're a wonderful person."

His mouth tightened. Abruptly, he stood. "They're here. Guess we'd better go in."

And he moved to the French doors that separated the little arbor from the living room and went inside.

I hesitated, then squared my shoulders and followed him into the house.

Lance

He tried to ignore the pang of jealousy that went

through him as he saw Grayson come in from the patio, followed immediately by Kara. Did the guy have to look quite so much like an underwear model?

But her gaze caught his, and she smiled slightly and nodded, as if to tell him it was all right. Obviously, whatever she'd told Grayson hadn't been good news for the hybrid; he looked as if someone had just stolen his dog.

But Lance didn't have much time to think about the hybrid's feelings, because Persephone and Paul were urging everyone to come into the dining room. Michael, who as usual had hitched a ride with Lance, looked from Kara to him and back again, then nodded, as if confirming something he'd already suspected.

They arranged themselves around the dining room table, Paul at the head and Persephone at his right, with Michael taking the seat at the foot. Somehow, Kara ended up across from Lance, with Grayson next to her. Lance wasn't too thrilled with that arrangement, but there wasn't much he could do about it. There were two seats remaining, one on his left and the other on Kara's right, presumably for whenever Jeff and Kiki showed up.

Persephone, playing hostess, had a grouping of pitchers on the sideboard for everyone. "There's iced tea and water and lemonade," she said. "I suggested a pitcher of margaritas, but Paul voted me down." She shot a mock-angry glare in her husband's direction, and he just grinned.

"I figured this was going to be tough enough without getting sauced into the bargain."

"True. So let me get your drink orders before we get started."

That took up a few minutes, with Paul and Michael opting for lemonade, and Lance and Kara taking iced tea, and Grayson murmuring that he just wanted water. Then everyone settled back in with their respective drinks, and an uneasy silence fell.

Lance was willing to wait it out. This had been Paul and Persephone's idea, so let them take the lead. And it seemed they'd come to the same conclusion, because once they'd exchanged a glance, Persephone nodded, as if giving Paul the go-ahead to get things started.

"Okay, then," he said, after taking a drink of his iced tea and looked briefly regretful that he'd denied Persephone her margaritas, "we figured the best thing to do would be for all of us to sit down and try to hash out exactly what's been going on, try to get everyone more or less up to date. Maybe then we can begin to decide on our next course of action. Kara, why don't you go first?"

She started, and for a second, her deep blue eyes met Lance's, wide and more than a little worried. Obviously, she hadn't expected to be called on the carpet first. He gave her what he hoped was a reassuring nod. What he really wanted was to be the one sitting next to her, so he could take her hand in his and lend her some of his strength, but that wasn't going to happen. Besides, the group already had enough to talk about as it was; he really didn't feel like discussing the change in his and Kara's relationship. That would be out in the open soon enough, if he knew anything about how this group operated, but that didn't mean he had to push it.

After fortifying herself with a sip of iced tea, Kara said, "Well, I was out walking Gort last Wednesday...." From there, she explained how she'd come home and found Grayson lying in her living room, how she'd revived him and given him a place to stay, tried to help him recover some of his memories. She didn't go into a huge amount of detail—obviously, she didn't want give too many particulars as to how her relationship with Grayson had progressed—but it didn't take a rocket scientist to put two and two together.

As Kara finished her little speech, Persephone stepped in right away, as if she could feel all of her friend's embarrassment, her continuing worry that she'd been a fool to take in Grayson the way she had. "Something's been bothering me—"

"Just something?" Lance drawled, and Persephone shot him an irritated look even as Paul appeared to smother a grin.

"One thing in particular." She turned toward Grayson. "Your eyes."

"My what?" he replied, obviously startled. That was probably one of the last things he must have thought she would mention.

"It's been nagging at me, but it hit me this morning when I could see you in clearer light. Your eyes are green."

He hitched his shoulders, clearly uncomfortable being the center of attention. "So?"

"All the hybrids' eyes were dark. I remember that very clearly. So if Grayson is supposedly genetically identical to all those other hybrids, how can his eyes be a different color?"

Good question. Kara frowned as she appeared to mull over the puzzle, while Paul leaned back in his seat a little, tapping his chin. All he needed was his beloved tweed sport coat, and he could have been back in a university office somewhere, pondering a particularly thorny question some grad student had just posed him. But, for better or worse, Paul's days as a professor were long gone.

Michael had been quiet this whole time, absorbing everything everyone had said, but he sat up a little straighter and remarked, "I think it's something you did to him, Persephone."

"I—what?" She glanced from Grayson to Michael, and then over at Paul, as if seeking some reassurance from her husband that Michael didn't know what he was talking about. "How could I change the color of someone's *eyes*? Well, without handing him a pair of colored contacts or something, that is."

Not even a blink. "How could you wipe out an entire base full of hybrids and infected humans?" Michael asked. "If someone had asked you before it happened whether you were capable of something like that, you would have said no. And you would have been wrong."

Another one of those uncomfortable silences fell. Grayson was frowning, as if trying to process what Michael had just said. Now he looked like a perturbed underwear model, and once again, Lance found himself wishing that he'd figured out a way to sit next to Kara, instead of her being in the chair beside that—well, whatever he was.

In the middle of this, the doorbell rang, and everyone started. Well, the Olivers and Kara and Grayson jumped a little. It would take a lot more than that to unsettle Lance, and Michael remained stoic as always, as if he had been expecting the doorbell to ring all along.

Who knows—maybe he had.

Persephone glanced at her watch. "I'll bet that's Kiki and Jeff. Let me go let them in."

She got up and hurried away from the table, leaving the rest of them to wait. A little smile touched Kara's lips as she apparently heard Kiki's breathless voice from the hallway: "Hope we haven't missed too much. Jeff dragged me into the van at, like, five-thirty or something, and I hope you have something with caffeine in it—"

Persephone assured her that she did as the trio entered the dining room, Jeff lagging a little bit behind. Something about the hacker looked different to Lance, and he scowled a little, trying to figure out what it was. Different haircut? He appeared as if he'd actually shaved, but it was something more than that. Oh, well. Jeff Makowski's personal grooming habits really weren't the issue of the day.

Kiki helped herself to some tea, and Jeff got water, before they took their respective seats. The hacker plunked himself down on Lance's left, while Kiki pulled out the chair next to her sister. "Okay," she announced, "we're here. So what did we miss?"

Lance replied, "You mean besides your sister's houseguest turning out to be a hybrid soldier from the base in Secret Canyon?"

Even as Kiki's cornflower-blue eyes—a few shades lighter than Kara's—opened wide, Persephone said hastily, "That's the main gist of it. But until a short time ago, he didn't remember anything of who he was or where he came from, so we're trying to figure out how that could have happened."

Michael folded his hands on the tabletop. Even a quarter-century after losing his wife, he still wore a plain silver band on his left ring finger. "It was Persephone."

Everyone's head swiveled toward the psychic, and Lance, who had sparred with her on more than one occasion, couldn't help feeling a slight stab of pity for the woman. She looked both perplexed and embarrassed, as if caught in some transgression she really couldn't explain.

"Care to elaborate?" Paul leaned forward, eyes keen. In that moment, he looked far more like a scientist on the trail of some tantalizing piece of evidence than a man trying to defend his wife.

Michael appeared serene and untroubled, as if he was conducting one of his medicine wheel ceremonies instead of explaining how one slight woman could single-handedly knock out a whole base full of hybrid soldiers and alien-possessed humans. "Well, not Persephone completely, but the force of Gaia working through her."

Trust Michael to come up with some mumbo-jumbo, New Age–sounding explanation. Lance tried not to snort and was only partway successful, instead producing a sickly sounding cough, which he tried to hide by drinking some more iced tea. Kara lifted an eyebrow at him but said nothing, while Kiki's mouth dropped open a little. Next to him, Jeff breathed something that sounded suspiciously like "bullshit," but the word didn't come out loud enough for anyone to call him on it.

"Gaia working through me," Persephone said, her tone flat.

"It may sound crazy," Michael replied, "but I think that's exactly what happened. You felt it when you came here, down by the creek. Our world senses these intruders, doesn't want them here any more than we do. So she used Persephone as a conduit."

From across the table, Kara shot Lance a quick "do you really believe this stuff?" sort of look. He felt his mouth twitch slightly in reply, but he tried to keep his expression impassive. Michael had some kooky ideas, true. That didn't mean his instincts weren't scarily accurate most of the time.

"And so when I channeled this energy, it...what? Changed Grayson's eye color, just for shits and grins?"

That was one thing about Persephone—she didn't hold back. At the moment, she was staring at Michael with her arms crossed, eyebrows slightly raised.

"I doubt that was the real reason." The shaman unclasped his hands and spread them wide, as if to indicate that he understood her disbelief. "There must have been something about Grayson, some small difference, that made him react to the energy differently."

"A sport," Paul murmured absently.

Kiki turned toward him. "A what?"

"An organism markedly different from its parents, or, in this case, the stock it came from."

Persephone made a throat-clearing noise, and Paul added quickly, "I mean, the stock *he* came from."

Grayson shrugged, looking as if he was past caring which words people used to describe him. For a second or two, Lance almost felt sorry for the guy. It wasn't his fault he'd been grown in a lab.

"So because Grayson is different somehow from the other hybrids..." Persephone began.

"...the rush of power that came from you—or from Gaia—didn't affect him the same way," Paul finished for her. He glanced over at Michael, as if for confirmation.

Michael nodded. "I can't speculate on exactly how it happened. But something allowed him to survive that blast of power, and at the same time wiped his memories clean."

For the first time, Grayson spoke. His brow was knotted. He looked as if he was trying to digest what had just been said. "Maybe that's true. I still don't remember a lot. But when my memories were wiped —why didn't I lose everything? Or, more specifically, why is it I know how to ride a motorcycle, or jet a carburetor—or hell, even talk and tie my shoes?"

That was a good one. Everyone looked over at Michael, who regarded them all with that same imperturbable expression. Talk about your great stone face....

"I can't say for sure. Maybe something about that same blast of power opened your mind to the world around you, let you absorb knowledge that you'd never been exposed to during your time at the Secret Canyon base. You became a conduit as well, but for human experience instead of the earth mother's power. I don't know. Only the mother knows, and she's not telling me."

Next to Lance, Jeff moved abruptly in his chair, as if made uneasy by all this talk of earth mothers and powers and conduits. Lance couldn't really blame him; even though he'd had his own experiences with what some people might call extra-sensory abilities, he'd never had much use for all the talk of earth spirits and vortexes and channels that drifted around Sedona like the cottonwood fluff blown on the town's air currents. But something weird had happened, and since Michael was the only one who seemed able to put together any kind of a theory, Lance would go with it for now. It didn't change the fact that aliens still occupied the base in Secret Canyon...and that they were probably still looking for their one lost soldier.

"Fine and good," he said, and everyone looked in his direction. All the swiveling heads reminded Lance of spectators at a tennis match. "But unless the earth mother is going to butt in again and drop a tactical nuke on Secret Canyon or something, we're the ones who have to figure out what to do next. Ideas?"

The silence that followed this pronouncement would have been absolute if it weren't for the soft hum of the A/C in the background. Lance hadn't expected much, but still it was a little disconcerting to have them all staring at him as if he was supposed to be the one to come up with the plan to save everyone's asses.

"We should do some reconnoitering—" Kiki began, and he sent her a quelling look.

"In what, the Scooby van? I don't think so. They're watching all of us."

"Not just the aliens, either," Kara put in. "Let's not forget our friendly neighborhood men in black. I bumped into one of them again today on the way over here."

"You what?" Lance demanded, his tone sharper than he had intended. "Were you going to mention this any time soon?"

"I *am* mentioning it. Besides, he didn't have much to say. Still, it's pretty clear they're watching my comings and goings...and if they're watching me, they're most likely watching the rest of you, too."

No one bothered to deny it. Kiki looked as if she wanted to, but after getting the stink-eye from Jeff, she shut her mouth without saying anything.

"But not me," Grayson said.

Kara shifted in her seat, an expression of dawning consternation spreading across her features as she seemed to process what he'd meant by that statement. "Oh, no, you don't—"

He ignored her, saying, "They're looking for me, true, but they don't know where I am. If you can get me inside, what am I then? Just another one of a hundred men who look just like me."

Everyone was silent, apparently processing Grayson's offer. It did make sense, but Lance wasn't about to voice his agreement, not when Kara might think he had a vested interest in making sure the hybrid was safely out of the way.

Finally, Paul spoke. "I guess Grayson is going to need some contact lenses after all...."

.

CHAPTER FOURTEEN

Kara

THEY COULDN'T BE SERIOUS. THEY COULDN'T really be thinking of letting Grayson walk back into that place, into a base filled with inimical alien presences, back to the creatures who'd been hunting him for months.

My mouth was dry. I made myself drink some of my tea before I said, "This is nuts, and you know it."

Grayson wouldn't look at me. His gaze seemed to be fixed on something outside the French doors as he said, "Well, it's probably the last place where they'd be looking for me."

"He's right," Jeff put in. "Wouldn't be the first time someone slipped right into a place like that because the bad guys were so busy looking for threats elsewhere."

My gaze went to Lance, but he was wearing his poker face, and I knew I wouldn't get any help from that quarter. He was probably kicking himself for not being the one to think up the insane scheme.

"Fine," I said. "So what's the big grand plan?"

"I'm working on it," Lance replied, an edge to his voice. The steel-gray eyes were equally sharp. "This isn't the first time I've planned something like this, you know."

"No, I don't know," I retorted. "Because you never tell any of us anything!"

All around the table, everyone seemed to find something fascinating in the bottom of their drink glasses. Okay, so maybe I'd let a little bit too much slip with that last comment. But how the hell was I supposed to keep it together when they all seemed intent on sending Grayson right into the lion's den?

Lance didn't blink, though. "You're probably right. But let's just say I have some experience in these sorts of things. It's not as if we're just going to send him in there in a T-shirt with a sign that says 'Kick Me' pinned to the back."

"So what are you going to do, precisely?"

He didn't answer, but merely gazed at me with that stony expression I knew all too well, the one that hid everything except what he wanted to reveal. Which at the moment was basically nothing.

I got it, on some level—I couldn't betray secrets if I didn't even know what they were. Realizing that unwelcome truth, however, didn't make this any easier.

The weight of everyone's watching gazes suddenly seemed too much. I stood, then bent to retrieve my purse from its resting place on the floor. "Then I guess I'm done here. You boys have fun storming the castle."

And ignoring Grayson's worried, "Kara," and the other murmurs from around the table, I turned and strode out.

The light and heat hit me in a wave as soon as I opened the front door. Blinking, I dug in my purse for my sunglasses and then stuck them on my nose. And where were those damn car keys....

The voice that stopped me was not Lance's, as I'd hoped, or even Grayson's, but Kiki's. "Kara —wait up!"

I really didn't need to deal with this right now. "I'm leaving, Keeks. It's pretty obvious that my opinion doesn't count for much in there."

"Well, I'm not sure that's really what's going on—"

I pushed the button on the remote to unlock the car doors. "I can't sit there and listen to them talk about sending Grayson into a dangerous situation like that."

"Sounded more like he was volunteering."

Oh, screw this. I yanked open the door and slid into the driver's seat, only to see Kiki climb into the passenger seat. "What do you think you're doing?" I demanded.

"Coming with you," my sister replied. "It sounds like we have a lot to talk about."

Lance

He supposed he should have expected a reaction like Kara's, but it took a good deal of willpower for him to remain seated, to not get up and hurry after her. A display like that would only lead to questions he didn't feel like answering, so instead he drained the rest of his iced tea and asked, "You still have what you were wearing when Kara found you?"

Grayson blinked at him, his thoughts obviously on the woman who had just fled the room. "What? I —I don't know. You'd have to ask Kara."

Who had just split the scene. Well, Lance knew he'd have to confront her sooner or later. Following up on Grayson's jumpsuit at least gave him an excuse to go talk to her. "Okay, I'll check on it. From what I could tell from my last viewing, the base hasn't changed materially from the last time we were all in there. Only difference is, no humans."

"None?" Persephone asked. Obviously, she was recalling the support staff who'd hightailed it to the four winds after her psychic blast killed off everything in the place that wasn't human.

"None," he repeated. "And I saw aliens—*real* aliens, not just the ones who've taken over human bodies. They're clearly not too worried about anyone with earth DNA finding out about their little operation. So that means none of us can go in with Grayson for a ride-along. He's got to do this on his own."

Everyone was silent then, and conspicuously trying not to look too hard at Grayson...or at the empty seat next to him. Even though Lance knew Kara's true feelings, knew she'd made her choice, it was obvious that she didn't want anything bad to happen to Grayson...and that she just might hold Lance responsible if something did.

Great.

"Do we go in the same way we did last time?" Persephone asked. Her tone was too deliberately casual, as if she knew she was supposed to act as if all this was no big deal even though she was actually scared shitless.

"*I* go in," Grayson corrected her. "Lance just told you that no one else can come along."

She gave a defeated little shrug and exchanged a quick, uneasy glance with Paul. Lance thought the scientist might have a word or two to say on the subject if Persephone tried to push the issue.

"I'm not sure yet," Lance said. "I'm going to talk

to one of my buddies over at Arizona Helicopter Adventures, see if he can do a little reconnoitering for me. Those guys fly that area all the time, so it's probably the best way of detecting any obvious activity. It probably won't be that easy, but it's someplace to start."

They all nodded, even Jeff, who had a tendency to want to argue everything even when he knew deep down that you were right. Funny how everyone seemed to recognize the need to defer to Lance, the only one who had any combat experience. Well, Grayson had been bred to be a soldier, but who knows if he'd seen any real action—or remembered enough of his training for it to do any good. It was pretty obvious that lately he'd been in "lover, not a fighter" mode.

Not that Lance was doing much better himself. He rattled on, talking about what he'd seen in his last remote-viewing session, discussing scenarios with Paul and Jeff, trying to pry what little knowledge he could out of Grayson, but only half his mind was on what he was doing. The rest of him was thinking about Kara and wondering what she and Kiki might be saying to one another.

Kara

It was amazing what a glass or two of pinot grigio could do to improve your mood. Kiki and I sat in the living room of the house we'd both grown up in, sandals kicked off, Gort twitching in ecstasy as Kiki rubbed his tummy with one bare foot.

"So," she said at length, "do you want to talk about it?"

"Not really."

My sister withdrew her foot and sat up a little straighter. Gort whined and rolled over onto his stomach, looking wounded.

Despite everything, I couldn't help smiling. There was nothing like a dog to keep you grounded.

"I mean," Kiki went on, expression contemplative, "if I'd known the hybrids were that hot, I might have been a little more upset when I found out that Persephone had blasted them all to kingdom come."

I shot her a warning look. "That's not funny."

"I wasn't trying to be funny." She tucked her feet up under her legs so she was sitting Indian-style on the sofa, then sipped at her pinot grigio. "I'm just saying that no one is going to give you crap for falling for Grayson. Especially since you didn't have any idea who he was."

I could think of a few people. Then again, that wasn't fair. Lance had been surprisingly gentle on the subject, for him. Especially when I considered his own feelings for me. I didn't reply, though, but only stared across the room at the dark fireplace, wishing summer was over so I could feel the heat of a real fire again instead of all this ceaseless air conditioning.

Something made me shiver then, and I reached over to set my half-empty wine glass down on the coffee table.

"There's more to it than that, isn't there?" probed Kiki. For all her seemingly airy—some might say airheaded—ways, my sister could be amazingly perceptive. Then again, for some time, I had thought a good deal of her breeziness was just an act. God knows the girl could whip a computer into shape like nobody's business.

"I really don't want to talk about it," I said.

Of course, Kiki wouldn't let me get off that easily. "I thought I saw a few sparks flying with you and Lance back there. Smells like somebody's jealous."

Goaded, I replied, "I really wish you wouldn't talk about Lance like that," and then wished I'd kept my mouth shut.

Kiki didn't say "a-ha!," but the gleam in her eyes indicated that she knew she'd scored a point. "So Grayson isn't the problem. It's Lance."

"I don't want to see anything bad happen to Grayson, and they're just going to let him walk in and—"

"They're not 'letting' him do anything. Sounds to me like he volunteered. So great, that's very noble of him. "'Tis a far better thing I do now' and all that. But what's going on with you and Lance?"

That was a really good question. The kiss we'd shared the previous night had told me things should have been different between us—and yet today Lance was his usual hard-ass self, barely even looking at me. Or was he only trying to keep everyone else from guessing that something had changed? Good luck with that. It was sort of hard to keep secrets when a good chunk of your personal circle just happened to be psychic.

"He kissed me last night," I said absently, recalling the feeling of his mouth on mine, the taut strength of his body, even the warm, delicious scent of his skin. Remembering it just made me want it all that much more, and the cramping ache had returned, the need, the desire to be back in his arms. God, how could I want him so much and be so irritated with him at the same time?

Kiki's eyes widened. "Shit, seriously? This is world-shaking. So, how was it?"

"I am not going to discuss my love life with my little sister, thank you very much."

A very indelicate snort. "You don't have to. I can tell just by looking at you that you've got a bad case of what Stephen King described in one of his books as 'hot thighs.' I don't really get it—Grayson is much hotter—but whatever."

"Grayson is an alien. Or at least part alien."

"Who cares, when he looks like that?"

I shook my head ruefully and said, "I missed you, Keeks. I'm glad you're back in town."

"Well, if I'd known things were going to be this crazy, I wouldn't have left."

"What, and miss out on shacking up with Jeff Makowski?" I cracked.

"Get your mind out of the gutter. Jeff was a perfect gentleman."

Okay, that was a little rich. "You know, there are a lot of words I can think of to describe Jeff Makowski, but 'gentleman' really isn't one of them."

Kiki flipped her hair back over her shoulders and shook her head. "You guys are all so down on Jeff, just because he isn't pretty."

"I really hope you don't think I'm that shallow," I replied, a little nettled. So Jeff wasn't going to win any beauty contests. Big deal. It wasn't that at all. Tone sharpening, I continued. "No, it's more because he seems borderline Aspergers to me, and I don't want him to develop some weird crush on you that ends badly because he doesn't know how to cope with his feelings."

"I don't think there's much risk of that. Most of the time, I'm not sure he even notices that I'm female. I think he just enjoys being Obi-Wan to my Anakin, programming-wise."

"Well, that's not a very good precedent, is it?"

Kiki stared at me blankly for a few seconds, then

burst out laughing. "No, I guess it isn't. So pour me another glass and tell me more about how Grayson showed up on your doorstep."

Lance

He left the Olivers' house several hours later, once it was pretty clear he couldn't do much else until they had a better idea of the best way to insert Grayson into the Secret Canyon base. Right before he left, Kiki had apparently texted Jeff to come pick her up at Kara's place, so Lance figured the coast would be more or less clear.

And Grayson, surprisingly, had gone with Michael to crash at his house, the shaman explaining that his home's proximity to Oak Creek provided a shielding effect, and that Grayson would be safer there. Whatever. Grayson hadn't seemed too put off by the idea—maybe being around the Olivers' domestic bliss was getting to him—so that all seemed to be settled for now.

Lance wished he could say the same about himself and Kara.

The driveway was empty when he pulled up into it. Jeff must have already retrieved Kiki so he could drive her back to her apartment. God knows where that was going...not that it was any of his business. One Swenson woman was enough for him to deal with at the moment.

He got out of the 4x4 and went up to the front door. It had to be the heat that started the sweat along his temples and down the back of his neck.

A rush of cool, welcome air greeted him as Kara opened the door. Surprisingly, she didn't look at all hostile as she greeted him with an airy, "Oh, hi, Lance."

Once he was inside, he discovered the probable reason for her current insouciance—an empty pinot grigio bottle sitting on the coffee table next to a pair of equally empty glasses. "You and Kiki get all caught up?"

"More or less." She bent and scooped up the empty bottle and glasses, then headed into the kitchen. He heard a *thunk* as she dropped the wine bottle in the trash.

"You don't recycle?"

"Oh, right." She began to reach into the trash can to retrieve the empty bottle, but Lance reached out and caught her by the wrist.

"I think it's okay if you let one go."

A pause then, as she stood there looking up at him, his hand still wrapped around her wrist. Her skin was smooth and warm against his fingertips. She didn't try to pull away. The dark blue eyes caught his, and held. "What do you want, Lance?"

Good question. What did he want? He wanted....

He wanted this to all be over so it could just be him and her. No aliens, no conspiracies, no plans to try to save the world. Just a chance to come home and have it actually mean something more than an empty condo.

Without thinking, he pulled her toward him, pressed his mouth to hers, tasted the lingering sweet-sharp taste of the white wine on her lips, her tongue. Maybe in the back of his mind, he'd worried that she'd try to pull away, but she didn't. Instead, she pressed into him, her breasts soft and full against his chest, her hair falling with a scent of warm peaches against his cheek.

"I want you," he said roughly, after they finally came up for air. "That's all I've wanted for a very long time."

Her mouth curved into a smile. "You've got a funny way of showing it."

"Well, if you knew why—"

"Then tell me."

She was dead serious, he could tell. Maybe she'd been slightly tipsy when he first showed up, but she looked sober enough as she stared up into his face, as if trying to read his secrets there. He hesitated.

"I mean it, Lance," she said, her tone quiet but firm. "If you want to be with me, then you need to tell me the truth. About your past. About why we've been doing this stupid dance for the past six years. I need to know if you had a good reason for it."

Oh, he'd had a very good reason. But he knew the time for evasion was past if he wanted to have a future with this woman. And he did. God, he wanted it.

"All right," he said heavily. "But I think you may want to pour us both another drink first..."

Kara

"God, I'm so sorry," I said at length, my neglected glass of pinot noir still clutched in one hand. "If I'd only known—"

"It's all right," Lance said, his expression blank. Too blank.

All this time, his only thought had been of protecting me. Of making sure I didn't meet the same fate as the woman he'd wanted to marry all those years ago. My heart ached for him, but all the usual words of condolence sounded false and hollow. He'd suffered already. I shouldn't drag him back through it now.

"Are they...?" I hesitated. "You don't really think they're still after you? Not after all this time."

He lifted his shoulders. "They know where I am. I'm not going to kid myself about that. But by now,

I'm guessing they think I'm harmless. Just some washed-up ex-operative spending his pension on booze, bullets, and the occasional lay."

I blinked. "Spending on—you're kidding, right?"

A smile lit his gray eyes, brought out the laugh lines that bracketed them. "Not that way. I meant more like buying drinks and the occasional dinner. I haven't exactly been living like a monk."

"Yeah, I kind of got that." A pang went through me at the thought of all those casual liaisons. Here I'd been all alone, while Lance had hooked up with an alarming number of attractive tourists.

"They didn't mean anything. You know that, right?"

I summoned a smile to answer his. "I do now."

He bent to kiss me again, and I reached out to deposit my wine glass on the coffee table before I forgot myself completely, lost myself in the taste and feel of him. His weight pressed me into the sofa cushions, and I twined my legs around him, pulling him that much closer. Even through my jeans and the cargo pants he wore, I could feel his arousal, knew he wanted me just as much as I wanted him.

It was crazy for us to be groping each other here on the couch like a couple of overheated teenagers. On the other hand, I didn't want to take him into the bedroom, into the bed I'd so recently shared with Grayson. Sure, I'd changed the sheets, but—

Lance didn't seem too worried about niceties

such as location. His hands went under my tank top, found the clasp on my bra, unhooked it. And then his fingers were on my breasts, stroking, and I moaned and arched my back, pushing myself against him. The soft fabric slipped up and over my naked torso, and his mouth was on me, suckling, tongue teasing at me.

I needed to be able to feel him as well. My eyes were half-closed, but I still found the buttons of his shirt, worked them open with feverish fingers. Then it was the warmth of his chest against mine, both our bodies flaring with heat despite the room's chilly A/C. Almost with a single thought, we reached for the other person's belt buckle, yanked down pants and underwear like the irritating barriers they were.

Only then did Lance pause, scrabbling through one of the pockets of his trousers and pulling out a small foil-wrapped package. He hesitated for the barest second, but I nodded. I hoped we wouldn't have to use those for too long, but now, when I knew how many women he'd been with—

No, I wasn't going to think about that. I wasn't going to think about anything but the feel of his hands on me, the touch of his fingers against me, so delicate and deft, a contrast to the hard muscles of his arms and chest and stomach. Then he was stroking me, seeming by instinct to find the exact right place to touch me, to tease me close to climax and then pause before continuing the relentless featherlight stroking until at last I was gasping, crying out his name as the orgasm shuddered its way through me.

It wasn't enough, though. It wouldn't be enough until he was inside me. I heard him rip the foil package away from the condom, and I reached down to touch him, to help him roll the thin membrane on, feeling the tantalizing incongruity of silky-smooth skin with the rock-hard flesh beneath. He moaned a little at my touch, his breath coming in short, fierce gasps, and then he was ready, pushing against me, sliding into me at last, my whole body seeming to thrum and pulse with the heat of him, with the culmination of so many years of hopeless longing.

I ran my fingers down his back as he moved in and out, felt his muscles contracting and expanding, encountered the unexpected roughness of a scar high up on his shoulder blade. Then there wasn't anything else but our bodies moving together as if we'd done this a hundred times before, as if every chance fantasy or fevered dream was the preparation for here and now, for the time we could finally leave everything else behind and meld into one being, one dream, one hope.

Maybe the climax hit me a fraction of a second before it hit him. It didn't really matter, because we clung to one another as the orgasm swept over both of us with the strength of a tidal wave, washing us to the far side of ecstasy to a place where neither of us could do anything except lie there and cling to the other person, breath coming in harsh gasps, flesh slick against flesh, until finally we came back to now, to the realization that nothing could be the same for us, that we'd crossed a line that had been drawn in the sand years earlier.

"I love you," I breathed, and then thought probably I shouldn't, it was too soon, and even if he knew how I felt, he wouldn't want to hear it, not yet—

But then his breath came warm against my throat, the irony gone from his voice for once as he murmured, "I love you."

That was all, but it was everything. He said it almost in wonder, as if it had taken this for him to finally recognize what I was to him. In truth, daydreams aside, I had never really expected him to say it to me. He didn't seem the type.

My arms tightened around him. I wished I could hold him there forever, but that was silly, of course. He'd have to pull away eventually, go get cleaned up and get a drink of water and do all those prosaic things that inevitably followed sex. Not that I really wanted to call what we'd just shared "sex." It had been lovemaking in the truest sense of the word.

At last he did get up, but gently, pulling away from me with a reluctance that was clear in his every movement. As he stood, I could see the round scar on his shoulder that I'd felt earlier. It looked like a bullet wound.

I swallowed then, remembering what he'd told me of Natalie, the things he'd said about his time in the Army with the remote viewing program. It had been easy to forget everything as I lay in his arms, but now it all came rushing back to me—the aliens, the men in black, the lurking danger in Secret Canyon, coiled there like a rattlesnake hiding in the brush.

First things first, though. I reached down and retrieved my underwear and jeans, then drew on my bra and tank top. One good thing about using a condom; the aftermath wasn't nearly as messy.

Lance returned to the living room, water still glittering on the tanned planes of his face from where he must have splashed it in the sink. For a long moment, we stood there, watching one another.

At last he came to me, took my hand in his, and brought it to his lips. The gray eyes watching me had some of their old wariness, but beyond that was a kind of terrible hope, as if by getting the thing he'd wanted for so long, he'd unwittingly created a whole new set of problems.

Well, that was understandable. I didn't quite know what to do next, either. For one thing, it was barely two o'clock in the afternoon. It wasn't as if we could just retire for the night and figure out what to do with each other the next morning.

So I flashed him a grin, stood on my tiptoes, and gave him a quick kiss, then said, "Buy you a burger?"

CHAPTER FIFTEEN

Lance

HE HAD THOUGHT HIMSELF FAR PAST THE STAGE where he could be surprised by anything. But the woman sitting across from him at the Red Planet Diner was the most amazing thing he'd seen in a long time.

She sat there, sipping her iced tea with airy unconcern, as if both their worlds hadn't just been rocked to their foundations. He didn't know what to say. He wasn't even sure how he should look at her. Her lovely mouth was the slightest bit swollen; he must have kissed her harder than he'd realized.

Somehow, though, he found it easier than he thought to fall back into their old familiar patterns. "I can't believe you brought me to this place."

"What?" she replied, widening her eyes in mock innocence. "Kiki loves it."

"She would."

The diner was the height of kitsch—UFO tchotchkes and souvenirs everywhere, topped off by a huge bug-eyed green alien that loomed over one of the booths, although thankfully not the one they sat in. Lance had always avoided the place like the plague, and winced every time he drove by. He knew the aliens all too well, and they weren't cute or funny in the slightest. The people sitting in the restaurant and drinking their milkshakes or eating their cheeseburgers would probably have a heart attack if they knew what really lurked only a few miles away in Secret Canyon.

Kara smothered a grin and said, "Their burgers really are pretty decent. And I figured you probably didn't want to wade through the crowds in Uptown."

"You'd be right about that."

A waitress drifted by, inquired as to their orders languidly, as if she had much more important things on her mind, then jotted down their requests and disappeared into the back.

Lance lifted an eyebrow. "We may be waiting a while for these burgers."

"You have someplace else you want to be?"

For a few seconds, he just watched her, noted the graceful line of her throat and the way her deep gold hair fell against it, the way her breasts moved under the tank top with every breath. A tightening in his loins told him he could think of someplace else, very much—back at her house, in her bed this time, or at his place, or....

A glint in the blue eyes told him she had more than an inkling of what was going through his mind. "Later. I need to refuel, even if you don't."

"You're probably right." He drank some of his water, then asked, "You still have Grayson's jumpsuit?"

"Wow, topic change." Kara's expression sobered, and she nodded. "Shoved into a dark corner of the garage. I tried to follow up on it with the manufacturer and was totally shut down."

"You what?" Alarms started going off in his head, but he managed to keep his tone even as he said, "Tell me about it."

And then he sat there, trying to keep the irritation at bay as she related her failed attempt at getting more information from the Patriot Uniform Company.

Obviously, she sensed his annoyance, because she laid her hands flat on the Formica tabletop and said, "I really don't think it's a big deal, Lance. If I'd tripped any alarms, they would have been on me by now."

"Maybe they are. Or do you think it's just coincidence that those two MIBs are suddenly hanging around?"

That got her, he could tell. She seemed to sag a little, but then she rallied and replied, "I don't think so. I think they're here because of Mr. Sun Devil's video. Or at least, that's what sent them to Sedona in the first place. I don't know why they keep hanging around."

He didn't, either. Things had been pretty placid the last few days...at least on the surface. No strafing UFOs or other close encounters.

Kara's lips curved into a wicked little smile. "However, I'm starting to get the distinct impression that one of them wants to ask me out."

That wasn't even funny. He glared at her, and of course she burst out laughing. After a second or two, she subsided, saying, "I'm kidding, Lance. Only he does seem a little too friendly for the proverbial Man in Black, so I'm not quite sure what his game is."

"Roswell burger," said a voice above him, and Lance couldn't help starting a little. Damn, he must really be losing it.

"Mine," he replied automatically, and the waitress set his plate in front of him, then delivered Kara's mushroom swiss burger with an abstracted air, as if bringing them their food had just taken her away from something vitally important. *Who knows,* he thought, taking in the girl's blue-streaked hair and severe eyeliner, *maybe she's just visiting here, too....*

Despite his earlier disparagement of the place, the food did smell good, and his stomach told him it needed some kind of sustenance even if his brain thought it had more important things to do. So he let the matter of the MIB-on-the-make go for now and concentrated on taking a few bites, getting some protein into his system.

After a minute or two, he said, "I wish you'd called me before you did that, though."

"Mmm," she said through her own mouthful of meat and cheese and mushrooms. Once she'd finished chewing, she added, "And what, confess I'd let some strange man who'd collapsed on my living room floor take up residence in Kiki's room?"

Ah. So that told him they hadn't tumbled into bed together right away. Not that he'd expected anything less of Kara, but you never knew. She'd been single for a long time, and Grayson had the kind of movie star looks that might have made her forget a few of her scruples.

"Okay, maybe not. But still...."

She swirled a French fry in some ketchup with a meditative air. "Lance, the phone I used is completely untraceable. You and Jeff have seen to that. So even if that call sent up red flags somewhere, how would they ever have been able to track it down?"

"I don't know. But—"

"But nothing. I think it's going to be okay." A hesitation, and she set down the fry without eating it. "That is, I don't know how all of this is going to shake out, but I'm pretty sure the uniform angle is a dead end. You won't be able to buy another one like it."

"I'm not going to buy one," he told her, and picked up his burger once more. "I'm going to have one made."

Kara

Lucinda Torres lived over in Cottonwood, and she ran a business doing custom embroidery for various uniform suppliers and sporting teams. She was also an accomplished seamstress.

I watched as Lance handed over the tattered jumpsuit and explained that he needed a duplicate made. How he'd known about Lucinda, I had no idea, but it really didn't surprise me all that much. Lance always had been a font of unexpected knowledge...a good deal of it supplied by Jeff Makowski, no doubt.

"Okay," Lucinda said, turning the jumpsuit over in her hands and then actually pulling it inside out so she could inspect the seams. "I don't carry this fabric in stock, so I'll have to order it."

"How long?"

She shrugged, shoulders plump and bra strap slipping out just a little from underneath the sleeveless polyester shirt she wore. "Two, three days to get the material, then another two days to take a pattern off this one and make a new one."

Lance didn't look too thrilled by the delay, but inwardly I was relieved. Four days at least until we could follow up on this insane scheme to send Grayson back into the Secret Canyon base. Maybe by then I could come up with a really good reason for them to abandon the plan and try something else.

Right.

I wanted to see Grayson again, needed to talk to him, but the opportunity hadn't really presented itself. Lance had stayed over last night but again melted away before dawn, presumably so I wouldn't be caught in the compromising position of having his Jeep sitting in my driveway all that time. Neither one of us had said anything about the shift in our relationship, although something in Michael's voice when I called that morning to check on Grayson told me that the shaman already guessed something had changed about me.

He'd also told me that Grayson wasn't available, was down by the creek, and I didn't know whether to believe Michael or not. Okay, maybe the hybrid soldier was out communing with nature, but more likely, he just didn't want to talk to me. I couldn't even blame him. I'd all but abandoned him, hadn't I?

Now I know why the whole love triangle thing is such a nightmare, I thought as I watched Lance lay down a respectable stack of twenty-dollar bills and

Lucinda pick up the money and secret it somewhere in a drawer in her sewing table. *Because you don't stop caring for the one just because you've decided to be with the other.*

However you looked at it, the situation was a mess. True, maybe I hadn't cheated on Grayson, because I'd broken things off before I'd gone to Lance, but it still felt like cheating. Sort of. Or had I been cheating on Lance when I went with Grayson, since I'd known in my heart that Lance was the one I really loved?

I didn't know what to think anymore. I just wished I could think of a way to let Grayson understand that I had never meant to hurt him.

The blazing heat of the August afternoon hit me the second I stepped outside Lucinda's small shop in a shabby little strip mall. For some reason, I felt dizzy for a second or two. Then the spell passed, and I shook my head slightly as I climbed into Lance's Jeep.

Just a temperature change, and too much on my mind. The heat had never really bothered me before, but I'd had a rough couple of days.

"You okay?" Lance asked, shooting me a sideways look before he pulled out onto the highway.

"Oh, sure," I replied with a lift of my shoulders. "My only problem is that someone hasn't been letting me get enough sleep."

At that response, he gave me one of his rare grins,

a flash of white teeth brilliant in the bright sunshine. "First time I've heard you complain."

"Who says I'm complaining?"

Another smile, accompanied by a shake of the head. Then he was aiming the Jeep northeast, back into Sedona, which, though hot, somehow didn't feel as oppressive as Cottonwood. It had always seemed too bare and flat to me, accustomed as I was to the red rock formations and juniper-studded hillsides of my hometown.

He dropped me off at the house, saying he needed to go meet with Brian Henderson, a pilot with one of the helicopter companies that ferried tourists around the area. I almost asked if I could go along, but then realized it was probably better if Lance handled those negotiations on his own. Besides, this would give me a chance to drop in at Michael's place unannounced. I had a suspicion that was the only way I'd get a chance to see Grayson, since I'd gotten the distinct impression everyone in the group was trying to keep the two of us apart.

So I went back inside and brushed my hair and repaired my lipstick, which had gotten more than a little smeared from my goodbye kiss with Lance. Then I took a few deep breaths, picked up my purse, and headed out.

Surprisingly, Michael's battered old El Camino wasn't in the driveway. I didn't think I'd ever seen him actually drive it, but I supposed this answered the question as to whether it ran or not. Unless, of course, he'd finally gotten around to having the thing towed away.

I parked more or less in front of the house, in a spot that wasn't too close to the driveway. This part of town didn't have sidewalks or streetlights, but Michael had stepping stones set in amongst the rocks that made up most of his front yard, so it wasn't too hard to get around.

Down here, the heat didn't seem quite as intense. Maybe it was the creek's influence, or just the tall cottonwoods and pines and sycamores that seemed to crowd everyone's lots. The breeze soughed through them, echoing the faint chatter of the creek.

For some reason, I knew not to knock at the front door, but instead opened the gate into the side yard and moved on past the back of the house and the little trail that wandered through the trees until it dead-ended at the creek. I'd been this way often—barbecues in Michael's backyard seemed to end up more often than not with evening walks along the water's edge—so my footsteps didn't falter until I got to the creek's bank and saw the man sitting there, staring out at the water.

He didn't turn. "Hi, Kara."

How he'd known it was me, I couldn't guess. My perfume, maybe, carried on the wind, or maybe the light fall of my footsteps, probably very different from Michael's. Or maybe he had super-attuned senses, half-alien warrior that he was. I wasn't brave enough to ask.

Instead, I stopped a few paces away from him and said, "I think you've found the one cool spot in Sedona."

A lift of the shoulders. I saw that he held a smooth black stone in one hand, as if he'd been contemplating chucking it across the quick-moving waters. Oak Creek never ran dry, even at this time of year, although its level was far lower than it would be in the spring, or after the first snowfall up on the San Francisco Peaks in Flagstaff.

He set the rock down and spoke, still without looking at me. "What do you want, Kara?"

"To talk."

"I don't know what we have to talk about."

There was no bitterness in his tone, and yet something in his voice sent a chill down my spine. Well, what had I been expecting? I'd left him when he needed me the most. Never mind that I had my own crap to deal with. It hadn't been fair, even if I'd known we had no possible future together.

My legs seemed reluctant to move, but I forced myself to take a few steps toward him, to stop and sit down on the creek's bank next to him. At least it was dry enough. The air smelled of damp leaves and warm stone.

"Where's Michael?" I asked. That seemed safe enough.

"Said he had to run over to Prescott for something."

That was news. I wondered what could be in Prescott that would make Michael leave Grayson here all alone. No point in asking, though. They all kept their own secrets, apparently.

"Oh."

At last, Grayson did shift his position enough so he was looking basically in my direction. Nothing about him seemed materially different, and yet there was a shadow to his eyes that hadn't been there a few days ago. God knows what he'd been brooding over, sitting there alone.

"I don't blame you," he said.

I said nothing, but only waited. Maybe I'd come here for some sort of absolution, but now I wasn't sure if I wanted to hear it.

"But I also don't want you to talk me out of... whatever they end up planning." His face tilted upward, and the fresh green of the cottonwood leaves reflected in his eyes.

"Grayson, I—"

"Don't." To my surprise, he reached out and laid a hand on mine where it rested on the sandy shore. "This couldn't have worked for us. I know that now. At least I know you won't be alone when I'm gone."

My throat tightened. Had he already consigned himself to oblivion when he didn't even know what the plan was, whether he would even be required to put himself in harm's way? "Grayson, you don't know it's going to shake out like that."

"Maybe not, but I can guess." He let go of my hand and stood, fine chin lifted into the breeze.

I got to my feet as well. This conversation was difficult enough without him looming over me like that. In a small voice, I said, "I never meant to hurt you."

"I know." He turned toward me. To my surprise, he smiled. "Actually, you've made it easier for me."

"I—what?"

"You have." With one hand, he made a sweeping gesture that seemed to take in the lacy, ruffling foliage of the cottonwoods, the solemn stillness of the pines, the bright, sun-laced chatter of the creek. "I know now what I'm fighting for. The aliens made me, put some of themselves in me, but I know I'm human, too. You showed me how beautiful this world can be. Maybe I can't have a place in it, but at least I can make damn sure it's safe for the rest of you."

The tears came then, and I couldn't stop them. It was too much. In that moment, I knew there was nothing I could say to stop him, nothing to change the quiet determination in his voice. Head bowed, I felt him move closer and take me in his arms. There was nothing sexual in his embrace, and I felt no answering heat at his touch. But something seemed to pass between us then, some understanding. I wouldn't try to argue with him anymore. If he wanted to do this thing, that was his decision. All I could do was let him know that someone in this world cared very much what happened to him.

Time passed. From somewhere far off, I heard the crunch of car tires on the patched asphalt of the road, and realized Michael must have come home. Grayson released me, but gently, as if trying to show that he was only doing so because he'd sensed in me the need to move away.

I reached up to wipe my cheeks and realized they were already dry. "It's going to be a few days at least," I told him. "Lance is having someone duplicate your jumpsuit, but that isn't something that can happen overnight."

He nodded, accepting the information without comment.

Slow, quiet footsteps came from the direction of the house. Michael Lightfoot stopped a few yards away and regarded us with no surprise. Then again, he would have seen my Prius parked in front of the house. It wasn't as if I'd tried to hide it.

His dark features showed no anger, no irritation that I'd intruded on Grayson's solitude. Maybe he understood better than I did my reasons for coming here.

"Kara," Michael said.

"Hi, Michael." So banal, but it was about all I could manage right then. "I was just filling Grayson in on some of our progress."

"Ah," was all he said, although I guessed he knew my conversation with Grayson had involved much more than that.

"Anyway," I continued, a false brightness in my voice that I was sure fooled no one, "we'll keep in touch. Lance said something about all of us getting together again tomorrow night."

"Yes."

There seemed to be nothing else to say, so I summoned a brittle smile, said my goodbyes to both men, and followed the path back up into Michael's backyard and then on to the street. As I got into the car and leaned over to fasten my seatbelt, a sudden wave of nausea assailed me, and I had to shut my eyes and gulp down a few deep breaths before it passed.

What the hell?

But then it was gone as suddenly as it had come. I shook my head. *That conversation must have gotten to you more than you thought.* I couldn't seem to erase the image of Grayson's sad eyes from my mind, the quiet resignation in his voice. It seemed he was already making his goodbyes.

Not if I have anything to say about it, I thought grimly, and pointed my car toward home.

Lance

Just like all the other helicopter tour outfits in Sedona, Arizona Helicopter Adventures had its home base at the Sedona airport, high atop a mesa. Conveniently, there was a pretty decent restaurant with an even more decent bar located a stone's throw from the tour company's office.

Lance waited there, nursing an extremely dry martini and trying to think of the best way to explain to Brian Henderson that he needed him to steer his helicopter closer to Secret Canyon than most pilots dared. It wasn't that they were scared of aliens...at least that they'd admit openly. No, most of them only said the air currents in that area were tricky, and besides, boxing yourself in a canyon wasn't the best way to show off panoramic vistas of Sedona to tourists who were paying four hundred bucks an hour for the privilege. Henderson knew better, though. He wasn't exactly active in the UFO group, but he also didn't try to deny that there was a lot more going on in Sedona's airspace than a bunch of general-aviation flights and air tours.

About twenty minutes after he said he'd be there, Henderson sauntered into the restaurant. He exchanged a few words of greeting with the hostess—he was well-known in the place, after all—before walking up to the bar and taking a seat next to Lance.

"Hey, Lance."

"Brian."

Henderson waved the bartender over. "Luis. Soda water and some lime, okay?"

The bartender nodded and went off to fill the order.

"Got another flight?" Lance inquired. Henderson had never met a martini he didn't like, but he also never drank on the job.

"Yep," the pilot replied, taking the glass of soda water from Luis. "Sunset flight. So I've got to cool my heels for a while."

Well, that explained why Henderson had been willing to meet him at four-thirty in the afternoon. Most people would be almost done with their day by then, but he had to go out when the tour company told him to.

Stirring the straw in his drink, Henderson asked, "So, are you going to tell me something that's going to make me wish this was a little stronger?"

"Maybe," Lance said. "You seen much out around Secret Canyon lately?"

"Define 'much.'"

Lance didn't bother to say anything, but just lifted his shoulders.

Henderson let out what might have been a sigh and swigged at his soda water. "You know I stick around Boynton mainly."

"Yeah, I know."

"Up until about five months ago, there were black helicopters out that way. And they weren't ours or from any of the other tours, if you know what I mean."

The timing matched. It was in early March when Persephone blew out the base. Lance supposed the airspace around Secret Canyon had been pretty quiet since then. He nodded.

"The past few weeks, though...." Henderson trailed off and looked regretfully into his half-empty glass of soda water as if he really wished it was a martini, or possibly a gin and tonic. "Not that I've really seen anything, but...."

"But what?"

"It's probably my eyes playing tricks on me. Just don't tell anyone else I said that. I need this gig. But I've seen...something...like heat shimmers out of the corner of my eye. When I turn to really look, though, nothing's there."

Some kind of cloaking technology, Lance guessed, although he didn't bother to voice that particular speculation aloud. Henderson was willing to go along with the whole UFO thing up to a point, but the minute Lance mentioned a cloaking device, he knew the other man would start making *Star Trek* cracks, and the whole conversation would only go downhill from there.

For a minute, Lance didn't say anything, but only drank his own martini, devoutly glad that Luis didn't mix them weak. *The past few weeks.* So whatever the aliens were up to out in Secret Canyon, it hadn't been going on for very long. That might be a bit of good news. Maybe the UFO hunters' own particular monkey wrench—in the shape of Grayson, the perfect infiltration agent—could actually do some good. Still, shimmers where alien craft might or might not be didn't help all that much. He needed to know if they were still using the old entrances to the base, or whether they'd done a bit of remodeling when they came back to take up residence.

"So...if there really isn't anything there, then it couldn't hurt for you to get in a little closer."

Henderson's eyes narrowed. The guy was no fool. Unlike some of the kids they had piloting those aerial tourist traps, he knew what he was doing. He'd flown med-evac in the first Gulf War, wasn't someone to get easily rattled. "And how am I supposed to explain that to the tourists? From the air, Secret isn't nearly as interesting as Boynton."

"I'm pretty sure most of them won't even notice the difference."

"You're probably right. Okay, I'll do a short buzz-by and see if I can scope out anything. But I'm guessing it's going to be a big fat zero."

"Probably...but you never know."

"You never do."

And Lance slapped a twenty down on the bar for Luis to cover both his and Henderson's drinks, then got up and left. He knew he didn't need to extract any more promises from Henderson. The man would do as he'd offered. And then?

Well, Lance could only hope he'd actually get something out of it besides some wasted fuel and a couple of disgruntled tourists.

———

Kara

I didn't go straight home, but spent a few hours at Persephone's house before finally pointing the Prius homeward. It had been good to sit down and talk— not about anything important, only topics like Ginger's wedding and how L.A. already seemed so ungodly crowded, even though Persephone had moved away a scant four months ago. Just the sort of cheerful, inconsequential chatter any two friends would have, with nary an alien nor a government conspiracy in sight. When I left, my spirits were considerably improved.

As I drove home, a series of emergency vehicles passed me on 89A, sirens blaring, lights flashing against the sunset sky. More than once, I had to pull over, letting first an ambulance, then a pair of fire trucks, and finally a couple of police cars go screaming by. Pile-up out on the western edge of town? House fire? It had to be something major to get that sort of response.

Still, it wasn't something I needed to be worried about. I pulled into the garage and got out of the car, patted Gort as he came bounding up to me the second I walked into the kitchen, and turned off the alarm. "Soon, Gort," I promised.

No messages on the answering machine, which was a relief after everything that had been going on. But I hadn't been in the house for more than five minutes before I heard the doorbell ring.

"What now?" I muttered to Gort, who cocked his head and wagged his tail doubtfully. "You think it's Martin Jones, the semi-hot man in black?"

The dog whined, and I couldn't help smiling slightly.

But it was not Martin Jones who waited outside, but Lance, looking positively grim.

"You hear the sirens?" he asked, moving past me into the entryway.

"Um, yes. Saw them, actually, as I was coming home from Persephone's."

He stopped in the middle of the living room and ran a distracted hand through his short-cropped hair. I couldn't remember the last time I'd seen him this agitated. "My fault," he said.

I blinked at him. "Your fault? Was there a car accident or something? Are you okay?"

"I'm fine. I can't say the same for Brian Henderson or the three tourists he had on board his helicopter when it went down."

The words didn't seem to make sense at first. I stared at him, at the obvious consternation on his features, and a second or two later it clicked into place. "He—he crashed? Oh, my God, Lance...."

"I'm sure that's what they'll call it. Mechanical failure or something plausible. Only I know that wasn't it at all. He got too close."

"Too close?"

"To Secret Canyon. To whatever it is that they're doing out there. They wanted to make sure we got the message—and they didn't care if it cost four innocent lives."

My heart began to pound at the thought of Brian Henderson's helicopter dropping from the sky, only to smash on the red rocks below. There was no way he could have possibly defended himself against such an attack. I swallowed, then asked, "A warning?"

"More like a 'fuck you.'"

Lance's eyes were narrowed, his jaw clenched. If any of the aliens had been around, he looked as if he could have reached out and wrung what passed for their necks. But of course they were all safely miles away, and I guessed they would have done something similarly lethal to Lance if he'd tried anything.

I wished I could have thought of something simultaneously bracing and soothing to tell him, but words seemed to have failed me. Somehow, though, I made myself say, "It's not your fault, Lance."

"It isn't? I'm the one who sent him out there."

"You couldn't have possibly known—"

"That's not the point. I sent him into harm's way, and now four people are dead because of me."

Without replying, I went to him, put my arms around him, and pulled him close. At first, he seemed to resist, but then I felt him tighten the embrace, crush me to him, as if he needed to feel my warmth, the life in my body, to know that I was here with him, was safe. We stood that way for several minutes, until I murmured,

"Those people aren't dead because of you. They're dead because of the aliens. It's horrible. It's a tragedy. But you can't blame yourself. If the aliens are on hyper-alert for some reason, they would have gone after anybody. It could have been someone else flying too close to Secret Canyon."

"But it wasn't."

I knew he'd never allow himself to cry, was channeling his hurt and sorrow into anger, into blame. That was all right; I could understand that.

"It's horrible," I said. "But this just means they're up to something, something big. We've got to stop them."

Lance grasped me by the upper arms and held me away from him, just far enough so he could study my face. Whatever he saw there seemed to steady him, because he nodded.

"I know." His voice was hard now, cold and

edged with steel. "I'm going to make sure Brian's death means something." He shifted, those flinty gray eyes fixed on a point beyond me, gazing westward, toward the aliens' base. "They're going to be very sorry they ever tangled with us."

CHAPTER SIXTEEN

Lance

"I'm so sorry, Lance, but it's going to be at least another three days," Lucinda Torres said, and she did sound truly apologetic. "But my supplier is out of that cotton canvas I needed, and he's waiting for his supplier to restock. From what he told me, it sounds as if it's sitting in a container at the Port of Los Angeles. Something about a dockworkers' strike, I hear."

He managed to refrain from swearing and even muttered something along the lines of, "I know it's not your fault," before he touched the screen to end the call and tossed the phone on the passenger seat of his Jeep.

A delay was the last thing he needed. What he

really wanted to do was load up the 4x4 with every gun and incendiary device he owned, drive out to Secret Canyon, and stage a commando raid worthy of a 1980s Schwarzenegger film. However, all that would accomplish would be to kill him off in some kind of spectacular fashion, and, angry as he was, he sort of wanted to stick around for a while.

He finally had a reason to care about his existence. If he bought it now, the timing would not just be ironic; it would be cruel.

Kara had gotten him more or less calmed down, partly because he realized there wasn't anything he could do at the moment, not until they were able to infiltrate the base and find out what was really going on. He'd attempted another remote viewing, but he was so agitated that nothing scanned. No images, just the darkness inside his skull.

And now any attempt at getting inside Secret Canyon was going to be put off for nearly a week, just because some dockworkers in L.A. didn't think their pension was big enough or something. And what was with everything having to come from China, anyway? Did no one grow or make anything in the United States anymore?

Still fuming, he pulled up into the driveway of the Olivers' house. Persephone had suggested a session with Grayson to see if she could extract any information.

"I had some hypnotherapy training when I was

getting my master's," she'd explained. "It's worth a try, since we obviously can't run the risk of an outside therapist having access to this information. And maybe if I'm really lucky, Otto will show up and give me some advice."

Otto, the not-so-magnificent. Okay, so her spirit guide had turned out to be some sort of extra-dimensional being instead of a long-dead Turkish eunuch, but whoever or whatever he was, "reliable" didn't seem to be in his vocabulary, especially lately. Not that Lance and Persephone had a lot of what you could call heart-to-heart talks. However, from certain things she'd let slip, he got the impression that lately she'd been depending more on her own powers of clairsentience than on any input from Otto. What that all meant, Lane didn't know, but he guessed it was nothing good.

Kara's Prius was already parked in front of the house, behind Jeff Makowski's '70s-vintage Chevy van, which looked as if it could have barely made it up the hill, let alone the five-hundred-plus miles from Southern California to Sedona. Lance shook his head a little at the thought of driving that distance in such a rattletrap, but again, not really his business.

Paul had picked up Grayson and Michael earlier, so now the gang was all here. Usually, they'd all be chattering about something—with Kiki's clear soprano tones riding on top of the general hubbub—

but this time, everyone seemed more than a little subdued. Maybe it was because they knew Lance had come here directly from Brian Henderson's funeral.

Working his tie loose so he could shove it in his pocket now that it was no longer needed, Lance went over and sat down next to Kara on the couch. A few of the dining room chairs had been pressed into service, since the Olivers' living room didn't normally have seating for this many people.

Grayson had already taken a seat in a leather recliner, with Persephone perched next to him on one of the dining room chairs. Kiki was sitting cross-legged on the Persian rug, but Jeff had taken a position on the love seat next to Michael Lightfoot, looking more than a little uncomfortable. The kid probably didn't enjoy being around so many people.

"You okay?" Kara murmured as she reached over to touch Lance's hand. She'd offered to go to the funeral with him, but he'd said there was no reason—she'd met Brian once, maybe twice, but it wasn't the sort of acquaintance that necessitated her presence at his funeral.

Closed-casket, of course.

The other three to perish had been a retired couple from Colorado Springs and their newly divorced daughter, vacationing in Sedona as a way of getting the daughter's mind off the breakup of her marriage. She'd been just twenty-nine. Kara's age.

Lance squeezed Kara's fingers, glad of her touch, her reassurance. Let the others think what they wanted. He wasn't going to tiptoe around forever, like some teenager afraid of introducing his new girl-friend to his parents.

The anger was still there, of course, but banked down. If he had to wait, then he'd wait. But he'd never forget.

Persephone gave him a brief piercing look, as if she knew all too well what he was thinking. Maybe she did.

"I talked to Lucinda on the way over here," he said. "Looks like she's not going to get the fabric for at least another three days. So we have more time to plan than we thought."

"Can't she just order it from someplace else?" Paul asked.

"Not according to her. I guess there aren't that many manufacturers that make the kind of heavy-grade stuff used in military gear. She tried to track some down but didn't have any luck."

"Maybe it's a blessing in disguise," Persephone said. "It gives us some more planning time, anyway."

Planning for what, Lance wasn't sure, since the original thought had been to have Grayson do the advance recon so they could devise a plan based on his findings. But maybe they'd get enough today, they'd be able to use that instead.

Through all this, the hybrid had sat quietly,

watching the interchange among the group. Well, among most of them, anyway; Lance couldn't help noticing that Grayson's gaze kind of skipped over Kara, as if he didn't want to look at her sitting there, holding Lance's hand. It had to be rough for the guy.

But if he was experiencing any inner turmoil, it didn't show on his face as he told Persephone, "Then let's get started. I want to know if I've got anything important locked up in here."

She smiled a little. "Okay. I know Janelle Russo already put you under once, so I don't have to explain how this works. This session will be basically the same, but I'd like to hold your hand during the process. I'm hoping that will help spark things."

"No problem."

Even if it had been a problem, Lance sort of doubted Grayson would have declined. The hybrid seemed just as eager to push ahead as Lance did.

Persephone looked over at Paul. "Ready?"

He nodded.

For the first time, Lance noticed that Paul held a small digital voice recorder. Made sense to get everything down in a permanent record.

"And it probably goes without saying," she added, "but please, no comments, no reactions, during the session. I don't want anyone to do anything to compromise our findings."

Everyone either nodded or murmured something along the lines of "okay"—even the ebullient Kiki, who seemed unnaturally subdued for her. She sat on the rug, fingers knotted on top of her crossed ankles, clear brow slightly knotted in concern.

Persephone nodded in approval. "All right. Let's get started, then."

And she began the sequence of counting back from ten, her tone soothing, soft. Lance knew better than to fall under its spell, although he thought he saw Jeff blink furiously, as if to prevent the hypnotic suggestion from affecting him.

At the end of the countdown, Persephone said, "Grayson. Can you hear me?"

"Yes."

"Can you tell me where you are?"

"In Persephone and Paul's living room."

"Very good. Okay, I want you to go back now. Go back to the time you were in the desert. Do you remember that?"

A reluctant nod.

"Good. Can you tell me how you got out into the desert?"

"Went out through a door."

"The door in the motor pool, right." Lance saw her pale fingers tighten around Grayson's sun-browned ones for a second or two before they relaxed again. "Do you remember any other entrances to the base?"

A frown. "The small door in the ravine."

Lance remembered that door all too well, hidden

in a crack in the cliff wall, obscured by manzanita and low-hanging junipers. He'd rather not have to go back in that way, all things being equal.

"Anything else?"

"The main entrance, through the box canyon."

Again, a known quantity. Of course, the "main entrance" was almost as small and piddly as the hidden door through which he and Michael and Persephone had first gained entrance to the base... and just as useless.

"...and the service entrance."

Persephone perked up noticeably at that tidbit. "The service entrance?"

A nod. "It's lower...you come in through the back, in another ravine. They would land there, off-load supplies."

This was promising.

"Is it guarded?"

"Yes."

"How many guards?"

"Four."

That wasn't so good. It was possible for one person to take out four...if he got the drop on them and had some other advantage in terms of skills, weaponry, or training. But Grayson would be going up against a group of men who were identical to him, so there went any individual advantage. Maybe the element of surprise would be enough.

Maybe.

Persephone likewise appeared somewhat concerned, but the small frown that had creased her brow smoothed itself away as she asked, "And the door? Is it operated by a key card like the interior doors?"

"No. Biometric thumbprint scan."

Well, that was a piece of good news. In a way, it made sense. Inside the base, there were probably rooms that not all of the hybrids would have access to, hence the key cards. But keeping them out of the base itself didn't make much sense.

Everyone else obviously thought the same, because Lance heard a little rustle go through the group as people shifted or nodded or let out a breath. It wasn't enough to disrupt the session, although Persephone did shoot everyone a quick glance of warning before she continued.

"And how do you make the approach to this service entrance?"

"A canyon...come in through Boynton."

That was interesting. Lance would have said he thought he knew the area pretty well, but he'd had no idea there was a way to cut through from Boynton into Secret Canyon.

"If you're coming overland, that is. A lot of drops were by air."

It figured. All that country was either part of or backed right up to U.S. Forest Service land, so no one would be around to see any comings and goings.

Not that the aliens had too much trouble with that angle. The memory of Brian Henderson's death brought a sour taste to his mouth, and Lance felt himself grimace. The pilot had never seen them coming.

Very soon—if everything went well—the aliens might get a taste of their own medicine.

"And what do you see when you first come in through that entrance?"

"Loading dock. Storage areas. There's one exit that leads to the rest of Level Ten."

Meaning this service entrance came in on the lowest level of the base. Good for stealth, not so good if you were trying to make a beeline for a more vital part of the base. Still, beggars couldn't be choosers.

He glanced over at Kara. She stared forward, attention fixed on Grayson. Lance couldn't guess what she might be thinking. It wasn't the gaze of a woman staring at her lover, true, but worry was clear in the taut lines of her fine throat, the slightly pursed lips. Maybe she was worried that Persephone was pushing the hybrid too hard, even though the questioning didn't seem all that taxing to Lance.

Persephone nodded slightly, as if she'd heard some sort of internal suggestion as to what should come next. Maybe she had. Just because Otto had taken a powder for the past few months didn't mean he might not show up now when they really needed him.

Wouldn't be the first time.

She leaned forward as she asked, "Why are they here, Grayson? Can you tell us what they're planning?"

Seemed like a stupid question to Lance. The group already knew the aliens had been trying to enslave the human population of the earth, make them their servants through a particularly nasty form of mind control.

For some reason, though, the question seemed to bother Grayson. He looked upward for a second, and his mouth compressed. Then he shook his head.

"You don't know?"

He shook his head again, and Persephone waited. In a detached way, Lance admired the way she handled herself, all business, cool, calm. This was a side of her he hadn't seen too much, but he supposed she would have been trained in this sort of thing when she got her counseling certification.

At length, Grayson said, "The power."

"'The power'?" Persephone repeated, clearly mystified.

"Want it. That's why they came back."

A lift of the eyebrows, and Persephone looked over at Michael. He frowned but then shook his head.

"Must stop them," Grayson ground out, the cords in his neck showing as he uttered the words painfully, as if every one of them was being torn from his throat.

"We plan to, Grayson. We will—"

But then the hybrid erupted from his seat, almost knocking Persephone over. He looked around, wild-eyed, and Lance wondered if he was going to have to tackle the guy to keep him from going on a rampage. Just as suddenly, though, Grayson subsided, falling back into his chair. His eyes went wide, and fastened on Persephone.

"What happened?" he asked.

Her gaze didn't flicker, but Lance noticed the way her shoulders slumped a little, as if in disappointment. She knew, as Lance did, that Grayson was now out of the hypnotic trance.

"You gave us some great information," Kara said quickly, as if daring anyone else to contradict her.

"Yes, you did," Paul added as he clicked the "stop" button on his micro-recorder. "Very helpful."

The hybrid didn't look altogether convinced, but then he nodded. "Good. So what's next?"

For some reason, everyone turned to look at Lance. He didn't much enjoy being the center of attention, but he also knew he was the one who had to figure out what to with the information they'd just gathered. "Wait for the jumpsuit to get made, and plan like hell in the meantime."

Paul and Michael both seemed to absorb that reply

with no noticeable change in expression. Grayson scowled a little, but Lance couldn't really blame him for that. Kiki looked worried, and Jeff, as usual, appeared as if he was thinking of something happening roughly a million light-years away. Kara seemed a little green around the gills for some reason. Was she still more attached to Grayson than she'd let on?

Hell, he didn't know how attached she'd been in the first place. They'd talked about a lot of things, but so far, she hadn't seemed too eager to go into the gory details of what had happened between her and Grayson. Not that it took a rocket scientist to figure out that sort of thing.

He'd worry about that later. She was with him now, and that was what counted.

That, and making sure they all survived this somehow.

Kara

I begged off going over to Lance's condo after the get-together. He'd offered in the most casual way, as if it hadn't mattered to him one way or another whether I came over or not, though somehow I knew that was how he protected himself. Of course, he'd wanted to spend more time with me, and it hadn't been easy to decline, despite the nausea that had reared its ugly head again.

For some reason, I felt positively ill, and really just wanted to go home and lie down. Maybe I'd picked up some sort of bug or another, even though I hardly ever got sick. Still, what with all the stress I'd been under lately, it didn't seem too implausible that something had managed to infiltrate my normally tough immune defenses.

So I went home and climbed out of my close-fitting jeans and into an infinitely more comfortable pair of yoga pants, kicked off my platform sandals, and wandered into the kitchen. For all my biliousness, I also was strangely hungry, and a bowl of mint chip ice cream seemed just the ticket.

I'd taken all of three bites, though, before the nausea overwhelmed me again. Pushing the bowl away of ice cream away, I got to my feet and bolted down the hall to the guest bathroom, where I bent over the toilet, retching. Nothing came up. As quickly as it had come, the queasiness subsided, and I got a Dixie cup and made myself drink two cupfuls of water.

What the hell?

A hand to my forehead told me that my temperature seemed pretty much normal, although I supposed I should go to the medicine cabinet in my own bathroom to retrieve the thermometer and see if I really was feverish. After drinking one last cup of water, I crumpled up the little cup and threw it in the trash, then went to the bath off the master bedroom.

The thermometer told me what I'd already suspected—nothing. Temperature of ninety-seven point nine, which was normal for me. I always ran a little low.

So...what? Not the stomach flu; I'd have a temperature with that. Maybe that burger at Red Planet Diner had been a little off, but you'd think if that were the case, I would have started to feel sick a lot sooner than this.

Just a bug, I told myself. *Just because it doesn't fit the parameters of something you've had before doesn't mean it's anything except a nasty little virus that slipped under your defenses.*

The T-shirt I was wearing suddenly felt too hot, despite my apparent lack of a temperature. Time to slip into a tank top and my oldest, loosest bra, and then curl up on the couch and ride out this thing, whatever it was.

I went to my dresser and pulled out a faded blue tank and the bra in question, and yanked the T-shirt over my head. After that, I reached back to unhook the bra I wore, and gave a sigh as it came off.

Freed, my breasts almost felt worse. heavy, aching. I grabbed the alternate bra and slipped into it, frowning. My breasts shouldn't be hurting like that. Sometimes, they were sore a day or two before my period started, but that blessed event was still a week off. No reason they should feel so swollen, so strange....

I stopped then, the fear blossoming like an ice-cold flower somewhere in the pit of my stomach, spreading out to fill every vein with something roughly akin to antifreeze. There was no way....

Slipping the tank top over my head, I stumbled into the bathroom, pulled my packet of pills out of the medicine cabinet, feverishly inspected the interior of the little plastic case. There were no missing days; taking a pill at night just before I brushed my teeth had been part of my regimen for so long that I didn't even think about it anymore.

It had to be something else.

The pill isn't one-hundred-percent foolproof, my brain told me, and I shook my head. That didn't matter. Grayson had always used a condom, and so had Lance, for that matter. He'd gone to get tested so we could dispense with those things as soon as possible, but he was still waiting on the results.

But then it hit me. That one time, when Grayson had come back from his ride, just after the MIBs had left. I jumped on him like an animal, not thinking, just wanting him, wanting him inside me. Of course, he hadn't stopped me, and I hadn't hesitated, maybe knowing somewhere in the back of my mind that it was perfectly safe, that Grayson was no risk in terms of disease, and I was on the pill anyway....

A frightened little moan escaped my lips. No, it had to be something else. Just a bug.

But what kind of bug would make my breasts hurt like this?

Barely a hesitation, and then I was shoving my feet into a pair of flip-flops, grabbing my purse, running for my car so I could go to Walgreens and get the test that would put my mind at ease.

No point in wearing sunglasses; everyone at the drugstore knew me, of course. All I could do was slap the pregnancy test down on the counter and pray that professional courtesy would keep Jerri, the cashier, from commenting.

Thankfully, Jerri didn't say anything except, "Hi, Kara, how's business?" before scanning the barcode on the pregnancy test and dropping it promptly in a bag, as if she instinctively knew that the less time it was visible, the better.

"Fine," I managed, before handing Jerry a twenty. This was one transaction I definitely didn't want on my debit card.

And then I was done and was out, hurrying back to my car and tearing out of the parking lot at a speed that was definitely not safe. Good thing Sedona's finest all seemed to be occupied elsewhere at the moment.

I pulled into the garage and rushed into the house, ignoring Gort's inquiring brown eyes, dropping my purse on the coffee table in the living room, practically sprinting into the bathroom. No need to look at the instructions; I'd had to use one of these things years ago, in a scare when I was still with Alan and I was sure the pill had failed me then, too. *That's all this will turn out to be,* I told myself. *Just nerves.*

Just jumping to conclusions because I'd been so on edge lately.

Peeing on a stick was not a graceful endeavor no matter how you looked at it, but I performed the task with a minimum of mess and somehow managed to wait the required three minutes. Then I bit my lip and looked down at the little pale pink stick.

Two lines.

The bile rose in my throat again, and I choked it back. After swallowing, I looked back down again, but those two lines were still there, staring up at me like a pair of evil, slitted eyes.

It was impossible. It *had* to be impossible. But the test claimed to be ninety-nine-percent accurate.

Yeah, well, they say the same thing about the pill.

Then again, the pill had never really been designed to stand up to alien super-sperm, had it? Or maybe I was forgetting how it really worked.

Logically, I knew the test could still be wrong. Somehow, though, I realized it wasn't, that despite my precautions, something had happened. Something I had never imagined in a million years.

Shaking, I bent my head, unable to tear my gaze away from those two accusing little lines. Finally, I shut my eyes, although I knew that wouldn't make them go away.

Oh, God. What do I do now?

CHAPTER SEVENTEEN

I debated between going to the Planned Parenthood in Flagstaff or the one over in Prescott, then decided there was less chance of running into anyone I knew over Prescott way. True, it had been years since I'd gone to college or lived in Flagstaff, but you never knew. And there was no way I was going to my regular G.P., Lisa Michaels, for this. If it turned out I really was pregnant and not just having a screaming case of the heebie-jeebies, I'd figure out what to do then, but in the meantime, I wanted to keep things as much on the down-low as possible.

So I got in my car and headed out at roughly nine the next morning, after asking Kiki if she could watch the store until I got back. Of course, I didn't say where I was going or why, but Kiki somehow seemed to sense that any questions she asked weren't going to get answers. She'd only said, "Sure, no problem," and then asked if it was okay if Jeff hung out at the store for a while.

By that point, I was feeling so wretched that I really didn't care if Jeff took up residence in the place, so I said that would be fine and hung up. What was really going on between those two?

With a head shake, I dispelled nightmarish visions of Jeff Makowski as my future brother-in-law and pointed the car south on 179. This route was slightly out of the way, but I just didn't feel like dealing with the switchbacks on 89A as it went over Mingus Mountain on its way to Prescott. Besides, I had no wish to go back through Jerome and be reminded of my idyllic day with Grayson there.

I brought along some bottled water in case the nausea returned, but it seemed to have retreated for the moment. My thoughts jumped this way and that, not settling on any one thing. Foremost among them, though, seemed to be, *What the hell am I going to say to Lance?*

Worry about that when you need to, I told myself sternly, and made myself look at the dry golden fields passing by, the rock formations, the bruise-colored mass of clouds piling up to the south and east. It might be raining by the time I returned home, but I couldn't worry about that now. The Prius had new tires, and I was a good driver. A monsoon storm was no big deal.

The miles blew past. I knew I was speeding,

although I couldn't seem to ease off on the accelerator. Stupid, really, because if I got there too early, all I'd end up doing would be sitting and waiting with a bunch of pregnant women, some of whom—maybe most of whom?—would have small children with them. Not that I minded kids, but dealing with a horde of screaming toddlers was really not what my nerves needed right then.

I came into Prescott, drove through its quiet streets, past the historic downtown area, and pulled into the parking lot for Planned Parenthood. The building was new and modern and very clean, and it helped put my mind at ease somewhat. Also, the waiting room wasn't too crowded—just two other women sat on the chairs there, one who looked as if she was about to pop at any moment. The second woman was barely more than a girl, and she didn't appear any more pregnant than I myself did. She looked around furtively in between bursts of rapid-fire texting on her phone. I wondered if she was there for a pregnancy test, just as I was. No need to come to Planned Parenthood for a Plan B pill, not when you could get it over the counter.

Too late for that for me, I thought as I signed myself in and sat down to wait.

The pregnant woman was called almost immediately, which was something of a relief, since that seemed to indicate the staff there was dedicated to making sure patients were seen quickly. Instead of staring down at my watch, I forced myself to look over at the closed-circuit TV with its ongoing round of bite-sized shows with information about pregnancy, sexually transmitted diseases, family planning.

What about family not-*planning?* I wondered, and had to bite back a small, nervous giggle. Luckily, Texting Girl didn't seem to be paying me any attention.

The minutes crawled by. After a bit, Texting Girl got up, had a brief whispered convo with the receptionist, and scurried out, looking both frightened and relieved at the same time. Once again, I had to wonder why she'd come here. Something as extreme as a D&C, or maybe just free birth control pills after being pressured by a boyfriend?

Impossible to know, although worrying about someone else's problems helped me take my mind off my own troubles for a while.

Then the receptionist, a comfortable-looking redhead in her fifties, said, "Kara Swenson?"

Taking a breath, I got up and followed the woman to a place where I was weighed, then guided into an exam room and given a cup.

"Just put it on the ledge over here when you're done. A nurse will be in to take your blood pressure in a moment," the receptionist instructed me.

So which was worse, peeing in a cup or peeing on a stick? I really didn't know, but I performed the procedure with too much trouble, placed the cup on its ledge, and headed back into the exam room, where I put on the paper garments they'd left for me and waited.

A minute or two later, the nurse came in, asked the standard questions, then took my blood pressure and temperature. "So, what are your symptoms?"

"Nausea, sore breasts. And an over-the-counter pregnancy test was positive."

The nurse made a few notes. "Got it. We're going to run the test, and then the doctor will be in to see you."

I nodded, not quite trusting my voice right then. Every passing moment in this place seemed to make the possibility more real, that I could actually be pregnant. I'd wanted to think it was just a mistake, that the home test had thrown back a false positive for some reason. Never mind that those things were actually highly accurate.

So I sat there with my feet dangling off the exam table and stared down at my toes. The polish was starting to chip, I realized. I'd have to schedule a pedicure sometime soon.

Oh, yeah, I'll just squeeze that in between handling an alien invasion and having E.T.'s baby, I thought, and made an odd little hiccuping noise, halfway between a sob and a laugh. Maybe coming here alone wasn't such a great idea. Maybe I should have told Persephone, had her come along—

The door opened, and the doctor, a pretty Filipina probably around my own age, came in. She smiled, her brown eyes warm and sympathetic. "Hi, Ms. Swenson. I'm Dr. Santos."

"Hi."

"We just ran the test, and you are pregnant."

The bottom seemed to fall out of the world, or at least it tilted on its axis, swung crazily around me. I gripped the edges of the exam table and told myself, *You will not pass out. You will not pass out....*

Dr. Santos' voice was very kind. "I take it this wasn't planned."

Somehow, I managed to nod. "I'm on the pill."

"I see." A pause, then, "If you're planning to continue with the pregnancy, then of course you need to stop taking it immediately."

Was I planning to continue with the pregnancy? I couldn't think about that right then, couldn't seem to think about anything except those three words swirling around in my brain. *You are pregnant. You are PREGNANT. You ARE pregnant....*

Hazily, I realized Dr. Santos had said something else. "I'm sorry, can you repeat that?"

The doctor paused. "Are you all right, Ms. Swenson? Did you bring someone with you?"

"No, I'm fine. Really. What did you say?"

"I said that, based on the level of HCGs in your system, you're about three weeks along. It's still very early."

What the hell? Three weeks ago, I hadn't been with anybody, let alone a hybrid alien soldier. Maybe the test was off. "Is this where you start to talk to me about my options?"

"Do you need me to?"

Wearily, I shook my head. "No, I think I know what comes next. But I've got time to decide.'

"Some, yes. But in the meantime, you should still take care of yourself, rest, eat healthy, avoid alcohol."

Naturally. Never mind that at the moment, I wanted a margarita roughly the size of my head. "Thanks, Dr. Santos. I'll be careful."

The doctor didn't appear entirely convinced, but she just made a notation on her chart before adding, "We can set you up for a follow-up appointment in a few weeks, or if you have a doctor back in"—she stopped to read my chart—"Sedona, we can forward the results there."

"I'm not sure yet. I'll have to get back to you on that."

"Not a problem. Take care, Ms. Swenson." And she went out, no doubt to see a patient who wasn't pregnant with an alien's baby.

I peeled off the paper examination gown, got dressed, and headed for home.

If possible, the drive back seemed even longer. As I

turned off Highway 69 onto I-17 northbound, rain began to fall. I turned on the windshield wipers. With every scratch back and forth across the windshield, they seemed to be saying, "You're pregnant! You're pregnant!"

Angrily, I switched on the radio, but of course out here, I couldn't get much more than static, and I wasn't about to try pairing my phone with the car's audio system, not in the rain and with my hands shaking the way they were. Nothing to do but push grimly northward, heading home, even though it didn't seem to be the refuge it once was.

Over the years, I'd reconciled myself to the fact that I didn't have any kind of mother figure in my life, but I found myself longing for someone like that, someone I could just fall upon and weep, someone who would tell me it was going to be all right, even if it wasn't. Yes, Kiki was very dear to me, but I was my sister's mother figure, not the other way around.

As I turned off the freeway and onto 179 to head up into Sedona, I pulled out my cell phone and called Persephone. Persephone would listen to me, would help me figure out what I was supposed to do next. Persephone wouldn't judge.

She sounded a little surprised to hear my obviously shaky request for a meeting at the Secret Garden Café, but she agreed right away. "Paul and Michael and Grayson are all huddled in Paul's study, having some sort of council of war. I'd complain about the sexism of them locking me out, but I know I suck at strategy. So you'll be there...when, a little after one?"

"Something like that," I replied, relieved beyond measure that Persephone didn't have a client scheduled. She actually kept pretty busy, had even retained a few of her L.A. clients, who would make the trek out to Arizona once a month to receive her pearls of wisdom. One of them was some sort of big-shot producer who flew in on a private jet and then hired someone to drive him around Sedona for the weekend. I couldn't really wrap my brain around that kind of extravagance, but it didn't seem to faze Persephone.

The café was a little crowded, since it was the tail end of lunch, but luckily, Persephone appeared to have gone early so she could snag us a shady table in one corner of the patio. The rain hadn't gotten here yet, but the heat, instead of feeling oppressive, seemed to wrap itself around me, helped to still the shakiness of my limbs.

I'd barely slid into my chair when Sharon, one of the restaurant's co-owners, came up and asked what we'd like.

"Iced tea," I said automatically, then realized I probably wasn't supposed to be drinking caffeine. *Sorry, kid...you'll just have to suck it up this one time.*

Persephone ordered the same, and then sat back

a little and watched me with speculative eyes. "You've just had some bad news."

"Seph, please don't do the psychic thing right now. I called you because I needed a friend."

At once, she leaned forward and clasped her hands on the tabletop. "Sorry, Kara. It's just—it's coming off you in waves. It's hard not to pick it up."

Sharon emerged then with our iced teas and asked if we wanted to order anything. My appetite seemed to have deserted me, but Persephone came to the rescue and said we'd like to split an order of bruschetta while we made up our minds.

"So, what is it, Kara?"

There was no way to say it easily. I blurted, "I'm pregnant."

That revelation obviously shocked Persephone. Her hazel-green eyes widened, and she sat silent for a moment before venturing, "How is that possible? I mean, you've only been with Lance a few days, and even Grayson...."

She trailed off, and I said, "According to the test, I'm about three weeks along. Never mind that three weeks ago, my only sexual partner was a vibrator, and I'm pretty sure those don't go around knocking people up."

Persephone's cheeks flushed, but she replied steadily enough, "Then how is this possible?"

"I don't know!" I replied, probably too loudly, since the couple at the next table shot us a curious glance. "I don't know anything, except I've been feeling sick, and my boobs feel like a couple of sandbags, and two separate pregnancy tests are telling me I'm pregnant."

"But you...you were careful, weren't you?"

I smiled humorlessly, and wondered if the expression made me look a little bit like a shark. "I'm on the pill. And I used a condom with Grayson every time. Every time...except one." My voice faltered a little as I recalled those moments of abandon, when all I'd wanted was him, just the feel of him inside me. I'd thought the pill would be protection enough. Guess I thought wrong. Those suckers weren't designed to stand up to alien super-hybrid sperm, apparently.

Wow. I'd actually managed to render Persephone Oliver speechless. She just sat there, staring at me, obviously searching for something appropriately comforting to say and coming up empty.

"It's okay," I said. "I'm feeling pretty gobsmacked right now, too."

The bruschetta showed up then, and surprisingly, it smelled great. I picked up a piece and bit into it, while Persephone appeared to gather herself before saying,

"So...have you thought about what you're going to do next?"

Well, since I can't drown myself in a margarita, not really. I set down my half-eaten piece of bruschetta, then hesitated a long time before answering. The answer had begun to surface all during the drive here, even though at the time, I hadn't wanted to acknowledge it, didn't want to face what I knew I had to do.

"I'm...well, I guess I'm going to stay the course. Not because I'm some sort of holier-than-thou right-to-life person, but because of Kiki."

"Kiki?" Persephone asked, surprise once again lifting her eyebrows.

I reflected on how much we still didn't know about one another, despite becoming friends over the past five months. "Kiki wasn't exactly planned, you might say. And my mother, being the mess she was, sort of waffled over whether or not to get an abortion until it was too late for her to do anything about it. And if she had, well, I wouldn't have a little sister. So I just don't think I could get rid of this baby and be able to look at myself in the mirror in the morning, not when I know that about my sister."

Unexpectedly, Persephone reached across the little wrought-iron tabletop and gave my hand a quick squeeze before releasing it again. "I understand. But if you're already supposedly three weeks along when it's only been a few days...."

"I know," I said, and forced myself to take another bite of bruschetta, although my mouth at the moment felt drier than the desert outside town. "It's not going to be a normal pregnancy. But if I can't get help for this sort of thing from a group of UFO chasers, then where can I?"

Persephone stared at me for a second or two, then actually laughed. "You're right. Guess I hadn't thought about it that way. I'm sure Paul has some connections."

And I'll have to hope they know how to keep their mouths shut. But I didn't give voice to this worry, instead drinking my iced tea and then managing a smile. Of course it was fake; my insides felt like ice. This talk with Persephone was the easy part.

I still had to face Grayson and Lance...and I had no idea which of those interviews was going to be the worst.

Lance

He watched Grayson as the hybrid and Paul went over an aerial map of Boynton Canyon, and wondered whether he'd be quite that calm if he was planning his own death.

Oh, no one had come out and said it in so many words. But it was pretty clear that Grayson didn't expect to come back from this mission, no matter how he might phrase things when Kara was around. They might be talking about reconnoitering and gathering intelligence, but the basic subtext was this:

Get in, find out what you can, relay any information you find...until they catch you, or you blow the place up.

Because that was what Grayson had asked for, quite calmly, as if requesting pepper on his salad. *I'd like as many explosives as I can carry, if you can manage it.*

Lance had replied that he could manage it without any problem, to which Paul gave him a sharp look but said nothing. The astrophysicist might appear to have his head in the clouds half the time, but he had a fairly practical streak for all that. After what had happened to Brian, Paul knew the aliens were playing for keeps. And Michael...well, he sat quietly in the corner of the office, observing but not saying anything, as if he knew that any protests he might make would be ignored.

Luckily, Persephone had excused herself from this meeting, saying she knew as much about planning an infiltration mission as she did about baking a cake—namely, nothing—and Kara had said she was going to be away part of the day, since she had to run over to Prescott. She gave no other details, and Lance didn't press her, but he could tell something was up. On the phone, her voice had that too-bright, almost metallic quality that usually indicated she was upset about something and desperately trying to conceal it. He didn't like the feeling that she was hiding something from him, though he knew better than to ask for any more information. If she wanted to talk about it, she would...in her own time.

And Kiki probably was grinding her teeth right now and wishing she could be putting in her own two cents on the plan, but since Kara had drafted her little sister to mind the store, there wasn't any worry that she'd be butting in any time soon. Oddly, Jeff had opted to hang out with Kiki at the UFO Depot rather than come over here, but Lance couldn't worry about that right now. If Jeff wanted to play footsie with the girl, that was his problem.

"On the map, it looks as if the canyon dead-ends, but it doesn't." Grayson was tracing his finger along the paper, pointing to the spot in question. "You can continue on through here, come in through this narrow ravine until you're at the upper end of Secret. From there, it's only about five hundred yards to the service entrance I told you about."

"Hmm," Paul murmured, then looked up from the map and frowned at Lance. "You getting all this?"

"Sure." Just because it might have looked as if he was woolgathering didn't mean he hadn't been paying attention all along. "So we drop Grayson in Boynton, have him go in wearing normal hiking gear. He can carry the jumpsuit and other...items...in his backpack, and then change inside the ravine where he can't be spotted from the air."

"Sounds good," Grayson said. His whole

demeanor had begun to subtly change, his jaw harder, eyes narrower. Despite the shocking difference of the green eyes, he was beginning to look a lot more like the hybrids who had been shooting at Lance and company back during their first encounter with the aliens. "From there, I'll just wait until I have an opening. With any luck, there'll be a shipment coming in. Usually that involves enough people coming and going that I should be able to join in without anyone noticing."

"You sure about that?" Paul asked. "Because Persephone was pretty clear about how the hybrids all seemed to be psychically linked somehow. Won't they be able to tell that you're no longer...like them?"

Damn. Lance hadn't even thought of that. He scowled at this new complication, but Grayson appeared untroubled.

"No. At least, I don't think so. We—they aren't telepaths, not in the true sense of the word. We can link consciousnesses to achieve some common goal, but it isn't as if we—they—are connected at every moment. And the thing is, I can still feel them out there."

"You *what?*" Lance demanded. "Since when?"

"Since yesterday, when Persephone put me under. I don't know why, but for some reason, the trance she initiated affected me differently from the one the other hypnotherapist performed. Maybe it's because Persephone is a psychic. Anyway, when I came out of it, I could sense them again. Faintly, just like a pulse at the edge of my mind, but definitely there."

"So why the hell didn't you tell us?"

"You didn't ask."

Paul made a noise that was probably meant to sound like a throat-clearing but which Lance guessed was a smothered laugh. In his corner, Michael smiled serenely, like the world's first Native American Buddha impersonator.

"Okay, fine," Lance gritted. "So maybe your change in mental status isn't going to register with them. If you do manage to get in, what then?"

For the first time, Grayson looked a little hesitant. "Well, the lower levels aren't going to do us much good. They're storage, holding cells, that sort of thing. Levels Four and Five are where most of the labs are located. I don't know what they're up to—"

"Power," said Paul.

"What?" Grayson responded, obviously confused.

"In your session yesterday, you said they were here because of power. What power? What does that mean? The vortexes?"

"I...I don't know."

Somehow, Lance managed to keep his eyes from rolling. "No clue at all."

Grayson didn't so much shake his head as lower it a little, as if he found something intensely fascinating in the contours of the topographical map spread out on the table below him. "I don't know where that came from. Sorry. Maybe it didn't mean anything. Anyway, I know where the labs are, but I was never assigned to those levels, so I don't know what's actually in them. It just seems to me that would be a logical place to start. That, or the power-generating station on Level Nine."

"Which is...?"

"A fusion reactor."

Paul swore under his breath, then said, "I'm not going to contemplate the irony of us wanting to blow up a fusion reactor when it's the sort of technology our world so desperately needs."

Lance shrugged. "The world's in more immediate need of saving right now. We can figure out the whole environmentally friendly energy thing later. "

The physicist looked more than a little pained, but he didn't bother to contradict Lance.

Grayson said in neutral tones, "If I can get to the labs, of course they're my first choice as a target."

"Okay," Lance replied.

So...drop Grayson off at the far edge of Boynton, make sure he gets on his way to the ravine that connects the two canyons, hope he can get himself inside and to an area where some high-level explosives can do some good. Piece of cake.

He didn't bother to articulate the many things that could go wrong with this plan, starting with

Grayson getting captured the second he emerged from the ravine and going downhill from there. But Grayson was the only viable asset they had. Lance knew he didn't stand a snowball's chance in hell of getting inside himself. They'd managed that once. Once. And he still didn't know whether that was blind luck or Persephone's guardian angel—or whatever he was—doing his own version of the Jedi mind trick so the aliens wouldn't notice the interlopers getting inside. Somehow, though, he had the feeling that guardian angels might not look on an infiltrate-and-destroy mission in the same light as they would a simple rescue.

"Okay," he said. "I think we're getting there. The soonest we'll have Grayson's replacement uniform is Friday, so I suggest we all just hang tight until then. And if anyone comes up with any enhancements to the plan, any more ideas, we can reconvene here. All right?"

The other three variously nodded or murmured their assent, and the meeting broke up, Michael driving Grayson back to the shabby house down by the creek, Lance heading home to his condo. He wanted to talk to Kara, but she hadn't said when she would be back in town. Besides, the UFO Depot didn't exactly lend itself to private conversation.

Waiting. More waiting. He didn't like it, but he'd survive.

Somehow, he always did.

CHAPTER EIGHTEEN

Kara

IT WAS WELL PAST TWO BY THE TIME I PULLED into the parking lot of the UFO Depot. I saw the store's UFO Night Tours van parked there, but not Jeff's equally shabby Ram van, which meant he must have gotten bored with hanging around the shop and taken off for greener pastures, whatever those might be. Thank God. I felt a little bit better after spending more than an hour with Persephone, getting reassurances from my friend that everyone would stick with me no matter what happened, but still, the knowledge of what I carried within me seemed to weigh down every footstep. Better to not have to deal with Jeff Makowski on top of all that as well.

I was a little worried that Kiki might be irritated by how long I'd been away, but she looked remarkably cheerful as I entered the store, which was otherwise empty.

"Hey, Kara," she called out, "you just missed your friend."

"My 'friend'?" I echoed, puzzled. But at least I could assume from Kiki's breezy demeanor that she hadn't noticed anything odd about my expression or manner.

"Yeah, one of our friendly neighborhood MIBs. You might have told me he was that cute, though."

"He—I—what?" Somehow the remark didn't seem to want to process through my already muddled brain cells.

"Yep, he stopped in for a little chat. Seemed a little concerned that you weren't back from Taos yet."

"'Taos'?" I repeated.

For the first time, Kiki's grin slipped a little bit. "Yeah, you know, where our mother is supposedly hanging out these days. Don't worry—I covered for you. I don't think he noticed anything."

I didn't quite sigh in relief. Kiki might have had her faults, but she'd always been pretty good about thinking on her feet. "Oh, that."

"Yes, *that*."

It was pretty clear that Kiki was less than thrilled I hadn't bothered to tell her about our mother's latest location. With everything that had been going on, it had completely slipped my mind. Besides, I didn't know for certain whether the agent had even been telling me the truth.

Hedging, I said, "Okay, he might have said something about that, but I had no reason to believe him. Besides, you swore to me on your twenty-first birthday that you wouldn't stop to dump a bucket of water on her if you found her on fire in the street. So maybe I just didn't see the point in relaying information about her whereabouts that might or might not even be accurate."

A scowl creased Kiki's brow, but then it smoothed itself away as she sighed. "Yeah, okay, I guess I did say that. But it was after about four shots of Cuervo, if I recall correctly."

Actually, I was sort of surprised that my little sister remembered even that much of the evening, considering the way the beer and tequila had flowed during her birthday party. "Was Jeff here when the agent came in?"

"Nope. He got bored, said he was going back to the apartment so he could do a remote login, check on some stuff he left running in L.A."

From Kiki's expression, I got the impression that she wasn't too happy with Jeff's defection. However, what had she expected? There was only so much you could do while hanging out at the UFO Depot; I didn't even have wifi set up, but plugged my laptop directly into the cable modem when I needed to use the internet.

"Well, I'm sorry my trip took me longer than I thought it would," I said. "But I'm here now, so you can take off if you want. Looks like it's been pretty quiet."

For a few seconds, Kiki didn't say anything, but just rustled a few papers on the counter. Then, "Are you going to tell me what's going on?"

I blinked. "What?"

"Sorry, Kara, but you're not a very good liar. I can tell something's bothering you. And then you take off for hours and don't say anything about where you're going or what you're doing, and that isn't like you."

No, it wasn't. Kiki and I shared almost everything, although there had been a gradual moving apart ever since she got her own place. Which was to be expected, but now I hesitated. As much as I wanted to confide in my sister, I knew I needed to talk to Grayson first, and then Lance. After that....

I'll worry about that after I've survived those two encounters. Everyone will know sooner or later, but....

"Just stuff," I said lightly. "I'm worried about what they're plotting, what they're going to try to make Grayson do. Or rather, what he's going to volunteer to do out of some misplaced sense of nobility. That's all."

Kiki looked spectacularly unconvinced, but she just shrugged and pulled her purse out from its hiding place in a cubbyhole beneath the sales counter. "If you say so." And she slung her bag over her shoulder and marched out, obviously annoyed.

Well, there wasn't anything else I could do at the moment. I could only wait for the day to end so I could close up the shop and go talk to Grayson. What the hell I was going to say to him, I had absolutely no idea. I had a feeling that no matter what I came up with, it wouldn't be enough.

———

At least at this time of year, the light lingered until almost eight o'clock, which meant the sun hadn't even begun to set by the time I locked up the shop and got on the road at a little past six-thirty. I'd called Michael on his cell and confirmed that he and Grayson were back home at Michael's place. Better to do this there, where we might have a little privacy. It sounded as if Lance had stayed behind at the Olivers' to go over a few more things, and I was fine with that, too. If he was still with Paul, then I wouldn't have to worry about him calling me, wanting to see me.

Apparently, Michael had told Grayson I was on my way, because he was standing in the open front door, watching me as I locked the car and made my way up the front walk. His expression was curiously neutral, expressing neither happiness at seeing me nor irritation at the intrusion. In fact, as I looked at him, for the first time I could see something of the blankness Persephone had described in the hybrids but had never before noticed in Grayson's features.

I swallowed. This was probably going to be even harder than I'd thought.

"Do you mind if we walk down by the creek?" I asked.

He didn't appear surprised by the request. "No."

Instead of leading me through the house, he stepped outside and then went down the driveway and through the gate into the backyard. From there, we picked up the narrow trail that wandered through the cottonwoods, sycamores, and pines until it reached the creek bed. The chatter of the water seemed somehow reassuring to me, as if telling me that it was continuing as it always had, and that there was no real reason for worry.

I wouldn't go so far as to say that, I thought, and smiled grimly.

"So, what is it?" Grayson asked after we'd paused a few feet from the edge of the stream. "If you're going to try to talk me out of going back to the base, don't bother. You and I both know they have to be stopped."

"No, I know that." I swallowed, wishing I'd thought to bring a bottle of water with me. For some reason, my throat felt horribly dry, even though it was relatively cool and moist here next to the creek.

"I just wish you didn't think the only way to go in there is some sort of suicide mission."

A muscle in his cheek tightened as he looked away from me. His eyes seemed even greener here as they reflected the shifting hues of the cottonwoods all around us. "I've been in there. I'm remembering more and more every day. Believe me when I tell you that I'll be lucky enough just to make it inside. I can't expect my luck to hold long enough to let me get back out again."

If there had been a note of defeat in his voice, of worry or sadness, it might have been easier to take. But he spoke calmly, without a trace of self-pity, as if he'd just woken up to the fact that he'd been designed as an expendable soldier and so couldn't hope for any other outcome.

I looked away from Grayson then. If he was so eager to walk away from this world, then maybe it would be better if I didn't tell him at all. What difference would it make? He wouldn't be around to see the child he'd helped to create.

No. That was the coward's way out. He deserved to know. He *should* know, even if in the end it changed nothing.

Voice steady, I said, "I'm pregnant."

Clearly, that had been the last thing he'd expected me to tell him. He turned back toward me, eyes widening, gaze fastening on me as if he was waiting for me to deliver some sort of follow-up, some explanation as to why the child couldn't possibly be his.

No, it can't possibly be anyone else's....

"I went to get an official test today, just to be sure," I continued. "They said I'm about three weeks along. I'd say that was crazy, but since I know it's yours, I suppose anything is possible."

He didn't say anything for a few seconds, then murmured, "Accelerated growth."

"What?"

His mouth pulled into an unwilling smile before he replied, "That's how they do it with us hybrids. You don't think they're going to wait twenty, thirty years for us to reach the peak of our physical development, do you? No, they make sure we're ready to go in just about six months. I don't know for sure, of course, but I'm guessing I'm only about eighteen months old."

The nausea returned out of nowhere, and I stumbled a few paces to a cottonwood tree, put a hand out to it to steady myself. If I'd stopped to think about it, maybe such a notion would have occurred to me. But to realize that Grayson, who had all the outward appearance of someone in his early thirties, might have been in existence for only a year and a half simply floored me.

If he was unnerved by my lack of a reply, he didn't show it. He went on, speaking simply, "So I guess it makes some sort of sense that the development of your unborn child would also be accelerated. Not to that extent, since it's half human, but some alteration of the gestation period is to be expected."

"Alteration of the—" I broke off, staring at him. "Grayson, I'm carrying your child. How can you be so—so—"

"So what? Cold? Detached?" That grim smile had never left his lips. "We both know I won't be here to see this child grow up, so what do you expect me to say? I'll admit I'm a little surprised—you'd think the aliens would have made sure all their hybrids were sterile—but maybe they simply thought the opportunity for one of us to interact sexually with a human female would never arise."

The wave of sickness passed as quickly as it had come, and I made myself breathe deeply several times before I dared to say anything. "So don't—don't you feel anything at all about this?"

"Are you going to keep it?"

"Yes."

For the first time, the mask of indifference slipped a little, and I could see the desperate hope in his expression, the realization that this one part of him would somehow survive. I took a little heart from that, and let go of the tree and moved toward him. Without stopping to think, I reached out and took his hand, placed it against the still-flat contours of my stomach.

"Whatever happens, some part of you will always be with us," I said.

He moved his fingers against me, wonder in his eyes. I realized then that what I'd feared was a regression to the behavior and personality—or lack thereof—from the time when he was only a simple drone for the aliens was really not that at all. It was only a desperate defense against the fear gnawing at him, the knowledge that he would have to give up the humanity he'd gained so as to make the world safe for everyone else.

"Thank you," he said.

I stared up at him.

"Thank you for not hiding this from me. It would have been easy enough. In a few days...." The words trailed off, the resulting silence lying heavy between us. "I already knew what I was fighting for, but this just strengthens that belief." He took my hands in his. "They can't ever find out about this child, Kara. If they did—if they knew such a thing was possible— I don't want to know what they'd do with that information."

Such a thing hadn't even occurred to me, but as I gazed into Grayson's taut, strained features, I realized he was right. The aliens had already shown they were more than happy to pervert the natural order of life on earth. What use they could make of a human/hybrid child, I had no idea...but I did know I would do whatever I must to conceal my child's origins.

"They'll never find out," I told him, voice firm even though worry had already begun to gnaw at me. True, Lance and Jeff and everyone else were experts at keeping secrets, but a baby wasn't something you could exactly hide. I'd just have to trust that they would come up with some kind of explanation for my child. "We can take care of things. I promise."

He nodded, although he didn't look all that convinced. "Does anyone else know?"

"Just Persephone," I told him. "I—I needed a friend to talk to. But I knew I should tell you before I talked to anyone else."

His fingers tightened around mine, just for a second or two, and then he let go. "I wish...." He shook his head. "Never mind. I'm just glad I could know you, if only for a short time." He bent down and kissed me very gently on the forehead. Before I could respond, he had turned and begun moving swiftly up the path, back toward Michael's house. It was abrupt, but I thought I understood.

I had never been all that great at goodbyes, either.

Lance

He left the Olivers' place just after seven, declining an invitation to stay to dinner—"We're getting deli takeout from Whole Foods, so no worries about Persephone's cooking"—at which comment Persephone had shot Paul a mock-evil glare but then shrugged. After so many hours sequestered in Paul's office, though, Lance needed a change of scenery. Besides, he hadn't heard from Kara all day.

He called the house, since he figured that was where she should be at this time. The shop closed at six, although sometimes she got stuck there late if she had enough of a crowd at closing time and wanted to see if she could squeeze a few more bucks out of the tourists at the end of the day. But the house phone just rang and rang before rolling over to the ancient answering machine she still used for her landline, so he called her cell.

Kara picked up on the third ring. "Hi, Lance."

She sounded tired. No, she sounded drained, as if whatever she'd gone through that day had put her through the wringer.

"You all right?" he asked.

A pause. "Yes, I'm okay. It's been a long day."

"Apparently. I thought you'd be home by now."

"I'm almost there. I was planning to call you when I got in."

Her conversation still felt strange to him, as if she was saying the things she thought he expected her to say and not what she was really thinking. "Do you want me to swing by India Palace and get some takeout?"

A little sigh. "Um, sure. Actually, that sounds great. Chicken korma?"

"You got it."

"Great. I'll see you in a little while."

He pushed the "end" button on the phone and tossed it on the passenger seat, wondering exactly what was going on. Well, he supposed he'd find out soon enough.

India Palace was crowded—apparently he and Kara weren't the only people with a yen for takeout that evening—so he didn't arrive at her place until almost half an hour later. He parked the Jeep in the driveway and got out. It had rained late that afternoon while he was at the Olivers', and the warm air was thick with the peculiarly pungent smell of damp asphalt, overlaid with a sweet scent that must have been the roses blooming in her neighbor's front yard.

He went to the front door and rang the bell. Kara hadn't offered him a key yet, and he hadn't asked. Too soon, probably, and it was a step she would have to take. He wouldn't presume anything, no matter what might have passed between them.

Gort barked on the other side of the door, and a minute later, Kara opened it. Surprisingly, she didn't look as wrung out as he'd been expecting. She'd pulled her hair back into a ponytail, which was unusual for her, but otherwise, she seemed to be more or less herself. Maybe she'd gotten her second wind.

"Dinner," he said, and raised the bag of take-out in a half salute.

"Great," she replied, moving out of the way so he could come inside. "I'm starved. Gort, get out from underfoot."

The shepherd mix obliged by moving a scant ten inches off to one side, his nose working overtime as he tried not to be too obvious about sniffing at the riches of chicken korma and brown rice and naan and samosas.

"Not a chance in hell, Gort," Lance said, and the dog backed away a little bit more.

Kara looked almost guilty. "Well, sometimes I let him lick the take-out container afterward. Korma isn't spicy enough to bother him."

That was Kara for you. The way she spoiled that dog was nuts, but also sort of endearing. Or maybe he thought it was endearing now because of the way he felt about her.

He wasn't sure what to think of that, so he only followed her into the dining room, where she'd already set out plates and silverware. A wine glass sat by his place setting at the head of the table, but he noticed Kara didn't have one for herself.

"Not drinking tonight?"

For some reason, she flushed slightly. "No—I'm so tired, I think I'd pass out with my head in my food if I tried to drink anything. But I've got a bottle of pinot grigio already open in the fridge, so if you want some...."

"Sure," he replied, mostly because he couldn't think of a good reason to say no.

She went to get it, and he got the take-out food set up using the large serving spoons she'd already laid out on the table. Gort took up his position on the rug, perfectly centered between their two chairs. Lance smothered a grin.

"Here you go," she said, coming back into the room. She poured him a little more than half a glass, then sat down in her own seat.

He watched her as he settled the napkin in his lap, took his first sip of wine. On the surface, she seemed fine, but he noticed the way her movements looked just a little jerky, as if she was filled with some sort of nervous energy that had nothing to do with her overall level of weariness.

"So how was the council of war?" she asked before spearing a chunk of chicken and putting it in her mouth.

"I think we have things mostly worked out," he replied carefully. If there was any way of keeping the details of the mission from Kara, he'd try to do so... but he sort of doubted she'd let herself be kept in the dark for too long.

"And you all are just fine with sending Grayson off to his death?"

The set of her jaw told him she was a long ways from giving up on the subject. "Kara, you don't know that's what's going to happen. None of us know."

"But it's a distinct possibility."

"Yes."

She didn't reply, instead stabbing at the korma with sharp little movements of her fork. Her eyes were suspiciously bright.

He really hadn't wanted this confrontation, but he knew he'd have to have it out with her sooner or later. "Kara, he's the only one who can do it."

"According to you."

"According to all of us. The aliens know what Paul and Michael and I look like. They know what Persephone looks like. None of us are going to get within a hundred yards of that place, and you know it. Hell, I doubt we could get within a half mile. Grayson can because he looks like every other one of their soldiers."

"But not his eyes."

"Colored contacts. Luckily, the biometric scans are for the hybrids' thumbprints, not their eyes. It should work."

She didn't reply, but reached out for a piece of naan and tore it viciously in half, dunking a piece in the korma sauce and then pausing with it partway to her mouth. At length, she said, "*Should* work."

"Nothing is guaranteed. But it's the best shot we have. And we should all be glad that Persephone apparently made them more than a little cautious about us and what we're capable of, or we'd be having to worry about alien-infected agents roaming the streets of Sedona. They're not here, which means they're not really surveilling us. Not yet. But if we let them keep going, let them build things back up to where they were in March—well, we're all going to be in a world of hurt. Not just you and Paul and Persephone and Michael, and probably Kiki and Jeff, but everyone in Sedona. Everyone in the world. Grayson seems to understand that. So why don't you?"

Her shoulders slumped, and she dropped the piece of naan on her plate. Then he saw a tear roll down one cheek, followed by another. They dripped onto the tablecloth, making dark, muddy-looking splotches on the clay-colored fabric.

Oh, shit.

It wasn't her crying. He wasn't one of those men who freaked out if a woman dared to shed a few tears over something. No, it was that those tears must mean she still felt a lot more for Grayson than she'd let on. That she hadn't really let him go.

Even though he hadn't meant it to, his voice hardened a bit. "You're not over him, are you?"

She looked up then. Her nose was a little red, but otherwise, she didn't appear to be the type who completely fell apart when she cried. "It's not that."

"Then what is it?"

A pause. Then she stared straight at him and said, "I'm pregnant."

It really didn't sink in at first. He gazed back at her, noting how the tears had already begun to dry up, that her full mouth was uncharacteristically tight. Then it hit him, those two words that could change your life in a way no others could. "You're *what?*"

"I went to Prescott today, to Planned Parenthood. They confirmed it."

"But we—it's only been—"

"It's not yours, Lance. It's Grayson's."

He'd been through too much in his life to let anything completely unnerve him, but even so, he had to force himself to sit still, to let himself absorb the idea. Kara, carrying the child of a human/alien hybrid.

"Even so—" he began.

"Accelerated development," she said, in a tight little voice that didn't sound very much like hers. "At least, that's what Grayson told me."

"So he knows."

"Of course. He has a right to know."

Probably he did, but what would this knowledge do to the hybrid? Would he be able to follow through with their plans, knowing that he'd be leaving behind the woman carrying his child?

Something in his face must have betrayed his thoughts, because Kara shook her head and said,

"Don't worry, Lance. It hasn't changed anything for him. If anything, it's only made him more determined."

"It has?"

"I guess he wants to make the world is safe for his child."

"So you're...that is...." Lance stopped himself before he could complete the sentence. Jesus, how was he supposed to ask her if she was going to get an abortion?

"I'm keeping the baby, if that's what you mean. I don't expect you to understand."

Proud words, but as he looked at her, he knew she wanted more than anything for him to understand, for him to tell her it was all right and that he'd stick with her no matter what happened. And, crazy as it might sound, he knew he would. He'd never expected to have children, thought all that business about having someone to carry on the family line was just stupid. If Kara had had a child with that jerk Alan, Lance would have accepted the situation. Everyone had their baggage. Some of it just weighed more.

He smiled at her, noting her surprise at the alteration in his expression. "Well, let's hope the baby doesn't come out green or gray or something. But if it does...."

"If it does...." she said, hope beginning to light those gorgeous dark blue eyes of hers.

He reached out and took her hand, felt how chilly her fingers were. She needed some warming up.

Soon.

Tone casual, he finished, "If it does, I can't think of a better place than Sedona to raise a pale green quarter-alien baby. Can you?"

In answer, she got up out of her seat and went to him, wrapping her arms around him, the soft scent of her perfume or her hair or whatever it was filling the air. He held her, pulled her close, tried to let her know by his embrace that he wouldn't lecture or condemn, wouldn't do anything except show her that he would be there for her.

By the quick, jagged little breath she took, and the tightening of the embrace, he thought she did.

CHAPTER NINETEEN

Kara

WE DESIGNATED SUNDAY AS THE DAY TO infiltrate the alien base, partly because Lance wanted more time to go over the plan, but also because I put my foot down and told everyone in no uncertain terms that I refused to be stuck at the store while something so important was going down. I knew I could have closed the shop on Saturday if necessary, but it would have looked suspicious after so many closures in such a short amount of time. The thought of Agent Martin Jones hanging around, asking more questions, did not appeal. Never mind that Kiki thought he was cute. Cute or not, he didn't need to be poking his nose into our business any more than he already had.

By that time, everyone knew about my situation,

and luckily, no one had really commented on it... maybe because Lance made it clear that he'd make things extremely unpleasant for anyone who tried to question me too closely. Kiki had been flabbergasted, but apparently she saw from my expression that I wasn't going to be talked out of my decision.

"So I'm going to be an aunt," she mused. "'Kiki' doesn't sound very aunt-ish. I've been thinking about going back to Kirsten. Maybe people will take me more seriously as a Kirsten."

"Maybe," I said cautiously. What I really thought was that a small child could manage "Kiki" better than "Kirsten"—my sister's nickname had come about in the first place because as a toddler, she kept lisping her given name. But I wasn't going to worry about it. For all I knew, the baby would emerge with its intellectual development far ahead that of a normal human infant's and would be doing differential equations during potty training.

All that aside, I did feel better now everyone knew about my situation, especially after Paul informed me that he was acquainted with a woman in New Mexico who "specialized in this sort of thing."

"That is, she's an RN with midwife certification who's helped other women who've had half-alien children." His voice was matter-of-fact as he told me this, as if such a thing wasn't completely nuts. Thank God for scientific detachment. He hadn't bothered to add, *Those women who were allowed to keep their children.* We both knew that for every woman who actually managed to bear such a child and raise it, there were many more whose pregnancies were mysteriously terminated, or who remembered giving birth but never saw their children. He said, "I'll make contact with her after—that is—" And there he broke off and looked almost confused, for him.

After the mission is over and Grayson is dead, I thought, but of course I didn't say the words out loud. No, I managed to smile and reply, "Thank you, Paul. Obviously this isn't going to be a normal pregnancy, so knowing that I'll have an expert to help me through it makes me feel much better."

Not that I really felt all that great. The nausea came and went, along with spells of weariness that seemed to drag down my every movement. If it was this bad now, when no one could even tell I was pregnant, what was it going to be like as the baby got bigger and bigger? Such accelerated development would have to take its toll somehow. But even though I relayed this information to Paul, who passed it along to the R.N. in New Mexico and got in reply that these things were perfectly normal, all things considered, and that I should switch to prenatal vitamins and get plenty of rest, I couldn't help worrying. I was in uncharted territory now, and even though I instinctively felt I was doing the right thing, I couldn't help being more than a little freaked out.

Thank God for Lance. I hadn't expected him to be so understanding, so seemingly free of jealousy over me carrying another man's child. And when I'd tried to press him on the issue, he'd only shrugged and said, "I want you, Kara. I've wasted enough time already. I won't let this come between us."

It should have been enough. Maybe it would be, one day.

Now, though, I sat with the others in Paul and Persephone's living room and tried not to notice most of them watching me, as if they'd halfway expected me to already be sporting a noticeable baby bump. That would come soon enough, probably, but even if the baby was developing at roughly three times its normal rate, it wouldn't be enough for me to be showing yet.

Grayson came into the room, and I had to force myself not to gasp. Persephone had vaguely mentioned something about "making sure he looked the part," but I hadn't realized what that meant until now. His hair was cut short in a severe military style, and he wore brown contact lenses to hide the brilliant green of his eyes. Although I knew the plan was for him to change into hiking gear as part of his disguise, now he wore the black jumpsuit Lance had ordered, probably to check the fit and overall look of the outfit one last time.

Even though I hadn't been with the group that infiltrated the alien base the first time, I could tell

Grayson's current appearance was just a little too close to the mark. Paul's eyes narrowed, and Persephone paled before reaching out to take her husband's hand. Michael nodded, as if in approval. And Lance—well, he only sat up even straighter next to me on the couch before saying,

"Looks good. Seph, looks like you've got a second career as a hairstylist lined up if the whole psychic thing doesn't work out for you."

She made a sour face. "Very funny. Not much involved—we got some clippers at a beauty supply store, and I looked up how to do it online. I don't think I'm going to give my stylist a run for her money any time soon."

Grayson looked a little puzzled, but then he glanced down at himself and smoothed his hands over the waist of the jumpsuit. "It's really close. Your seamstress did a good job."

Lance's tone sharpened. "Close, but not exact?"

"The fabric feels a little softer, but it looks right. I doubt anyone will get close enough to feel it...and if they do, I'm going to have more important things to worry about."

The words were spoken carelessly enough, but I knew the bravado was only for show. His muscular frame seemed to fairly radiate nervous energy, like a spring that had been wound too tightly. And what would happen when he finally blew?

I wished I could go to him, put my arms around

him and let him know that I didn't consider him expendable, that someone in this world cared about what happened to him. Right then, though, that didn't sound very feasible, and besides, something in the set of his jaw told me he probably wouldn't be too receptive to that sort of display. No, I would have to hold on to what had passed between us at the creek and hope it would be enough.

Lance looked at his watch. "It's almost two. Are you ready?"

Grayson nodded. "Yes. I'll go and change."

He left the room, and I crossed my arms and said, "So you're really going ahead with this."

My words had been directed at Lance, but, surprisingly, it was Persephone who answered. "I don't think we have much choice. Grayson knows what he's doing. I don't feel anything from him but determination."

Of course you wouldn't, because that's what he is feeling. Never mind whether it's right or wrong.

I knew any further protests would only be met with more of this unwavering calm, this certainty of the path ahead. From where she sat on the love seat, Kiki looked troubled. She wouldn't protest, though, not when everyone else seemed so determined. I couldn't even say whether that was a good thing or not. At some point, you just had to let things take their course...whatever that meant.

Grayson returned, this time wearing a T-shirt,

khaki cargo shorts, and brown hiking boots, a Sun
Devils baseball cap covering his freshly shorn hair.
From one hand hung an innocuous-looking gray
backpack. You'd never guess that pack carried more
than twenty pounds of C-4.

Before I even realized what I was doing, I'd risen
to my feet and gone to Grayson. "You get in and out,"
I whispered fiercely. "No heroics. Got that?"

He nodded, but I could tell from his expression
that he did so only to humor me. For a few seconds,
he hesitated, and then he placed his hand on my
stomach, so quickly, an onlooker would have missed
the movement altogether if they hadn't been
watching closely. "You be careful, too."

And then he turned and said to Paul, "I'm
ready."

Paul had already been standing at the edge of the
room, car keys dangling from his hand. They'd
decided Paul would be the one to drive Grayson to
the drop-off point. Lance would remain here, to be
their remote lookout, as it were. Not much fun for
Paul, who would have to loiter near the hiking trail in
Boynton in case Grayson actually did make it back
out again, but Paul had already said he wouldn't just
dump Grayson there and then leave.

Persephone wasn't overly thrilled with this part
of the plan, although she'd kept her protests to a
minimum. The risk for Paul wasn't all that huge—
he'd be near a known hiking trail, in an area that got

enough traffic that he should be safe enough during daylight hours. Still, I understood all too well the strained expression on the psychic's face, the worry that the man she cared about was putting himself at risk.

Whereas Lance....

He stood off to one side, next to the fireplace, and he was giving Michael a run for the "great stone face" competition. Whatever he might be thinking, he wasn't showing it. Maybe he'd been willing to put himself in harm's way. But he was more valuable here, because he was the only one with even a chance of seeing what was going on and reporting back on it. Persephone's clairvoyance wasn't reliable enough for something as important as this.

I stared across the room at Grayson. He looked more like himself in his current getup, but dark contact lenses covered the green eyes I'd thought so striking, and his regular features were so still, they might as well be a mask. For an instant, I thought I saw something pass over his face, swift and subtle as cloud shadows racing over the desert floor, but I couldn't begin to say what it was.

He pulled a pair of sunglasses out of his pocket and put them on, covering those unfamiliar dark eyes.

"Let's do this," he said.

Lance

He'd been less than happy about being left behind, even though he understood the reasoning behind the decision. As Persephone had said many times, she wasn't technically a clairvoyant. She could see things sometimes, but the visions came and went at their own whim, and not by her control. So naturally it fell to him, the only one with this sort of training, to give the group their sole window into what was happening out beyond Boynton Canyon.

They sat around the Olivers' dining room table, hands clasped together as if they were holding an old-time séance. This had actually been Michael's idea.

"Transmit it to Persephone and me," he'd told Lance, "and we'll pass it along to the rest."

Lance had been more than a little skeptical, especially since he wasn't sure he'd be able to maintain focus while experiencing that sort of contact, but damned if he hadn't felt something similar to a small but powerful electric current running down his arms and into Michael's and Persephone's fingers. That charge seemed to make its way around the group as they laced their fingers in one another's, eliciting a startled gasp from Kara and a muttered "what the hell?" from Jeff Makowski.

But Lance didn't have time to think about any of that, didn't have time to do anything but let his mind drift free from his body, let that finely tuned part of his consciousness break loose, moving across the hot sand and scrubby mesquite and juniper, focusing at last on a narrow trail, hardly more than a track, and the silver pickup truck moving along it. A sign announced the location of the trail head, and there was a slightly wider spot in the road where you could park. The pickup stopped there, and two men got out.

Paul wore the Aussie digger hat that no one had the courage to tell him made him look more than a little foolish, while Grayson still had on the Sun Devils baseball cap. They appeared to converse for a moment, and then Grayson set off along the trail. Paul removed his hat, ran his hand through his hair, and replaced the hat. He was probably wishing the monsoon rains from the day before would return.

No such luck, though; the day was mercilessly bright. Paul leaned up against the pickup, on the side that afforded a little shade because of the junipers growing next to the trail head, and settled down to wait.

Shifting focus, Lance watched as Grayson moved sure-footed over the rocky trail, rising as it headed farther back into the canyon. The rock walls to either side seemed to move ever closer to one another as the way narrowed, and the spot was further choked with manzanita and even the odd scrubby pine. But the hybrid kept walking quickly, pack slung casually over one shoulder as if he carried nothing more threatening than a few spare water bottles, a fresh T-shirt, and a GPS tracker.

At length, though, he reached the spot they had determined would be best to change out of his hiking gear and into the uniform all the hybrids wore. He did so with an easy economy of movement, stripping off the shorts and T-shirt, removing the baseball cap...and strapping the C-4 to his body, around his waist and to each thigh, before pulling the jumpsuit over everything. The little blocks of C-4, designed to be inconspicuous, did not even show up as bulges once he was fully dressed again.

Down the table, Kara made a frightened little sound, but Lance ignored it. No, they hadn't told her about that part of the plan, but really, what had she expected? It wasn't as if the hybrids walked around carrying backpacks, and Grayson had to get the explosives into the base somehow.

The image wavered slightly, and Lance set his jaw, focusing only on the half-alien man, on the way he carefully stuffed the backpack out of sight among several clumps of manzanita before he headed back up the trail again, moving ever closer to the junction with the narrow ravine that would lead him down into Secret Canyon and the back entrance to the base. It felt darker here, although the sun was still high in the sky. It was only the canyon walls leaning in toward one another high above. Or maybe it was something else...the dark energy from the alien stronghold flowing outward and touching the territory all around it.

A fancy, and one Lance wouldn't allow himself to entertain. Watch. Observe. He was only a set of eyes, a camera to transmit the images to everyone else in the group. Faintly, he was aware of Michael's rough, firm grip on his left hand, and Persephone's warm, delicate fingers on his right. Because of them, he could feel his own power amplified, strengthening and sharpening the vision so it was clearer than any remote viewing he had ever done.

Grayson's steps slowed. It seemed he had begun the final approach to the base, and so he moved with extreme caution, going from one outcropping to the next, using the stunted manzanita bushes as cover as he inched ever closer. At last, he came to the spot where the ravine opened out into a narrow little canyon, a place that should have been just as deserted as the narrow defile through which he'd just come...but which hummed with activity.

Two soft-sided trucks, obviously some kind of Army surplus vehicles, were backed up to the loading dock, which yawned open. Because of the angle of the light, you couldn't see what was inside, but there was no mistaking the forms of the men loading boxes off the truck, putting them on some sort of odd hand trucks that floated a few inches off the rocky ground rather than rolling along it, and moving the hand carts inside.

Every single one of those men looked just like Grayson.

Persephone's fingers tightened on Lance's, and from across the table, there was a sudden intake of breath that could have only come from Kara, but other than that, everyone remained still, their minds turned inward, focusing on the impossible images flowing into their brains. Lance breathed in as well, maintaining the focus, not allowing himself to think of anything except the scene playing itself out on the flickering movie screen inside his mind.

Grayson was hesitating, watching the ebb and flow of the men who wore his face as they went about their business. After a few minutes, they seemed to be finished with unloading the truck. Two of them closed it up, got in, and drove away, down a barely perceptible track that seemed to lead back toward Boynton. Four remained in place to guard the entrance, just as Grayson had described in his last hypnosis session with Persephone.

That stance Lance remembered all too clearly— feet slightly apart, hands on the guns at their hips, dark eyes blank and yet at the same time piercing, scanning the area like a laser-guided burglar alarm. The hybrids weren't the kind of soldiers who would get bored and start chatting about baseball scores or getting drunk or their last lay. No, they would remain fixed in place, implacable, unswerving.

Once again, he could feel Persephone's grip tensing on his, and this time it didn't relax. He didn't blame her for being worried, but he couldn't think about that right now. There was nothing any of them could do for Grayson, except hope that the combination of his hybrid reflexes and strangely human mind would be enough for him to get the drop on them.

Even as this thought passed through Lance's mind, Grayson walked out of the ravine, in full view of the four hybrids guarding the service entrance. What the hell?

Something must have passed between them mentally, because none of them made any hostile moves or did anything but acknowledge him with a nod so faint, it was barely perceptible. He approached them, hands obviously empty, nothing but another of their brethren, come perhaps to beef up the detail or to relieve one of them.

And then....

So quickly Lance still wasn't sure exactly what he was seeing, a knife came flying from seemingly nowhere and buried itself in one of the hybrid soldiers' throats. The other three reacted swiftly, soundlessly, closing on Grayson at once, but with another flick, this time of his left hand, a second knife flashed through the air and lodged itself in yet another jugular. The soldier dropped, and the remaining two were on Grayson.

Or rather, they were on the space he had previously occupied. He'd dropped to the ground, swung out with one leg, toppling the soldier closest to him. A muffled blast, and the hybrid fell away, blood pouring from a gaping hole in his chest. This time, the last soldier standing did manage to draw his weapon, but another muzzle flared, and he fell, too, bleeding from the stomach. For good measure, Grayson reached out and snapped his neck with one swift motion before rising to his feet. A quick glance downward—apparently to make sure none of his erstwhile compatriots' blood had gotten on his uniform—and then he was dragging them away from the door, shoving the bodies behind a pile of boulders that sat to one side of the back entrance. He returned, straightened his jumpsuit slightly even as he slipped into his breast pocket the key card he'd lifted from one of the dead men, and put one thumb up to the faintly glowing blue scanner next to the large metal door.

Lance didn't quite hold his breath, though he knew if this part didn't work—if something about Grayson had changed forever when Persephone's energy blast passed through him—then all that virtuoso killing would have been for nothing. But the door slid open at once, and Grayson moved inside.

They had successfully infiltrated the base.

Kara

Maybe it hadn't really sunk in, even after all this time. Maybe I had just managed to convince myself that Grayson wasn't like all those other hybrids, was different on some fundamental level. Seeing it all play out, though, in those too-sharp images somehow filtering through from Lance's own remarkable mind, brought home to me that, whatever else he might have become afterward, Grayson had been created to be a finely tuned killing machine.

I sat rigid in my chair, eyes tightly closed, and watched as Grayson slipped inside the base and shut the door behind him. As soon as it was closed, his entire body language changed. He straightened, and his shoulders went back as he stared ahead with an all-too-convincing facsimile of the same blank gaze as the soldiers he had just killed. A few strides, and he was in the corridor and moving eastward, to his left.

According to what Grayson had told Lance and Paul about the layout of the base, the level with the reactor was located directly above this floor. No access there for the hybrids, but detonating approximately twenty pounds of C_4 directly beneath it would be enough to blow right through the roof and into the reactor. Since a fusion reactor depended on an extremely delicate balance of perfect conditions to continue operating, chances were it wouldn't be in any shape to power anything for quite some time to come...if ever.

In the hallway were more hybrids, but none of them seemed to pay any attention to Grayson. Why should they? He was one of them, after all.

I swallowed, thinking of how I had once been cradled in those powerful arms, felt those tight, grim lips pressed against mine. Amazing how a shift in expression and demeanor could change him so much that I wasn't sure if I would have recognized him if I'd passed him on the street.

He stopped at a door and ran his stolen key card through the lock next to it. The door opened without a pause. Why shouldn't it? This area was only more storage, something innocuous, safe.

Funny how Persephone and Lance and Michael had spoken more than once of their own adventures inside the base, and yet I had never gotten a very clear image of it. The place was strangely prosaic, proportions and technology—aside from those strange hover hand carts—not so very different from what I would have expected to see in any military installation. Were the aliens really not as advanced as I had feared, or did they borrow human technology when it suited them? It would be that much harder to prove anything strange was going on in the base, should they ever have to abandon it to be discovered by human beings.

I had a feeling I'd never find out the real truth.

The room Grayson entered was filled with more packing crates and large metal boxes, all neatly stacked on one another, with perfectly straight aisles between them. He paused in the center of the room, looking upward as if to gauge the best spot to plant the explosives. Then he nodded, and pulled himself up on one of the stacks of crates so he could reach up and touch the ceiling. Moving quickly, he unzipped his jumpsuit and pulled it down so he could access the blocks of C4 that had been hidden under his clothing. Once they'd been removed, he drew the jumpsuit back on and zipped it. From one of his pockets, he removed the detonator and the electric leads, and set it down by his feet before gathering up the C4 and flattening it in a largish semicircle against the ceiling. Once that was done, he retrieved the detonator and leads, inserted them into the explosives, and nodded.

The remote was a small black object that looked like something you'd use to open a garage door. For all I knew, that was exactly what it had been in another life; I'd never had the courage to question Lance too closely about his explosives knowledge, or exactly what items he had in his possession. A whole lot of highly illegal somethings, based on what he'd managed to scrounge up for this operation.

I wanted to hold my breath as Grayson dropped lightly onto his feet from the stack of packing crates and moved back toward the door. Surely it couldn't be this easy—slip in and slip out, heading through the service entrance and back down the ravine, to be safely away before he even pushed the button?

Maybe it would be. Maybe I'd been all doom and gloom for nothing. Maybe Grayson really would be around to see his child come into the world, to be a part of its life—

The door opened, but it wasn't Grayson who had opened it. Four more hybrids entered the room, guns drawn. Their silence was more frightening than any barked commands could have been, but it was obvious enough what they wanted. They gestured for Grayson to put his hands up, and he did so, also without speaking, although a small smile played around his mouth. In that instant, he looked like the man I thought I'd loved once...and I also knew what he was about to do.

Oh, no, Grayson.

No.

His hand closed around the black remote, and the world exploded in fire.

CHAPTER TWENTY

Lance

He blanked out the vision as quickly as he could, but even so, the shockwave seemed to ring in his ears. Neither Michael nor Persephone seemed willing at first to let go of his hands; finally, Michael pulled his fingers away, and then Persephone did so as well.

From across the table came the sound of quiet sobbing, and Lance opened his eyes to see Kara with her face pressed into her hands, her shoulders shaking as she wept. Kiki already hovered behind her, expression an odd mixture of worry and awkwardness, as if she wasn't quite sure what her reaction should be.

Good question. Lance really didn't know, either.

That explosion had to have knocked out the reactor and everything within at least a hundred-foot radius around it, but was it enough? Had Grayson's sacrifice meant something, or would it turn out to be a hollow gesture, nothing more than the sting of a single bee?

Time to worry about that later. For now, he could only force himself to rise, legs feeling as stiff as if he'd been sitting in that chair for seven or eight hours, and not the scant forty-five minutes that had actually passed. Everyone at the table watched him as he moved toward Kara, Persephone grave and white-faced, Jeff a little stunned, Kiki mute with worry. Only Michael seemed unperturbed, although his dark eyes held a sadness that Lance had never seen before. And then Persephone stood, murmuring that she needed to call Paul and tell him it was time to come home.

None of that seemed to matter. The only thing Lance could think of was the woman who still sat at the table with her head bowed, hair falling in a spill of gold over her shoulders. He wanted to reach out and touch her, pull her to him, but did he dare? Maybe she would hate him now, hate him for his role in Grayson's death. Never mind that the hybrid had willingly walked down that path, as if he'd known this world had no place for him. If Kara blamed him for Grayson's death, Lance knew he wouldn't be angry. He would understand...and maybe someday she'd be able to forgive him.

He waited next to her chair, hands knotted into impotent fists at his sides. For a long moment he stood there, staring down at her, as Kiki hesitated a few paces away and no one else said anything.

Finally, Kara raised her head and stared up at him with blurred blue eyes. She said, "Oh, Lance," and lifted her arms to him.

And he took her hands and pulled her against him, holding her, letting her spend her grief as she wept into his shoulder, knowing that he himself would have willingly died for her, and realizing with sudden wonder that somehow, for whatever reason, he had been spared so he could be with her.

Kara

It turned out that the earth tremor was felt for miles around, though everyone thought it was a minor earthquake and nothing more. We didn't have many of them in that part of the world, and so the quake was a topic of conversation for several days...until a particularly severe monsoon storm hit the town, flooding the streets for almost a day, and that became the star subject of discourse until yet another oddity came along to take its place. And so it went.

The numbness of grief was a weight in my heart, a grief I knew I couldn't openly express. Oh, Persephone offered an understanding shoulder to cry on, and Lance had been more than patient with me. Maybe it was stupid to feel such sadness over someone I'd only known for such a short time. Somehow, I knew it was more than the loss of whatever had begun to blossom between the two of us. It was the loss of a life that someday might have offered this world a great deal, if he'd only had the chance to do so.

And maybe it was guilt as well, at the quiet happiness of having Lance in my life as something more than the casual acquaintance he'd tried to be all these years. No more bothering with any pretense; the Jeep was parked in the driveway all night most of the time, and Lance only went back to his condo every couple of days or so to check on things and make it look as if the place wasn't totally unoccupied. What exactly he planned to do with it, I didn't know; we hadn't discussed that yet, as we hadn't discussed a lot of things. Well, time enough for that later. At least now I was fairly sure there would be a later.

Lance had attempted a remote viewing the day after the explosion, just to see what the aftermath was. This was no group effort, but simply him sitting back at his condo, focusing his mind on the base a few miles away. The image wouldn't hold for very long—he claimed it was weariness, and that he usually didn't try to do this sort of thing so quickly in succession—but he was startled by the destruction he saw before the vision blanked out again.

"Grayson didn't say anything to me," he told me as we sat on the couch next to one another, still weary, still a little unsure around each other. "But I see now why he was so certain that he could do some serious damage to the base. I thought we'd take out the reactor, but that amount of C4 isn't enough to level a regular building, let alone an underground base carved out of rock. I don't know what was in some of those crates, but it had to be highly explosive. Far as I can tell, the back entrance is completely caved in, and the service area and several floors above it are destroyed as well. And it looks like the explosion went right up though the elevator shafts and caused a lot of collateral damage. They're going to be digging that place out for months."

I pushed myself a little closer to him, needing the reassuring warmth of his touch to help dispel some of the chill that seemed to find its way along every vein. "Did you see...*them?*"

"They're not all dead, if that's what you mean." He shrugged, but carefully, so he wouldn't shift me away from him. "But they sure seemed *pissed.*"

As well they should be. I could only hope that this additional blow would help convince the aliens that Sedona and its environs really weren't the most hospitable place for their operation, and maybe they

should move their base someplace a little friendlier...
like to Antarctica, or the middle of the Gobi Desert.

I didn't bother to say that, though. Lance knew
how I felt...we all felt the same way. What was it that
Kiki liked to say? *Don't let the door hit you in the ass
on the way out.*

If only it was that easy.

Days passed. Labor Day came and went, and with it,
a temporary lull in the tourist activity. I could almost
feel the shift in the world around me, the change in
the quality of the light outside the windows, the realization that autumn would be here soon, and after
that winter.

Plans had to be made, because I'd felt the
changes happening in my body, knew that I wouldn't
be able to conceal things for too much longer, not
with the rapid pace at which the tiny being within
me was developing. The R.N., Lola Montenegro,
had made a trip to Sedona to check on me. Everything seemed to be progressing just fine, but she told
me just before she left, "Don't put it off until the last
minute. I want you out of here and settled in Santa
Fe before too much longer."

It was Lance, aided and abetted by Paul, who'd
come up with the idea. I let it be known that I'd
been in the process of adopting a child from Roma-

nia, and the approval had finally come through. That sort of thing often got hung up in paperwork and bureaucracy, so no one should think it strange that a trip which was only supposed to last a few weeks would end up stretching into several months. And at the end, I would come home with my "adopted" child, and no one would be the wiser.

Unless, of course, said child came into the world an odd shade of gray or green. They didn't have too many of those in Romania.

Time to worry about that later. Lola said everything was fine, that none of the half-alien babies who'd been brought to term were anything except baby-colored, so I just had to make myself believe that.

I finished locking up the shop and turned, then barely bit back a little squeak of surprise. Standing directly in front of me was Martin Jones, the man in black...who'd been scarce the past few weeks. I'd thought he and his partner must have gone back to Washington, D.C. or wherever MIB Central was located. That particular point was still hotly debated in conspiracy chat rooms and UFO forums across the nation.

"Sorry, we're fresh out of 'I had a close encounter in Sedona' T-shirts," I said as I slipped the heavy ring of shop keys into my purse and withdrew the remote for my Prius.

"That's too bad," Agent Jones replied, tone almost amused. "Tourist rush over?"

"Not really. This is just a breather before they start descending for autumn festivals and wine tastings and balloon rides. Before you know it, they'll be putting up the lights at Tlaquepaque."

"I wasn't planning on sticking around that long."

"Oh?"

It was barely a shrug...just the slightest lift of the broad shoulders under the black suit. "Looks like our tour in this part of the world is done for now."

"Oh," I said again. What was he expecting me to say? That we'd always have Paris? "Does this mean I'm no longer under surveillance?"

For a few seconds, he didn't reply, only watched me carefully with a pair of gray-blue eyes that were just a little too keen. I had to resist the temptation to cross my arms across my stomach, to hide something that wasn't even really showing yet. Well, not much. My belly was pushing against my loosest jeans, telling me that their days were numbered, but even so, that little bit could always be attributed to too much pizza and not enough time on the treadmill.

At last he said, "I'll let you in on a little secret."

"What's that?" I asked.

"You and I are on the same side, Ms. Swenson." And he pulled his sunglasses out of his pocket, set them on his nose, and sauntered off across the parking lot to his might-as-well-be-marked black sedan, then got inside and drove off.

I stared after him for a long minute, wondering what the hell that was supposed to mean. Did he know what had gone down at Secret Canyon? Was this his oblique way of thanking me?

Who knows? I shook my head, and got inside my own car.

On Saturday night it rained, not the sudden downpour of a monsoon storm, but an early autumn shower, unexpected and yet gentle and healing. I lay in bed, listening to the rain patter down outside, hearing beneath it the regular breaths of the man who slept beside me. I wanted to reach out to touch him, but instead I lay still, willing myself to be content simply with his presence. He did not fall asleep easily, and when he finally did slumber, it was often restless, as if he recalled things in his dreams that were far from pleasant. Since he slept so peacefully now, I didn't want to disturb him.

It was all right. It was fine to simply know he was there, to recall the miracle of him loving me the way I had always loved him, to know that he had said he would be with me no matter what. I didn't question him, or his love for me. If Lance said he would do something, it got done. Even if it was being father to the child of a dead half-alien soldier.

And that made me love him all the more.

When I went out the next morning to clean up some of the fallen leaves from my driveway and snip away the dead flowers from the bed that bordered the walkway, I saw I wasn't the only one with a similar idea. Felicia Martinez was out in her yard as well, ubiquitous basket over one arm as she worked to deadhead her prized roses.

She smiled when she saw me, and gestured me over with a hand that held a pair of clippers. I wasn't much in the mood for conversation—I'd managed to avoid any encounters with Felicia over the past few weeks, which was fine by me—but there was no way to avoid this one with being actively rude.

"Morning, Felicia."

"Morning." She looked past me to where Lance's Jeep sat in the driveway. "He's been over a lot lately."

Talk about nosy. But I couldn't just brush Felicia off; I'd known the other woman for more than half my life, even if our acquaintance had never been close. "Yes, he has," I agreed, somehow managing to keep my tone noncommittal.

"So what happened to the other one?"

"Grayson?" My throat tightened. I managed to reply, "Oh, he had to...go away. He was just visiting."

"Oh." Felicia was visibly disappointed. "Too bad. It was nice to see him riding around on Bill's bike."

You will not cry. Not here, not now. You've cried enough. Lifting my chin, I smiled a little, even though the expression made my face feel as if it was going to crack. "Yes. Yes, it was."

At first, Felicia didn't reply. She raised her head a little, too, the fresh morning breeze ruffling the loose strands around her face, drifting away from the careless barrette she'd used to pull back her heavy gray-streaked hair. Finally she said, "Can you feel it?"

"Feel what?"

"It's not here yet, but it's coming. Change is coming."

I knew Felicia was only referring to the shift of seasons, with the equinox less than ten days away. But in that moment, I could feel it as well, in the currents of energy underfoot, in the feel of the wind, the angle of the sun. And within my own body as well, every day a little different as the life within me stirred and made its presence felt.

Once again, I had to resist the urge to press my hands against my belly. Felicia's eyes were too sharp, and already I was wondering how much my neighbor had begun to guess, after I'd started wearing my baggiest jeans every day and had likewise had switched over to peasant-style tops instead of my usual close-fitting tees and tanks.

It was good that I would be leaving soon. I needed to be away from here, away from anyone who might begin to guess, might begin to think something was definitely up with that Kara Swenson.

"Yes," I said, and looked past Felicia, up to the red rocks that towered above the subdivision, strong and bright in the morning sun. "Soon, everything will change."

The Sedona Files series continues with Kiki's story in *Angel Fire*.

ALSO BY CHRISTINE POPE

PROJECT DEMON HUNTERS
(Paranormal Romance)

Unquiet Souls

Unbound Spirits

Unholy Ground

THE WITCHES OF CANYON ROAD
(Paranormal Romance)

Hidden Gifts

Darker Paths

Mysterious Ways

A Canyon Road Christmas

Demon Born

An Ill Wind

Higher Ground

THE WITCHES OF CLEOPATRA HILL*
(Paranormal Romance)

Darkangel

Darknight

Darkmoon

Sympathetic Magic

Protector

Spellbound

A Cleopatra Hill Christmas

Impractical Magic

Strange Magic

The Arrangement

Defender

Bad Blood

Deep Magic

Darktide

Books 1-3 and Books 4-6 of this series are also available in two separate omnibus editions at special boxed set prices. Chronicles of Cleopatra Hill includes the series' two "back in time" novellas, *Bad Blood* and *The Arrangement*.

Or get the entire series in one enormous, specially priced boxed set! (Not available on Amazon.)

THE DJINN WARS

(Paranormal Romance)

Chosen

Taken

Fallen

Broken

Forsaken

Forbidden

Awoken

Illuminated

Stolen

Forgotten

Driven

Unspoken (June 2019)

Books 1-3 and Books 4-6 of this series are also available in two separate omnibus editions at special boxed set prices!

THE WATCHERS TRILOGY*

(Paranormal Romance)

Falling Dark

Dead of Night

Rising Dawn

The Watchers Trilogy is also available in a specially priced boxed set!

THE SEDONA FILES*

(Paranormal Romance)

Bad Vibrations

Desert Hearts

Angel Fire

Star Crossed

Falling Angels

Enemy Mine

Get the first three books of this series in an omnibus edition, or read the complete six-book series in one super-low-priced boxed set!

TALES OF THE LATTER KINGDOMS

(Fantasy Romance)

All Fall Down

Dragon Rose

Binding Spell

Ashes of Roses

One Thousand Nights

Threads of Gold

The Wolf of Harrow Hall

Moon Dance

The Song of the Thrush